A NOTC

ROUGH
rough
AND
RICH
rich

Harper —

Enjoy Sunshine

HAYLEY FAIMAN

Rough & Rich
Copyright © 2017 by Hayley Faiman

Editor: Rosalyn Martin, The Green Pen
Cover Cassy Roop, Pink Ink Designs
Formatting: Champagne Book Design

ISBN-13: 978-1976073748
ISBN-10: 197607374X

A rich man is nothing but a poor man with money.
W.C. Fields

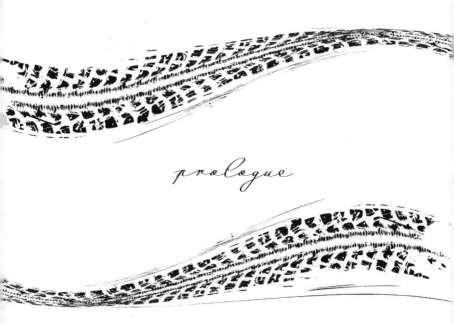

prologue

Imogen

I call his cell phone. *Again.* He sends my call straight to voicemail, and I glare as his voice barks out orders to leave him a message. He calls himself *Soar*, and all of his little buddies call him that too. I've even got it tattooed on the front of my hip—some misguided act of love and encouragement.

God, I'm such a fucking idiot.

Soar.

How stupid.

His name isn't Soar. It's Sloane McKinley Huntington, *III.* I doubt any of his *brothers* know that, though. Just like none of them know that my name isn't *Genny*, it's Imogen. We're frauds, the two of us. I'm not some badass biker bitch. I'm Imogen Carolina Stewart-Huntington.

We're both from well-to-do, upper class families. Not just upper class. No, more like elite. Our parents are trust fund babies, as are we. Neither of us has to work a day in our lives. We could both spend to our hearts content and still have plenty of money to give our children.

I met Sloane when we were in high school. We went to a private school, where we were famous for our parents' titles, our hand-me-down last names, and our breeding lineage.

Sloane was a bad boy. He was beautiful in every way a boy could be beautiful to a fifteen-year-old. His blond hair was never out of place, yet he looked as if he couldn't care less about it. His leather jackets were expensive, yet looked like he beat the shit out of them—his jeans the same.

He started running around with the club right after he graduated high school. During the week, he would stay in Shasta, a couple hours from San Francisco, where the club was based.

He always reserved his weekends to spend with me. I loved it. I felt so special, considering I was in high school and he was older than me. I thought I was really something. He even took me to all of my formal dances after he left school.

When I turned eighteen and he was twenty-one, we were married.

That's when things started to change.

I didn't know what being a *Notorious Devil* meant.

I didn't know about the women, the booze, the drugs, and the constant parties.

I didn't know about being left at home, all alone, for days at a time.

I didn't know that my husband would sleep with other

women while he went away on runs, whatever *that* meant.

"Sloane, where the hell are you?" I snap once his greeting is finished. "I'm not taking this shit anymore. I'm done."

I always say that too.

That I'm done.

Then he comes home and sweet-talks me into accepting him back. I hate myself a little more because I allow it, and allow him into my bed, every single *fucking* time.

I stay with him instead of leaving and going home to my parents. They were pissed when I married Sloane. They didn't understand why I wouldn't go after someone else, *anyone* else. His reputation for being a bad boy was known far and wide in their circle of friends they surround themselves with. Unfortunately, I'm extremely stubborn, and have no problem suffering for my pride.

Now, fourteen years later, I see exactly why they were so angry. Sloane hasn't grown up; he hasn't changed; he hasn't taken on the responsibility of his father's company. He's still running around, getting high, fucking whores, and has zero ambition in life. At this rate, his little brother will be running his father's company, and everything will completely bypass him.

I hear something in the next room, and I know it's Cleo. She's been staying with me for a few days while her man and Sloane have been gone on this run together. I feel like a bitch for ignoring her, but I'm so angry that I'm not good company anyway—not that I ever really am these days.

The phone rings in my hand, but it's not Sloane on the other end—it's MadDog, his president.

"Need you to come down to the clubhouse, darlin'," he murmurs on the other end.

MadDog. Now he's a member of the club I can respect. One of the only ones. He has ambition, he's in charge, and he doesn't take shit from anyone. He's also fiercely loyal to his woman, Mary-Anne. God, they're so cute and perfect; they make me sick and bitter.

"What's wrong?" I ask, my heart racing inside of my chest.

"Just come on down here. Bring Cleo, too," he says and then ends the call.

"Cleo, we're being summoned to the clubhouse," I call out as I walk out of my room. Her head jerks and she looks at me, giving me a sad smile and a nod.

We take separate cars, probably because she thinks I'm a bitch. I am. Or at least I am *now*. I wasn't always. When I was young, I was fun, always down for a good time, and always smiling.

Sloane used to call me his *Sunshine*.

He hasn't called me that in at least ten years, and for good reason. I don't feel very happy and sunny anymore.

I walk into the clubhouse and MadDog tells me, with regret swimming in his eyes, that Sloane's been arrested.

"What did he have?" I ask.

"I'm sorry, babe, I don't know. I only know they hooked him up and carted his ass off," Torch, Cleo's man, says, keeping his voice soft and gentle, like I'm some kind of wounded animal.

I nod, understanding filling me. He's gone. I'm done. The entire room watches me like I'm some kind of freak show, waiting for me to go insane. I look around until my eyes catch MadDog's.

"I'm leaving. I'm not coming back. I'm going home

4

to my family, and I'm sorry, but I'm divorcing his ass," I announce.

"Now, Genny, we don't even know if the charges will stick," MadDog murmurs.

"No, fuck that. He doesn't give a *fuck* about me. He cares about the club, the drugs, and the whores. I'm not on that list anywhere. So he can have it all, and he doesn't have to worry about me anymore," I state as I tamp down my emotions. I'm on the verge of tears, so I take a step toward the front door.

"Babe, you know that's not true," Colleen says.

"Do I?" I ask, arching a brow. "I know he doesn't come home for days, sometimes even weeks. I know he'd rather fuck those whores then come home to me. I know that what I want—it doesn't *fucking* matter."

"What do you want?" Colleen asks.

I shake my head. No way am I telling this room full of people what I want out of my husband. No way am I telling them that I want him to come home at night, to hold me, to whisper to me that he loves me, again.

No way am I telling them that I want him to slide inside of me bare, make love to me, and fill me with a baby. No way am I going to be that vulnerable in front of these people. These people who have it all. No way in hell.

I'm thirty-two years old.

I want a family.

I can't let my own husband have sex with me without a condom because I literally do not know where his dick has been. No way am I telling them that I don't want to lie awake at night, crying because my husband doesn't want me.

The only man I have ever been with doesn't want

anything to do with me. The man I love with everything that I am can't stand to look at me. *Fuck that.*

"Everything," I whisper, giving them *that* and nothing else.

Colleen's eyes widen, "That's too much."

"Then. Fuck. *Him.*" I growl before I turn and walk out the door.

"Genny," Mary-Anne calls out, chasing after me.

"What?" I ask, whirling around and giving her a dirty look. I don't mean to be a bitch, but it's basically just my personality anymore.

"Don't leave. The club will help you out. We're your family," she says, reaching out to wrap her hand around my forearm for comfort.

I know that she's been really sweet, helpful, and kind, but she doesn't know *shit.* I let out a humorless laugh and shake my head.

"I don't need the clubs help," I snort.

"Don't leave like this," she whispers.

"I envy you. A man like you've got, who obviously loves the hell out of you and would do anything to keep from hurting you, it's more than I've ever had. I want to hate you, but you're too damn sweet," I laugh softly. "I'm glad you have MadDog, but please, don't put Soar in the same category."

I open my car door and slide inside, start the engine, and drive to my parent's house. I leave everything in Shasta, not wanting one single memory to come with me. Sloane's fancy ass muscle car is in the garage of our house, as is everything else of ours. He can throw my stuff away, or give it to one of his whores. I don't give a shit anymore.

Sloane McKinley Huntington, III, is nothing but the past.

Soar

"I'm sorry, man," MadDog says as he sits across from me.

It's visiting day. I'm stuck in fucking prison for a minimum of the next three years on a drug charge. It's my own fault. I knew how much was too much to have on me, but I did it anyway. I was high and cocky. Now that I'm in forced sobriety, I can see a bit clearer.

I fucked up.

Big time.

"Why? Because I'm in here? Brother, I did this shit to myself," I laugh humorously as I lean back in my chair.

"No, Genny," he says. I sit up a bit straighter.

"She okay?" I ask as my heartrate speeds up and panic begins to consume me.

I haven't heard from her, but that doesn't surprise me. My woman, my *wife*, she's a bit temperamental, high strung, and high fucking maintenance, among other things. I've known her since she was a pretty little fifteen-year-old, and I snatched her up quick. I saw the way the other thoroughbreds in school were eyeing her. No way would she be with them. My blonde-haired sunshine needed wild freedom.

I just didn't know that we'd eventually be semi-miserable together. Love her, but the woman grates on my goddamn nerves sometimes. I hide out until she's over whatever snit she gets into, then I sweet-talk her down, and it's all good again for a while.

It's a cycle.

"Don't know. The day Torch came back and said you'd been hauled away, she said she was getting shot of you and she left. We've been keeping eyes on your place, but she hasn't come back, not even for her shit. We've had to up our security on the Old Ladies, shit is in limbo. Brother, we got no clue where she is."

I close my eyes for a beat. She wouldn't need her shit. She has enough money to buy herself a new outfit every day for the rest of her life and never repeat it. I know where she's gone. She's gone back to Frisco, back to her parents, back to *society*.

Fuck.

"Don't worry about her," I say with a shrug, trying not to look as affected as I feel.

"Soar…"

Clearing my throat, I mutter, "Seriously, Prez. She's got so much fuckin' security where she's at, she's safer than the fucking president."

"You sure?"

"Yeah, Prez. I'm sure."

MadDog leaves a few minutes later, leaving a photograph on the table. I snatch it up before I'm taken back to my cell. I look at the photo. It's a picture of Genny. Imogen. She's about twenty-one in it. She's smiling, but the expression doesn't reach her eyes.

That's my fault.

She hasn't been happy since the day she walked in on me fucking a whore while I was high off my ass. It's not that I want to hurt her, but *fuck*, nothing I ever do has made her happy.

I bought her a house. It's about a quarter of the size house she grew up in. It's not fancy and perfect, but honest to fuck, I don't give a shit about that material stuff, so I didn't think she would either. She started complaining about it almost immediately. She wanted to build something bigger and fancier, but I told her no.

Then she wanted me to come home every night. I have shit to do at the club, I couldn't come home every night. I was young, and I wanted to party—she didn't, so I left her ass at home. She'd accuse me of cheating constantly, and started holding out on me as a form of *punishment*. I hadn't actually done anything with another woman, until she kept accusing me of it. We'd been married for two years when she started that shit.

That was when I actually started fucking clubwhores.

I hadn't been with another woman in over five years. I stooped, I fucked the bitch out of spite and anger. I didn't get caught, so I kept doing it. It was just another high for me to chase. When she caught me, she threatened to leave. I charmed her back to me, and she stayed.

It became a game; it was a high. I played her, and played *with* her. I pushed her as far as I could, manipulated her anyway that I could. The fucker of it all was that I liked it. She didn't show emotion, she was cold as ice sometimes, so I'd push, and push until she was at her breaking point. Then I'd reel her ass back in, with a fucking victorious smile.

Now that I'm sober, I realize that it wasn't rational or even fucking nice, but I did it nonetheless. I was high, and the drugs, the women, and fucking with her were all highs I chased.

Fuck, I'm always chasing the next head change.

Always.

The realization that I'm so much like my own father, it slaps me in the face and makes me sick. He does the same shit, just in a different way. The fucking apple doesn't fall far from the tree. I hate myself for it.

Now, Genny's gone and I'm stuck here. No charming her, or sweet-talking her back home anytime soon—at least not for the next three years.

Fuck.

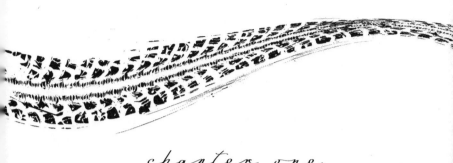

chapter one

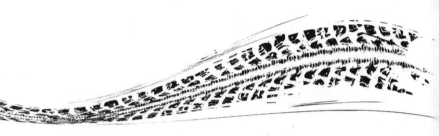

THREE YEARS LATER

Soar

"How's it feel?" MadDog asks as I step into the sunshine.

"Fuckin' good, brother," I murmur as the heat of the sun pounds down on me.

It's not as if I haven't been outside in the sun these past three years. It's more like I haven't been outside of the prison's gates. Now I'm free.

Free.

Fuck.

I didn't think the day would come. Thirty-eight years old and I just wasted three years of my life behind bars because I had too much dope on me. Intent to sell.

Luckily, the guys have been keeping me posted on the

goings on in the club. The Aryan's are pretty much taken care of, and one of the guys from the Russian mafia cut off the head of the *El Patron*, the head of *The Cartel*.

Our club has been busy; but for the past year, they've been breathing easy, making money working with the Russians, and enjoying life, all while my fuck up has kept me locked up.

"Ready to get back to the club," I grunt.

He lifts his chin and smiles, but it doesn't reach his eyes. I wonder what he's concerned with. I look around for our bikes but I'm surprised when he heads toward his truck. My brows snap together and I climb inside after he unlocks the doors.

"No bikes?" I ask after he gets inside and starts the engine.

"Thought we'd talk a little," he shrugs. I nod, looking straight out of the windshield.

"Hit me, brother."

"What's your life look like now that you're out?" he asks simply.

I shrug, "I have to stay clean for the next three years. I'm on probation."

"Your personal life?" he asks after he nods.

"You mean Genny?"

He grunts, "Still your Old Lady until you say otherwise."

"She's gone—doesn't want me back. Don't see any sense in fighting that shit. She's too hard, anyway," I murmur.

The words come out easy enough, but I feel as though I'm being ripped in two just by saying them. Truth is, *I miss her.* I've missed her for years, and I was the reason she changed. It was all me. I fucked her up and fucked her over, which fucked *us* up.

I don't deserve her.

I've been sober for three years, and I've had time to think

about all the shit I did to her, all the games I played and the way I continued hurting her over and over. I'm a piece of shit. If I stay away from her maybe, just maybe, she can find a little happiness after the years of misery I dished out to her.

"If it were easy it wouldn't be worth the payout in the end," MadDog states.

"Not the same people we were when we met."

I think about her anger and hesitancy the first time I charmed myself back into her bed. I'd been high and she caught me screwing a clubwhore. She was devastated, broken. I didn't want to see her hurting anymore, because of me, because of what I did. I was numb, but seeing her hurting twisted me up inside.

I had to make it better, I had to make her smile again. When she did, when she accepted my apology and let me back inside, I felt like a goddamn king. It started a cycle, a cycle that I couldn't fucking break for the next decade, no matter how many times I tried.

I fucking tried too, more than once; but goddamn self-sabotage is no fucking joke.

"Not the same man I was when I met Mary-Anne either, and that was only a few years ago," he announces, breaking me out of my thoughts. I turn to face him and he continues to talk. "I still don't deserve Mary, never have and never will. For whatever asinine reason, she loves my old ass. She loves me enough to marry me, have my babies, and put up with my shit. Think maybe Genny put up with a lot of shit from you over the years to prove she loves you, too."

"I hate how much fucking sense you make when you get all philosophical," I grumble.

"Just telling you the truth, kid," he laughs.

I turn back to the windshield before I speak again, "It's been three years. She never tried to contact me, and I never reached out to her, either. I fucked her up, man."

"She serve you those divorce papers?" he asks as we pull into the clubhouse parking lot.

"No," I admit.

Closing my eyes, I think about MadDog's words. Can I change enough for Genny to be able to forgive me? Can that urge to find a high, be tamped down enough to be a good enough man for her, to make her happy?

"Maybe all ain't lost then?" he asks, lifting an eyebrow.

"Pretty sure it is, but who the fuck knows."

"Enjoy your welcome home party, Soar. We're glad as fuck to have you back—but think about this conversation, yeah?" he rumbles.

I turn to face my president—the man I've looked up to since I was an eighteen-year-old kid, a kid who thought he was tough shit. MadDog proved I wasn't as badass as I thought I was. While it pissed me off when he did it, I grew up a little more each and every time.

Twenty years later, I still feel like a punk-assed kid. He's not really knocking me on my ass anymore; but his conversation on the way here, about Genny, about how she obviously loved me all those years I put her through hell, that has definitely thrown me for a loop.

"Thanks for the ride, prez," I mumble.

His words continue to dance around in my head, even as I walk through the clubhouse doors. I can't shake them. I walk over to the bar and am greeted by my brothers with slaps on my back and tequila shots. I smile and do the shots, one right after the other. It feels hollow. I feel hollow.

Fuck.

Nothing's the same.

Genny's gone. Some of my brothers have started settling down and having kids. I'm surprised to see Torch with his arm wrapped tightly around his woman, Cleo, her belly heavy with pregnancy. Teeny is standing next to Mammoth, pregnant as well. Mary-Anne walks up to me and wraps me in a hug.

"Welcome home," she says sweetly.

"You look good, babe," I say.

"Oh, I look fat," she says waving me off. "I'm pregnant again, if Max didn't tell you," she grins and my eyes widen.

"Number three?" I ask in surprise. They've only been married about four years.

"Number three. The final one," she laughs. "Riley and Finley keep me on my toes enough. I can't do anymore after this," she says shaking her head.

"Do you know what it is yet?" I ask.

Tears shine in her eyes before she whispers, "Just found out. A boy." Riley and Finley are baby girls, so I can tell she's excited for a boy.

"Happy for you," I murmur, wrapping her in my arms.

She looks up at me, biting the corner of her lip before she whispers. "Are you bringing Genny home, Soar?"

I shake my head. "Don't know, Mary," I murmur. She grabs my forearm, giving it a gentle squeeze as her kind eyes roam over my face. "Bring her home, Soar."

My chest aches at her plea. *Bring her home.* She wouldn't have me if I tried. I need to forget her, save her from me and my brand of fucked up.

"Ready for a show?" Camo asks, interrupting our

exchange and my thoughts. I'm pleased as fuck. Mary's pleading eyes are too fucking much.

"What?"

"Serina and Grease," he grins.

I cringe as I see them. Serina is Grease's Old Lady now, but he shares her—liberally. Not a dynamic I could get down on, but they are certainly putting on a show and not giving a flying fuck. I sway as I stand up from my seated position.

It's getting later and later. The room is starting to thin out as I continue to talk to my brothers and drink. *Fuck.* There's so much tequila being thrown at me. I'll probably still be drunk for the next three days.

Then the girls start to show off, and I smile as a new girl makes her way toward me. She's a cute young thing. Looking at her, an image of Genny fills my mind. I try to ignore it. She's not here, she's not waiting for me, and this time I'm doing nothing wrong. This time it's not a head change, I'm chasing, it's not me being fucked up and falling down the rabbit hole, this is just a good time, nothing else.

"My name's Destini," she whispers as she straddles my lap before she takes her top off.

My eyes widen when she bares her tits for me. Then she gives me a coy smile before everything goes black.

Imogen

"He got out today," Kip says. His voice is deeper sounding through the phone.

Kipling Huntington is Sloane's little brother, eighteen

years old, and already accepted into Harvard University. He's the exact opposite of his big brother, and yet he loves Sloane with everything he is. He looks up to him. I'm not sure why. Kip is going places. Sloane is probably only going back to prison sometime in the future.

"Are you going to see him?" I ask.

"You know I can't," he mutters. "They have trackers on my car and monitor my every fucking move," he murmurs, sounding more like his brother than he should.

"Your graduation party is next weekend," I point out.

"He won't come."

"I'll be there, though," I whisper.

Kip is like my own little brother. I've known him since he was a baby. I'm an only child, and he's the closest I'll probably have to a sibling in my life. I'm so damn proud of him for graduating high school with honors, and being accepted to Harvard. He's going to become a wonderful man, and he's going to take over their father's company. I know, with his drive, he's going to be so incredibly successful.

"Yeah, with Graham," he grumbles.

"What's wrong with Graham?" I ask, arching an eyebrow that he can't see.

"I like you with Sloane," he states. I swear, I can see his shoulder shrug and his furrowed brow in my head.

"Sorry, Kippy," I whisper.

"Me too. Anyway, I thought you should know he's out or whatever," he mutters.

"Thanks."

I end the call and then walk over to the door that leads to my upper balcony. I bought a house in San Francisco a few months after I left Shasta. It was built in 1928, but it's been newly renovated, with panoramic views and a contemporary and modern inside.

It's gorgeous, but four thousand square feet and seven bedrooms of *empty*. I don't know why I decided I needed all of the space. I'm a thirty-five-year-old woman separated from her husband and childless, living completely alone.

Kipling was right when he said I had Graham, but he was also wrong at the same time. I don't really have Graham. Not because he wouldn't want it, he would—but I don't feel anything for him. I'm seeing him because he's in business with my father, he's my age, he's handsome, and he's ready to settle down.

When Graham touches me, I feel absolutely nothing. When Sloane even looked at me, I felt absolutely *everything*. Maybe that was my problem. Maybe I just felt *too much* for Sloane, it made me stupid.

Being with him was exhilarating, and the highs were off the charts; but the lows, they were the lowest I have ever felt before. There was no middle of the road with him, always extremes. With Graham, it's all middle of the road. No high and no lows. It's all easy and, well—boring.

I pick up my phone and call the dress shop. I have a fitting today for the dress I'll be wearing to Kip's graduation party. No matter what my status with Sloane, I will attend the party, as will my parents and the rest of *society*.

The first party I attended without Sloane at my side, there were whispers, pointing, and staring. Even though Sloane hated society, he always went to his parents' yearly New Year's Eve parties, or any event they had for Kip. Then we always attended my parents' summer event, something he probably only did for me, so that I wouldn't bitch and scream and act totally crazy—something I had been known to do on occasion throughout our marriage.

Sitting down on the patio furniture, I lean back and close my eyes. That disappointment washes over me for the millionth time. It doesn't go away. It always comes to me, and I always feel a wave of guilt and sadness.

"I saw you with one of your whores," I whisper as tears stream down my face.

Sloane looks at me and I see regret swimming in his gaze. His hand reaches out and tucks some of my hair behind my ear. "It was nothing, baby. You know how it is, shit got out of control," he says with a gentle voice.

I narrow my eyes on him before I push his hands off of me. "Fuck you, Sloane. You're such a piece of shit. You're just like all of the other men I know. Fucking bimbos behind their wives backs and hoping that your money will keep me here and quiet," I ramble as I stand up and walk toward the entertainment center.

I grab a candy dish and feel the weight in my hand as I watch him turn and run his fingers through his hair.

"Baby, you know I love you. Shit just gets out of control, and I can't stop myself. I can't help it," he practically cries.

God, he looks so remorseful. I want to believe him but I'm so pissed. This isn't the first time or even the twentieth.

Without thinking, I inhale a deep breath and throw the glass dish toward him. His hand reaches out and catches it midair before he throws it on the ground. I gasp as my eyes widen.

He stalks toward me so quickly that I don't even have time to turn away and run from him. His hand fists in the back of my hair and tightens, holding me still. His other hand clamps around my waist as his face lowers to mine.

"Cut the shit, Imogen. You're mine. You aren't going anywhere," his hips press against my stomach and I feel his hard length.

I whimper, "Sloane." The wetness pools between my legs and I hate myself for it.

His nose slides alongside mine as his lips hover over my mouth. "There's nobody else for me but you, baby. Nobody. I can't breathe without you at my side. I'd die," he whispers.

"I hate your fucking club," I sneer right before his lips crash against mine.

My body jolts with the flood of memories. I wasn't a good enough wife for Sloane. I should have accepted the man he was; should have given him what he wanted, like Colleen suggested, so he didn't go out to look for it elsewhere.

I should have been okay with him being in his club, because it made him happy. I shouldn't have tried to change him.

I should have loved him just for him, and told him so.

I never did stop loving him, though; even if I stopped saying and showing it.

We were both so young. Looking back, there were so many things that I would have done differently—if I could go back and redo it all.

When he didn't do what I'd expected after a few years, which was leave the club and go work for his father, I shouldn't have bitched at him about it. I should have talked to him. I was young, immature, and disappointed—not only in him, but in myself.

Why couldn't I be enough for him?

Why did he need the club and the drugs? Then later, why did he need all of the women?

Sloane is the only man I have ever been with. He's the only man I have ever *wanted* to be with, but I'm not enough for him. As hard as it was for me to leave him, I needed to. I want to live a good life. I want to be happy and have a family and children—*god,* I want children more than my own breath.

If I don't start now, I'll probably never have them. Graham is my chance at a family, but I don't love him. I don't even know if I *like* him.

My life is nothing like I planned.

I'm just trying to pick up the pieces and salvage some kind of future for myself, a future that doesn't include Sloane. I wipe the tears away from beneath my eyes and stand.

I have a dress fitting and lunch with my mother and her friends. Then I have dinner with Graham. I have a full day ahead of me, and I need to stop thinking of Sloane, or I'll lock myself in my room and cry all day long, *again.*

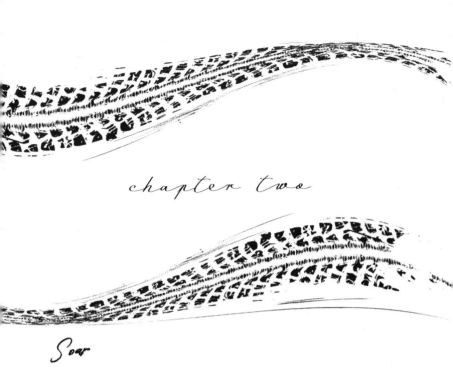

chapter two

Soar

I groan into the pillow, feeling a heavy weight against my back. Opening my eye just a crack, I see a mass of hair, and I realize there's a woman halfway draped along my back. I slide out from beneath her and she moans but doesn't move.

I reach for my pants and pull them up as I walk around my room. I spy a quarter full bottle of tequila on the floor, so I pick it up and take a swig, swishing it around in my mouth a little before I swallow.

Making my way to the bathroom to take a leak, I try to ignore the fact that there's a naked whore in my bed, *again*. Imogen left, so I shouldn't feel guilty for fucking another girl, but I do—just like I always have. I wash my hands and look down at my finger. My wedding band is tattooed on and serves as a permanent reminder of what a piece of shit I am.

"Soar," a voice calls as I stumble back to my room.

I look up to see Torch standing there, his eyes reading me, but I'm not sure what he sees.

"Torch," I grunt.

"You need to talk about any of it, I'm here," he states.

My eyes widen and I nod my head, but it comes out more like a jerk.

"Nothin' much to talk about. Fucked up, got caught, served my time, and now I'm out. After my probation is up, I'll be free," I shrug.

"You went to prison, Genny left, and you're drinkin'. Lots of shit to talk about if you feel the need, brother," he states.

"Genny left because we treated each other like shit. I went to prison because I fucked up. I'm drinkin' because I just got out yesterday," I respond, grinding my teeth together.

He rubs the back of his neck before he speaks, "I spent a lot of years hiding from the truth. I acted like an ass, and I ran from the one person I loved and needed the most. If I would have gotten my shit together sooner, I could have been as happy as I am right now for all those years I was fucking miserable."

"We're toxic," I say with a shrug.

"Are you toxic because of actions and reactions? Or have you always been?" he asks. My eyes widen again at how fucking on point he is.

Imogen and I haven't always been toxic. My sunshine was the sweetest thing on earth. We went to shit slowly. It wasn't an overnight thing. We hurt each other, made up, hurt each other again, and then continued on that cycle until she walked away from me, but only when I couldn't drag her back to start the cycle all over again.

"Actions and reactions," I begrudgingly admit.

"You gonna fix that?" he asks. My answer is to shrug. He wraps his hand around my shoulder, giving it a squeeze, causing me to lift my eyes to his. "You're coming up on forty, Soar. Ain't a young kid anymore. If she's what you want, you need to make that shit happen."

"She's my wife, but it's been so long," I say, unsure of what I'm admitting to. Lots of things, maybe.

It's been a long time since we've fucked. A long time since we were happy. A long time since I told her I loved her, and an even longer time since I showed her how much she meant to me. I run my hand through my shaggy hair, irritated at how long it is.

"Get your shit together, lay off the booze and the dope, think about what you really want," he suggests. "If it's her, get her back."

"She hasn't showed up in three years. I'm sure she's moved on."

The words make my chest ache, and I don't know how to feel about that. I don't *like* how it makes me feel. Numbing this pain would be a fuck've a lot easier.

"She serve you with papers? Cause she knew exactly where you were to do that shit," he grunts. I shake my head and he chuckles. "Sort your shit and get your woman back."

Torch turns and walks away, leaving me in the hall to watch after him. I let his words sink in. All of them. Do I want Imogen back? If I do, I definitely don't want it the way we had it, but I don't know how to change our dynamic. I don't know if I can change, truly change, and be the man I need to be for her.

We've both hurt each other, and I can't pretend the way

I hurt her wasn't more than the way she did me, because it was. I demolished her self-confidence, and I didn't give a fuck while I was doing it. It was all a game to me.

I didn't even feel guilty about it until I sobered up, then I'd get baked, all over again to make that guilt go away. When I was sitting in a prison cell, alone and sober, there was nothing to mask the feelings and the realization of what I did to her. Nothing could mask that guilty feeling while I was in there. I don't deserve her.

Walking back into my room, I tell the whore to scoot off the bed, and she does. "Soar, baby," she groans as she stands on wobbly legs. "You promised we'd have fun this morning," she wines, stumbling naked around my room.

"I lied," I grunt.

My phone buzzes from my nightstand, and I grin when I see who's calling me. I don't answer until the whore stomps out of the room and slams my door.

"Kippy," I rasp.

"You're coming next weekend, right?" he asks, sounding more like a man and less like my kid-brother.

"Wouldn't miss my baby brother's valedictorian speech or his party for the fucking world."

"Imogen will be at the party," he announces. My spine straightens.

"Okay," I say slowly.

"With a date," he practically growls.

"Date?"

"Graham Bayard," he announces. It's as though fire and rage instantly fills me.

That fucking weasel prick. "Graham? She's dating Graham?" I roar.

25

"Knew you wouldn't like that," he says, sounding as though he's trying to hold back his laughter.

"No. Fuck, no, I don't like it. Imogen is still my wife," I hiss.

"It's black-tie, of course. See you then," he calls out before he ends the conversation by hanging up.

I narrow my eyes, thinking about *fucking* Graham *fucking* Bayard's hands anywhere near Imogen, *my Imogen*, my fucking wife.

Yeah, Torch and MadDog are right.

I need to get my wife back.

I'll be damned if she makes a life with that piece of shit over me.

Imogen

I let out a heavy sigh as I straighten my dress. It's a sleeveless, fitted, bright red bandage dress. I can hardly breathe in it. When I turn to the side, I can really see just how much weight I've lost since leaving Sloane.

I look really thin. I should be excited about how tiny I am now, but I'm not. It's just another reminder that I'm alone, that Sloane isn't with me, and that he doesn't care. He's all about curves, or at least he claimed he was, always making sure I ate when he was around; always grabbing me and telling me just how hot he thought I was.

Thinking about him, as I eye my shoes on the floor, I cringe. I recall one of the last times I saw him. He had swayed into the house, drunk and smelling like a brothel. I was so pissed. It was our anniversary, and we were supposed to be going out for the evening.

I took off my shoe and threw it at him, screaming like a banshee as I started throwing everything I could get my hands on toward him. I wanted him to hurt as much as he hurt me. He fucked me against the wall that night, broken glass all around us, as tears stained my cheeks.

Closing my eyes for a moment, I can almost hear his voice as he whispered in my ear, his cock buried deep inside of me, my back pressed against the wall. *I'm no fucking good, Genny. Goddamnit baby, I'm so fucking sorry. I wish I could be better."*

Shaking my head, my straight blonde hair flying around me, I try to rid myself of the thought of him. I step into my nude high heels and grab my coat off of the bed. I have a date tonight. As much as I want to stay home and wallow in my self-pity, Graham has been so patient and kind to me, I owe it to him, and myself, to give us a chance.

My doorbell rings, and I suck in a deep breath. Graham and I haven't been intimate yet, but I can tell that he's anxious for that step in our relationship. Though he's been incredibly patient, a man can only *be* so patient—a lesson learned from my failed marriage. They need sex, and Graham and I have been seeing each other for four months. He's without a doubt at the end of his rope with me. There's just something that doesn't feel right though. Maybe it's me, or possibly him. I don't know, but I can't seem to go there, yet.

"Hello, darling," Graham greets as soon as I open my front door.

I watch as his eyes do a sweep of my body. When they land on my face, his lips curl up in a sexy smirk. I wait for my belly to do flips or to clench, or for my skin to heat at his perusal of me, but it doesn't. I feel like I'm looking into the eyes of Kip, or maybe even my oldest cousin, Dale.

"Hello," I respond with a fake smile as I take his outstretched arm.

"I brought the BMW," he announces, "It's easier for you to get in and out of your heels."

Inwardly, I roll my eyes. His other car is a Land Rover and just as easy for me to get inside of. I don't care about cars, about *stuff*, not anymore. Life isn't about stuff, it's about love and living and being happy. I learned a long time ago that stuff wasn't what I wanted to make me happy. You can have the worlds *things* at your fingertips and still be miserable.

"We're going to *Gary Danko* for dinner," he announces. I gag a little as he closes the door and goes over to the driver's side. "You'll enjoy it."

I won't enjoy it. I don't like French food, not even a little. I don't know why, but I never have. Caviar is not for me, and the only truffles I enjoy are the chocolate kind, not mushrooms.

"So, how was your day?" I ask as we drive toward fisherman's wharf. I don't know why we don't go somewhere with less tourists, but I don't say anything. I choose to bite the inside of my cheek.

"Long and full of things that would bore you," he murmurs.

I hate it. He acts like I'm too stupid to talk about his work. Although I probably am too stupid to understand every aspect, I don't know why he can't just talk in generalizations. It's annoying. Maybe I'm just on edge tonight, with all the talk of Sloane earlier with Kip, but Graham is getting on my nerves more than he ever has.

"Did you get your dress situation handled for the party?" he asks casually as he pulls up to valet.

"Yes. My final fitting was this morning, then I had lunch with my mother afterward," I state.

He turns to me, giving me a bleached white toothed sparkling smile. It still does absolutely nothing for me.

"Excellent. You're going to be the sexiest woman there, I already know it, and you'll be on my arm," he announces before he opens the door and exits the car.

The valet attendant helps me out, and I can't help but frown at Graham's words. I watch as he tosses the attendant his keys before he slides up to my side and presses his palm against my lower back. I don't want to be a trophy *anything*. I've seen what happens to trophy wives in our circle. Once their beauty fades, they're traded in for a younger, sexier, childless, *perky* model. I don't want that. I never have. I've always wanted love, real soul shattering love.

"Can I help you?" the hostess asks.

Graham tells her his name and that he has reservations. She smiles kindly and suggests that we follow her. Once we're seated and Graham orders some ridiculous champagne, I decide to ask him exactly what is happening between us.

"Why are you dating me, Graham?" I ask. He lifts his head from his menu and furrows his eyebrows together.

"Why wouldn't I want to date you, Imogen?"

"I don't know, but I don't think I'd make a good trophy wife," I say, scrunching my nose up.

Graham throws back his head in laughter, and I stare at him, my eyes widening in surprise at his boisterous response.

"I'm sorry, Imogen, but you're far from a trophy wife. You're thirty-five years old, and by looking at you, nothing on you is fake?" he asks, arching an eyebrow as he stares at my chest. My face heats in embarrassment and shame.

"I like you, Imogen. But I'm not going to beat around the bush with you. This is as much because my family approves of you and of your family's status as it is because I find you attractive. You fit within my world in a way most women don't. You understand *society*, what's expected of you, and you're not as much of a bitch as some of those other girls. So, while I do find you attractive, very attractive actually, that is not my sole reason for wishing to date you."

I nod my understanding, because I do understand. There aren't many *society* girls that are single at my age. If they are, they come with a lot more baggage than I do. Graham is Sloane's age, unmarried, no children, and obviously wants more than a fling with me, especially since he's been dating me without pushing for sex for the past four months.

"Okay," I murmur, not wishing to embarrass myself further.

"You're beautiful, Imogen, and if he didn't see that after twenty years of having you, he's never going to," he whispers as he takes my hand in his from across the table.

"I know," I shrug, lifting my head and looking into his dark brown eyes.

They aren't the light green of Sloane's, and looking into them feels wrong. Every day I miss him, and I feel stupid for it—completely brainless.

Graham orders for us, not even asking me what I like. He orders caviar, scallops, shrimp, and several truffle tasting items, all of which I can't stand. I choke down what I can while he talks about his family, their many houses, and how he's getting ready to buy a country home, probably in Napa;

he doesn't want to raise a family in the city.

"Napa is beautiful," I offer. He nods.

"I'll always keep my place in the city and just commute on Fridays and Mondays," he announces.

"So, you want to live in the city during the week?" I ask as I choke down a scallop.

"Yeah, I mean, I'll be around on the weekends and you can hire a nanny. It's not as if you'll have to do everything," he shrugs. My eyes widen when he assumes that I'm going to be his wife and the mother of his children.

"Graham," I whisper.

"This is happening, Imogen. You need to file for divorce from his ass, and you're moving on, with *me*. Next weekend, after the party, you're staying at my place. Enough pretending like we don't know where this is going. We aren't young enough to mess around anymore. We'll have a small wedding in six-months and start trying for a baby immediately. It's time," he announces.

My eyes widen and my mouth drops open in shock. I don't know what to say. It's a big assumption, and we aren't in love. I'm not even turned on by him. Things could change after we move to the next level, but right now? He feels like my cousin.

"Do you love me?" I ask.

Graham's eyes narrow as his lips purse together. "I don't, but it doesn't matter. I respect you, your family, and I'm attracted to you. Our children would come from perfect breeding. It's the foundation of a successful coupling."

I scrunch my nose up at his words—*successful coupling*. How clinical, how unsexy, and how very much unlike Sloane. Graham stands and walks over to me, helping me up from my chair. He's poised and always a perfect gentleman. I can't help but think he's like this in bed, too, and that kind of makes me feel grossed out.

I'm used to hot, dirty, sweaty sex. I don't think Graham has worked up a sweat anywhere but on a treadmill his entire life. Plus, I feel like we're making an appointment to have sex, and that just makes it even more awkward and unsexy.

"I'm busy with work the rest of the week, but I'll be by your place at seven to pick you up for the party," he announces as we walk out to valet.

"Okay," I nod.

Graham helps me in the car, and we ride in silence back to my house. As ever the poised gentleman, he walks me to my door and I unlock it, reaching for the handle after murmuring goodnight when he wraps his hand around mine and tugs me away from the door. His finger slides under my chin and tips my head back so that I can look into his chocolate eyes.

"I'm sorry I won't be available the rest of the week. I wish that I was," he murmurs. "I'll make it up to you next weekend," he grins.

His promise and sly grin should make butterflies flit around in my belly, but they don't. When his face lowers and his soft lips touch mine, I close my eyes and wait for something to happen, anything. It doesn't. Graham doesn't deepen the kiss, lifting his head and biting his lips as if he's done something salacious.

"Just the taste of you has me wanting more, Imogen," he whispers.

I wish that I could say the same, but I'm as dry as the Sahara. I tip my lips in a small smile and he takes it as coy instead of disappointing, giving me a wide grin before he shakes his head slightly.

"I can't wait to have you underneath me," he rasps.

Inside I cringe. It can't happen. I have to end this before next weekend, maybe after the party. I can't leave him date-less, and I refuse to go to another society party alone.

"I'll see you Saturday," I offer.

"Saturday," he nods before he turns and walks away without looking back, leaving me standing on my front porch.

My house is in a good neighborhood, but he's left me on my porch, not ensuring that I'm safely inside.

What a dick.

I can say with all honesty, as much of a complete asshole my husband is, he's always ensured my safety.

Always.

With a heavy sigh, I walk inside of my house and unarm the alarm before I arm it again as I lock the door. MadDog left me a message several months ago saying that the threat of the Aryan's and *The Cartel* was, for now, gone.

I'm pretty sure that I'm safe and that none of Sloane's club stuff will follow me here, but this is the city, and I'm a single woman living alone, you can never be too safe.

Making my way upstairs to my bedroom, I flip on the light and look around. It's perfect. Not a single thing out of place. It looks like a magazine, and I despise it.

Not for the first time, and stupidly, my eyes sweep the floors and I miss it.

I miss the way Sloane would throw his shit around, not caring where it landed. I miss being annoyed as I picked it up and threw his dirty clothes in the hamper.

I miss him.

Even the asshole part of him.

I miss the way we really did love each other. Beneath all the pain we caused one another, there was love, and I miss it. I need to let him go. He isn't coming back to me. Even if he tried, he isn't changing. He'll go to other women and we won't have the family I desire; the family Graham is offering me on a silver platter.

So, I need to find a way to let him go, and to move on completely. Maybe I'll move away, somewhere where there are no memories of Sloane, and where Graham isn't—a place where I can completely start over.

chapter three

Soar

Walking into the house, the place I grew up and left, the place I haven't stepped foot into for the past three years, is sobering. It looks the exact same, which isn't normal, considering my mother usually redecorates the whole house yearly, but it's exactly the way it was the last time I was here.

"I see you decided to grace us with your presence." My father's harsh, booming voice fills the air.

Rolling my eyes, I respond to his statement, "I wasn't on vacation, it's not like I could just come over any time I wanted to."

"That bed of shit you made yourself, son. When are you going to get your fucking head out of your ass, be a man, and get a real job?"

I bite the inside of my cheek, not wishing to get into it

with him right now.

"Your wife is living alone, fucking other men, and here you are being a goddamn pussy. Do you realize how this makes me look? You were sent to prison for three years, and you can't keep your fucking wife on a leash? You know how many parties she's showed up to either alone or with another man? You don't think about anybody but yourself, Sloane. You're so goddamn selfish that you don't think about how that makes your mother and me look; you don't give a fuck about anybody," he shouts.

"Sloane," my mother slurs from the top of the staircase. She's looking right at my father, but he ignores her, which is par for the course "You don't know what they're going through. It's just a rough patch."

My father turns his head, and I can practically see the lasers that he attempts to spear my mother with, coming from his eyes. "Why don't you get back to your bottle? Doesn't it miss you?" he sneers.

She snorts. "Your whores missing your money? Because I know they don't miss that limp fucking dick you've got."

I close my eyes for a second. Listening to them is like a complete fucking flashback to my childhood, except my mother and I would both end the night with black eyes and bruises.

When my father's voice rises again, I shout at them to shut the fuck up. I can't listen to it anymore, and all I want to do is go in search of a high. I can't do that, though, and they're putting me on the fucking edge.

"You dare to talk to me like that?" my father spits.

"I do, because you're being goddamn ridiculous," I state. "Imogen and my relationship has zero bearing on your life.

36

We're adults. In fact, in case you didn't realize it, I'm almost forty fucking years old. Whatever happens between us, is just that, between us. I'm here tonight for Kippy and nobody else. So, you two can go fuck yourselves," I calmly state. I breeze past them and walk out into the back of the estate.

I need to fucking breathe.

Imogen

I smooth down the front of my dress and cringe. I can't believe I let my mother talk me into it. It's black silk fabric with a halter neck, and the front dips down so low in front that my entire chest—to almost my belly button—is exposed. Two triangles of black silk cover my breasts. Though, since I've lost weight, my breasts aren't as full as they used to be, so it doesn't really *show* anything.

A piece of gold ribbon wraps around right underneath my breasts and the middle of the dress is completely cut out, with another gold band that wraps around my waist, holding it together at my back.

The dress is completely backless. The black silk starts again at my hips and falls to the floor, but there's a slit on my right side, and it's cut all the way up to my mid-thigh.

I look like a slut.

Sliding my feet into my gold high heels, I smooth down my wavy, blonde hair before I apply my nude shimmer lip stain and cringe again. I feel like I should be going to some kind of party in Vegas, not a high school graduation.

The bell rings, and I exhale. This is going to be a long

night. Not only do I have to deal with society bitches, but I also have to break it off with Graham. I thought about it all week, and I can't be with him.

It isn't as though I'm not ready to move on from Sloane, because I think that I could be, it's that Graham does absolutely nothing for me. I can't even see being content with him, let alone remotely happy.

"Wow," Graham breathes as I open my door.

He's wearing a tuxedo, and it should make my belly do flips. Sloane in a tux always did things to me, but Graham, not so much.

"Hey," I smile as I step out of my front door and lock it behind me.

"Who picked that dress out?" he asks as his eyes narrow.

I thought he liked the dress originally, but now as I look up into his eyes, I can tell that he's not pleased at all. In fact, he's angry. He wraps his fingers around my elbow, his fingertips gripping me roughly, and tugs me to the waiting car. There's a driver tonight, and without being gentle, Graham practically shoves me into the back seat.

"My mother did," I state, though my voice waivers slightly.

"Of course your mother did," he snorts.

"What does that mean?" I ask, arching an eyebrow as I turn slightly toward him.

"Your mother is a classic aging trophy wife. I didn't realize from our conversation the other night that that is exactly what you wanted to be. I thought you were different," he shrugs.

"You do realize my mother comes from more money than my father, don't you?" I ask, narrowing my eyes.

"Money can't buy class. Your mother is classless, always

has been. She can't help it; her entire family is. Yes, she has more, but her family is *nouveau rich*. That money was built from luck, unlike your father's, which came from generations ago; wise investments of textiles was then rolled into other avenues. I know your family history, Imogen, as you I'm sure know mine. If I wanted a trashy trophy wife, I could have my pick."

I don't know his. I hate it all. The bullshit, the status, and exactly the way he described my mother's money versus my father's. Like my mother is cheap because her family's money is new money and not old money.

My eyes lower, as though I feel the weight of his words on my shoulders, "I'm sorry I'm not classy enough for you," I say, lifting my head and turning it to the side, avoiding looking at him. I can't wait until this party is over so that I can leave his pompous ass.

"Your father's family line is impeccable, and your mother's isn't atrocious, so there's nothing to be *sorry* for. Just, next time we go to a party, I want you to see my stylist instead of allowing your mother to help you," he says, taking my hand and giving it a gentle squeeze.

I roll my eyes to the window as he caresses my hand. His skin is smooth and soft, and it is another reason he does nothing for me.

Sloane's hands were rough. He enjoyed using them on his bike and with whatever else he did for the club. They were also scarred from fighting, and the way they would drag across my skin—the thought still gives me goosebumps.

"We're here," Graham announces, taking me out of my day dream.

The driver helps me out of the back of the car, and I

wait for Graham to walk around and join me. His hand slips around my waist, and he squeezes me as we walk up the steps into the Huntington mansion. As soon as we're inside, I look around for Kip. I have something for him, and I want to make sure that he gets it before he takes off to Harvard.

I see him, and he smiles widely.

"I'm going to say hello to Kipling," I murmur, disengaging from Graham's grasp on my waist.

"I'll be right there," he mutters, not even turning away from Mr. Shilling. I don't like Mr. Shilling anyway. He has always leered at me, and he's older than my grandparents' age.

"Kip," I say as soon as I reach his side.

He turns, and I have to keep from breathing funny, the closer I get. He looks exactly like Sloane did the day I met him. His blond hair is a little wild, but still not out of place; his face is clean shaven and young; his green eyes pierce me, and his full lips tip in a cocky grin.

"Imogen," he whispers as he wraps his arms around me in a tight hug.

He's even tall like Sloane, and with long lean muscles of a boy-man, *just* like Sloane was when I met him. It sends my mind spinning back twenty-years.

"I'm sorry, you look so much like him," I whisper against his ear.

"He's not dead, Genny," Kip chuckles as he straightens.

He keeps his hands on my waist and continues to give me his cocky as shit grin as I shake my head.

"I know," I murmur. Isn't Sloane dead, though? To me at least? It feels like I've been mourning him for years.

"You look hot as shit, big sister," he laughs softly. I roll my eyes.

"I have something for you. I wanted to give it to you before you snuck off with your friends and got into trouble," I say.

"Never," he gasps, but his green eyes twinkle.

"Anyway, I just thought you might like this," I murmur as I pull the ring from my clutch.

He holds out his hand, "What is it?" he asks.

"This is Sloane's class ring. I don't know, I thought you might want it," I shrug. "You think it's dumb, right?"

"No way, Gen," he says as I drop it in his hand. I watch as he slides it onto his finger. "I didn't get one. Mom forgot to turn in the paperwork," he shrugs.

She didn't forget. Kalli Huntington is a drunk.

"Now you do," I grin, looking up at him, my eyes filling with tears.

"Don't give up all hope, yet," he mutters, sounding far too mature for his age.

I feel a warm, soft, hand on my back, and I twist my neck around to see Graham just behind me. His heat is against my body and still, nothing. I exhale and look over to Kip while rolling my eyes.

"Congrats on graduating, and Harvard," Graham says, his voice deeper than usual.

"Thanks," Kip says, not looking at him.

Graham is stiffer than normal standing next to me, and I look up to him, and notice that his gaze is focused across the room. I follow it, and my eyes widen at the sight.

Sloane.

Soar

Bourbon. I always drink it at my parents' parties, mainly because they think tequila is tacky. My mother prefers bottles of wine, hidden beneath her bed, but that's a totally different scenario. Right now, I'm leaning against one of the back walls, halfway hidden in the shadows, watching and drinking.

Then I see her.

Imogen.

Goddamn, her dress shows so much skin that my slacks tighten, and my cock presses against the zipper at the sight of her. I stuff my hand into my pocket so nobody notices my semi as my eyes track her. She's walking alone toward Kip, and her right leg peaks out through the high slit of her dress with each step she takes.

Her hair is longer than it was three years ago, her body dangerously thin, and that causes me to scowl. She and Kip hug, and I watch as she pulls something out of her purse and places it in his hand before giving him a small smile. Fuck me. She's still the prettiest woman I've ever laid eyes on. Then I watch as Graham *fucking* Bayard walks right up to her, his hand sliding around her waist and his eyes pinned to mine.

I give him a grin and lift my chin in his direction as I push off of the wall and make my way toward them. Genny notices me and her eyes widen, as she obviously sucks in a breath. Fuck me, her lips are shiny, and I can't help but remember just how well they fit around my cock when she sucked me off.

"Huntington," Graham practically sneers as he eyes me.

"Imogen," I rasp, ignoring the fuckwit.

"Sloane," she breathes. It goes straight to my cock.

I grin at her, tipping my lips the way I know makes her tremble, and she does. Graham notices. I can feel his eyes narrowing on me, but I only have eyes for my wife. I reach out and let my fingertips trail down her shoulder. I watch as she shakes, and I can't help but bite on my bottom lip, thinking about how wet she must be right now—for me, and not for the man she came here with.

"Darling, will you excuse us? I'd like to talk to Sloane alone," Graham says through clenched teeth.

Kip snorts slightly, but he takes Genny's hand and tugs her away. When she turns around, my eyes widen at how bare her back is. Fucking hell, she never dressed like that before. The dress has her mother written all over it, but I could give a fuck less. She looks like one hot as fuck piece.

"Stay away from her," Graham announces.

"Or what?" I snort. "She's my wife," I point out.

This fuck has been trying to best me since we were in first grade. He couldn't throughout school, and he can't now. He refused to accept the fact that I'm better than him in every way possible.

"She'll be sending you divorce papers, since she's marrying me in six months. You know, as soon as they're final," he laughs as a giant smile appears on his face.

I want to punch him, but my father would have my ass for it. Honest to fuck, I do not feel like dealing with him tonight.

"You want my wife? For what? I've had her, man, you aren't the winner here," I say, bringing my drink up to my lips and tipping it back, acting as though I could give a fuck. I'm goading his ass, and he'll bite, he always does.

"I'll be the winner," he says slowly, giving me exactly what I knew he would. "I'll give her what she wants, a family, and

I'll take all her money while I'm at it. Her parents love me; her father has already agreed to release her entire trust fund and let me *invest* it for her," he states pompously. "Once it's all transferred to my off-shore accounts, I'll let you have her back and you can take care of my brats."

"When you kiss her, can you still taste my cum in her mouth? She loves to swallow," I say, ignoring the rage that's building inside of me at the way he plans on using Imogen and stealing her money.

His eyes widen and he jerks back slightly. That's when I know that she hasn't done that for him. By the looks of him, I'm wondering if he's touched her at all.

"Say what you want. I'll have the last laugh. I'll ruin her body and leave her penniless," he laughs.

"Good luck with that. Remember, *I'm back*, Bayard," I bark walking past him.

I make sure to ram my shoulder into his when I pass him, causing him to stumble back slightly.

I don't walk up to Genny like I want to. Instead, I turn and walk over to a group of people I went to school with to shoot the shit. I have to act unaffected. If I don't, then he'll think he got to me—and I make it a point to never show Bayard that he's gotten to me. He can go fuck himself.

"You pissed him off. What'd you say?" Kip asks a few minutes later, after I've made my way back to the bar for a refill of bourbon.

"Asked him if he could still taste my cum when he kissed Imogen," I shrug. The bartender coughs as he hands me a glass.

"Sloane," my brother groans.

"Proud of you, Kippy," I offer, wrapping my arm around

his shoulders and slapping his back lightly.

"Thanks," he shrugs as his cheeks pink in embarrassment. "You don't think I'm a big fuckin' loser, do you?"

"For what?" I ask, knitting my eyebrows together in confusion.

"Valedictorian, Harvard, all that shit?" he asks.

"Being smart doesn't make you a loser. If anything, I wish I could have been more like you when I was younger. School was not for me."

"You don't give a shit what anyone else thinks. I want to be like you. I always have, but I'm so afraid of fucking up. Mom and dad, they won't allow it," he says.

That guilt that I usually feel when it comes to my little brother washes over me again.

My parents had him when I was twenty. It wasn't an accident; he was supposed to replace me. He was their do-over because I'm such a colossal fuck up in their eyes.

"So, don't give a shit about what anyone else thinks, but do it your way. You wanna take over dad's company and run it the way you want, a different way than he has, then you go to school you prove you're competent to take over. Then you do what you want when you take it over," I suggest.

Kipling smiles. It's huge, and it's pretty fucking scary, because it's like looking in a mirror. He has plans, and I hit the nail on the fucking head.

"Yeah," he grins. "What are you gonna do about Genny?" he asks, changing the subject like fucking whiplash.

"What do you mean?" I ask, arching my brow.

"You're not going to let her be with Graham, are you?" he asks, looking completely disgusted. I shrug, taking another sip from my drink. "She doesn't love him," he mutters.

"She might," I murmur as I watch Graham's hand rest against her back from across the room, dangerously close to her ass.

"She doesn't," he insists. "But if you aren't going to treat her right…"

"Then what?" I challenge.

"Then you need to let her go," he says. Without another word, he walks away from me.

I don't think about how much fucking smarter and more together my baby brother is than me. I choose to order another round from the bartender instead, and I watch. I watch how Imogen is stiff, how she's not touching Graham back, and how Graham, aside from the hand on her back, is pretty much ignoring her. She tugs on his sleeve, and he leans down to give her an ear. He then nods and releases her as he talks to someone.

Imogen walks away from him, and I know where she's going as she makes her way through the crowd. I slide into the hallway, without being seen, then I make my way toward the bathroom, slipping into the dark room before her.

I bite my bottom lip when I hear her high heels walk inside, then she turns on the light as she locks the door. Before she can even turn around, I'm pressing my chest against her back.

chapter four

Imogen

I gasp as someone's hard chest presses against my back, but as soon as I inhale, my body relaxes. I know exactly who it is. *Sloane.* My belly heats and flutters at the exact same time, just as it always does when he's around. Something I haven't felt for the past three years.

One of his arms wraps around my stomach. I shiver when his hand slides up the center of my chest and beneath my dress, to curl his fingers around my breast. His mouth goes to my ear, his hot breath and rough fingers gently brush against my skin.

"Imogen, baby," he whispers.

My entire flesh breaks out in goosebumps, and I shiver. Then I close my eyes. *Damn him.* I love it when he whispers to me, his body so close.

"Sloane," I respond shakily.

"Missed you," he rumbles as his hand squeezes my breast roughly.

My body betrays my mind, and I moan as I let my head fall back against his shoulder. I feel his other hand on my thigh, at the slit of my dress. Then, in a single breath, it's beneath my panties and he's cupping me.

"Sloane," I whimper. "This is wrong."

"You're my wife," he informs me as he fills me with two fingers. I'm wet, but I haven't had sex in three years—not since him—so it's a little painful.

"Fuck, baby. So tight and warm, just like I always remembered," he murmurs against my neck. His tongue snakes out and he tastes me while his fingers gently pump in and out of my pussy.

I push my ass slightly against his slacks and moan when I feel his hard cock against my crack. Sloane's thumb presses against my clit, and I gasp, turning my head to press my lips just on the underside of his clean-shaven jaw.

"Still so sweet when I touch you," he rasps. "Come all over me, Imogen," he groans as he curls his fingers inside of me, grinding his palm against my clit, just like he knows I love.

"Oh, god," I say through trembling lips. My body shakes, and I come.

I feel him gather my dress in his hands, turning me around to face the mirror, and then his tuxedo rustles behind me. Without a word, he yanks my panties down before he fills me from behind. He grabs my face and turns it toward the mirror, his green eyes connecting with my brown ones; his jaw set hard and looking like the most beautiful man I have ever seen.

"You're my wife, Imogen, *mine*," he grunts as he fucks me.

I can't do anything but gasp as his hips thrust and slap against my ass. He continues to hold my face so that I'm forced to look into his gorgeous eyes.

"No man touches you," he growls as his hips pump harder. "Not ever."

I want to push him away and then pull him closer. No matter how pissed I am at him, he feels so damn good. I reach up behind me and thread my fingers into his hair, tugging hard on the strands, which causes him to suck in a breath. It only urges him to fuck me harder and faster.

"Keep looking at me," he demands.

His hand slips between my legs again, and he starts to rub firm circles against my clit. My second climax rushes through me, and as soon as I cry out, he moans with his own release. I feel his seed fill my body, and instantly I regret it. This should have never happened.

"This can't happen again," I whisper, still looking at him in the mirror.

"You let that piece of shit touch you, and I'll kill him," he growls.

"Yeah, well, if we were playing the same game I'd have to kill hundreds of women," I announce.

Sloane's jaw clenches and his eyes narrow on me, but he doesn't respond. He pulls out of me, and I feel his cum slide down my legs. I turn to face him, tired of looking at him through the mirror, and then I reach back and slap him across the face. It stings my palm as his head flies to the side.

"You get one pass, Genny, but only because I deserve a hell of a lot more. You hit me again, and we'll have words," he growls. I'm too fired up to care.

"How dare you come here, to a party, and try to piss on me like this, and then tell me who can and cannot touch me," I grind out as I pull my panties up, trying to ignore the fact that Sloane fucked me with *no condom* just a few minutes ago.

"You have my last name. You're legally my wife; and if I lift your dress, my brand is assuredly still on your hip. I can tell you whatever the fuck I want," he growls.

"Fuck you, Sloane Huntington," I whisper as tears fill my eyes. He takes a few steps toward me and my back presses against the door.

With his nose practically touching mine, Sloane wraps his hand loosely around the front of my throat. His lips are just a hair's breadth from touching my own.

"You are mine, Imogen. That fuck touches you, and I'll kill him. You are not marrying him. You are not having his kids. I won't allow it," he whispers harshly.

My eyes widen in surprise, "Allow it?"

"Yeah. You have any kids, they'll be mine," he murmurs.

"You have got to be kidding me right now. Is this some kind of joke?" I laugh out humorlessly.

"Fuck no, it's not a joke," he says, straightening but keeping his hand around my throat.

"I don't see you for three years, and for the decade before that you stick your dick into any wet hole you can find, and I'm supposed to, what, just accept that and start a family with you? I don't think so," I snort.

"There she is," he growls stepping back from me.

Narrowing my eyes, I ask, "Who?"

"That bitch you like to bring out. That bitch inside of you that you save just for my pleasure," he shrugs.

His words cut deep, and for the first time in years, I don't throw up a shield. I let him see just how deeply he's cut me with them. I know he notices when his brow furrows and he runs a hand through his perfectly, albeit a little too long, hair.

"I'm a bitch because I won't fall at your feet? I'm a bitch because I don't accept you fucking around with a smile on my face? I'm sorry, Sloane, I'm sorry you don't think I'm good enough to be faithful to. Most of all I'm sorry that we've both spent years wasting each other's time."

"Genny," he whispers, his head tipped down but his eyes open and focused on mine.

"We don't work, Sloane," I choke. "I've loved you since I was fifteen years old, but you don't love me the same way," I murmur.

"Imogen," he growls as he crowds me against the door again, his hands slapping down on either side of my head.

"It's been twenty years. We haven't been happy for a long time. I don't think it could ever be possible at this point."

"And Graham will make you happy?" he says, sounding disgusted.

"He wants to have a family—children," I shrug.

"Offered to give you those more than once, baby," he says, sounding cocky and pissed off all at once.

"Yeah, while you were out getting blitzed and fucking every whore who would spread for you. Sorry, that doesn't really put me in the mood to have your baby."

"Fucking shit, Genny. What do you want from me?" he asks. To his credit, he looks serious.

I lift my hand to cup the smooth skin of his cheek as a tear falls from my eye. I haven't cried in front of him in at least ten years. I refused to show him how much he hurt me, or any emotion at all. His eyes track the tear as it falls before they clash with mine again, and I can see the obvious concern on his face.

God, if he'd only looked at me like this ten years ago.

"There was a time where I wanted you to grow up and leave the club, but that's not you. I get that now, and I'm sorry I tried to change that part of you, Sloane. But in the end, the cheating killed us, killed our chances," I whisper as more tears streak down my face.

"You're still legally my wife. We aren't dead yet," he growls.

"We've been dead for a long time." Even I don't believe the finality of my words. They're weak as hell.

"Nope," he says, popping the *p* before he presses his lips to mine in a hard kiss.

Moving me over to the side, he then walks out of the bathroom, leaving me alone. I take a moment to clean up and then look at myself in the mirror. I can't hide the fact that I look freshly fucked, but there's more that I can't hide—and that's the *hope* I stupidly feel.

Why I'm allowing myself to feel hope toward Sloane? Why do I have a small smile curved on my lips just thinking about him, I don't know—but I do.

It's probably foolish, and he'll probably break my heart again; but the truth is, Graham won't make me happy. He was never going to make me happy. Only one person can truly do that, and that's Sloane McKinley Huntington, III.

My husband.

Fuck.

I hate him right now, but most of all, I hate my fucking self.

Making my way out of the bathroom and slowly back into the party, I take a deep breath. My eyes glance around the room, and I don't see Sloane anywhere.

I let out a heavy sigh as I walk toward Graham, who is glaring at me. Once I reach his side, he wraps his hand around mine tightly before he mutters something to the man he's talking to and he tugs me hard behind him.

"Imogen," a woman's voice calls out. I turn to see Kalli Huntington wobbling toward me.

"Graham, stop," I plead, pulling hard on his arm.

He stops, but his lips are in a straight, angry line, and his eyes are focused on mine.

"Kalli," I say softly as I smile. Unless she's drinking at a party, she's usually locked up in her room, drowning in a bottle or five of wine.

"My daughter," she slurs as she wraps her arms around me. "Don't let that son of mine treat you badly, now, you hear me," she mutters as she always does.

"Kalli, Sloane and I have been separated for three years," I gently remind her.

She sways, her eyes widening slightly before she waves her hand at me in a dismissal.

"You're good for my boy. He'll get you back. He always does," she murmurs, causing Graham to growl behind me.

"How about I come by tomorrow afternoon and I bring brunch?" I offer, knowing the woman probably won't even eat tomorrow and simultaneously trying to shut her up. In all honesty, she'll probably still be drunk.

"Oh, I would adore that, simply adore that. You know you're one of the only good girls to come out of all these society sluts," she cackles.

I can't help but smile. I bite the inside of my cheek, so that I don't burst out in laughter like her. In a different world, if

Kalli weren't such a complete disaster, I have always thought that we would truly get along wonderfully.

"I'll see you tomorrow, Kalli," I say gently as I take a step back from her.

"Not too early now," she warns.

"Of course not," I agree.

Graham doesn't let me say another word. He tugs me along and doesn't stop until he's throwing me in his car. I cry out as I fall into the back seat, twisting my ankle slightly. "Go to my place," he growls to the driver.

"No, please, take me home," I call out.

The driver nods as his eyes flash to mine in the rearview mirror.

"You fuck him?" Graham asks.

I turn to him in surprise. "Excuse me?" I say, trying to stall. "Graham, this isn't going to work."

"You needed that closure, that's fine. You're mine now, Imogen," he announces. I scrunch my nose up.

"Graham, did you not hear me? This isn't going to work," I announce.

"Because of Sloane?" he asks on a growl. "Because he's a worthless fucking piece of shit. You've done nothing but waste your life with him. He's trash, Imogen." I flinch at his hard words.

"No, it has nothing to do with Sloane. It isn't going to work because I can't force my feelings, and I'm not attracted to you," I blurt out.

"I don't care. We're getting married, and you're having my children," he announces, acting completely unruffled.

"Graham, no. I'm telling you *no*," I say standing firm.

Then his hand flashes out and slaps me across the face,

sending me across the back of the car. All of a sudden, the car stops. I'm frozen in place, my eyes focused on Graham's aloof ones.

His hand reaches out to wrap tightly around the front of my throat. "I'll let this slide this one and only time, Imogen. But if you know what's good for you, you'll come to heel, and do it like fucking lightning," he grinds out.

Before I can respond, the driver opens my door and hauls me out by my bicep. His grip is firm, yet gentle, and I teeter on my heels before he places his body in front of mine, between Graham and me.

His voice is deep, but I hear him clearly, "Go inside, ma'am." I turn around and see that I'm home.

"Th-thank you," I stutter, holding my face.

"I'll make sure you're safely inside and he won't follow you," he says, pressing his back to me.

I turn and run, ignoring Graham's angry voice, listening to him struggle against the driver and threatening to have him fired as he calls me a whore.

Once I'm inside, I set my alarm, lock my doors, and sink to my ass, my tears flowing down my cheeks. I press my shaky palm to my heated cheek as my body trembles uncontrollably. I have completely fucked this whole thing up.

I don't drive back to the clubhouse after the party. Instead, I climb inside of my *'67 Shelby GT500e Super Snake* and speed back to my house. I haven't stayed here since I've been back from prison. I came here long enough to grab my tuxedo and my car before tonight's party. For whatever reason, I feel the need to be here tonight.

Walking inside after I've parked my car in the garage, I look around. It doesn't feel like my home. I didn't stay here often. I stayed at the clubhouse more, and that makes me feel like a fucking dick.

Genny left everything here; kitchen appliances, dishes, decorations, fucking everything. It's like she wanted zero reminder of our life when she walked out the door.

Making my way to the bedroom, I notice that everything has a thick layer of dust over it, every single surface. I walk toward her closet, needing to see her space for whatever fucked up reason.

All of her clothes are hanging up perfectly, by color order. *Fuck, she's so goddamn anal.* I laugh to myself as I open a drawer in her closet, it's full of sexy little nighties and silk stockings.

My fingertips run over them and catches on something, a tag. In fact, almost everything in the drawer still has the tags on it. I don't want to know what she was thinking when she bought all of this shit, but she never wore it. Knowing what was going through her mind would probably just make me feel like an even bigger asshole.

Furrowing my brow, I decide I'm going to get my wife back. No way in fuck am I going to let a prick like Graham take her from me. She's not his, she's mine, my property. I'll do whatever it takes to ensure that I'm the victor, just as I always am when it comes to him.

I can't deny the pull that I have toward Genny. She's much more than just some conquest for me. Spending three years to think about all I did wrong with her, made me truly appreciative of the woman I had at my side, all those years.

When I got out, I decided I was going to let her go and find her happiness; but I'll be damned if it's with Graham *fucking* Bayard. She's mine, being inside of her tonight proved just how much that is still true. I'm bringing my baby home, where she fucking belongs, as my wife and my Old Lady.

No man touches Imogen but me.

chapter five

Imogen

Looking at myself in the mirror, I grimace at the sight before me. My cheek is swollen and there is bruising just underneath my eye. I still can't believe that Graham hit me. He has always seemed indifferent; patient, but not angry or forceful by any means. We've been seeing each other for months, and he's never tried to push me further than a good-night kiss, until last night.

As soon as he saw Sloane standing across the room, he changed. He started groping at me a little more than usual, holding me closer to him, and his grip was firmer than ever. Then he hit me when I tried to end things. The anger that came pouring out of him was more emotion than I have ever witnessed in the years I've known him.

I feel out of sorts and frazzled—not just my face, but the

rest of my appearance, too. I throw on a loose tank, tucking the front of it into my tight, dark wash jeans. I slip my feet into a pair of sandals and slide a big pair of sunglasses on my face to cover my bruise.

I promised that I would go to my future-ex-mother-in-law's house today. While she probably won't remember, I always make good on any promise I give. Plus, I want to see Kip again, find out if he knows anything else about Sloane.

Calling ahead to the place I know Kalli loves brunch from, I order for take-out. It's not something they would normally do, but I'm a Huntington. I don't have to even go inside. They send someone out to deliver the bags of food to me. My credit card is on file, so I don't even have to pay for it right then. I hand the delivery girl a twenty, and then I'm off and heading toward the *Huntington Manor*.

The mansion is quiet, nothing like the hustle and bustle of the party last night, and I know that Kalli has requested that cleanup not start until after noon so that she can nurse her hangover. Looking down at my watch, I shake my head. It's eleven, so she shouldn't be too angry that I'm here.

Ringing the bell, I shift the bag of food to another hand and let out a breath as the door opens. I expect to see a staff member, but instead, I'm met with Kipling. I smile and he shakes his head slightly as he opens the door to let me inside.

"You left with Graham," he points out. I nod as I walk into the kitchen, Kip on my heels.

"I also broke up with him," I say, reaching for a few plates. "You want some brunch?"

"Nah, I ate," he shrugs.

I don't remove my glasses as I move around their kitchen. I'm all too familiar with the Huntington home. I spent my entire teenage years rooting through this kitchen with Sloane. I try not to let the happy memories flood my mind as I look for all of the things I need.

"You and Sloane, you're going to work all this out, aren't you?" he asks, sounding far too hopeful.

"Probably not. There're just too many bad years between us," I whisper, the heavy weight of that knowledge settling in my chest.

"Genny," he rumbles, sounding so much like Sloane it makes me ache.

"When do you leave for *Hah-vahd*?" I jokingly ask, trying to lighten the mood.

"Couple of weeks."

"Kipling, sweetheart, why are you still here? Don't you have Rugby at the club?" Kalli asks as she floats into the room, wearing a floor-length nightgown and robe, looking as though she belongs in a soap opera.

"Yeah," he grunts before he turns and runs off without another word.

"He's a good boy," she murmurs. I nod my agreement.

Her gaze swings to me and I watch as her eyes are scrutinizing as she looks at me, "Why are you wearing glasses? Take them off," she demands. I take them off but keep my head down. "Let me see."

Lifting my head, I let my gaze crash with hers. She doesn't gasp in horror like I expect. Rather, she grabs ahold of my chin with her hand and assesses my face.

"Bring those plates upstairs and I'll fix your face," she announces as she turns and floats away. I stand for a moment in shock, then do as she's ordered.

I've been with Sloane for years, and yet I've never stepped

foot inside of Kalli and Sloane II's master suite. It's lovely. A little cold for my taste, but very lovely. I know that she's had it styled by an interior decorator and probably changes it every couple of years, as my mother does with her entire house. Except for my childhood bedroom, something she hasn't touched since I left home for whatever reason.

"Come in here and sit," she orders from her bathroom.

I walk in and notice she's standing at a makeup vanity. I set the plates down before I sit in the chair as I watch her arrange her makeup.

"Sloaney's father has been known to have a heavy hand from time to time. Let me fix this so that nobody notices," she says. My eyes widen in surprise.

"Sloane didn't do this," I inform her. She nods.

"Oh, I know my boy didn't do this. Why do you think he hates coming here so much? Why do you think he's always rebelled? His father hasn't hit me in years. Kipling doesn't know he ever has; but when we were younger, Sloaney saw much more than a child should have," she says, sounding sad as she dabs makeup on my face.

"He never told me," I whisper, feeling sad, so fucking sad.

"I know he didn't. He wouldn't. Sloaney is like me. He keeps everything inside. Probably why I drink and he does the many things he does," she says, giving me a knowing look. "Those things being the reason you left him, I'm sure."

I bite my bottom lip and worry it with my teeth as she works on my face. I feel sad and guilty. How did I not know this part of my husband's life? All these years together and I didn't know he'd been raised in an abusive household.

I know that in society we don't speak of such things. They run rampant and everybody just turns a blind eye and gossips behind each other's backs. A husband's hand that's a little heavy, a wife asking too many questions and getting put in her place, it's common, but nobody mentions it.

Yet, how did I not know that Sloane had witnessed it first hand? How did he not trust me enough to tell me any of it? The thought makes my stomach ache. I don't really know my husband at all.

"There. Flawless," she whispers. I turn around to look in the mirror. I am, indeed, *flawless*. "Are you staying with Graham?" she asks as she picks up her plate. She leans against her vanity before she begins to nibble on her food.

"No," I shake my head. "I broke up with him last night."

"Good. He's an asshole, just like his father," she says, scrunching up her nose. I can't help but giggle.

Spending the afternoon with Kalli turns out to be extremely pleasant. Maybe it's the fact that I suffered at Graham's hand and she opened up to me about herself and about Sloane, but something has shifted between us. Not that we ever didn't get along, but now, it feels like a friendship has formed.

"Don't let Sloaney walk all over you, but don't give up on him completely either," she whispers as she gives me a hug later that afternoon.

"I'm so tired," I admit.

"I know you are, but you're good for him," she says as we separate from our embrace.

I purse my lips together, "What if he's not good for me, though?"

"If you didn't love him, you would have left a long time ago. Trust me," she nods. "And if he didn't love you, he would have let you."

After our time together, I now see her in a completely different light. She's not just some sloppy drunk, she's nursing some deep hurts inside of her. I don't necessarily agree, because her drinking has always made her a neglectful parent; but I now have a compassion for her that I never did before. You truly don't know how someone else's life is behind closed doors.

On my drive home, I think about her words. She's stayed with Sloane's father, not out of duty or standing, but out of love, no matter how much he *didn't* deserve it.

In our world, love isn't necessarily a factor in relationships; it's about breeding, money, and power. It's very aristocratic, and in a sense, we're the American version of royalty.

Women are urged to marry men their fathers approve of, and men are urged to marry women whose families can help their careers or tie businesses together through marriage.

Sloane and I both rebelled, not only with being together, but for leaving society as well.

"Hello," I say into my phone as I disarm my alarm, walking inside of my home.

"Graham called me this morning. You need to come down to my office," my father announces.

I feel fear and panic prickle over my skin at the mere mention of Graham's name. I've held it together so far since he hit me, but I can't deny that I'm waiting for him to do more, to hurt me again. I'm terrified of what will happen if he gets me alone. I feel as though a rock has settled in my stomach, and I wheeze at his words.

My father doesn't hit. He never has. Lifting a hand to do *anything* would be beneath him. No, my father mentally abuses and tortures. Before I had control of my own trust, he would try to control me monetarily.

I still don't have complete and total access to my money, so he could very well still try that—but I have more than enough to live the rest of my life comfortably, so he can honestly keep the rest for all I care.

"I can't today," I lie.

"Of course not *today*. I don't have an available appointment time for you today. Tomorrow. Lunch. Eleven-thirty. Meet me at *Boulevard*," he announces before he ends the call.

I let out a heavy sigh and re-set my burglar alarm before I make my way upstairs. I'm completely and totally drained. I didn't sleep much last night, and although it's not even six in the evening, all I want is a hot bath and my warm bed.

Opening my eyes, I wait for that pounding pressure that usually follows, except it doesn't. My head is completely clear. I'm completely sober, for the first time since being out. I had a few bourbons last night at my brother's party, but I didn't get tanked, knowing I had to drive home and having no desire to stay in the city for longer than I had to.

My phone rings and my brow furrows at who is on the other end.

"Mother?" I ask in confusion.

My mother never calls me. She's usually too lost in her bottle to concern herself with anyone else.

"Are you going to let her get away?" she asks, not bothering to even greet me.

"Wasn't planning on it," I grunt, though its none of her fucking business.

"Good. Whatever you do, you need to do it quickly."

"Why?" I ask.

"Graham and her father are plotting something," she states.

"I know. The fucking idiot told me everything himself," I chuckle.

"You need to see your wife in the next day or two," she says before ending the call.

I look at the phone in my hand, confused by her words and her insistence. My mother usually calls me for one reason and one reason only, to appear with her for whatever functions where we're required to look like a happy family. Nothing else.

I get dressed and head down to the clubhouse on my bike. Shit is not sitting well with me. The things Graham said, the things my mother's said—none of it. I'm not about to walk into a situation blindly. First, I need some information.

"Soar," Camo greets as I walk into the clubhouse.

His woman, Ivy, is perched on his thigh, and I'm surprised to see that she's pregnant.

"Hey, brother, congrats," I say, lifting my chin to Ivy.

"Thanks," he grins, placing his hand on her swollen belly.

"We just found out it's a girl," Ivy squeals. I can't help but smile.

"Get your guns out, brother," I murmur as I walk past them to MadDog's office.

He should get his guns out, too. If his daughter is half as pretty as Ivy, he's in deep fucking shit.

"C'mon in," MadDog's gravelly voice calls out.

Walking inside, I'm surprised to see he's got a toddler in his arms. I can't tell which daughter it is. I don't know either of them, and it's then that I realize exactly how long I've been away. MadDog has two toddlers and another baby on the way. My whole life stopped while everyone else's kept moving right along.

"You still in contact with Russian's tech guy, Oliver?" I ask, my eyes unable to move away from the little dark-haired girl in his lap. It hits me out of nowhere, I could have a whole brood of my own, if I wasn't such a colossal fuckup.

"What's wrong?" he barks. My eyes lift to his.

"My mom called me to talk about Genny. Normally my mom doesn't care much what I do, but she sounded funny. Last night I confronted Genny and her new man, who I've known my whole life," I explain. MadDog's eyebrows rise in surprise. "He's talked her father into releasing her entire trust fund to him to manage. He already told me he was going to transfer it to his off-shore accounts and leave her penniless," I explain, leaving the part about giving her a couple of his kids out.

He doesn't say anything for a beat, but I can see the cogs working behind his eyes, "I've never asked you details about your life, Soar. I know you come from some money. Especially based off of your car and Genny's. But I think it's about time you come completely clean with me about how much money we're talking about here."

"Genny and I both come from old money. I'm a Huntington," I say. MadDog's mouth gapes slightly.

"Fuck," he rasps.

"Genny's family has just as much as mine, if not more. We were raised in society, private schools, vacations to Europe, the whole bit," I shrug.

"This guy wants her money, that it?"

"He's from old money, too. Graham Bayard. He's hated me and has competed with me since we were kids. Genny is just another competition to him, but he'd break her. He'd not only leave her broke but break her mind and body too," I explain.

"Unlike the way you've treated her?" he asks, arching his brow.

"Never said I was a saint, prez; but what he would do, I can't let that happen. I need more info. I don't even know where she's living right now. I need everything on her, her father, and Graham."

"I do this for you, what are you going to do with it? Aside from deal with the situation. What are you going to do about Genny?"

I want to tell him to mind his own fucking business, but I don't. I need him. I take him in. He looks a little older than he did three years ago, but he looks a fuck of a lot happier than he did before he married Mary-Anne. He doesn't fuck whores that I know of, and he's got a third baby on the way, in four years. Instead of looking miserable, he looks more content than I've ever seen him.

I wonder if I'll ever be content. If I'll be able to be that kind of man, now that I'm forced into sobriety. I wonder if I can do it, if I can really do it. Or if it will all come crashing down around me like a goddamn avalanche of shit.

"Getting her back and bringing her home," I mumble, ignoring the churning in my gut.

"Going back to the way it used to be?"

I let out a breath and slide my palms against my jeans

before I tap my fingers on my knees. "Can't get fucked up, so no," I bark. He stays stony faced and waits for my real answer. "Genny's mine. Has been since she was fifteen years old. I haven't been good to her, but that doesn't mean I don't love her. I do. I can't let her go to some douche that I know is intent on causing her harm."

"What you didn't tell me in any of that is that you want to change or that you want your relationship to change. Don't string her along for another twenty years and make her completely miserable, or yourself," he says, cocking his head to the side.

"I'll get you the info. Leave me their names. I'm doing this because I see past the bitch-shield Genny's had up for years. I remember the pretty, sweet, young thing she was when you brought her here. I watched her change because of *whateverthefuck* you guys have going on between you. I'll do this for Genny and because you're a *Devil*—but I'm warning you, get your shit straight with her. Don't waste anymore of hers or your own time."

I leave his office. Without a glance at anybody else, I leave the clubhouse. I have to meet with my probation officer, but my mind is consumed with MadDog's words. He remembers the young eighteen-year-old Genny, and it's not lost on me that he attributes her bitch façade as being my doing. He's not wrong, that's the fucker of it all.

I did all this shit.

Me.

Sloane McKinley Huntington, III. A giant fuck up, just like my father. A name that hurts women one way or another for no reason other than they are supreme assholes. A name that I've never been proud of, not since I was a kid—not since

I discovered just how fucked up my father is.

Not since I walked in on him fucking his secretary in the ass, her dead eyes aimed at the door. He didn't stop, either. He finished, put his dick away and threw an envelope of cash at her head before he told her to get her whore ass out of his office.

Degradation, my father's favorite fucking pastime. I was ten years old. He never once apologized. He told me when you have money you can do whatever you want, to whoever you want, and nobody can say a goddamn thing.

You fuck, you steal, you lie, you cheat, and you beat the shit out of your family—no consequences. Those were my life lessons as a kid. Those are the reasons I'm fucked in the head. Those are the reasons I rebelled and found dope, found a way to forget it all; and yet, it didn't help me one fucking bit. Here I am, still a complete fuck up.

chapter six

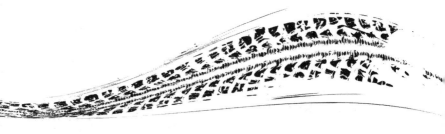

Imogen

Day two of my bruised face is by far much worse than day one. It's darker, and there's no way I have the magical powers of Kalli Huntington when it comes to makeup, so I don't even bother.

Graham hasn't made an appearance yet, but it seems like he's going to try to get to me through my family, which doesn't surprise me at all. What scares me is what my father will say and do. I know that he and Graham are buddies.

If my father wants to ask me about my eye, then I'll tell him the truth. I have nothing to hide, and I already know that this luncheon is about Graham. If he sees my face and still wants to push me with Graham, then I don't even know what to think.

My father and I have never gotten along. No, that's a lie.

When I was a child, he doted on me. He doted on me to the point where my mother would get jealous. She'd say snide things to me, narrow her eyes, and just be cold toward me in general. By the time I was a teenager, it had gotten so bad that I started to rebel so that my father wouldn't think I was perfect.

It worked.

Throughout my adult years, my relationship with my mother and father has been tolerable. They never cared for Sloane, but they supported our marriage because Sloane is from proper breeding, though they weren't happy about it at all. They couldn't say much. Since I've been back the past three years, things have improved between my mother and I; however, they've only stayed distant between my father and me.

My mother wants grandchildren, and both of my parents were ecstatic when I started dating Graham. My father deals with his father's company often, and I know they had been making plans on being in-laws. Sloane's father can't stand my father and vice-versa. I don't know why, but they've never been able to be cordial to each other.. Another reason my father didn't want us to be married.

I smooth down my cream pencil skirt and adjust the straps of my deep purple tank top before I put on my matching cream blazer. My feet are encased in pale pink, sling back, four-inch-high heels.

My outfit screams that I'm *together*, my face looks completely opposite of that. I don't have time to worry about my face a second longer. Hurrying downstairs, I slip into my garage and start my car, with only twenty minutes to make it to the restaurant. It's going to be a time-crunch, that's for sure.

The restaurant is bustling, but I spot my father immediately. I ignore the hostess' wide eye's when she sees my cheek, and hurry past her to my father's table.

"Father," I say as I remove my blazer and sit down.

"Sloane do that to your face?" he asks immediately as I adjust myself in my chair and place my napkin at my lap.

"No, Graham did."

"Don't lie to me. I know all about Sloane's father and his heavy hand. No surprise his son is cut from the same cloth. I know that you and he met up at Kipling's graduation party," he states coolly.

I'm not surprised that he knows. He was probably watching me from across the room the entire time—my every move.

"We did have a discussion, yes, but Graham did this to my face when I refused to go home with him. Sloane has never hit me."

"Why *didn't* you go home with Graham? He *is* your fiancé," my father says accusingly.

"Graham is not my fiancé. I actually don't wish to see him any longer. Not that it's your business, but I'm not attracted to him," I announce.

"Who gives a shit if you're attracted to him? You're old, Imogen. No man in our social circle would take you at the age you are. You've got one unsuccessful marriage beneath your belt, everybody thinks you're sterile, and you're lucky a man with such impeccable breeding like Graham is even considering taking you," my father snorts as he lifts his hand to call over the waiter.

I listen to my father order, *for us*, and then shoo the waiter off. I didn't even hear what he ordered, knowing it wouldn't matter. I'm not planning on staying here long enough to eat.

"That wasn't nice, father," I whisper. "Sloane and I, we have our own set of issues, but we never tried for children, so I'm fairly certain that I'm not infertile."

"Well, that's good. At least you might be able to have children; but that window of time is narrowed as it is. That doesn't negate the fact that you're old, Imogen. Men my age have their children already, so you couldn't secure yourself in a family with a man my age. Graham is your only hope."

"I would rather be alone than be with Graham. Why are you pushing this so hard?" I ask.

"I'm not going to repeat myself again. Graham comes from a good family, much better than the man you married," he grunts.

"I'm sorry to ruin all of your plans, but I won't be marrying him, father," I say standing firm. "Aside from the million other reasons why I don't want him, I won't be with a man who takes his anger out on me this way," I say pointing to my bruised face as I stand. "I'll see you at your summer party in a few weeks," I state before I turn and walk away.

I've never turned my back on my father in the middle of a conversation, and I can feel his narrowed, heated gaze on my back with each step I take, but I refuse to allow that conversation about Graham.

It's over with, finished.

There is no *Imogen and Graham*, and there never will be. To be honest, there never really was. I tried, but there was always something lacking, either in me, or him, I'm not sure—but I know one thing is for certain, I don't want him.

It doesn't take me long to get home, and I'm grateful for

the lighter traffic of the mid-afternoon. I make my way inside and kick off my shoes in the mudroom before I bend down to gather them in my hands.

Slowly, I make my way upstairs and change out of my luncheon clothes and into a pair of soft, faded holey jeans, and an oversized *Notorious Devils* shirt before throwing my long hair into a pony-tail.

The shirt is Sloane's, and it's a complete comfort piece. I used to wear it when I wanted to feel close to him, when he would be gone or I just missed him in general. It's probably stupid, but I don't have much to grasp onto when it comes to Sloane, so this shirt, I'm keeping it close to me—*forever.*

Making my way downstairs, I freeze when my doorbell rings. With a frown pulling at my lips, quietly as I can, I walk over to the door and look through the peephole. I expect to see Graham standing on the other side, but what I don't expect is Sloane. He's standing with his hands in his pockets, looking almost nervous as he shifts from side to side in his boots.

"What are you doing here?" I ask as I open the door, my eyes trained on his green ones.

"What in the fuck happened to your face, Imogen?" he barks as he barges past me into my living room.

After closing and locking the door, I turn around to see him standing in the living room, his angry gaze on me, his jaw clenched and his balled fists resting on his hips, waiting for an answer. I inhale a deep breath before opening my mouth to speak, but he can't stand waiting.

"He do that to you?" he asks as his arms move and hang loosely at his sides, attempting to appear relaxed, although he's anything but.

"After the party," I admit with a nod. "I broke it off with him."

His eyes narrow, "He hit you because you broke up with him?"

"Graham assumed I was breaking it off with him because you were back," I state. "The driver held him back once we were in front of my house. I ran inside and set the alarm."

"Fuck," he bites. "Why didn't you call me?"

I look up and into his eyes, which are focused on me and still angry; but I have a feeling he's as much angry with me right now as he is with Graham, and that pisses me off.

"Why would I call you?" I huff.

"Maybe because I'm your husband, and it's my job to protect you, and he *fucking hit you*," he roars.

I jerk back as though he's the one who's just hit me and stare at him, my mouth agape before anger builds inside of me.

Fuck. Him.

"Your job is to protect me?" I say with harsh laughter.

"*Imogen*," he hisses, his tone one of warning.

"No, really, explain to me how you've protected me? Were you protecting me while you were high as a kite, fucking whores, and I was home alone? I mean, I'm curious as hell," I say, crossing my arms under my breasts.

"I never hit you," he grinds through clenched teeth.

"No, that was the one shitty thing you never did. But you cheated on me, probably more times than I could even count," I say, tipping my head to the side and watching as his eyes cloud over, knowing I'm right.

In a flash, he's in front of me, one hand gently cupping my bruised cheek, the other clamped firmly around my waist.

His thumb traces my bruise, and his lips are so close they're almost touching mine when he speaks.

"I'll kill him for marking you, sunshine," he whispers.

It's as if all of the breath has left my lungs. They burn and my eyes sting as they water. Peace washes over me, as though my body suddenly feels warm and safe in his arms.

I swallow the lump in my throat and try not to cry. I feel like I can finally breathe for the first time since Graham's hand lashed out against my cheek. *I'm safe.* I won't admit that he's right, that he makes me feel safe and protected—but right now, I do feel just that.

Then his words repeat in my head and my breath is lost for a while other reason—*Sunshine.* A name he hasn't called me in at least ten years. As much as I love it, I hate it at the same time.

"Sloane," I warn.

"Baby, I don't give a fuck what kind of bitchy attitude you threw at him. A man doesn't put hands on a woman, especially not *my* woman. My cum was still inside your pussy and he hurt you," he rasps.

I fight to get out his grasp, but he only holds me tighter. If I don't fight him right now, that blanket of safety will consume me completely, and I'll give in to him—again.

"I'm not yours," I growl.

"My name's on your body, my ring on your finger, and you have my last name. I explained this shit to you; makes you one hundred percent mine, Genny," he growls right back at me.

"We don't work, Sloane. I'm not yours, and the divorce is happening," I practically plead. I need him to release me, he makes me feel way too much.

I watch as his eyes alight with humor and he laughs, his voice deep as it washes over me. Dammit, I love it. I hate that I love it, too. His scent, his warmth coming from his body, and then his damn laugh makes my body feel hot. Not to mention the way the rough pad of his thumb gently runs over my bruised face over and over. It's too much.

"We work, sunshine. We've always worked where it counts," he rasps. "I was too fucking baked, searching for the next high, too fucked up in my head, to be any good to you before, but we work. We *fucking* work, baby."

"What's different now?" I ask, trying not to sound as breathless as I feel, staring up into his green eyes. "Why are you saying all of this? Why do you *care*?"

"I'm sober," he says simply.

"Yeah? For how long?"

I watch as he bites his lip and studies me. Stupidly, my body wants all of him, right now. Saturday night was not enough. It'd been so long. Now that I've had a taste, I want more. I always want more when it comes to him. So much more.

As much as I should hate myself for it, I can't—my heart has always wanted Sloane and nobody else. My body has always craved him, as though it can never get enough of him, no matter how badly he's hurt me, time and time again.

"Can't tell the future," he states.

I feel supremely disappointed. It's not the answer I wanted from him, but it's probably more honest than the answer I crave.

"I can't waste any more years," I murmur. "I'm over it all."

"Imogen?"

"I'm thirty-five, Sloane. I want a family. I've wanted a

family for a long time. Graham was offering that to me, and I'm not going to lie, it was tempting. As my father says, I'm old, and nobody will want me anymore. I can't help but feel that there's something out there for me; but at the end of the day, I want a baby, and I want a husband who loves me," I admit.

I feel as though a weight has been lifted off of my chest just by saying the words out loud.

"But you don't want those things with me?" Sloane asks, taking a step back from me and dropping his hands from my body. That fear climbs up my throat again, threatening to choke me just at the loss of his hands on my skin.

"I waited for those things for years, Sloane," I whisper.

"I can't just let you go, knowing you'll be going to another man. Not when you're right here, wearing my old *Devils* shirt—not when you're still mine," he rasps. Without another word, he closes the distance between us and crashes his lips against mine. "Not when my sunshine is still inside, burning. Not when my stupidity didn't completely extinguish that flame."

Lifting my hands, I place my palms on his chest to push him away, but he's solid and doesn't even move a millimeter. Sloane's tongue tastes my lips as his hands wrap around my ass and squeezes me roughly. I moan, and he takes the opportunity to slide his tongue into my mouth.

His stroke his firm and warm, and I can't help but think about the stroke of his cock as his tongue takes over. One of his hands slides up my back and tangles into my ponytail as he twists my head to the side to deepen our kiss. He groans before nibbling on my lips and then presses his forehead to mine.

"Don't walk away from me, sunshine," he whispers.

"Too much has happened between us for this to work out," I say, my voice trembling.

"We're too good together for it not to work."

Closing my eyes, I admit, "I'm tired of hurting."

I've never admitted to Sloane how much his actions hurt me. I've always withheld sex or acted like a bitch to him, but I've never come right out and told him how his actions truly affect me. I'm not the same person I was three years ago, and I'm willing to admit the truth to him now. He needs to know.

When he went away, I felt free. I took a good two-years to work on me, to reflect and really examine the woman I had become. I hated myself, and that wasn't all because of him, it was me too.

I'm definitely not the same woman as the one he left three years ago; and yet, I'm not much different, either. I'm still vulnerable and scared, strong and independent—except now, I want to voice my feelings rather than bottle them up.

Soar

I'm tired of hurting.

Genny's words ring in my ears as I press my forehead against hers and just breathe. I did this to her. Nobody but me. I hurt her. I knew I did, and yet I didn't stop. I couldn't stop. And had I not been locked up, I *wouldn't* have stopped.

"I've worked on myself for the past three years, done a lot of soul searching, and I want it all, Sloane. But I don't know if you can give it to me," she murmurs against my lips. My chest aches at the pain in her voice and the accuracy of her words.

I don't know if I can give her everything, either.

But I'm not about to let another man give it to her.

I'm a selfish fuck, and Imogen is mine.

So, I take another deep breath and give her the words she needs to hear.

"I won't hurt you anymore, sunshine," I lie. I'll hurt her. It's inevitable—I don't know how *not* to.

"Sloane," she moans, sounding pained.

I move my hands, sliding one underneath her shirt, and then shove it down her jeans to cup her ass and squeeze her soft flesh. The other hand I move up her side, beneath the shirt, and wrap it around her ribs, sliding my thumb over her nipple from the outside of her bra.

"You're mine, Imogen," I remind her. Her body trembles against me.

When her eyes meet mine, I know she's relented, like she always does. I give one more squeeze at her tit and her ass before I release her. I then reach down and pick her up by her thighs before I carry her to bed.

"And I'm going to show you right now, just how *mine* you fucking are."

chapter seven

Imogen

I let out a squeak as he carries me to my bedroom. I have to direct him once he's up the stairs, but then, as soon as we enter the room, he tosses my body across it and onto the bed. I expect him to pounce on me, but he doesn't. He stands in the middle of the room and looks around.

My master bedroom is decorated in all extremely pale greys and bright whites, except for a few medium gray decorative pillows on my bed and my dark grey sheets.

I have an all metal gold nightstand with a glass top and two white club chairs in front of the three windows that look out at the valley and city around us.

"This fits you," he murmurs, looking around before his green eyes connect to mine. "It's light and soft, like you," he says, tipping his lips in a grin.

I shake my head slightly at his words.

"Why are you wearing my shirt, sunshine?" he asks, using that fucking nickname again as he prowls toward me.

My only answer is to shrug. I'm not about to really tell him why it's the only thing I took with me from our life together in Shasta. That and my gigantic wedding ring that sits on my finger, since I'm unable to let it go. I don't dare tell him why I still wear it, just enjoying the weight of it on my finger.

"You miss your man?" he asks as his hands slide up the outside of my thighs and underneath said shirt. He drags it up and over my body, causing me to shiver.

I watch as his eyes take in my torso, my bra covered breasts, my ribs, and my stomach. When they get back to mine, I expect to see them heated with desire, but instead he looks angry.

"You look too skinny, baby," he murmurs as he unbuttons my jeans and yanks them down my legs, leaving me in just my bra and panties.

I don't bother responding to his words. I've lost weight, and I haven't decided if I hate it or love it. Graham loved it, but he's a piece of shit, so I'm leaning toward hating it.

I suck in a breath when he lowers to his knees, his lips touching below the center of my ribs. He then kisses his way down my stomach, his tongue swirling around my belly button before he reaches the top waistband of my panties.

He gently tugs my panties down my legs, and without a warning, his tongue licks my entire slit before it swirls around my clit.

"Sloane," I moan.

His tongue dips inside of me while his hands move to

my ass and lifts me up slightly, pulling me even closer to him.

I gasp when his teeth graze my clit, one of my hands flying behind me to hold onto the comforter, and the other diving into his thick, blond hair. I spread my legs a little wider and arch my back, pushing my pussy even closer to his face.

He moans and starts to devour me, his mouth and tongue working me to the brink of a climax. Just when I'm about to fall over the edge, he sits back, moving away from me.

"What? Why?" I practically cry.

"Want you to come on my cock," he murmurs as he slowly stands.

I watch him undress, a whimper escaping my lips when he's completely naked. His body is bigger than it was three years ago, his muscles more defined.

My eyes dart down to his hard cock, and I bite my lip at the sight. When my eyes go back up his body, I notice that he's got his cocky grin in place at my obvious ogling, and I roll my eyes.

Sloane leans over my body and presses his lips to mine before he moves them to my ear.

"Come ride me, sunshine. I want to see that body I've been dreaming about for three years above me," he whispers.

My entire body breaks out in a shiver, and I nod. He throws back my comforter, sending pillows flying everywhere before he props his back up against the ones that didn't go skidding across the room. I roll over and lift myself to my knees, removing my bra as I make my way toward him, then straddle him.

"Fuck," he rasps as his hand slides from my stomach, up

between my breasts, and around the back of my neck.

"Condom?" I breathe.

Sloane grunts, before he shakes his head. "No more of that, sunshine. It's just us now, only us." I make a noise in the back of my throat and close my eyes, wishing that his words could be the truth. "Baby," he murmurs shaking me gently and I open my eyes. "I'm fucking serious, nobody else. Just you and me, from now on."

He squeezes my neck as I take him inside of me, sitting until I'm completely full of him. Sloane is focused on me, and maybe it's just me wanting to see it, but the truth to his statement is there. Damn if I don't want to believe every word, every single freaking word.

I look down and into his green eyes, which are now full of desire, need, and want. His hands wrap around my waist, and I expect him to force me to move, but he doesn't. He just watches me, his head slightly tilted, his eyes roaming over my face but nowhere else.

"You're mine," he rumbles, giving my waist a squeeze. "All of you. It was meant for only me."

I fight back the tears that threaten to spill at his words. I want to ask him if all of me was meant for him, then why wasn't all of him meant for me, but I don't.

Instead, I close my eyes, unable to look into his for another minute, and I ride my husband. It doesn't take long for the orgasm that I had been on the brink of only a few moments ago to return.

Sloane moves one of his hands from my waist to press his thumb against my clit. My entire body shakes as my head drops back, and I let everything else wash away and only *feel*. I feel the way our bodies fit together, the way his hands slide over my skin—his fingers rough. When I come, my entire body locks up and I let that orgasm roll through me.

Without skipping a beat, Sloane flips me onto my back and drives into me, his pelvis thrusting against mine as he fills me over and over until his muscles tremble above me and he lets out a moan with his own release. His body sags, and he buries his face in my neck with a long groan as his thrusts continue, slowly and languidly.

"You aren't leaving me," he whispers against my neck.

I try not to react, but my body must tense because he lifts his head and his eyes meet mine before he tips his head to the side in question.

"Tell me, Genny," he murmurs as he lifts one of his hands and traces my hairline, with his fingertips.

I shake my head, but he doesn't let it go. He urges me again to tell him what I'm thinking, and so I do. I can't hold it in.

"If all of me is meant for you, then why isn't all of you meant for me, Sloane?" I ask.

He freezes as his eyes meet mine, his cock still inside of me, and his weight on me. I know he's angry because his jaw clenches, and I watch a muscle in his cheek jump.

"Sloane?" I hesitate when we sit in silence for what feels like a lifetime.

"You know the life, babe," he says as though its no big deal.

"Get off of me," I grind out.

One of his hands moves to wrap around my hip, and I know exactly where he has it. He squeezes the tattoo that says *Soar*, in pretty black lettering with black birds around it. Then his eyes meet mine and he gives me a cocky grin.

"It's the life, Genny. You don't get to just run away when you don't like something. We make it work. We always make it work," he grunts as he slips out of my body and sits back against the headboard.

"While that is fine and dandy for you, because you get to do whatever you want to, it doesn't *work* for me anymore," I state. He only laughs.

"Sunshine, it takes me less than five minutes to remind you just how much we do work together just fine."

I narrow my eyes on him and decide to get out of bed and away from him. I don't get far. He sits up and reaches for me, pulling my front against his and holding me against his body. I look up at him, giving him my most evil eye, but he only laughs.

"Lay it out for me, babe, tell me what you want," he offers. I narrow my eyes on him, but he is the epitome of cool, calm, and collected.

"You really want to know?" I ask, sounding bitchy but not really caring at the moment.

"Yeah. Wouldn't have asked if I didn't," he smarts back at me.

"Like I said, I want a baby, more than one if its possible. I want a husband who loves me."

He shrugs, "Already love you, Imogen. You want a kid, it's yours," acting as if it's no big deal.

"No," I shake my head. "I want a husband who *loves* me, who would do everything in his power not to hurt me—and that doesn't just include physically, but emotionally as well. I want a husband who doesn't fuck every pair of tits he comes across who offers it up. I want devotion, and I want him to want a family as much as I do. You don't, Sloane, and that's okay. Maybe there is a woman out there who will love you and be okay with you being with other women; maybe there's a woman out there that you couldn't imagine cheating on, but I just know that that woman is not me. If it were, you wouldn't have cheated on me repeatedly for over twelve years."

"Imogen," he rasps as his hand moves to cup my cheek, his eyes searching mine. "I can't change the things I did, baby. All I can do is be better for the future."

"What does that future look like to you? What do you want?"

"You, sunshine, and whatever comes with you. Whatever you want," he murmurs.

God knows that I want to believe all of these sweet words, but this isn't anything new. Sloane knows how to sweet-talk me, and I believe him every single time. I buy all of his sugary words every single fucking time.

Even right now, I want to believe him, I want to believe *in* him, but I'm not sure if my heart can handle it anymore. There isn't much left of me, and I'm afraid to hope one last time and have there be absolutely nothing of me left when he betrays me.

"You're so risky, Sloane," I whisper.

"Give a sober ex-con a chance, sunshine," he murmurs.

"I know I'm going to regret this," I whisper, mostly to myself. I know he hears me because his fingers flex and he grimaces.

"I hope not," he grunts before his lips press against mine.

I don't bother to get up. Rather, snuggling closer to his hard, warm, body, I do something I haven't done in days—I close my eyes, and I sleep.

Soar

Imogen's breathing evens out and her body becomes heavier against mine as she falls asleep. *Guilt.* It's an emotion I should feel on a regular basis, but I don't. I never really have felt it before, except when it comes to Genny. I've felt bad, angry, regretful, but never truly guilty. I've just lied to my wife, again, and not only a small white-lie, I've downright fucking lied to her.

A family.

I've never really wanted one, and I still don't. Yet, to keep her, that's one of the major things she needs from me. Something she's mentioned more than once, twice, or even a dozen times to me over the years. I offered it to her, half-heartedly throughout our marriage to appease her, but I never really thought she'd push for it. She didn't, until now. I had a shitty childhood. I'm aware that I never did without financially, but emotionally, I was extremely destitute.

My father has never shown any other emotions toward me but disappointment and anger. He's selfish, fucked up, and abusive.

My mother has always been so worried about upsetting my father, about being perfect for him, and then later about drowning in a bottle, that she never had time to nurture me. She spent my entire childhood trying to save her own ass that she had no clue how messed up our whole family dynamic was for me.

In order for me to keep Imogen, I'll have to knock her up. That I can do, the fidelity thing I'm not so sure I can do. I'm not scared of fucking someone else, or of being able to say no because I could. I just don't know that I would say no when the opportunity presents itself.

In fact, it's not really the desire for other pussy, it's the desire to get blitzed. When I'm stoned, I don't give a fuck what I'm doing or how it'll make anybody feel. When I'm wrecked, all I care about is climbing higher and higher.

Then I crash, and fuck me, the resentment I feel toward myself is too much, so I search for that dope again and I end up fucking whores, drinking, and doing stupid shit that I know is wrong. I end up acting just like my goddamn father. Isn't that the fucker? I act exactly like the man I despise. I treat my wife the way he treats my mother.

I squeeze my eyes closed and can't get the image of the look on her face the first time Genny caught me with another woman out of my mind. She looked devastated. I was blitzed as fuck and just brushed it off, because I literally didn't give a shit in the moment. It's so hard, to be what she needs and what I need, and being high, that thrill and that escape from reality, it was easy. It was always easier to escape through dope and booze.

Fuck, I'm such a dick. Even now, I'm not sure I could keep from fucking around. It's not that I don't love her, because I do. I love her as much as I'm capable of loving another person, but sex is sex, and I need it—the thrill, the escape, just like with dope.

I need it all. Without it, I don't know who I am. I've been rebelling and fighting for so long, I'm not sure how to just be. I don't want to lose her, either. Sitting in that cell, thinking about her and how much she means to me, and how much I truly missed her, I know that I need her in my life.

Opening my eyes, I look down on her sleeping against me.

I should let her go. I should let her find someone who could make her happy, someone who can stay faithful and give her those kids she wants without reservation or hesitation.

Fuck.

Her doorbell rings, and I slide out from underneath her sleeping body before gathering my jeans. I yank them up my legs and hips, zipping them only as I make my way down-stairs to the front door. I pull it open without looking through the peephole, and I'm met with the angry gaze of Graham.

I can't contain my smirk as his eyes widen and then nar-row on me. Taking in the fact that I'm shirtless, barefoot and answering Imogen's door in the early evening, he practically growls at me.

"So, it's true. The whore lied to me, then," he grunts.

"Genny doesn't lie."

"So you didn't get back together?" he asks.

"We did, but not until about an hour ago. I have more important things to talk to you about, you prick," I growl.

He chuckles. "And what's that?"

"You hit my wife," I state. He winces but stands firm and doesn't respond. "Do you have anything to say for yourself there?"

"You think you've won, but you haven't. Her father doesn't want you with her, and he's going to make life really fucking difficult for her, and you, if she doesn't toe the line. Just remember that," he says, lifting his chin.

"Oh, I've won, Graham. Haven't you realized yet? I al-ways win; and with Imogen, I always will. My dick is the only one she's ever known. You aren't getting even a taste of her, you piece of shit. You come anywhere near her again, and I'll kill you," I rumble.

"We'll see," he winks before he turns and jogs away. My entire body jolts as I watch him go.

I close the door and turn around on a heavy sigh as I make my way back up to Genny. I'm done. I decide right here and now. This worry about other women, this worry about staying sober, this worry about me chasing a high, it's done.

Maybe it took Graham coming over with his cocky as fuck smile, maybe it was the fact that he's threatening to take the only woman who has ever loved me away. Maybe it's that he represents the fact that I was on the verge of losing her forever. I'm done.

Gathering her in my arms I inhale her sweet scent and press my lips to the top of her head. From now on, I fight, but I don't fight her. I fight *for* her and for *us*. I'm going to fight my demons, and I refuse to be my mother, to drink myself to death, or to get blitzed anymore. I refuse to be the bastard my father is. What I am going to be is a better man. Starting right fucking now.

chapter eight

Imogen

I groan and stretch, my arms colliding with a hot body lying next to me. Opening one eye, I see Sloane's sleeping form next to me. His hair is a mess, and his full lips are facing me. I stare at him and wonder what exactly is going to happen next. Before I can even think about any scenarios, one of his eyes opens and he grins.

"Morning, sunshine," he murmurs, wrapping his hand around my waist and tugging me closer to him. He throws one of his legs between my thighs.

"Morning," I whisper before my breath hitches when he presses his thigh against my center.

"You ready to pack your shit and come home tonight?" he asks as his fingers tweak my nipple.

"What? No," I breathe as I arch closer to him. He repeats

the motion then adds a tug to my hardened nipple.

"Why the fuck not?"

I shrug, "I don't want to rush anything. I'm not ready for anything serious, not with you."

I watch as a storm passes through his green eyes, and then he shakes his head.

"Sunshine, I've been your man for twenty years. We aren't really rushing anything, and we're fucking married. That shit's as serious as it gets," he quips.

"I'm not ready to move back up there. I'm not ready for everything that the club includes. Plus, I want to make sure this is going to work before I leave the city again," I whisper as I hitch my leg around his waist.

Sloane slips his hand between my thighs, and I shiver when two fingers dive inside of me and curl immediately.

"Genny," he rasps as he works me up, his thumb pressing against my clit while his fingers fuck me.

Moaning, I whisper, "I'm serious, Sloane," I roll my hips as I search for more from him.

"How long?" he groans as he moves his hand and then thrusts inside of me, rolling me onto my back while he slides to his knees.

"I don't know," I admit as I spread my legs as wide as I can and wrap my hands around his forearms.

"We can't move on with what you want, the way you want it, if you keep your pussy here, sunshine," he grumbles, his head dipped down and focusing on our connection.

"Maybe I want to see if you can keep your dick in your pants," I sigh as he starts to thrust a little harder.

"Not big on being tested, baby. Either I get full access or we go back to the way it was and you spread for me when you're feeling horny," he grinds out.

"You fucking asshole," I gasp as I reach up to slap him across the face.

Sloane catches my hand and starts to pound inside of me. His grip on my wrist is solid, his strokes firm and hard. His eyes blaze into mine with a heat and anger he shouldn't be allowed to possess, since he was the one being a dick.

I feel my orgasm rush through me, and I know that Sloane feels it, too. His fingers flex and he fucks me *wild* until he's coming inside of me with a roar. He doesn't stay inside for long. He pulls out and stomps toward my bathroom before slamming the door. I don't know what I did to piss him off so much, but I'm not his puppet.

I may not be the cold-bitch I was three years ago, but I'm not about to follow after his every whim either. If this is a *real* relationship, a marriage, then there has to be compromise. Plus, I don't think that I'm being unreasonable in not trusting him and his roaming cock.

A few minutes later, he emerges, still naked. I've slipped on the soft Devils shirt that I had been wearing earlier, along with my panties, and I have the covers pulled up to my waist. I watch him move around the room, silently. He grabs his phone from his jeans pocket and pokes at it for a few minutes before he finally walks over to me.

"What do you want, Imogen?" he sighs, almost in defeat, as he sits down.

"I want this to work. In order for that to happen, I need to trust you. It's been a long time since I've trusted you, Sloane," I admit.

"I don't see how we can change anything with you living here and me there," he says, running a hand through his messy blond hair. He's calm and rational, his green eyes bright and intent looking at me.

"I'm willing to discuss something different."

"What if you lived at the house and I lived at the club-house?" he asks. I can't help it, I burst out into a fit of laughter.

"What?"

"Tell me something." He nods for me to continue. "When was the last time you fucked a clubwhore?"

I watch as his face pales and he winces.

Yeah. Exactly what I thought.

"So what? You're gonna keep me on a leash now? I told you I'd give you want you want. Fidelity is one of those wants. I'm willing to put in the work, try to be the man you need me to be, in order to keep you and keep us together"

"That's all fine and dandy, but I'm sorry, I would never be able to trust you living down there," I say. He nods and looks down at his feet. "How about I live here until my parents' summer party, and we see if this is what we want? I can come to Shasta for a few days here and there, and you can stay here?" I suggest.

Sloane lets out a heavy sigh and runs his hand over his face before he turns to me. I watch as his green eyes roam over my face, and land on my bruise. He reaches out and his fingertips touch it.

"I don't want you here without protection," he murmurs softly.

He looks so worried that it hits me somewhere deep inside. As long as I've known him, I've never seen him worry like this about *me*.

"Can you arrange that for a couple weeks, or do you want me to hire someone from daddy's firm?" I ask.

"I'll arrange protection for my own fucking wife," he growls.

"Okay, Sloane," I murmur.

He leans down and presses his lips to mine. His tongue sneaks out to taste my lips, but he doesn't take it further.

"I have to head back to the club tonight," he murmurs. "I don't want to leave you," he says, closing his eyes and resting his forehead against mine.

"Why do you have to leave tonight?" I ask.

"I have a meeting with my probation officer tomorrow morning first thing," he admits.

"Yeah?"

"Gotta piss in a cup and all, sunshine," he grumbles as he sits up.

"So that's why you're sober? Because the state is forcing you to be?"

"Sober for three years in prison, sunshine, not exactly a big deal to keep at it," he shrugs.

"It is for someone who uses it as a crutch to deal with other parts of their past," I point out. I then watch as his face turns red in anger.

He opens his mouth to say something, but I cut him off. "I saw your mom the other day. She did my makeup for me. She told me about the abuse. Why didn't you ever tell me?" I ask.

Sloane stands and grabs his clothes, quietly and quickly dressing while I watch and wait for him to speak. He shakes his head after he pulls on his boots and looks over at me.

"It was a long time ago. My mother shouldn't have said anything," he growls. His body is stiff as he moves around, and I know this is a topic he has no desire to discuss.

"It may have been a long time ago, but Sloane, it's affected your entire life. It's affected us," I murmur. His eyes flash with unbridled anger. He's completely shutting down on me.

"I'll see you tomorrow, Imogen," he says as his eyes shutter closed and he turns to walk away from me.

If I let him go right now, I know that he won't talk about this ever again. We need to talk about it. We need to have discussions like this or we'll forever be two separate people living in a house together, when he's around, that is. I climb out of bed and hurry down the stairs after him.

"Sloane, stop," I demand as his hand reaches for my front door handle.

"What?" he bites without turning around.

"You can't ignore this. We need to talk about it," I call out.

I watch, waiting for him to leave me standing in the living room alone. To my surprise, he doesn't. He turns and looks at me. His eyes are completely blank, and he looks the way he always did when I would bitch at him. *Bored. Indifferent.* Walls built so fucking high not even a professional rock climber could get over them.

"What do you want to talk about?" he sighs.

"Sloane," I whisper as I close the distance between us.

He doesn't watch me, his gaze focused on the windows that look out at the city in my living area.

Once I'm directly in front of him, I wrap one of my hands in the back of his hair and I tip his head down to look at me. That angry muscle in his cheek jumps, but I don't let myself become bothered by his anger.

No matter how angry he's been toward me, he's never once hurt me. I may not trust him in many aspects, but I do trust that he would never physically hurt me.

"Your father hurt your mother when you were a child. Don't act like it doesn't affect you now. Don't act like that wasn't a reason you did drugs and drank, like it wasn't an escape for you. And don't pretend that sex wasn't a way to have affection. It all ties in together," I say.

His eyes go from blank to angry. I welcome that anger, because at least he's not completely impassive.

"Fine, you want the truth?" he barks. I stiffen at his tone, but I don't move away from him.

"The drugs and booze helped me escape when I was young, but he didn't just hit her, he hit me too, Genny. As I got older, dope and booze, they helped me escape from your bitching. I know they were the reason you bitched, but I didn't care. The higher I got, the more I really didn't give a fuck.

The pussy was easy and you weren't. I didn't give a fuck what I was doing when I was blitzed. I didn't think about how you would feel, or about anything else. Getting caught was just another high. I wanted to. I wanted you to see me fucking those whores, to know. I got off on being able to talk my way back into your bed after you'd seen me inside of another woman. It was all a goddamn game."

"Sloane," I whisper as tears fall from my eyes at his hurtful words.

"You wanted to talk about it. You fucking got it, sunshine," he bites out. I find that I hate the way he uses the nickname in anger.

"I've always loved you, Sloane. Since the moment I laid eyes on you across campus—you in your beat-up leather jacket and your jeans. The way you didn't give a shit what anybody else thought. Then the way you would be so sweet to me. I felt like the luckiest girl in the whole world to be on your arm. After you graduated and you left, I thought that I'd lose you; but you came back every weekend, and I fell deeper in love with you with each passing day. That boy, he's still inside of you, he's just hurting. I'm here for you, baby," I whisper.

"What if I told you I fucked clubwhores all week long, then I'd come home and fuck you on the weekends?" he asks, arching an eyebrow with a smirk. I stumble backward, unable to be close to him.

"Why are you saying all of this?" I ask, holding my hand to my lips, trying to keep from sobbing loudly.

"You wanted to talk. You wanted to know," he spits.

"You're purposely being mean."

Giving me a cocky grin, he continues, "No, I'm telling you the truth. I could be mean if you wanted me to."

"Fine."

"Anything else you want the truth about?" he asks, sounding like a smart ass.

The next words come out of my mouth on a whisper, "Have you ever loved me?" I'm unsure if I want the answer. I square my shoulders to hear it anyway.

"You're mine, Genny," he states.

"That doesn't answer anything," I murmur.

He grunts before he turns and walks away, his voice nothing but a lingering echo, "That's the answer you get."

He leaves me standing in the living room, wearing nothing but one of his old shirts and my panties. Tears stream down my face, and I wonder why the hell I thought getting back together with him was a good idea. This is all a flashback to three years ago, just in a different house. Me, alone and crying, and him walking out of the door to go to his fucking club.

I pick up the crystal coaster on the side table and hurl it at my front door. It doesn't break, and lands on the floor with a bounce. That pisses me off even more. I pick up everything that I can find that isn't nailed down and I throw a fucking temper tantrum. I'll pick it all up later, or maybe hire someone to do it for me, but right now I don't care. I want to hurt something as badly as I hurt on the inside.

Fuck him.

Fuck Sloane Huntington.

I leave Imogen standing in her living room, probably crying, and definitely feeling like fucking shit. I don't know why I eluded to fucking whores while we were still dating. I said the lie to hurt her even more, as if I needed to lie to make her ache. I straddle my motorcycle and throw on my helmet before taking off down the road, aimed for the clubhouse, which is a few hours away.

I'm such a fucking dick.

I'm lost in my head as I drive, and I don't check my phone until I stop for gas and I see my brother's called me. Without listening to his message I call him back.

"Sloane," he murmurs, and my brow furrows.

"What's up Kippy?" I ask.

"It's dad. He's had a heart attack. I'm at the hospital right now. Mom didn't want to bother you, but it doesn't look good," he chokes out. I know that he must be on the verge of tears.

"I'll be right there, I'm in the city," I state before I hang up.

I know exactly which hospital they're at because only one is good enough for the Huntingtons. As I drive, I think about one of the last encounters I had with him before I went to jail. He'd called me to his office, wanted to talk to me about something. It was about money, money laundering to be specific.

I walked in, knowing he was probably banging his newest secretary since she wasn't at her desk. I was right. There she was, her ass cheeks spread, and he was fucking her hard, except this one didn't have that dead look in her eye. No, this bitch was getting off on it.

When he finished fucking her, he didn't just throw an envelope at her. He helped her up and rearranged her skirt before cupping her cheek and kissing her, the kiss looked more intimate than the actual act he'd been performing. I watched him slip her the envelope of cash, then he handed her a bag from Tiffany's. He whispered to her and she giggled before she walked out of the office.

"Wanna tell me what that's about?" I ask.

He grunts. "Not really, but I will. She's a good little lay, tight pussy and tighter ass. I've decided I'll be keeping her around for a while. If you want to know how to keep a woman, you'd pay attention to your old man. I could teach you some shit."

Rolling my eyes, I ignore him before asking him what the fuck he wants from me. "I have some money I need cleaned up," he admits as he sits down behind his desk.

"Money from what?"

"Can't tell you that, son," he murmurs.

I let out a harsh laugh, "Old man, if you want me to do you a solid that could land my ass in the clink, you're going to have to elaborate on just where you got the money," I state.

He sighs, "Fine. I had a one-time opportunity to make some cash. I invested and it was profitable, but I can't claim that shit on my taxes, I'll get locked up."

"Don't you have any off-shore accounts?"

He shakes his head, "I did it for you and Kipling. Its enough that it will set your children up for life."

"I don't need it," I grunt.

"I know you don't, but I'm giving it to you anyway."

I think about his words and his actions, then I rub the back of my neck. "I'll do it, but only for Kip."

Once my gas tank is full, the signal that goes off shakes me from my memory. I did what he wanted and he was right, the amount is enough for Kip and I to set our children up for life if we wanted to. One day, I'll give it to Kip. Now there's a true possibility that I'll be able to give it to my own kids, but I'm not touching it, not ever. I don't fucking need it, and honest to shit, I don't *want* it.

I turn around and head to my father. It's true, I can't stand the man, but he's been a good father to Kipling. He also leaves my mother alone to her own devices, which is more than he did when I was a kid. So for Kipling, I'll be at the hospital, and for no one else.

Once I park my bike, I hurry inside, asking the receptionist where my father is before I head toward that floor. He's in surgery, but Kipling and my mother should be in the waiting room. As soon as I step off of the elevator, I see my little brother sitting in a chair, his elbows on his knees and his head hanging low.

"Kippy," I murmur.

His head shoots up before the rest of him does, and then he runs to me, crashing into my body and wrapping his long arms around me in a hug.

I hug him back, my baby brother. My hurting baby brother.

"It's gonna be okay," I rumble.

"It isn't," he whispers against my neck.

He straightens and looks over my shoulder, a smile breaking out on his face. His eyes rimmed in red from his tears, he abandons me for whoever has just stepped off of the elevator. I slowly turn around and watch as my brother embraces my wife with the same affection he just embraced me with. I know they're close. She's known him since he was a baby; but seeing them hold onto each other, I wonder exactly how close they are.

I fold my arms over my chest and stare at them when a cool hand wraps around my arm, giving it a squeeze.

"When you don't communicate, Imogen is our only link to you. When she refused to communicate with you the past three years, she and Kipling became very close. They talk on the phone often. Usually, it's him telling her how much he wants the two of you back together. They have a very special sibling bond," my mother murmurs before she releases my arm and walks back to her seat.

Genny's head lifts, and I watch her. When she sees me, I watch as surprise, and then anger, and finally hurt settles into her features. I've earned the anger and hurt from her—more than earned it. Kip turns away from her to go back to his seat, but his eyes flash to me and they look disappointed.

"I'm here for Kip and your mother. I figured you'd be almost back to your *home*," Genny announces as she starts to brush past me.

I wrap my hand around her wrist and gently tug her back

toward me. I massage her wrist with my thumb before I lean down to whisper into her ear.

"When you get feisty, it makes me hard, sunshine. I'm here for Kip, same as you."

"Well," she says breathlessly. I can't help but smile as she clears her throat. "That doesn't mean you need to be in my space."

"Oh, but your space is my favorite place to be," I murmur, giving her wrist a squeeze.

"That's not what you were saying an hour ago," she snaps, narrowing her eyes on me and trying to tug her wrist out of my grip.

"Out of all the shit I said to you, none of it was that I didn't like being with you, Genny. In fact, I clearly remember telling you that you are mine," I say, tipping my head down and making sure to keep my eyes even and level with hers.

"You broke my heart, for the millionth time," she whispers, sounding just as broken as she says.

My eyebrows pull together and I let out a breath. "Sunshine."

"No, fuck you, Sloane," she states, yanking her hand out of my grasp. I let it go.

I watch as she walks over to my mother, bending down to embrace her. My mother reaches up and touches Genny's face and shakes her head. Genny just shrugs before she sits down next to her. As always, from the outside looking in, I watch my family.

I've never really been part of my own family; from the time I was a child, I refused to be part of it. As I grew older, I only grew more distant. Now, they're all strangers to me, even my own fucking wife. I've alienated everyone.

chapter nine

Imogen

I'm thankful when Sloane stays away from me after I walk over to talk to his mother. It doesn't take long for the waiting room to fill up with society people, and I'm too exhausted to turn myself on.

Sitting in my holey jeans and a plain, navy blue t-shirt, with sandals on my feet, no makeup on my face, and my hair in a messy ponytail is how my parents find me.

"You look awful," my mother gasps, walking straight up to me.

"I've been here for four hours," I respond.

"A lady should always look her best. Look at Kalli. Her own husband is fighting for his life, and not a hair is out of place," my mother hisses. Kalli squeezes my hand in a show of support.

"Mother, I've had an awful day. Please, no rules," I mutter.

"Why is your face like that? Did that horrible husband of yours do that?" she gasps.

Kipling growls next to me, but I stand and wrap my hand around hers, tugging her away from Kalli and Kip.

"No, Graham did this to me, did father not tell you?" I whisper.

"Graham would never do that. He comes from proper stock, Imogen. Now hush, and don't cover up for that *thing* you married," she says, waving her hand around.

Thing.

She just called my husband a—*thing*.

This is exactly why I stay at my parents for as little time as possible. I disappointed them by marrying Sloane, and they don't hide that disappointment or their disdain for him even slightly. They accepted the marriage in their own way, but they still staunchly disapprove and don't hide that at all.

"Well, Graham did it," I hiss.

"I'm sure it was just a misunderstanding," she says flippantly. It pisses me off.

"Yeah, I broke up with him and wouldn't marry him."

"See, completely fixable. He's here, too. Go and fix things," she says, pushing me away from her and toward the middle of the room, where Graham is now staring at me.

The room suddenly feels as though all the air has been sucked out of it as I stare at Graham. I know that Sloane is somewhere amongst the people, and he's got to see Graham, but my feet are frozen to the ground as Graham's cool and calculated gaze pins me to my spot.

When he starts to walk toward me, my entire body stiffens. Before I can even say a word, he's right in front of me. He lifts his hands, and I wince at the action. Instead of hurting me, he cups my cheeks as his eyes take me in, looking regretful. I don't think he regrets anything, though, just the fact that he can't force me to do what he wants.

"Imogen," he whispers.

"Please step away from me," I grind out.

"We had a fight, darling. Things got passionate and out of control."

I open my mouth to speak when Sloane's deep voice vibrates right beside us. "If you don't take your hands off of my wife right now, I'm going to cut them off," he growls.

Graham takes a step back, letting his hands fall to his sides before he turns to face Sloane. He snorts as he looks over Sloane and shrugs.

"She's technically your wife, but not for long," he chuckles before he turns and walks away, going directly to my father's side.

"Why were you entertaining that asshole?" Sloane asks. I slowly turn to him. His angry gaze is focused on me, and my mouth gapes slightly.

"You can't seriously be mad at me right now?" I hiss.

"I sure as fuck can, sunshine."

"Stop calling me sunshine when you're pissed," I demand. A smile tips his lips as he lowers his head so that his lips graze my ear.

"You like it when I call you sunshine with my cock deep inside of that sweet pussy?" he whispers as his hand wraps around my waist and gives me a squeeze.

"Sloane, stop," I exhale.

"Mmm, you do. I'll remember that, my sweet sunshine," he breathes. I hate that I love it, too. My entire body shivers as his other hand wraps around my hip and his lips touch the skin just below my ear. "There she is, my sunshine."

"Sloane," I sigh.

"Mr. Huntington's family?" a doctor calls out, interrupting Sloane and me. I breathe out a sigh of relief as I turn and walk toward the doctor.

As soon as I reach Kip and Kalli, I wrap my hand around Kip's. I can feel Sloane's heat at my back, and I try to restrain my shiver as his hand slides around my waist while his warm front presses against my back.

"I'm sorry, Mrs. Huntington, but Mr. Huntington didn't make it. We tried, but the blockage was too great. The years of cocaine abuse and drinking, his heart was just too weak," the doctor explains. At the same time Kip's hand squeezes mine, Sloane's fingers squeeze my waist.

"If you'd like to come in and say your goodbyes before he's taken, you're more than welcome," he murmurs.

"I would," Kalli announces and walks away from us without a word, following behind the doctor.

"You want to go in, Kip? I'll go with you," Sloane rumbles. Kip shakes his head.

"No, I don't want to see him like that," Kipling whispers. I watch as his eyes fill with tears.

"Take care of Kippy, I'll get rid of these assholes," Sloane whispers in my ear.

I turn to Kip and I wrap my arms around him. As soon as I do, he shoves his face in my neck and he cries. He's eighteen-years-old, getting ready to leave for college in just a few weeks, and he's just lost his father. A man he's looked up to his entire life. My heart aches for him.

A few minutes later, Sloane returns. "We only have

about ten minutes before the brothers start to show up," he announces.

"What?" I ask, lifting my head to look over at him.

"I called them. They'll be here for support, just like they would be for anyone," he grinds out.

I run my hands up and down Kip's back soothingly. A few minutes later, he breaks away from me, wiping his eyes.

"I feel like a pussy," he mutters.

"You're not," Sloane announces before I can respond.

"You're not crying," Kip points out to his brother.

"Yeah, because I'm fucked up. Having feelings doesn't make you a pussy, means you aren't as fucked up as I am," he shrugs.

He sighs, his eyes focused on the ground, "Sloane."

"You think I'd be separated from my gorgeous wife if I wasn't a fuck up? You think I would have ended up in prison if I was stable? Face it, baby brother, you're the well-adjusted one. Nobody is gonna say shit to you because you cried the day your dad died," he grins as he shoves at Kip's shoulder lightly.

I look up at Sloane and he winks at me before he pulls his brother into his arms. There's something about him right now. He's always sexy, but I've never seen him like this before. Loving, supportive, and gentle. He can be all of those things when he chooses to be, but I've never seen them all at once.

It makes me think about what he would be like as a father. I bite my bottom lip and try to tamp down the butterflies in my stomach, but I can't. They're there, flying and alive until the room suddenly fills with people. I look around to see his club is here.

"Oh, Genny," Mary-Anne calls out as she hurries to my

side and wraps her arms around me.

Hesitantly, I hug her back. I'm surprised to see that she's pregnant again. When we separate, I look around the room and see so many familiar faces that it makes me feel uncomfortable. As an Old Lady of the club, I was untouchable. I was also a complete bitch at the end, before I left.

"Hey there, honey," Colleen says as she takes my hand and gives it a squeeze.

Colleen was one of the first women I met in the club. She's in her late forties, and had been around the group a while. She taught me everything about the club life, even the hard lessons—like when I walked in on Sloane fucking a whore for the first time.

She was the one who informed me of my place. Though I never hated her for it, I always took my bitterness out on anyone who came crossing my path, and that means Colleen had been the brunt of it often.

"Hey," I whisper back to her, squeezing her hand.

"How you doin?" she asks. My answer is to shrug. Right now, I don't know how I'm doing. "Hang in there. I know it's been a while, but I'm only a phone call away," she murmurs before she turns and walks over to her husband Texas' side.

MadDog, Mary-Anne, Bobbie, Roach, Ivy, Camo, Grease, Torch, Cleo, Teeny and Mammoth—they're all here and all looking at me questioningly. Then their eyes move to Sloane and back to me.

Nobody says a word as Sloane updates them on his father and how he's passed. I watch as he walks over to MadDog and whispers something to him. MadDog's eyes flick up to me for a few seconds before they return back to Sloane's and he nods.

"Kipling, do you wish to say anything?" Kalli asks, looking extremely put together for a woman who just went to talk to her dead husband's body.

"No, mother," Kip says, shaking his head.

"I've already called your father's attorney and he'll come to the house first thing in the morning. You'll be there Sloane, darling?" she asks, turning to Sloane.

I don't miss the looks of shock around the room at learning Sloane's name. Then I realize that these people probably have no clue how well-bred and well off Sloane is. He's always just been *Soar* to them.

"Yeah. Imogen and I will be there."

"Imogen?" I hear Teeny whisper.

Sloane and I are frauds, complete and total frauds. Nobody knows who we are in Shasta, and that's exactly the way Sloane wanted it.

Now there are going to be questions, and I know the women will turn to me to find out answers. Maybe it's bitchy, but I don't want to give anybody anything. I'm fucking tired.

I watch was Kalli and Kip walk through the throng of bikers and their Old Ladies like they don't even exist. Well, Kalli does. Kip is looking around kind of in awe at all these huge men that take up the entire space.

MadDog walks up to me and his eyes narrow on my cheek. "The fuck happened to your face?" he barks roughly.

"Someone didn't like the fact that I didn't want to date him anymore," I shrug.

His eyes flick up to Sloane and then back down to me. He cocks an eyebrow in question, and I shake my head.

"Not Soar," I admit. He bends down and gives me a big bear hug. "You look good, sweetheart. A little thin, but good," he murmurs against my ear before he kisses the side of my head.

I can do nothing but stand in shock at his actions. I've known MadDog since I was eighteen years old, and not once has he ever embraced me, let alone kissed me.

"We're stayin' at a hotel here in town for a few days to help out with funeral shit," MadDog announces before he turns and walks away.

Sloane presses his hand against my lower back, pushing me forward. Together, along with the rest of his club, we make our way out of the hospital.

"I have several extra bedrooms if anybody wants to stay with me," I offer.

MadDog's eyebrows shoot up in surprise, but he shakes his head.

"We got the kids with us. They're a little wild. Wouldn't want to mess up your place," he murmurs.

I get what he's saying. I don't have children, I'm a little bitchy, and obviously self-centered. He's being kind, but I can tell he doesn't want to ruffle my feathers, mainly because he's seen how I can react to things.

Like the time I walked into a party and some whore had her naked body pressed against, Sloane's. I started throwing beer bottles at them, hoping to hit Sloane but hitting her a few times as well. I gave not one fuck. She ended up having to go to the hospital, and two brothers had to restrain me before Sloane could drag me to his room to *deal* with me.

"Okay," I murmur, looking up and giving him a fake smile.

I turn toward my car and try to hurry away from the group, feeling like I'm seconds away from bursting into tears.

Today has been too much, too fucking much. Now Sloane's father is gone, and I feel like I can't breathe.

Soar

I watch her run off, and as much as I want to chase after her, I don't. I have to talk to my brothers first. I turn to MadDog, who is also watching Imogen intently. He turns to me with a furrowed brow. "Not how I expected to see her again. You're gonna need to explain some shit, brother," he murmurs.

"She was dating some prick. She tried to break it off, he got physical. That's the extent of the story," I shrug.

"It's not, but I'll let that rest. She's sickly thin," he announces.

I don't bother responding because it isn't his business, and I can see it with my own eyes. Imogen is thin, but once I get her pregnant, that shit will surely change.

"You haven't fixed your shit with her, either."

"Anything else you want to point out that I already fuckin' know?" I ask, getting irritated.

"You have to meet with your probation officer tomorrow," he grins, being a smartass. "And you're really fuckin' rich, aren't you?"

"I do have to meet with him; and yeah, Genny and I both are. I told you this."

"No wonder she was a snotty, pissed off little thing when you brought her to Shasta. I woulda been, too," he clucks. "But she looks like she's about to shatter into a million pieces, brother. Worse off than the day she left the clubhouse three years ago. How you plannin' on fixin' that?"

I shrug. "Doesn't matter. She's pissed at me. I threw some shit in her face that wasn't nice."

"Bitches?" he guesses correctly. I nod.

"If I learned anything from my first marriage, I know that living with guilt and regret isn't an easy thing. You need to make shit right. If you keep going the way you're going with her, it's going to ruin both of you," he murmurs.

"Yeah," I grunt.

"We'll see you tomorrow. Give me a call when you're up and moving. Go get your woman, and I'm sorry as fuck about your dad," he rumbles.

"Wish I could be sorry about him, too, but thanks," I state before I quickly walk toward my bike.

I put on my helmet and start my engine. There's only one place I want to be right now, and that's with Imogen. She may not want me, but she's my home. After losing my father and not feeling sad like I probably should, I need to feel something, and Imogen always makes me feel.

I'm not more than ten miles down the road when I get pulled over by a highway patrol cop. With a curse, I pull my bike over to the side of the freeway and close my eyes, waiting for what will assuredly be a pain in the fucking ass.

I hear his boots crunching behind me on the dirt and I wait. "Notorious Devils, huh?" he asks as he draws closer to me. I don't bother answering him, my cut says it all. He asks me to get off my bike and then requests my license and information.

"I'm on probation," I offer. His eyebrow lifts.

He walks away from me for a few minutes and then comes back with a grin on his face. "Well, now I never expected to pull you over. We're going to need to run some drug screens on you," he laughs.

Unable to protest, because the state of California has me by the balls, I follow him. I spend the next few hours being poked, prodded, and eventually released. I'm not drunk or high, and I didn't violate any fucking laws. He pulled me over claiming I didn't signal as I merged onto the freeway. Which was complete bullshit.

"Watch yourself, Huntington," he murmurs before he releases me. I don't think anything into it, my only focus on getting to Genny.

Her house is dark when I pull into her driveway, and I hurry up her steps. I lift my hand to knock, but her door opens and she's standing in front of me. Her face is bare, and she's wearing a sexy little silk nightie with a robe.

Silently, she holds out her hand, offering it to me, and I slip mine inside, my fingers tangle with hers as I step over the threshold. I close the door behind me, flipping the locks before we silently head upstairs to her bedroom. All thoughts of me being pulled over, and all the bullshit I just went through are gone with one simple touch from her.

I strip off my clothes while she drops her robe to the floor. Still without speaking, she pulls her nightgown up and over her head, dropping it beside her robe before she crawls beneath her sheets. I watch her before I finish disrobing, and then I join her.

"Please, stop hurting me," she whispers as I gather her in my arms.

"I don't know how," I admit as I close my eyes and hold onto her tightly.

chapter ten

Imogen

I wake to an empty bed and a note on the pillow next to me. Sloane's note explains that he had to leave to meet his probation officer. I stretch before getting up and dressed for the day. Today, we're also supposed to be meeting with the Huntington's attorney. Then there's the club that are all apparently staying here in town.

Just thinking about all of them being around makes me sick with nerves. I'm not the woman I was, and yet, I still am just that person. I don't know how to completely change. I don't know what Sloane and I are. We slept together last night, naked, but only slept.

I waited for him to take things further, knowing that after the evening he had, he probably needed it, but he didn't even try. He just held me. I wish I could read his thoughts. I wish that I knew what he wanted, and I wish I knew if he really loves me. If I knew he didn't, walking away would be so much easier. God, I wish I were some kick ass alpha woman.

I slip on a maxi wrap dress. It's navy with big, light pink and cream flowers on it and long sleeves. Then I slide my feet into nude high heels and finish my makeup before I apply serum to my hair to make it sleek and straight. My front doorbell interrupts my last-minute examination of myself, or rather my cleavage examination, to ensure that it's not too much for a meeting with attorneys.

Glancing through the peephole, what I see causes me to groan, but I open the door to find MadDog, Mary-Anne, Torch and Cleo on the other side. They're looking at me with questions, and I know they're going to bombard me as soon as I let them inside. It's been three years since I've seen any of them, and I was never particularly friendly toward any of them.

"Come on inside," I murmur as I stand aside and hold the door open. I might as well get this over with.

"Holy shit woman, this is a really great place," Mary-Anne says as soon as she takes in my living area, kitchen, and breakfast room. I watch as a trail of children run behind her. "Oh god, I'm so sorry," she groans. "I thought they would stay in the car."

"It's okay," I smile as I watch them. Walking over to the television, I turn on one of the cartoon channels. "Can I get you guys anything to drink?"

They all politely decline but make their way into my living space, the women sitting, with the kids, and the men standing, still taking in my expensive San Francisco home. It's worth at least five times what our home in Shasta was, maybe even more. I wait for them to speak, knowing that they aren't here for just a friendly little chat.

"How you doin'?" MadDog finally asks.

"I'm fine," I admit on a nod.

"You left three years ago and never came back. We walk into the hospital room, your face is bruised, and the tension between you and Soar is thick enough to cut with a knife. Then we find out you're like an heiress. None of us knew, not even Colleen, and she's known you since you were eighteen," Mary-Anne says, cutting to the chase.

"Sloane didn't want anybody to know. He doesn't like his family. They've had issues, except for his little brother Kipling. He's the only reason Sloane even has contact with his parents. I just found out that Sloane's childhood was rough. He refuses to talk to me about it," I say, spilling everything to these people—these people that I know love Sloane whole heartedly and without reservation.

"What about you?" MadDog asks.

"My family was angry when I ran away with Sloane. I was eighteen when we were married. I had just graduated high school and was head-over-heels in love. I didn't know anything about the club life. As time went on, I realized what he was doing, his involvement, it wasn't just a rebellious thing. He was the rebel, the bad boy, and I thought he'd change and want to take over his father's company eventually. As the years went on, I realized, that wasn't what happened, or that it was ever going to happen," I explain as I walk over to the windows, unable to look at these people, these genuine people that I'd been lying to for fifteen years.

"Then the women," Cleo guesses. I nod as I try not to cry.

"He admitted yesterday that he'd been with other women

since the beginning. The fifteen-year-old girl inside of me just broke. It's stupid of me," I choke.

"What is?" MadDog asks, his voice thick. If I look at him, knowing he's gazing at me with pity in his eyes, I'll surely break down.

"Loving him the way I do, the way I always have. Allowing him to continue to screw around on me like that. Wanting a baby, knowing the man I love doesn't want to give me that. I mean, he's just offered it to me, his concessions for getting me back for whatever reason. But he doesn't want it, not really. The man who hit me, he offered me that, a family. Sloane came barreling back into my life, and I broke up with the other guy. He got angry," I shrug.

"No matter how angry, he shouldn't have hurt you," Torch growls.

"I know. Sloane or no Sloane, I wasn't going to marry Graham. But his offer of a family, at my age, it was tempting, even though I'm not attracted to him," I admit, watching a few cars pass by my back street. "I'm stupid to complain. Look at all that I have," I say, waving my hand around before I turn to face them. "I have anything I could ever want. Money is no object."

"Money doesn't buy happiness," Mary-Anne says, her voice soft and quiet.

She was with a successful businessman hoping for security before she met MadDog, and she knows firsthand that money indeed does not buy happiness. A lesson that is sometimes never learned, and other times is a hard lesson to learn.

"I know," I murmur.

"So what happens now? With his father's company?" Torch asks, thankfully switching the topic.

"The lawyer will tell us what his will says. I doubt Kalli, his wife, knows what the will says. These men, they're all very secretive," I laugh softly. "The plan was that Kipling would take over, after he finished school at Harvard and probably worked for him a while. My guess is that the vice president will take over until Kipling is ready, but who knows."

"No matter what happens, we want you to know, Genny, that we're here for you. You're still family, no matter what," Mary-Anne says, giving me a sad smile.

"I appreciate that," I murmur. "I don't know when the funeral will be, but I should know by the end of today. I can let you all know," I offer.

"Okay, sounds good, darlin'," MadDog says solemnly.

"Sure wish you'd come home," Mary-Anne whispers as she envelopes me in a hug.

"Thank you," I mutter.

The group leaves a few minutes later, after the men are assured that I'm not too emotional to drive on my own. I feel stupid for spilling everything that I just did to them. It was as if the words just flowed and I couldn't stop myself. Once everything was out, though, it felt relieving.

Now they know pretty much everything, there's nothing else to hide anymore from them. I really do like them. I don't know Torch well, but MadDog is not the man he was when I met him. Mary-Anne has grounded him, and he's become a wonderful husband and father, proving that you can teach an old dog new tricks. I wish I could have faith that Sloane could truly change, but I don't think it's possible.

Sliding into the front seat of my car, I start my engine. After opening the garage door, I head toward the Huntington manor. The lawyer should arrive within the hour, and I want to make sure that both Kalli and Kip are okay.

I haven't heard a word from Sloane, so as much as I want to believe that he'll be here for his mother and brother, I'm not planning on holding my breath. I'm going to be there for my mother and brother-in-law, but at this point, I think I need to let Sloane go. I'll never be what he needs. After twenty years, that is painfully obvious.

"Imogen?" Kip's voice calls out as he knocks on my car window, making me jump. I didn't realize I was already here, driving the last few miles in a complete fog.

"Sorry," I call out.

I wipe the tears from beneath my eyes and gather my purse as Kip opens my door for me, ever the gentleman.

He looks to the seat next to me and I watch his shoulders deflate, "Sloane didn't come with you?"

"He had to meet with his probation officer this morning," I explain. Kip nods as he slides his arm around my shoulders. I, in turn, slide my own arm around his waist.

"How was last night?"

"Mom drank until she passed out while she cried," he admits. It kills me.

"Anytime you want to come over to my place, you just come right on over," I say, resting my head on his shoulder.

"It's funny. Sure, he was my dad, but he wasn't really around much. I mean, he was around more for me than Sloane I think, but it still wasn't often. It doesn't seem real yet," he murmurs as we climb the steps.

"It will when you pick up the phone to call him, excited to tell him something. It'll hit you then," I whisper. He makes a noise in the back of his throat before he clears it.

"Yeah."

Once we're inside of the house, we separate, and I walk straight to the kitchen to make something for Kalli to eat and drink. Today is going to be another long day, and she's no doubt hungover as shit.

Soar

"You will be tested each time you're scheduled to come to me. And I will come to you randomly to check on you. I don't want to hear of you getting pulled over again," Randall Lundorff, my parole officer, rambles, sounding bored as fuck with his speech. It's the same speech he gives all of us, just leaving one set of shackles for another.

"Do I have to stay in the county?" I ask.

"You have to stay in the state, and I would prefer if you stay in the county. Where else would you go?" he asks warily, his eyes narrowed on me, though he hasn't asked me why I wasn't in my county last night when I was pulled over.

"My wife and I are separated and currently living apart. We're trying to work things out. She lives in Frisco," I state. He nods.

"I'll give you permission to go from her place to yours, but I want all of her information," he murmurs, shoving a piece of paper and pen at me.

I write down Imogen's name, address, and phone number. I also give him the information for my mother's place.

"Who's this?" he asks after I give him the paper back.

"My father died last night of a heart attack, that's my mother's information. I'll probably be at her place often as well," I shrug.

"Okay. Don't get into any trouble. One toe gets out of line, and I can toss your ass right back in your cell. You can finish out your two-years there faster than you can say *Bobs your uncle*," he grunts.

"Yes, sir," I grind out.

I leave with a stack of paperwork, and what dignity I have left, before rushing to my bike. I don't typically use my car, unless its late at night, wet, or snowing.

I'm already late for the meeting with the lawyer, but hopefully Kip can fill me in when I get there. Then I have some talking to do with Imogen.

I try not to think about last night. About how haunted and sad her eyes looked when I walked into her house. About how silently she made her way upstairs and stripped naked. She looked resigned, as if her body was all I wanted and she was just going to give it to me.

Granted, it was a draining evening, but I couldn't fuck her like that. Even all those times she was pissed at me and I talked my way back between her legs, she was always white fucking hot for me.

I don't want to break her, but maybe I have. She's been so fucking strong all these years, putting up with me and apparently giving up on her dream of children, something I didn't even realize she'd wanted that badly. I feel like a fucking asshole.

Once I pull over for gas, I check my phone and am surprised to see that Torch has called me. I shove the gas nozzle into my tank and walk away, calling him back.

"You on your way to the city?" he grunts immediately after the second ring.

"Yeah, just stopped off for gas, then heading to my parents. I need to meet with you guys later today."

"About what?" he questions.

"Something that happened, need to talk to you all," I inform.

He grunts an *okay*, before he continues "Normally, I could give a fuck what a brother does with his woman. That's their shit, and god knows I have my own fucking shit going on. But I gotta tell you, if you aren't going to do right by your woman you need to let her go," he murmurs. I'm frozen to my spot in shock.

"Excuse me?"

"Never really knew your woman. Thought she was always some stuck-up cunt who thought she was better than everyone and spread her bitterness around like fucking confetti. I only let Cleo stay with her because we went together on that run before you went in, and it was better than the clubhouse for her without me around at the time," he explains.

I wonder what the fuck he's going to say next. What he's saying now is not the man I've come to know as Torch. "She deserves better than your selfish ass," he states. I can't hide the shock on my face, so I'm glad he's not saying this shit in front of me.

My anger rises before I grind out my next words, "Yeah, but I'm what she's got."

"Don't you think you've played with her long enough?" he asks, his voice deep and serious, even and not a bit angry.

"She's mine."

"I don't think you understand the meaning of a woman being yours, brother," he rumbles.

"Yeah? Why don't you explain that shit to me then," I growl.

"You're almost forty years old. Not something I should have to teach you at this age. I will say, when a woman is yours, no other woman compares. Now, if you're both into playing with other people, that's a totally different thing; but she doesn't want to play, and you're off doin' shit behind her back. A woman's yours, you kill yourself giving her the life she deserves, whatever that looks like. Kids, white picket fenced house, *whateverthefuck* that looks like, you give to her."

"So what? I let her go, I divorce her and let another man have my woman?" I ask.

"You still don't get it, brother," he sighs. "Time to grow the fuck up, Soar. Grow up or let her go."

The line goes dead, and I grip my phone, hearing it pop in my hand.

I'll be damned if I let my woman go. I'm a fuck up, and I've fucked up, but never again.

She's mine. I'll prove that I'm a man, and that I'm all the man she needs. I'll fucking make her so goddamn happy that nobody, not one single person will question the love I have for her.

No other man touches her. She wants kids and a white picket fence, I'm going to be the man who gives it to her. Not some other fuck, and especially not some fucking pansy in our parents shitty assed social circle. And definitely not Graham.

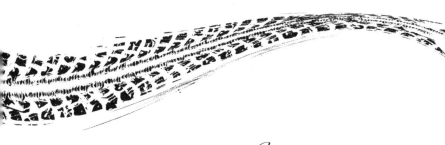

chapter eleven

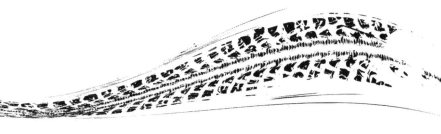

Imogen

The attorney walks out of the living room, leaving us sitting in the receiving room in shock. Sloane McKinley Huntington, II was an asshole when he was alive, but a major fucking *dick* in death. Kipling is the first to speak after the attorney closes the front door behind him.

"Dad was a piece of shit," he announces. I gasp and slide my eyes over to Kalli.

She nods before she speaks, "Always was, always will be."

The house has to be sold within a month. Kalli isn't going to get half of the estate, a loophole in their pre-nup that was written almost forty years ago. Instead, she'll get a stipend, monthly allowance from the estate.

The Huntington Estate will not be passed down to Kipling or Sloane. Instead, they'll only receive what is already in their trusts and not a penny more. Kipling won't even have access to his until his twenty-fifth birthday.

Sloane II's money will all stay in the business, and Kalli's stipend will only flow freely as long as the business does well. If the business fails, she'll get nothing.

As for the remainder of the estate, Sloane II, and his liquid assets, those will go to his other children, to be divided amongst evenly. Children nobody even knew existed, especially not Kalli.

Granted, there are six of them, so their money won't be even close to what Kipling and Sloane already have, but that's beside the point. He had a whole life that nobody knew about, a secret life, and it's then that I realize just how much Sloane is like his own father, a man he despises.

"How could he? And he knew. It wasn't like it was a surprise to him, he's always known," Kip says.

"Because, darling, he was a Huntington and Huntington's do what they want, when they want," Kalli announces before she stands and walks away.

"He's forcing us to sell the house. Who does that?" Kip asks. I wrap my arm around his shoulders and hold him.

"I'm so sorry, Kippy," I whisper.

"No wonder Sloane always hated him. I didn't understand it, not until now. I have siblings, six of them," he murmurs.

"Do you want to try and find them?"

"Never. It's not their fault, but no. I never want to know who they are," he says as he stands. "Sorry, Genny, I gotta go."

I nod and watch him race out of the house, worried that he'll get into an accident, but knowing him well enough to know that he needs the space.

"Where is everyone?" Sloane asks. My spine straightens.

Closing my eyes for just a second, I rise before I reopen them and make my way over to him. He's standing in a pair of jeans that hug his thighs perfectly, a black shirt, his cut, and his heavy black boots. I shiver at the sight of him, his blond hair messy from his helmet. I'll never *not* be attracted to my husband. If nothing else, I'll always physically want him.

From across the room, I explain to him what happened, and I watch as his face goes from shock to anger.

"That piece of shit," he growls. "Where's Kip? Is he okay?" he asks. This is one of the reasons that I've always loved him, his adoration of his little brother.

"He's shaken. He took off, needing some space," I whisper. He nods. "How do you feel?"

"I'm not surprised," he shrugs. "I walked in on him more than once fucking someone else."

I suck in a breath in surprise, but he looks as if it's no big deal. That makes my heart ache. No wonder he never had a problem stepping out on me, his father has always done it. I turn away from him, trying to tamp down my emotions, but they come bubbling to the top.

"Imogen," he whispers as his heat presses against my back.

His arms wrap around me, one around my chest the other around my waist. I feel his lips touch the side of my neck before he speaks.

"How are you doing, baby?" he asks.

"I'm tired," I admit.

"Sucks my dad was a giant fucking dick, but sunshine, it's not news to me. I just want to take you out of this city and go back to our lives," he states, his voice vibrating against my skin. "Start over."

I close my eyes and inhale deeply, smelling him, his scent another thing that drives me insane about the man. "I don't think we can start over," I murmur.

"Not letting you go, sunshine," he rasps. "I'll change."

I spin around in his arms and look up at him in surprise. He looks completely serious, and I wonder if it's true, if he really will change. I feel stupid for hoping, so damn stupid, but I can't help myself.

"Is it possible? Or are you just going to hide it better?" I ask. I want the truth. Since he's been being so honest with me lately, I expect it.

"Imogen."

"I'm serious, Sloane. I don't know if you've ever loved me, but I can tell you with certainty that I have loved you every day since I was fifteen years old. Don't promise me anything else that you can't deliver, *please*," I whisper with tears in my eyes.

"I want to try, for you," he admits. "Let me try to make you happy."

I bite the corner of my lip and nod. I should run far, far away. He's promising me changes, but then he turns around and says something hurtful. I'm foolish to hope that this time it's a real change, but I do. Again. Something inside of me must be just as broken as what's inside of him, because I weakly allow this shit over and over.

"Why do I always believe you?" I ask.

"Because you're mine."

Without another word, he bends down and presses his lips to mine, his tongue seeking entrance inside of my mouth. I open for him. As I always do, and as I always will. My Sloane, my husband, the man I've belonged to since I was just a girl.

There is no other man for me. As much as he hurts me, I keep going back for more, hoping, praying, and wishing that it will be the last time.

It's not lost on me that my relationship with him, the way I continue to go back to him, that it's nothing short of the definition of insanity. If I lose complete hope in him, and in us—what happens to me then?

"Let's get the fuck out of here," he growls against my lips.

"I should check on your mom," I murmur, my eyes still closed.

"No, baby, you should take your sweet ass to that car, drive home, and fuck your husband."

"Sloane," I whisper as my thighs shake.

"Go, now," he rasps.

I do as he instructs, but once I've reached his mother's front door, I turn around to face him. He looks at me with question.

"This is all real? Why the change, yet again?" I ask, needing to know more.

I can only hope that all of this has come about because he did some serious soul searching, that he realizes what he's done to me, to us, all of those years. That this is because he's, somehow, a reformed man.

His only answer is to shrug with eyes focused on mine. Then, when I don't accept that and simply keep walking to my car, he finally speaks.

"Torch called me, told me what an ass I'd been. Told me to let you go," he says. I'm surprised at his words. "I can't let you go, Imogen. You're the only constant I've ever had in my life. I don't know who I would be without you at my side."

His admission makes my step falter, because I feel the

same way. I don't know who I am without being Sloane's Imogen. "The other women?" I ask.

"You're the only woman who matters to me. Told you I'd stay faithful to you if it's what you want and, sunshine, I don't plan on failing," he says. I can see the sincerity in his eyes, a look I'm not used to from him.

"Okay," I whisper before I turn and walk toward my car.

It's probably foolish, and I'll probably end up in a shattered mess, but it's Sloane. I want him, and I want us to work. I want his children, and for us to live a happy life—a sober life.

If the club is what he desires, I'm okay with that, as long as I'm at his side and he's at mine. I wouldn't have been okay with it five years ago, but now, I fully accept that part of him.

As long as he gives me all of him, then I'll always continue to give him all of me as well. I have to accept all of him, just as I expect him to accept me and with that comes accepting his faults and learning to forgive the past. I'll never be able to forget, but hopefully one day I can completely trust and forgive him again.

Soar

"Don't break that sweet girls heart, Sloane," my mother's voice rings out from the stairwell.

"Mother," I warn, turning to face her.

She looks like shit. Normally, she's perfectly put together, but her hair is a mess, her face is splotchy, and her eyes are puffy from crying.

"I'm serious. Don't turn her into me. She's much too gentle of a soul," she whispers. "Your father had six other children, an entire secret life he hid from us. I'd always known about his dalliances, but never about the children. Don't leave her feeling the way I do right now. If you can't give her all you've promised, you need to let her go," she announces before she turns and goes back to her bedroom.

I wonder if that last woman I caught with my father was a mother of one of his children. He doted on her, gave her more than just a stack of cash. Shaking my head, my thoughts drift back to the money laundering he asked me to do, and I wonder if that had anything to do with his other life, too.

Fuck, I have no clue who my old man was. I'm relieved he's dead. No more schemes, no more lies, and no more pretending. Now, I have to focus on not becoming him—easier said than done.

Walking outside, I straddle my bike and put on my helmet. It's not lost on me that my mother isn't the first person, even just today, who has told me to give Imogen what I promised or let her go.

I would let her go if I could, but I can't.

I *should* let her go, but something inside of me forces me to hold onto her. Is it true unapologetic love? I don't know. I know that I haven't been sober for this long, since I was ten years old. I feel like a completely different person than I did the day I was locked up.

But I also know without a doubt that Genny's the best thing that's ever happened to me, and I can't imagine my life without her. That's all I know. So if that's what love means, then yeah, it's love keeping me from watching her walk away.

I sent a text a few minutes ago to find out where MadDog

and the rest of the brothers are staying, he just texted me his address. Turning my bike toward the hotel I send my own message letting them know I'm on my way over.

I need to tell them about the cop pulling me over. I know they can't do anything about it, but I feel like it was all too suspicious. Like maybe I was targeted. I don't know if it's because of me or the club.

When I pull into the hotel's parking lot, I'm surprised to see a couple cops standing outside of the front doors. I can feel their eyes on me, as though their gaze actually heats my skin, then a hard band clamps around my bicep. As much as I want to jerk out of his hold, I don't. I lift my chin and am surprised to meet the eyes of the cop that pulled me over.

"You and your buddies plan anything around here, and I will catch you. I'll take extreme pleasure out of throwing you back in jail. I'll also love knowing the fact that you'll be getting ass-raped while I fuck that sweet little wife of yours," he chuckles.

His buddy clears his throat, but I don't respond. If I even open my mouth, I know for a fact that I'll say and do something that will definitely put my ass back in jail just like he wants. My face heats and my blood boils as I stomp into the elevator and watch the numbers climb to the floor my brothers are on.

"Who pissed in your cheerios?" MadDog asks before I can even knock on his door.

I storm into the room and look around, noticing that its all the men and no women. MadDog answers my question before I can ask it, and tells me that they've all gone to the pool to get a little sunshine. Then he asks me again what the fuck is going on.

"I got pulled over the other night. It was because of my cut. He made me do the whole drug screen and shit. Nothing became of it, but I wanted to bring it up to you anyway, just in case it was something to do with the club. That theory was just blown out of the fucking water," I grind out as I clench my fists.

Torch lifts his head and his eyes catch mine as he waits for me to continue. When I don't, he speaks up. "What the fuck happened, brother?" he practically whispers as though he understands the gravity of the situation for me.

"He and a buddy are standing guard just outside the hotel. He made it clear his mission was to lock my ass up again for a parole violation. Then he told me how he was going to fuck my wife."

Every man in the room growls, and I feel the air start to fill with rage. It's so thick, it's practically choking me. A second later, MadDog speaks. His voice is low, yet lethal, and full of authority.

"I know you can't do anything, brother. You stay low and keep your nose clean. I'm going to make some phone calls and try to get to the bottom of this if I can. You keep your ass out of a cell and let us worry about the rest."

Giving him a nod, I lift my chin to the rest of my brothers. I tell them that I need to check on Genny and they all give me knowing looks. They all fucking know that I need to check on her not for her own safety but for my own sanity. My nerves are shot, and I've never felt so goddamn helpless in my entire life.

Making my way out of the hotel, I decide to go out the back instead of the front, hoping to avoid the dicks in blue and hurry to my bike. Then, I head to Genny.

Shoving thoughts of the cop, jail, and everything else out of my head, I make my way toward Genny's house. The door is unlocked when I arrive, and I quickly lock it behind me. I can hear her voice floating down the stairs. She's giving information on my father's funeral, which will take place in two days. I'm taking Genny right after, and we're leaving Frisco. I know I promised her until her parent's summer party, but I can't wait that long.

"I just told MadDog about the arrangements," she murmurs as I walk into her room. She's ditched her shoes, but she's still in her sexy as shit long dress.

"Nice of you. Thanks, baby," I murmur.

"I feel like I haven't slept in a year," she admits as she sits down on her bed.

"Stress," I point out. I walk over to her, sinking down to my knees in front of her, my hands sliding up the outside of her thighs.

"Sloane," she whispers.

"I want to be a better man for you. I *have* to stay sober to stay out of jail. I don't like the man I am and what I'm capable of when I'm blazed. I don't want to lose you again. I know that I can't live without you. I know that I'll kill any man that even thinks about taking you from me. I know that I'll die to keep you safe," I admit, feeling like a pussy, but telling the truth for the first time, ever.

"Oh, Sloane," she sighs as she cups my cheeks.

"Come back with me. After the funeral, come home, sunshine," I rasp.

I watch as her eyes search mine, and then she nods slowly as she bites her bottom lip.

"This is all really how you feel, for certain?" she asks. I

turn my head to press my lips to the inside of her wrist.

"Yeah. Bring my sunshine home to me."

"Okay," she says as tears fall from her eyes.

My gut reaction is to drop my pants and fuck her until she screams, but the vulnerable look in her eyes tells me that I need to move slowly—for her. So that's exactly what I'll do.

I untie the little bow at her waist and gently tug her dress open before I pull it down her arms. Wrapping my hand loosely around the front of her throat I slide it down the center of her chest to her belly, stopping just below her belly button.

"I'm ready to put my baby inside of you, Genny," I murmur as I feel her stomach tremble beneath my fingers.

"Sloane," she exhales.

I move my hands to her panties and tug them down. She lifts up, and I pull them down her legs before I press my hand to the insides of her thighs and spread her wide. I moan when her fingers comb through my hair and she forces my head back.

"When you're like this, I can imagine a beautiful life with you," she whispers. I wait for her to continue, knowing that she has more to say to me. "I want the beautiful life, Sloane."

I slide my fingers through her center, finding her wet and biting my bottom lip as I push two inside of her. Curling my fingers, my eyes connect to hers while her grip flexes in my hair. Her face is flush, her hair hangs around her face, and this is the moment it washes over me—*love.*

"I'm giving you the beautiful life you deserve, sunshine. No more women, no more drugs. You and me, our little house up in Shasta, and babies. A simple life," I rasp.

"It's all I've ever wanted," she breathes as her thighs shake.

"I know, sunshine."

I continue to fuck her with my fingers, my eyes trained on hers and watching as she climbs closer toward her release, her body moving on its own volition as she chases what I know is bubbling toward the top. Her pussy flutters around my fingers, causing me to groan, wishing my cock were deep inside of her instead.

"I love you, Sloane," she whispers as she throws back her head and comes, her pussy squeezing my fingers tightly.

I let her ride out her climax before I take my own clothes off, quickly. Leaving them in a pile on her floor, I instruct her to climb up the bed. She does as I've asked before she removes her bra, releasing her gorgeous tits for me.

Grasping her ankles, I let my hands slide up her calves, behind her knees and then to the backs of her thighs. I place her legs over my shoulders. She bites her bottom lip and grins, the heat in her eyes obvious as the head of my cock presses against her slick entrance.

"Ready for me, Imogen?" I ask, my eyes snapping up to hers.

"Sloane," she moans.

"Gonna fuck you, sunshine. You ready to take all of me?"

I watch as she nods. I've been rough with her, but nothing like I'm about to be. I've always held myself back a bit, thinking she can't take all that I need to give. She's got no choice now but to take it. There's not going to be anybody else, just her. Without another warning, I slam into her, as hard as I can in one thrust.

"Oh, shit," she gasps.

I place one of my hands on her headboard for support, my other on her shoulder to keep her in place, and I thrust into her tight cunt, hard and fast. It's rougher than I've ever fucked her before, but I can't hold back. She's mine again, and she's coming home. It feels *new, raw*, and fucking *right*—so goddamn right.

"Relax," I urge as sweat forms on my forehead.

My hips moving and my cock filling her over and over as she makes the sweetest fucking sounds on earth beneath me. She's wound tight, and I can tell by the look on her face that she's tensing with each thrust. I'm not slowing down, and I can't stop, so her only alternative is to fucking *relax*.

"Sloane, honey," she gasps as my hips grind against her clit. I lean my head down and press my lips against hers.

"Relax, sunshine. Feel, don't think," I whisper against her lips. I can feel the tension leave her body.

Returning back to my punishing thrusts, I know when she's finally feeling instead of thinking. Her back bows as her thighs relax further against her chest, allowing me more room. I take full advantage.

The tight glove of her pussy strangles me, and I know that she's close again. I don't slow down. I speed up my movements and slam against her. Genny's breath hitches until she gasps, and that's when she strangles my dick tighter than she ever has, crying out with her release.

"Christ," I curse.

My balls tighten and empty inside of her, my body giving no other warning that I was close. I fucking explode inside of my wife. Her pussy pulses as I slowly move in and out of her, allowing her to milk me dry before I collapse on top of her, her thighs wrapping around my waist and her body trembling beneath mine.

"Fucking hell, sunshine," I whisper against her neck as

her arms wrap around my back.

"I've missed you. Missed us," she murmurs. I grunt.

"This is our new beginning, baby."

"Sounds nice," she sighs. I nip the side of her neck with my teeth.

"Sleep."

chapter twelve

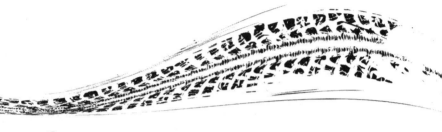

Imogen

The black dress I'm wearing is tight and hits to right above my knees, the neckline cut so high that not even a hint of cleavage is showing; the sleeves are three-quarter because that is what is appropriate. My high heels are black, four-inch, Jimmy Choos.

I finish pinning my hair into a low chignon, away from my face as is proper. My makeup is light; my lips, a dark berry color.

"You look gorgeous, sunshine," Sloane murmurs as he slides his hand around my waist from behind, his lips touching the back of my neck.

"I shouldn't be excited about today," I whisper, turning around and sliding my hands up his chest to wrap around the back of his neck.

"But?"

"I'm moving back home, and you're coming with me to stay," I say, licking my bottom lip.

"Yeah, I'm stayin' there, baby," he murmurs before his mouth touches the corner of mine, careful not to mess up my lips.

"It's all real?" I ask, not for the first time.

Sloane's hands slide down to my ass and give me a hard squeeze. His stiff cock presses against my belly. "All real, sunshine," he grins.

I smile as he shakes his head, and then the doorbell rings. We've spent the last few days helping Kalli with the funeral, along with Mary-Anne, Cleo, Colleen, Bobbie, Ivy and Teeny.

I didn't think that Kalli would want their help, but when nobody from her circle of friends even offered to lift a finger, she welcomed them with ease and grace. She's still sad, but deep down I think that she's relieved. Sloane's father had this hold over her. Now that he's gone, it's as though she's bursting through her shell. It's a beautiful thing to watch.

I wish that I could say the same for Kipling, but I can't. He seems to be retreating into himself more and more. Sloane has been talking with him, but I don't think it's helping. He had an image of his father built up in his mind, and it's been shattered. Sloane can't really help him too much with that aspect, as his image of his father being a good person was shattered when he was just a child.

Sloane walks downstairs to answer the door as I gather my purse from the bed. I look around my bedroom and shake my head with a grin. I'm completely insane, and absolutely crazy.

I don't know why I'm doing this, but I am. I'm leaping

into something that will probably crash and burn. There's something that feels so different this time. Hope—*hope* is the something that's different, and I'm going to grasp onto it with both hands.

All of my clothes are neatly packed and ready for the movers to load up and drive to Shasta. I don't know when I'll have the opportunity to wear my designer clothes much, but I don't really care. I'm more comfortable in jeans and t-shirts, anyway. I always have been.

"Movers are here, Genny," Sloane calls out. I hurry downstairs.

There are a few men standing around, big and broad, looking at my home in surprise. I don't have much packed, because I honestly didn't accumulate much in the past three years.

"The furniture all stays. The only things going are the boxes, and they're all ready to load up," I instruct. Their eyes widen even further in surprise.

Once they get the rest of their instructions from Sloane on when and where to drive the truck after they're finished, I notice the limousine pulling up, and then a couple of bikes behind it.

"Mammoth and Roach are going to stay here with the movers until they're finished," Sloane informs me.

I grab the small bag that's packed by the front door. It's a change of clothes for the ride home. Sloane hasn't left me for one second since his father died and we decided to get completely and totally back together. That also means that I'll be following behind his bike in my car, since he hasn't been back to Shasta to drop it off.

"Ready?" he asks. I nod jerkily. "You okay?" His brow

furrows as he looks at me with concern, and I wonder if I'm doing the right thing.

I know I'm not doing the safest thing. My heart is definitely on the line, again. I turn around and look at my house, my home for the past three years, and yet, it's not a home at all. There aren't any special personal touches, and no good or bad memories were made here. This was a place I slept, but I never *lived* here.

"Yeah, I am," I admit with a nod.

He takes my bag and walks over to my garage, punching in the buttons that automatically raise it. He then clicks my trunk open button and tosses my bag inside before he closes everything back up. Together, we walk toward the limo.

After he opens the door for me, I slide inside and am met with not only Kalli and Kipling but my parents as well. I blink in surprise, and my mother rolls her eyes at me before my father speaks.

"We're a family. We show as a united front no matter the circumstance," my father says. "Since it appears as though you aren't going through with a divorce from *him*, we're to remain family."

"No, you're right. I won't be going through with the divorce," I admit.

"I don't understand it," my mother says, shaking her head.

"You don't have to," Sloane replies, finally speaking.

He's always detested my parents but hasn't ever spoken against them. Both of our parents have their own sets of issues, and we've just always kind of ignored them. Fighting with them isn't ever worth it. We each listen to them and then do what we want. We're in our thirties, and they don't have control over us anymore.

"What does *that* mean?" my father asks, puffing out his chest.

"Means that you don't have to understand us. You aren't part of our marriage," Sloane shrugs.

I watch as my father's face visibly reddens at his words. "Listen here, you little prick, you aren't allowed to talk to me that way," my father growls. Sloane just snorts.

"I'm almost forty, old man, not a little prick anymore," he jeers. "Also, your big bad voice didn't scare me away from Imogen when I was eighteen years old, and it still doesn't. Genny's mine—my wife. I don't care what kind of *plans* you had with Graham Bayard, but they're done. She won't marry him, not even if I'm out of the picture," he rumbles.

"Sloane," I whisper, tugging on his arm.

"No, baby. Your dad and Graham had some master plan, and they're both pissed now because I'm back and they can't try to manipulate you. I won't let that happen," he announces.

"I still have a little control, Huntington, don't forget that," my father chortles.

"What? You have control over a portion of her money but not all of it. I know how much is in her trust, and I'll know if one penny goes missing, too. That trust is untouchable, and it's going to stay that way so that our children can have it. You can keep whatever money you want, I could give a fuck; we don't need it," Sloane announces.

"You'll be singing a different tune if it's taken," my father says, sounding high and mighty.

"Not singing any tunes for you, asshole. Wanna know what? My father's money is all but gone, and I didn't get what I should have. Do you know how much of a fuck I give? Not a single one. Its money. It isn't life or death if you don't have it, and guess what? I can always make more, and I make plenty."

"Bullshit," my father snaps.

"Which part?" I ask, interrupting them. "There's a reason you're pushing for Graham even though you know he hit me."

My father doesn't visibly show a reaction. He wouldn't. I'm convinced he has no soul. We pull up to the funeral home before my father can answer, and I fight rolling my eyes as the door opens and my father plasters on a concerned, yet calm face. It's his serious funeral face. My family's entire social circle is so damn vapid, it's disgusting.

"You gonna be okay, Kippy?" I ask as I squeeze his hand.

"Yeah," he lies.

"Well, that was hell," Kipling murmurs.

We're sitting in the front row outside in the cemetery after everybody has left the graveside service, other than immediate family.

Luckily, my parents are heading to the reception early to play host and hostess. Since they love that shit, nobody protested. Now it's just Kip, Kalli, Sloane and me staring at the casket in front of us.

"No, what he left for us, the way he did it, that's going to be hell," Kalli slurs.

"Whatever you need, we're here for you," I say, squeezing Kip's arm.

"I'm supposed to leave for Harvard in two-weeks. My first semester is paid, but nothing else," Kipling says, his voice shaky.

"Don't worry about money. I'll take care of you," Sloane says. I turn to him in surprise. "I don't spend even a fraction of what I get each month, Kippy. I have some of my own holdings as well. You need to go to school," Sloane murmurs. My heart fills with even more love for him.

I let my head gently fall onto his shoulder, and I wrap my hand around his upper thigh. He grunts before he stands and tugs me up as well.

"You want to come home with us for a while?" Sloane asks Kip.

"No, I'm going to help mom with packing and getting her settled in her own place," he says as he stands.

We walk away from Kalli, Kip behind us. When we're far enough away, Sloane speaks more freely.

"Mom's an adult. You don't need to take care of her. She's capable of calling people to hire that can help her. If you need to get to college earlier, or you want to crash with us before you go, nobody will be angry with you. Nobody expects you to take care of her," Sloane says.

I slide my hand around his waist, feeling nothing but pride in the way he's handling all of this. He so obviously wants to take care of Kip. Sloane's so sexy when he's in control; but when he's showing love, it's *the* sexiest thing I've ever seen. He doesn't show if often.

"Thanks. I'll help her, though. I'll feel better knowing she's all settled when I leave," he shrugs.

"Don't do it all on your own. Call me if you need me," Sloane murmurs.

"Me too," I chime in. Kipling looks down on me and smiles.

I step away from Sloane and wrap Kip in my arms. He does the same and hugs me tightly.

"Glad you're back with my asshole brother," he whispers

into my neck.

"I am, too… I think," I admit.

Sloane and I leave a few minutes later, and we tell Kip that we'll send the limo back to pick them up once it drops us off at my place. He nods his agreement and turns back to sit with his mother.

It's sad, the destruction that one stack of papers, a simple will, left behind. *Sloane McKinley Huntington, II* is a piece of shit—*even in death.*

Soar

"I have to work tonight, sunshine," I announce. Genny stiffens next to me. "Not at the clubhouse."

We're headed back to her place to pick up her car and my bike before we get the fuck out of this city. Everyone who came to support us from the club is waiting in front of her place, and the moving van has already left.

"Okay," she says and turns to look out the window.

"Sunshine," I bark a little too harshly, causing her to jump. "Talk."

"I'm just… I don't want to be in that house all alone *again*," she admits, refusing to look at me.

I ask her to look at me, and when she does, I see tears swimming in her eyes. Makes me feel like shit, but I have to do my job. It's true that I don't need the money from the club, but that's not why I have to do my job.

They depend on me, and they're my family. I can't let them down. I refuse to. Me being in prison for three years was enough of a goddamn letdown, not only to them, but also to myself and Genny.

"I'll be home right after I'm finished. Probably won't be until early morning, but swear to fuck, I'll come straight home," I say, cupping her cheek with my hand.

"It's stupid," she says, shaking her head.

"What's stupid?" I ask, my jaw clenching as I try not to become angry.

If she says the club is stupid, then we're going to have bigger problems then we already do.

"I shouldn't be so worried about being alone in that house, but I spent so many nights alone while you were…"

I don't let her finish her sentence. Pressing my lips to hers, I give her a hard kiss, effectively shutting her up before I whisper. "No other women. No whores—just you, baby. Swear, sunshine."

"I wish I could believe you," she says shakily.

I repeat my words, "Swear to you, sunshine." She nods, letting out a deep breath. "Now let's hurry home so I can make you come before I have to head out."

"Sloane," she breathes.

"Need to be inside you again," I murmur as I nibble on her lips. "I'll prove to you that this will work, baby."

"I love you," she says. I close my eyes. "I'll always love you."

I don't say it back, but holy fucking shit does it feel good every time the words tumble from her lips. The limo stops in front of her place, and I press my lips to hers quickly before I open the door and wait to help her out.

It doesn't take us long to load up on bikes, and the women all load up into Mary-Anne's SUV, since most of them are knocked up and can't ride on the back of bikes. My brow furrows when I notice that Imogen is alone in her car. I jog over to her.

"You want me to have one of the other girls come ride with you?" I ask. She shakes her head, but I can see her mind working behind her eyes.

"I want to be alone," she says, giving me a fake as shit smile.

"See you at the house. We'll celebrate," I grin, feeling completely uneasy about her going alone when the other car is packed full of women. "Maybe go for a ride?"

"A ride?" she asks in surprise.

I smile at her giddy excitement. It's been since before I went away that she was on the back of my bike. I can't wait to feel her against me again, her arms wrapped around me, her tits pressed against my back.

I grin. "Yeah, sunshine, a ride."

"Okay, baby," she whispers.

I swear to fuck, it hits me straight in my dick, making me hard and needing her even more than I did before.

I try to ignore my cock and bend down, pressing my lips to hers. I remind her to drive safe and let her know that her gas tank is full. Something feels wrong about separating from her right now, but I tamp that down. She'll be fine, there's no reason for me to worry.

Nevertheless, I can't get that gut feeling to dissipate. She nods and we separate, the nagging feeling that something isn't right still in the pit of my stomach. It stays with me as I follow behind her the entire trip home.

chapter thirteen

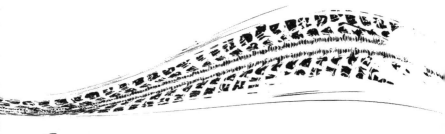

Imogen

It doesn't escape my attention that all of the other Old Ladies pile in one SUV while I drive all the way back to Shasta by myself. I was a bitch to them *for years*, so it shouldn't surprise or hurt my feelings. For whatever reason, it does just that.

My cell phone rings in the seat next to me. Without thinking, I accept the call. I regret my decision as soon as Graham's voice comes through the car's speakers.

"Where are you headed, Imogen?" he asks coolly.

"Home," I admit as my fingers grip the steering wheel.

"Back to the mountains, then?"

I don't bother responding. He knows where I'm going, and he knows it's not anywhere with him.

"I just had a long conversation with your father. You

know he's very upset by your choices. He feels as though you're not quite sane," he chuckles. "Going back with a habitual cheater, a drug user, and a felon in a motorcycle gang," he states before he makes a tsk, tsk sound.

My jaw clenches at his words, at his veiled threat, "What do you want, Graham?"

"Oh, you'll know when I'm ready to tell you," he ominously says before he ends the call.

My brow furrows, and I try turning up the radio to take my mind off of the strange conversation. I don't know what kind of game Graham is playing, or what he and my father have planned. I should probably be worried, but I'm so far removed from them up here in the mountains that I doubt I'll even hear from either of them again, until my parents' summer get together.

Looking in my rearview mirror, I notice that I've been separated from the rest of the group somewhere on the freeway. When I take my exit, I assume that we'll catch up, but then something flashes in my rearview mirror.

The blue and red lights have me pulling as far over to the side of the road as I can. I watch as a police officer approaches my window, and I roll it down, feeling nervous as my hands grip my steering wheel.

"Hey there, ma'am. License and registration please," he says, his voice soft and gentle. Except, when I glance up at him, I'm startled by the intensity in his gaze.

With shaky fingers, I reach for my glove box and pull out my registration then grab my wallet from my purse to find my license.

"Imogen Huntington," he murmurs. I watch as his eyes travel from my license, to my face, to my breasts. "You were going five miles over the speed limit, and in inclement weather."

My eyebrows snap together, and I look up at the sky. It's a gorgeous sunny day, a warm seventy degrees, and not a cloud in the sky.

"Inclement weather?" I ask.

He grins as his teeth sink into his bottom lip. "Yeah, sweetheart. Now, I can give you this ticket, but it'll make your rates go up, and probably not look too great to have the wife of a man on probation getting a reckless driving ticket—or I can make it all go away."

"Make it go away?" I whisper, pretty damn sure what he's implying, but unbelieving that this is actually happening to me.

He leans over, his wrists pressing against my window, his hands dangling in my car, and his face mere inches from mine. "You suck my cock, sweetheart, and I can make it all go away. You don't, and I'll have to pull you out of this car and do a search. Now, I would hate to see you go down because that husband of yours thought he'd be slick and put his dope in your car."

I press my lips together, unsure of what to say or do. There's no way in hell I'm giving this douchebag a blowjob; but since he's obviously dirty, I have no idea what lengths he'll go with his filth. He pauses and I watch him reach into his pocket, pulling out his phone.

"Yeah, I got her right here. No, he's not with her," he sighs before he continues. "Yeah, okay." He looks at me and presses his lips together as a muscle jumps in his cheek. "You get a pass today, sweetheart. But eventually, those sweet lips will be wrapped around my cock. You can guarantee that shit.

He stands, throwing my license and registration at me before he walks away. When he's in his car, he turns around and heads in the opposite direction of where I'm driving.

Only when he's gone do I start to shake. My entire body starts to tremble and my eyes water. I try to take calm breaths, but I'm on edge. Had he not gotten that phone call, there's no telling what he would have forced me to do. Out here, on this deserted road, I wouldn't have been able to stop him, no matter how hard I fought.

Sucking in a deep breath, I look around before I pull back onto the road. I should turn around and go back to San Francisco, get the fuck away from Sloane and whatever is following him. That cop knew who I was. He pulled me over to fuck with me for a purpose. I try to force the entire situation out of my head. Ignorance is bliss, and I just want to forget it even happened.

By the time I've arrived at the home I've shared with Sloane for the past fourteen years, I've completely forgotten the conversation with Graham and ignored the fear from the police officer. My house is looming in front of me, and I don't want to get out of my car.

My heart starts to race, and I find it hard to breathe as I look at the house I've practically lived in alone. I can't count how many tears I've cried, how many nights I laid awake imagining every disgusting scenario I could think of.

I don't want things to ever to go back to the way they were, not even a little bit. I feel like walking into this house will catapult me back in time, and I want no part of it.

"Imogen?" Sloane's voice calls out as he knocks on my car window.

I don't know where he came from, but seeing his green

eyes makes my tense body relax.

I jump slightly and turn to face him. He must see something on my face, because his eyebrows pull together and he yanks my car door open before he crouches down beside me.

"What's wrong, sunshine?" he asks.

Ignoring everything but my feelings about this house, I answer, "I thought I could do it. I thought I could go back inside that house and pretend that the memories were just that—memories. I thought that we could make new ones and everything would be fine."

"Genny," he murmurs as he lifts his hand and wraps it around the back of my neck. I search his light green eyes and wait for him to say something else. "I have to work, baby. I don't want you to be here if it's going to upset you like this. I'm workin' with Camo tonight. You can go and hangout with Ivy until we're off?"

I bite the inside of my cheek, not wanting to be a burden on Ivy, but also not wanting to go inside of that house. My eyes move from the house back to Sloane, and I nod.

"As long as it's okay, I'll stay with her," I mutter.

"I'll build you a new house, sunshine, one where we can make new memories," he states. I can't help the smile that plays on my lips. "But unless you want to live at the clubhouse while it's being built, you're going to have to go inside this place eventually."

"Yeah," I exhale.

"For now, you got some shit in your bag, and you can just go to Camo and Ivy's," he shrugs. I nod in agreement.

Sloane stands up, but before he straightens, he squeezes the back of my neck and brushes his lips against mine. When he walks away, I watch him in my rearview mirror. He walks over to the SUV.

The men are all standing around, and he points at my car, at the house, then shakes his head. Camo slaps him on the back, and then he turns and walks back toward me.

"Follow the SUV. They'll go straight to Ivy's, and I'll be right behind you," he gently states before he turns and walks back to his bike.

I start my car again. Once the SUV pulls out into the street, I back up and then follow behind. I feel like a big damn baby about the whole thing. I should just march my ass into that house, redecorate it or something, and suck it up. Just because it's filled with sadness and bad memories doesn't mean that it has to stay that way.

Life is what you make of it, and so is that fucking house.

Pulling up to the little green home trimmed in white, with a black door and a white picket fence, I sigh. This place is so cute, and it looks exactly the way I pictured my home would look like with Sloane when I was a teenager. It seems absolutely perfect. The only thing it's missing is a dog and maybe some kids' toys in the yard; but judging by Ivy's pregnant belly, that will be happening soon.

I open my car door and step out before popping my trunk and taking out my overnight bag. Sloane comes up behind me and slips the bag from my grasp while his other hand wraps around my waist.

I'm surprised when all of the women and kids climb out of the suburban, SUV and the men disengage from the bikes and follow us inside. I'd assumed they would have all just taken off toward their clubhouse.

The small living room is completely full to capacity by the time the last man walks inside, and they're all looking at me. It's completely and totally unnerving.

"Glad to have you back, Genny," Texas' voice booms. Everybody around us smiles encouragingly.

"I—I—thank you," I stutter.

The men break away and go out back to talk about whatever Sloane is doing tonight, I presume. That leaves me alone with all of the women. I inhale deeply before I let all of my oxygen out, then I speak.

"I'm sorry I was a bitch for so long," I start.

"You don't need to apologize," Colleen starts, "for anything. Every woman here understands exactly where you were coming from, and why you were as unhappy as you were."

"I was very unhappy, but that never made it okay to take anything out on any of you. And I did, often," I murmur.

"Honestly, if my man acted like Soar did for years, I would be a complete bitch. We understand," Mary-Anne says with a sad smile.

"Imogen, huh? How did we never know your real name?" Bobbie asks, arching a brow.

"When I came here, I was eighteen. I didn't want to be Imogen Stewart anymore. I rebelled against my family and I eloped with Sloane. I wanted to be unknown. Nobody knows Genny Huntington, and that's who I wanted to be—just Genny. But Genny ended up being a pathetic bitch," I laugh.

"No. See, you can't reinvent yourself. You're you, and you'll always be you. I've tried, trust me, and I wasn't happy. You weren't either," Mary-Anne says.

"Neither Sloane nor I were happy. It wasn't just him cheating, it was a million other things. But what it all comes down to is exactly what you said. I tried to reinvent myself;

Sloane happened to find himself here, and this is who he is.

"I didn't accept that, and I was playing pretend, waiting for him to change. When reality hit that he wasn't going to change, it made me angry. Nothing excuses him cheating on me, nothing at all, but we were both living lies. Lying to each other and to ourselves," I admit.

The men walk in and we're all quiet. The tension is thick, and I find it a little difficult to breathe. Sloane's brow rises as he looks between the women and me, but he doesn't say anything. He walks straight over to me and wraps his hand around my back tugging me into his chest as his face dips down.

"You'll be okay?" he asks as his green eyes search mine.

I nod, "I will."

"Be back as soon as I can, okay, sunshine?"

"Okay, Sloane," I whisper.

He dips his head slightly as his lips brush mine, and I shiver when his tongue slides along my lips. He doesn't deepen the kiss, but just the taste from his tongue is enough to make my body heat with desire for him. He grunts before he steps back and then the rest of the men say goodbye to their women.

"You'll drop everyone off in a bit?" MadDog asks Mary-Anne.

"Yeah, we're going to order some dinner, eat, then I'll take the girls home," she smiles.

"Okay, sweetness. See you at home," he rumbles. Then they all leave us standing in Ivy's living room.

"Well, I was going to ask you how you knew he'd changed, and how you decided to give him another chance. But that tender moment right there, I can see a difference in him,"

Colleen states.

I probably shouldn't tell them this. They'll most likely run and tell their men; but I don't really have any girlfriends, none other than this group. "I still don't trust it," I admit, shaking my head.

"What do you mean?" Ivy asks curiously.

We all sit down on the furniture and I let out a deep sigh.

"He's sober right now, which is different and new. I love it because he's the boy I fell for all over again. He's sweet and charming, but now he's honest. Sometimes brutally so. I hate that part, the brutal honesty. He's admitted things, and it hurts like hell. I'm just afraid that he'll go back to the man he was," I state.

"The drugs and women," Mary-Anne states. "It was hard for me to believe that Max could be faithful. He cheated on his wife, and he hadn't been in a relationship for years; not since her. I completely trust him now. He's proven to me time and time again that he is not that man anymore. I think with Soar it will just take time for him to prove himself."

"Yeah," I nod. "I'm just afraid I'll give him so much time that…"

"That you'll miss out?" Teeny murmurs quietly.

"I want a family. If I spend five more years with Sloane and it ends badly, what then?"

"We can't predict the future. Wouldn't it be great if we could?" Mary-Anne says with a smile as she places her hand on her rounded belly. "If I had followed through with leaving Max out of fear, out of what-if's, then I wouldn't have this life that I cherish so damn much. On the other hand, you have to do what's right for you," she says.

I nod, unable to really respond. I don't know what's right

for me. I know that Graham Bayard isn't right. I know that since he's been back, that Sloane has *felt* right. He's also said some things that have hurt me.

I always stayed with him because of how he made me *feel*, never using my head, which has screamed at me to run for years. I'm doing it all over again; putting myself in the same positon as I always have. Allowing myself to be vulnerable to him, to be hurt by him. I understand that the past is the past, but when it's the person who hurt you that brings things to light, it's a hard pill to swallow.

The fact is that I love Sloane, but I absolutely don't trust a damn thing about him. I want to. I really want to, but I don't. I'm not sure if I can stay with him without that trust. I hate feeling in limbo, and yet, that's exactly how I feel. I want it to work between us. I want the family and I just want *him*. Just because I want it doesn't mean that it's what will happen, or that it's what's best for me.

I hope that I'm not throwing all my chances at having my own children away, but I don't know who else I would rather have them with other than Sloane.

"It'll all work out," Colleen says with a smile. She doesn't look convinced.

I give her a slight head jerk and Ivy changes the subject to food.

Soar

I force my mind to clear as I ride toward the docks. The only place I want to be right now is inside of Imogen, but I have work to do. Since I was rotting away in prison for three years, I'm fucking behind.

Camo and I don't stop as we ride to our destination. There's a truck and trailer waiting for us there, and a prospect should already be behind the driver's seat, waiting for further instruction.

Once we pull into the dark area where we park our bikes, Camo and I discard our helmets. He stretches his neck from side to side before he lets out a long groan. We've been on these bikes far too fucking long today, and I can't say that I'm not stiff and sore myself.

"You remember the drill?" he asks as we walk toward the docks.

"Yeah. Load the shit up, make sure nobody is around, pay the dock worker when the work is complete," I mumble.

"Pretty much sums it up."

We walk over to the familiar dock, and the smell of the fish and salty air is disgusting, but it brings me back to fond memories. Out here, I didn't worry about Genny, about my family, about anything. This was busy work, and it kept my mind off of dope, pussy, and Imogen.

"This is way more shit than we moved three years ago," I announce as I see the stack of guns and dope we're supposed to load.

"Denver has expanded, rapidly," Camo shrugs as he walks over to the dock worker to talk to him.

I start looking at the crates of guns and am surprised to see some seriously high grade weaponry. Nothing like what we moved the last time I was here. Fuck, they are not messing around anymore.

"We still doin' this shit once every two months?" I ask

Camo when he returns to my side.

"Every two weeks now," he announces. My eyes widen and he grins. "So much fuckin' money coming in, brother. You've got a fat stack of cash in the safe."

"Christ, this is crazy," I mutter.

We spend the next three hours straight loading up the truck, with the help of the dock worker and the prospect. Once it's completely loaded, we lock the back of it and send the prospect off toward the clubhouse. Camo hands the dock worker his money, and we walk back toward our bikes.

"All this time and nobody has gotten wise to anything?" I ask out of curiosity.

"Not that we can tell. We have some of the local cops on our payroll now, so we schedule these loading times when they're on shift. Other than that, we just keep our heads down, noses to the grindstone; load up the truck, and get the fuck out," he shrugs.

"Seems too good to be true," I mutter.

"I have no doubt that we'll have to change shit up here soon. It's been over three years. We can't get too comfortable."

I nod in agreement and pull my helmet on before I straddle my bike and we take off. It'll be a couple more hours before we're back to Shasta, but I know that unlike any other time I made this run, Imogen is waiting for me.

We don't make it very far down the freeway before we come up on our truck and trailer pulled over by the California Highway Patrol. I don't stop, because I can't afford to go back to jail, so I signal to Camo to pull over to the nearest gas station.

"What the fuck?" Camo grinds out.

"Don't know, man," I say, looking behind us.

We have a clear view of the prospect, the truck, and the cop. Camo tells me that he's going to put a call into MadDog, and I nod without looking away from the scene before me. The last thing we need is more trouble. We've been flying without it for a while; and from what I hear, it's been pretty fuckin' sweet.

Sure, the men have been looking for and recovering some ex-old ladies, current old ladies, and widowed old ladies from the Aryan's, but that's been ongoing for years and completely under the radar. A national search, nothing only our club is involved in, and nothing that has been life threatening or war-threatening.

"MadDog says to keep him updated. The CHP is not on our payroll. We just have to wait for this to play out," Camo murmurs. He sounds as worried as I feel.

I watch as the prospect nods to the officer, jumps in the truck and then takes off. Camo and I look at each other in surprise before we hurry to our bikes and do the same.

We can't stop anytime soon to talk to the prospect about what went down, so we drive straight to the clubhouse. I promised Imogen that I would be back as soon as I could, but it looks like I have other shit to handle first. I know she'll understand. She'll have to. She has no fucking choice.

chapter fourteen

Soar

"Church," Texas rumbles from the parking lot of the clubhouse right after we turn our engine's off.

The prospect that was driving the truck hurries out of the warehouse, and we all file into the clubhouse toward the room where church is held. This will be my first church since coming back, and I can't deny that I'm a little nervous. Probably because this is also my first sober church, ever.

MadDog slams down his gavel as soon as the door closes behind the last person in the room. I look around at my brothers, and I can see the uncertainty in all of their eyes. Prospects aren't usually allowed in our meetings, but since it was a prospect who was pulled over, he's allowed to stay for the moment.

"Why don't you tell us what went down?" MadDog asks, looking directly at the prospect.

"I was doing the speed limit, driving in the slow lane, when I saw the bear come up behind me with his lights flashing. I pulled over, thinking he couldn't be pulling me over, because I knew I was following all of the rules to a *T*," he explains.

"What'd he say?" Torch asks.

"He said that he knew who I was, he knew what we were doing, and if we didn't watch our backs we'd all find ourselves locked up just like Huntington," he says. My back straightens.

"Thanks. You can go," MadDog says. We all wait until the door is closed behind the prospect before we continue.

"Do you think he was a real cop? I mean, he could have just searched the truck to nail the prospect," Mammoth mutters.

"He wants us all, not just one lowly prospect," MadDog says as he runs his hand over his bearded chin.

"It doesn't sit right with me. You said it was a marked CHP car?" Grease asks, turning to look at me.

"Marked, LED light bar; but I mean, fuck, it could have been a light bar he bought online, and it could have been a magnet on the car instead of the insignia painted on. I went by pretty quickly. Didn't want to draw attention to myself," I admit, feeling shitty for not paying close enough attention.

"I've tried to find out why they would target us, but there's nothing out there that I've come across. Regardless of who this guy is, we need a different route for next time," MadDog mutters.

We all agree and then we decide to meet up around noon to figure it out for the next run. Roach and Mammoth are going to take the truck to Denver early to drop the load off. They're going to go home pack and then head out. The longer it sits in our warehouse, the more vulnerable we are, especially if the cop was legit and not an imposter.

"Soar," MadDog grunts as the men leave. I turn to him. He motions for me to walk over, so I do. He then throws a large envelope on the table. "It's your portion of everything that we made while you were locked up, plus your payment for the Garcia job."

"You didn't have to pay me for that. Did that for Torch and Cleo," I mutter.

Garcia was locked up in the same facility as me. He was working for *The Cartel*, tried to kidnap Cleo and was planning on selling her to the Aryan's. Back then, the Aryan's were secretly buying club women through *The Cartel*, and using them for breeding purposes. Since then, they've gone to ground, and our club has been trying to get the women back one-by-one.

One of our own, our VP, Drifter, was in on the whole fucking twisted thing. When Garcia got locked up with me, I eliminated him for the club—for Torch—but also for Cleo. She didn't deserve that shit. She's one of the sweetest women I have ever met.

"It could have added to your sentence. You took a risk, brother, and that risk deserves payment. We all voted on it, and it's yours," MadDog grumbles.

"You know I don't need it. Any of it," I state.

"Know that. Doesn't mean you didn't earn it with your blood and sweat. You think I give a fuck, any of us give a fuck, what you have from your family? We don't," he says. "That why you didn't tell us?"

"The world I grew up in, everything about your history, about your family's history, it matters. What your great-great grandfather did matters. Every single move you make is recorded or handed down throughout the different families. It's bullshit, and I hated every fucking second of it. I wanted as far away from that world as possible."

"Yeah, you fuckin' got it," he chuckles. "This is where you belong. I see it in you, Soar. We're your family. No matter the size of your bank account, we'll stay that way."

"Thanks," I nod.

"I'll see you in a few hours and we'll figure out this whole fucking mess we have now," he says, lifting his chin.

I nod and grab the envelope on the table before I turn and walk away. I walk into the bar of the clubhouse and am not surprised to see a small party in full swing.

Since we were all called down here in the middle of the night, it seems like the girls were roused, and it's suck and fuck time. I don't blame any of them. I'm about to head back to Imogen for the same thing.

"Hey, Soar baby. Come on, let's have some fun," Destini coos. I recognize her as the girl I fucked when I first arrived back from prison.

"Sorry, babe, got places to be," I shrug as I walk away from her.

Straddling my bike, I can't believe how easy that was. I thought the first time pussy was offered to me at the club would be harder to turn down. The thought of hurting Genny makes my chest ache. I aim to be better for her—to be the best. With a grin, I head toward her.

Imogen

I hear the door close, and I sit up from my spot on the couch. My heart races inside of my chest, and I blink my eyes to see a figure looming above me. It takes a second for my eyesight to adjust, and when it does, I see Sloane standing right in front of me.

"C'mon, sunshine," he rumbles. "We'll take your car so you don't have to drive home. I can pick up my bike tomorrow," he mutters.

I hear another set of boots walking around the house and turn my head to see Camo disappearing down the hall toward his bedroom.

"What time is it?" I ask, my voice groggy from sleep as I stand.

"Four in the morning," he yawns.

I slip my feet into the sandals I brought, and watch as Sloane picks up my overnight bag as he opens the front door. He takes my keys from my hand and loads up my bag before he opens my door. He then waits until I'm inside before he closes it behind me. Once he's settled into the driver's seat, I turn to look at him.

"I didn't expect you back so late," I murmur, my mind going over a million different scenarios of where he's been.

"The job didn't go off as planned. We had to have an emergency meeting," he mutters as he focuses on the road ahead of us.

"Where'd you have to meet?"

"Went to the clubhouse, baby. Just a meeting with all of the brothers, then I came here to get you," he offers with a shrug. I feel my hackles rise at the mention of that *fucking* clubhouse.

"Just a meeting?" I ask, a little louder than I intended.

"Yeah, Imogen, *just* a meeting."

I stay silent, twisting my fingers together in my lap and

biting the inside of my cheek. I want to ask a million questions. I want to accuse him of a million things. I can't. I need to try and not jump to conclusions, but dammit, it's so easy to do.

"I was approached, offered a good time, but I declined and kept walking," he admits when he pulls into our garage.

"*Seriously*?" I ask in surprise.

"Seriously," he grunts as he opens the door and steps out of the car.

I do the same and hurry after him, ignoring the painful memories of the house. I'm too focused on Sloane's back as he walks toward our bedroom in front of me. I call out to him to stop, but he completely ignores me.

Only once we're in our bedroom does he turn around to face me. When he does, I see pure fire in his green eyes, making my step falter. I back up until I hit the wall behind me.

Sloane stalks toward me and presses his chest down to his hips against me. I can feel his hard length against my stomach, and I bite the inside of my cheek while my eyes stay pinned to his.

"Ask me," he grinds out as his head dips. His lips are so close to mine they're almost touching.

I shake my head, but his angry gaze doesn't dissipate at all. He growls, demanding that I ask him again. "Did you want her?" I finally ask.

"Fuck no," he grunts. "Not even for a goddamn second. Not when I have you waiting for me," he murmurs as his lips touch mine with each word he speaks.

"Sloane," I breathe.

"Only woman I want is you, sunshine," he rasps.

Sloane doesn't give me a chance to say another word. His

tongue fills my mouth while his hands tug my sweats down until they are past my hips and fall to the ground, my panties joining them. I step out of them when one of his hands slips between my center.

Two fingers quickly slip inside of me, curling and causing my head to fall against the wall with a thud. His lips travel down the column of my neck as I widen my legs, a moan escaping my lips.

"Fuck, baby, you're so wet," he murmurs against the hollow of my neck.

"Sloane," I rasp as my hips roll and I search for more from him, feeling wanton as my body heats from the inside out.

"What do you want, Imogen?" he asks, his voice rough as he fucks me with his fingers.

"You," I murmur.

"Yeah? Who am I?"

I whimper when he presses his thumb against my clit, "*Sloane.*"

"Who am I, sunshine?"

"You're my husband," I whisper, lifting my head to look into his green eyes.

"Fucking right, I am. Your husband, your old man, fucking *yours*," he hisses.

He wraps his hands around the backs of my knees and picks me up, his jeans rustling before he slides inside of me to the hilt. I hold onto his shoulders for stability as he presses my back against the wall with just his hips, his cock seated deep inside of me.

"Sloane," I gasp.

"Yours, Imogen. I'm yours," he grinds out as he pulls back slightly and thrusts against me, hard.

"For now."

Sloane pauses and his eyes alight with anger again, causing my breath to hitch. His jaw clenches, but he doesn't say anything. He takes a step back, keeping me close so that we're still connected, and he walks us over to the bed.

I watch as he completely divests himself of his clothes before he climbs onto the bed, our bodies still connected as he lays me down in the middle, while he looms over me. Then he starts to glide in and out of me, slowly and with purpose. His eyes stay fiercely connected to mine with each pump of his hips.

"For fucking ever, sunshine," he breathes.

He doesn't fuck me, he makes slow love to me, and my eyes water as tears leak down the sides of my temples with each and every move he makes. It's the most beautiful moment I think I've ever shared with him. I wrap one of my hands around the side of his neck as my body climbs closer toward my release.

"For fucking ever, Imogen. Just you," he rasps as he starts moving faster, his breathing pattern changing as he edges closer toward his climax.

"Sloane," I choke before my release completely takes over me, causing my entire body to shake.

"Fucking hell," he groans as he starts moving faster, more erratic.

Then he bites his lip, his eyes on mine, and groans as he fills me with warm spurts of his cum.

"Only you," he whispers, lowering his head and pressing his lips to mine as his hips continue to move in long lazy strokes.

"Just you, sunshine," he repeats.

chapter fifteen

Imogen

I roll over and touch the sheets beside me, but they're empty. Opening my eyes, I sit up slightly, just as Sloane walks out of the bathroom, his hair dripping and a towel wrapped around his waist.

I can't look away from him. He's mesmerizing with his muscular chest, unmarred by any ink. Just perfect. His back is a different story. He has his club's brand on his back, and it's super sexy, too. But there's just something about his chest and abs, his smooth skin, it does something to me. It always has.

"Look at me like that much longer and I'll have to fuck you before I go," he murmurs.

My eyes snap up to meet his, and I tug the sheet up my chest a little higher.

"Where are you going?" I ask, my voice raspy with sleep.

"Meeting. We didn't finish everything we needed to talk about last night," he says, dropping his towel.

His hard cock is jutting straight out toward me, and I can't stop myself from licking my lips at the sight. I shiver as he wraps his hand around himself and squeezes. I bite the inside of my cheek as I lift my eyes to meet his green ones, and he gives me his cocky smirk as he walks closer toward the bed.

"What do you want, sunshine?" he asks, his voice low and husky.

"You," I rasp as I crawl to the edge of the bed, letting the sheet fall around me, leaving me completely naked.

I lean forward and open my mouth. My eyes staying on his, waiting. Wrapping his hand around the back of my neck, he twists his fingers in my hair, never moving his intense gaze from mine, even as he sinks his cock down my throat.

"Touch yourself for me, baby," he whispers as his tongue pokes out and he wets his bottom lip.

I hum around him and it causes his fingers to tighten in my hair. Spreading my legs further apart, knowing without a doubt that he definitely likes to watch me touch myself when his cock is in my mouth, I slip two fingers inside of me, my eyes still on his.

Sloane slowly pulls out of my mouth and then thrusts back inside, his strokes slow and precise. He slips further down with each pump of his hips.

After a few minutes, his movements speed up, as do my own between my legs. I can't hold back the whimper. I'm on the edge of my release, and he quickly pulls out of me.

"Not coming down your throat, baby," he grins.

"Sloane," I whisper.

"Turn around," he orders. I quickly do, though I'm not fast enough.

His hand presses against my back and he pushes me down as he slams inside of me. His fingers wrap around my hips, holding me still. He pulls almost completely out of me before he slams back inside on a moan.

"*Fucking mother fucking shit,*" he groans as his hips start to wildly and roughly fuck me.

He doesn't slow, he doesn't stop; he fucks the complete *breath* out of me with each thrust of his hips. I try to push up on my elbows so that I can rear back against him, but his hand moves from my back to my neck. He wraps his fingers around the back of it, holding me to the bed while he takes his pleasure.

I close my eyes and accept all he gives. I can hear the sounds of our skin slapping filling the room, along with low moans from him every so often, as well. My thighs shake. I'm on the edge, but without something *more,* I won't come. I let out a cry of surprise when I feel his finger slide inside of my ass.

"Missed this sweet ass, sunshine," he rumbles as his cock and finger fuck me in tandem.

When he slips the second finger into my pussy, and starts to curl them inside of me, I don't hold back my cry. I feel so full of Sloane, so full that I can't keep from forcing my body up. He lets me, and I rear back against him, which causes him to moan. I reach one of my hands beneath me and touch my clit. On the second stroke, my entire body starts to shake, and I come.

Sloane doesn't stop fucking me until he roars out his whole climax, my pussy trying to clamp down around him to keep him inside. He removes his fingers but keeps his cock planted deep as he pushes me forward and rests his chest against my back.

"Imogen," he whispers against my shoulder. I don't move, waiting, knowing there has to be more he wants to say to me. Plus, my breathing is still erratic, and I'm completely out of breath. "I love you, sunshine," he murmurs.

I turn my head to the side and look at him in surprise.

"You do?" I ask.

I'm unsure of why after two freaking decades that admission makes my heart race. He's said the words before; not in a long time. I always treasured them.

Yet, as time went on, I discovered that he didn't mean them, so I asked him not to say them again until he did. He presses his lips to my shoulder before pressing them to my mouth.

"Yeah, sunshine. *Fuck*," he breathes as he slips out of my body and then gathers me in his arms.

Pulling me across his chest, our legs tangle together and his hang off of the side of the bed. "I knew I'd always felt love for Kipling. I knew I felt possessive over you, unable to imagine letting you go and be with another man.

"Until last night—until I saw that hurt in your eyes when you thought that I could have done something with someone else, I don't know. It hit me differently, and I just know that I can't hurt you like that again. Everything that I feel for you is so much different since I'm sober."

I'm surprised at his admission, or the fact that he's speaking it aloud. "I want to believe you," I say hesitantly.

"You don't have to, not yet. I'll earn it, sunshine," he murmurs as his face lifts and his lips touch mine.

We stay cuddled together for another twenty minutes, and then he tells me that he has to go or he's going to be late. Reluctantly, I sit up and allow him to move around the room.

I watch him as he dresses, and I don't feel the pang of sadness that I thought I would at being back inside of this house. I look around and nothing has changed, except for everything.

I've changed, he's changed—we've changed.

"If you want to go into Sacramento and go shopping for new furniture or whatever, please just don't go alone," he murmurs as he pulls his boots on.

"Furniture?" I ask in confusion.

"Figured you'd want to get rid of everything here and re-decorate. It's cool with me, baby. We won't be able to have another house built and ready for move in for at least a year. So whatever you need to do to be okay staying here, it's whatever you want," he shrugs.

My eyes water and he cocks his head to the side in confusion.

"I'm okay, Sloane. That's really, really, sweet," I whisper.

"Sweet?" he asks with a grin.

"Yeah."

"I don't think you've ever said I was sweet, not ever."

"Well, you just were," I grin up at him.

Sloane walks over to me and lowers his head, brushing his lips across mine. "Be home as soon as I can, and I'll bring some brothers with me to unload the truck. Feels good to have you home, sunshine, and to finally be home," he murmurs against my lips before pressing them against mine one last time.

He straightens his back, and I watch his ass, encased in

his jeans, as he walks away from me.

I stare at the empty doorway for a few minutes before I decide to get up and get dressed for the day. I may not want to completely redecorate this place, but I do plan on purging a bunch of stuff and moving things around.

This is a new life for me, for us, and I'm not going to waste anymore time thinking about the past. If I dwell on everything that Sloane's done to me, to himself.

If I dwell on all I've said to him, on the way I behaved toward him, which was shitty on more than one occasion, we will never move forward. I want to move forward.

Once I'm dressed in a pair of shorts and a tank top, I throw my hair up and get to work on the house. After I'm finished cleaning and rearranging, I'm going to take inventory of our food and head to the grocery store.

Today is going to be a great day, and I'm not going to let anything stand in my way of making it so.

Sloane loves me.

I love him.

We're going to make this work.

Leaving Imogen at home wasn't easy. I wanted to be buried inside her for the rest of the day, but church is non-negotiable, especially after what happened last night. It only takes me a few minutes to get to the clubhouse, and I cuss when I realize that I'm the last person here.

With a grunt, I swing my leg over the side of my bike and

take my helmet off, leaving it on my seat, knowing nobody will dare touch it while I'm inside.

The bar is empty, which means they're all in the room waiting, and that irritates me even more. Though, getting laid by Genny, the way I was so thoroughly satisfied, was completely worth it. I walk into the room with a grin on my face, and Camo's eyebrows rise as he grins over at me.

"Glad you could join us," MadDog grumbles as I close the door behind me.

"Sorry I'm late," I mutter.

"No you're not," he laughs, shaking his head. My answer is to shrug. "Okay, let's get started."

MadDog pulls out a map with two routes on it marked in different color marker. He shows us the route we've been taking from the docks, but then there's an alternative. He explains that this one is a little less direct, a little more dangerous and exposed. It doesn't sit right with me.

"I don't like this new route," I announce. Texas grunts in agreement.

"I don't either, but I also don't know how to get away from the docks any other way. Obviously, someone is onto us. It wouldn't take a super genius to follow our path," MadDog says.

"Are there any other docks we can come from, maybe? I mean, what about Humboldt? Maybe we can do that instead? It's about the same distance as Frisco," I suggest. MadDog's eyes snap up to meet mine.

"Let me call Kirill," he grunts.

We all sit in silence, each of us watching and waiting. MadDog explains the situation, explains that the heat were onto us, the altercation, and the obvious threats. A few minutes later, he grunts his goodbye and turns to face us.

"Soar, when you're not high as a kite, you're useful as fuck," he chuckles, making everyone else laugh.

I shake my head with a smile and wait for him to continue.

"Kirill is going to have the shipment redirected to Humboldt Bay with a worker on the inside. Same thing will happen. Truck will need to be there, one dock worker to accept payment, and two more men will have to load it up. Now I just need to figure out the best route to take. Hopefully, this completely different county, area, and bay will throw that pig off, *whoeverthefuck* he is."

MadDog excuses us, and we all let out a sigh of relief that it seems we have this shit handled for now. The men go straight to the bar, and I find my feet automatically following behind them. I accept an offered beer from a prospect and take a pull as the familiar whore slides up beside me.

"You ready yet?" she asks as she bites on her bottom lip, trying to look enticing.

"Nope," I say, popping my *p* for emphasis.

I watch as she pouts and then turns and stomps off, like the child she probably is.

"How you doing?" Texas asks from beside me. I hadn't noticed that he was even there.

"Good," I admit, lifting my chin.

"Any cravings?" he asks.

"Nah, man. Had all that detox shit happen when I was locked up."

He smirks before lifting an eyebrow, "Now that it's available, you good?"

"Got my wife back, got my brother heading to Harvard, got my *life* back. I'm fucking great," I state.

"Lots of shit went down with Genny, and then your dad."

"Genny walking away from me, I earned that shit. In fact, she should have stayed away. I'm happy she didn't, but the way I treated her for as long as I did—I don't deserve her forgiveness. My dad? He was never really my dad. I'm more worried about the way my little brother is handling it rather than me," I say. Texas nods.

"Just want you to keep your head on straight, brother," he warns.

"I get popped in a piss test for dope, I'm on a one-way street back to prison. I have no fuckin' desire to be back there again, so no need to worry about my head," I clarify before I walk away from him.

I ignore him calling my name, and I drop my beer on the nearest table before I head to my ride.

I start my bike, and without another thought, I take off. I don't know where I'm going, but I don't want to be around the clubhouse right now. I don't feel tempted by the bitches or dope, but Texas pissed me off.

It makes me wonder if everybody else is thinking like him. If they're all waiting for me to fail, to take that first hit of coke or whatever.

It's not like I don't have enough pressure with Imogen waiting for me to sink inside of some whore. I can tell that she's braced for it to happen. She's prepared to feel that hurt from me, and it kills me. I bought that shit with every shitty decision I made.

I automatically stop in front of the tattoo parlor, and I don't think. My bike knows me better than I do, and right now, it knows I need something. Ink. I don't have much, just my club's patch on my back, but now I think I need to add to my body.

"Hey, brother," Nick calls out from his stool.

He's drawing something and doesn't have anyone in his chair, so I ask him if he has a couple hours to spare for a smaller piece.

"You finally decide to mar the front of you?" he asks on a laugh. He's been trying to get me to add to my back piece for years.

"Outside of my forearm," I mutter.

"Old Lady's name?" he asks on a hunch. I nod.

"She's put up with my ass for almost twenty years, figure I should make a gesture to show her what she means," I shrug.

"Fuckin' hell man, twenty years?" he asks as he pulls out a paper. I watch him, pen-in-hand, start to sketch.

"She was fifteen when I met her. Name's Imogen," I grin.

"Robbing cradles," he snickers.

A few minutes later, he turns his sketchpad around and I'm blown away. It's Genny's name written in old English with a crown that looks like it's hanging off of the I.

I smirk at the crown because it's so her, "So you remember her?"

Grinning, he shakes his head a little, "Hard to forget that little blonde princess you brought in here all those years ago."

I get into position and close my eyes as he preps to tattoo me. I also ask him to freshen up my wedding band's ink. Fresh ink for our fresh start.

chapter sixteen

Imogen

I didn't miss this grocery store. Not a single freaking bit. I push my cart down the aisle and narrow my eyes at the box of pasta in front of me. It's the only veggie pasta they have, and it looks like it has about an inch of dust on the box. I let out a sigh and turn my cart right around, deciding to leave town and go to the good store, even if that's about an hour way.

"Oh, sorry," a young girl says as she bumps into my cart.

"Umm, sorry about that, I wasn't really paying attention," I mutter as I hike my bag higher over my shoulder.

"Aren't you Soar's Old Lady?" she practically sneers.

I take her in a little closer and I blink once. She's dressed slutty, really slutty. Without even thinking about it, I know exactly what she is. A whore. My back stiffens, and I narrow my eyes on her.

"I am," I state.

"I can't wait until he's finished playing nice with you. He's the best fuck I've ever had," she announces before she walks away, leaving me standing in the middle of the supermarket, completely shocked.

"What a little *see-you-next-Tuesday*," the cashier says from behind her counter, a few feet away, with a pop of her gum.

"I don't even know who she is," I murmur.

"Ignore her. Little girls like that?" she shakes her head. "Self-conscious and mean."

I nod but hurry out of the store, my eyes watering. I push thoughts of the little bitch out of my mind. I'll talk to Sloane when he's home, I promised him that we'd give this a fair shake. I can't start jumping to conclusions without giving him a chance, even if I really, really want to.

Once I reach my car, my step falters at the man who is leaning his ass against my driver's side door. Pressing my lips together, I continue to walk toward my vehicle. When he sees me, he pushes off of the side and takes a few steps in my direction before he stops and looks down at me.

"Imogen," his smooth voice murmurs.

My eyes shift from side to side before I close the distance between us. "What are you doing here?"

"Thought that I'd check up on you. See how your old man was treating you," he rasps, his hand wrapping around my shoulder, and giving it a squeeze.

I shake my head and my hair flies around a little in combination with the low winds. "I'm good," I practically whisper as my heart bangs against the ribs in my chest.

I don't know why I'm not running and screaming from him, why I'm not stomping on his foot and kneeing him in the balls, but after the mini-scene I just had with that whore, I feel vulnerable and weak.

Graham's finger slips under my chin and lifts my face so that I'm forced to look in his eyes. "Are you done being played by him again, yet?"

I open my mouth to respond, to tell him that I'm not being played. I open my mouth to defend him, because Sloane is mine and I'm his. I love him and he loves me, no matter what that little whore says. She probably knows about our relationship and our past. She probably knows exactly what buttons of mine to push.

Jerking out of Graham's hold, I take a step back. "Sloane is my husband. I already broke it off with you, Graham. I've told you, even if Sloane isn't in the picture, you won't be either."

He shakes his head as though he's disappointed before he lifts his face and smirks at me, his eyes sparkling in a devious manner. "I thought that I'd give you one last shot, darling. I thought that you would be smart and save yourself. I didn't peg you for a woman who would want to go down with her man," he shrugs before he starts to walk away.

"Go down?" I call out after him.

Graham stops and turns to face me, standing about ten feet away. "Darling, don't you know it yet? It may take me awhile, but I will win. The game may have changed, but I'm still going to take you away from him. It's just that I'm not going to keep you this time. I've offered you up to be played with, a reward of sorts."

"Why are you telling me this?"

His grin turns devilish and it makes my stomach hurt,

just at the sight of it. "Anticipation is fucking killer, isn't it? Besides, I know you won't tell Sloane. You'll be scared, wondering if that cop is going to pull you over and use you on the side of the road; curious as to when Sloane will get locked up again. When he does, I've decided I'm going to use your body as I see fit. A plaything of sorts. Do you know how many men want a taste of Imogen Stewart-Huntington? It's going to be great fun, darling. Just you wait and see."

My knees shake and my legs practically turn to jello at his words. My vision gets hazy, and I wrap my hand around the door handle of my car and try to keep my self standing straight. My eyes dart around the parking lot after I've gathered my wits, and I notice that I'm now alone. He's gone and, unfortunately, he left me with nothing but fear.

I should tell Sloane immediately. Graham is right, I won't. I don't want him to get sent back, and I have a feeling kicking Graham's ass will do just that. Sliding into my car, I grip the steering wheel tightly before I head toward home. I need a damn glass of booze. Not beer or wine, either. I need the hard stuff.

Pulling into the garage, I have one thought and one thought only on my mind—*packing*. I can't be here. I can't be the reason he gets sent back to prison. I know my husband, and I also know that he won't stand for Graham's threats. Once I walk inside, I shake my head.

The house looks different, and it should feel different, but suddenly it feels the exact same.

Sad, dark, dank, and fucking pathetic—just like I am.

I walk over to the sliding glass door that leads out to the backyard and I look outside. Fourteen years ago, when I moved in here, I imagined that my backyard would be full of

184

kids' toys, jungle gyms, and maybe even a treehouse.

It's empty.

The grass is barely alive, and there are no signs of life other than some plants and a tree. I turn around and press my back against the glass before I sink down to my ass. I bring my knees up to my chest and press my forehead against them.

The tears flow as I think about how, yet again, I've fucked up my life because I'm blindly, head-over-heels in love with Sloane McKinley Huntington, III. Then I cry because the promise of us, of what we could have, it is so bright, so close, and yet so far away.

The hours tick by, and I don't move. The sun goes down, and I stay planted to my spot. I don't know when, or even if, Sloane will be home tonight. My mind starts racing.

I need to pack my shit and get the fuck out as fast as I can. I need to move far away—away from Graham and Sloane and my parents. I need to hide, because this shit is never going to end.

"Genny, baby what's wrong?" Sloane asks. I jerk my head up, and he's crouched down in front of me.

"What time is it?" I ask.

"It's eight. Sunshine, what's happened? Are you okay?" he asks, concern written all over his face. I want to slap it off of him.

"I'm just peachy," I say bitchily, I decide to deflect and focus on the slut from the store.

Maybe if I pretend that she's why I'm upset he'll believe it. Then when he least expects it, I can sneak away—forever.

Sloane's eyebrows pinch together, and his jaw clenches, a muscle jumping in his cheek as his eyes narrow on me. "Talk to me," he demands.

"One of your most recent whores told me just how great you were in bed in the middle of the fucking grocery store today," I scream before clamping my mouth shut, afraid I'll say more.

I watch as he blinks slowly, and then his face relaxes as though he's relieved.

"Some slut said something in the store and it's got you in tears?" he asks in confusion. "I thought something *really* bad happened."

"You fucking asshole. She's new. I knew exactly who every whore was before I left, and I've never seen her before in my life. Plus, she looks young enough to be your fucking daughter," I screech as I reach forward and start to slam my fists on his chest.

Sloane presses his knees to the ground and wraps his hands around my wrists. He yanks me closer to him. Moving both of my wrists to one of his hands, he wraps his other hand around the back of my neck.

"Sunshine," he whispers. "Nothing's happened with anybody since we got back together," he murmurs.

"Don't fucking lie to me, Sloane," I grind out through my tears.

Sloane doesn't say a word. He stands and picks me up, throwing me over his shoulder while he walks toward the master bedroom. I brace myself when I expect him to throw me onto the bed, but he doesn't.

He walks into the bathroom, flips the light on, and then pulls me down his body, my chest brushing his until my feet gently touch the ground.

Spinning me around, he wraps one arm around my waist, the other just under my chin to hold my face where he wants it, pointed directly at the mirror.

"Baby, look at yourself," he rasps. My eyes lift as I look at myself in the mirror.

I look like hell. My face is pale, my eyes are puffy and red. I close my eyes, but Sloane shakes my head gently, making me open them again. I move my gaze to his.

"You're so fucking beautiful, Imogen. Even when you cry," he whispers, his head lowering to talk against my ear, his warm breath washing over me, sending chills over my entire body.

"You're mine, sunshine. Swear to fuck, I'm not going to hurt you like that again. I haven't been with anyone since we got back together, nobody but you."

"So she lied?" I ask, my voice timid and scared sounding.

"I was with her right after I got out. You knew I was with someone."

I close my eyes, letting the pain of his words slice right through me, but his fingers squeeze my cheeks and I open them again. His gaze is intent on me, but there is no anger, there is no pity, only concern. His hand moves from my waist up to just under my breast, and I feel his thumb slide along the underside of me.

"You were gone. I came here, and I didn't think I could get you back even if I'd wanted to," he murmurs.

"You didn't want to, did you?" I ask, knowing that he'll be brutally honest with me, even if it aches.

"I thought you'd be happier without me, sunshine. I'd hurt you so much, so fucking much," he says as his voice cracks.

I turn around in his arms and look at his face, into his gorgeous green eyes. I see nothing hidden, only the complete and total truth staring back at me.

There's no wall up, no bullshit in his words, no smoothing things over to make me complacent. Just truth. I hate it, and I love it, but I hate it because where he's got the truth practically spilling out of him, I'm full of lies. At the very least, I'm full of omissions.

"I thought that I would be happier after I left you, after I left here," I whisper.

"But…"

"How can I ever be happy when you have my heart?" I murmur.

He guffaws as he wipes a falling tear away with the pad of his thumb. "Baby, we're a fucked-up mess."

"We really are."

"We're going to make this work, sunshine. You and me, we're unstoppable, *unfuckingbreakable*, and we're going to have an unbelievable future. We fucking *deserve* it," he announces before he lowers his head and presses his lips to mine.

I moan when his tongue slips inside of my mouth, lifting my arms to wrap around his shoulders and pull him closer to me.

"I love you, Genny. I was too fucking blinded by my own shit before to really see it, really see *you*. But, sunshine, I fucking love you," he rasps against my lips.

I melt into him. I melt *for* him. This man, this man who has broken my heart more times than I can count. He's slowly starting to mend it back together again; and for whatever insane reason, I'm allowing it—I'm welcoming it.

I'm loving it. I only wish that it could last forever, but I plan on cherishing it for the time being.

"Swear, sunshine, and I'll prove it over and over again.

Swear to fuck, baby, nobody else," he murmurs as his lips move across my jaw and down the column of my neck. "Spent a whole fucking lifetime hurting you, never again," he mutters before his tongue snakes out and he licks my skin.

"Sloane," I whimper as my fingernails dig into the shoulders of his cut.

"Mmm," he hums as he slips to his knees and starts to unbutton my jeans. "No more talking, sunshine."

I suck in a breath as he yanks my jeans and panties down, simultaneously, before two fingers slide through my slick entrance and then plunge inside of me, curling the way he knows I love. Leaning forward, he presses his lips to my clit and kisses me as his eyes look up at me through his lashes.

"Want you to ride my face, baby. Can you do that for me?" he murmurs. "Miss this sweet cunt all over me."

"Sloane," I hiss.

He grins, removing his fingers from inside of me before he stands up. I watch as he undresses and my eyes catch something on his arm.

"What is that?"

Soar

Imogen is pointing at my tattoo, standing in nothing but her shirt while I'm completely naked in front of her. Honest to fuck, I do not want to talk about my new ink right now—I just want her pussy on my face. I want her to come, and then I want her to take my cock so that *I* can come. Nowhere in there do I want to discuss why her name is now on my arm.

I love her, that's why. Plain and simple.

"Your name," I shrug as I turn around to make my way toward the bed.

Her arm flashes out and she wraps her hand around my wrist, halting me from climbing into bed.

"My name?" she breathes.

I turn to face her, my hand wrapping around her hip where my road name is permanently etched. I run my thumb over my brand.

"Yeah, sunshine. Figured you've had my name on your hip, showing the whole world that you're claimed for years. Least I could do is the same," I mutter, giving her hip a squeeze.

"I—I—"

I watch as tears well up in her eyes again, but she blinks them back before she smiles. She twists my arm so that she can see her name clearly, careful not to touch the new ink. Then she shakes her head.

"A crown?" she asks, arching an eyebrow.

"My princess," I grin.

Bending down, I wrap my palms around the cheeks of her ass. With a grunt, I pick her up and turn to take her to the bed and toss her on it.

I climb up and lay down, my eyes focused on hers, on the way she strips out of her shirt, then her bra, before she straddles my thighs and crawls up my body. I wrap my hands around her hips when she's close, and yank her down on my mouth. My need to taste her is above anything else right now.

"Oh, fuck," she groans as she leans forward, wrapping her hands around the top of the headboard for stability.

Reaching up, I cup her breasts and tug on her nipples,

which only causes her to moan and move a little faster against my face. I want her cum. I fucking need it. I'm goddamn starved for it.

I watch her, the way her eyes widen, and her lips make that perfect O shape. Fucking shit, she's gorgeous. How I ever went elsewhere for pleasure, I'll never know. *Drugs make you fucking stupid.*

She comes, and her taste floods my mouth as her cries flood my ears. Holding her up, I move her boneless body until she's on her back. Sliding deep inside of her, filling her pulsing cunt with my dick, I groan.

I have the urge to fuck her until she can't walk, but I don't. The small smile tipping her lips, the satisfied and relaxed look on her face, plus the emotional drama of earlier—my woman needs slow tonight.

"I can't believe you put my name on your arm," she whispers as I slowly pull out before I slide back inside of her tight heat.

"I'm yours," I announce, wrapping my hand around the back of her knee to spread her legs further apart.

"Sloane." Her breath hitches and her hand wraps around the side of my neck. I tip my head down to look into her soft, brown eyes, and I grin.

"Sunshine, this shit is fucking real," I announce as I continue with my slow pace, though it's fucking killing me not to pound into her tight cunt.

She leans up and presses her lips to mine before she speaks against my mouth. "Fuck me, baby."

I rear my head back and look at her, her mouth and eyes smiling. I grin before I pull out and then drive into her with all of my strength.

"*Yes,*" she hisses.

I don't stop thrusting inside of her, slamming my hips against hers as I fuck her, harder than I should but unable to control myself.

She whimpers as she spreads her legs wider for me, and I can't help but moan as her pussy flutters around me.

I press her legs open with my palms, grasping onto her thighs harder than I should, surly bruising her tender flesh as I take her. Then I come, deep inside of her, while she cries out with her second release, the pulse and tight grip of her pussy telling me all I need to know—that she's satisfied.

My wife.

My sunshine.

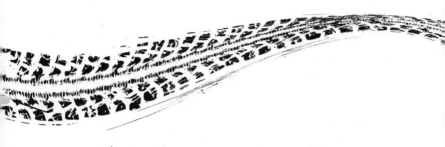

chapter seventeen

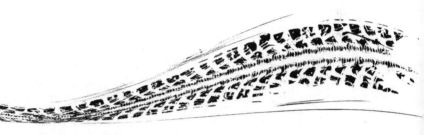

Imogen

Stepping into the shower the next day, I moan when the hot water hits my shoulders. I slept like a baby. I was completely emotionally exhausted after the events of yesterday.

Now my body is physically tight from all of the stress lately. I'm being selfish, I know. Selfish as shit for staying here, in his bed, and not leaving immediately. I just want a little more of this, of this Sloane that is so easily loveable.

I finish shaving my legs and turn the water off before grabbing my towel and wrapping it around my body. Then Sloane calls out from the other room. "Sunshine, you want to go to the store in a bit?"

"I don't like the one here. I was going to go into the city," I say, scrunching up my nose.

"Baby, I know you don't like the store here," he says

shaking his head. "I have to go out on another run in a few days, so I want to spend time with you. I'm planning on taking you to that natural bullshit expensive store you like, c'mon."

I stand, with only a towel wrapped around me, my eyes wide with wonder and surprise as I stare at him. He grins over at me and winks.

"You know which store I like?" I ask breathlessly.

"Yeah, I know which store you like," he says, his voice gruff as I walk up to him. "Go finish getting ready and we'll head out."

I rise to my toes and press my lips to his in a kiss before I do as he says. I hurry out of the bathroom and into the closet to find something to wear today. Looking around my closet, I take in the vast array of clothes that I have.

There are formal dresses for the gatherings with our families, expensive outfits for parties or just luncheons with them, and then all the things I bought and accumulated over the past three years that I just unpacked.

Then I look at my Shasta clothes. Jeans, plain tees, jackets, all things that I *cannot* wear in San Francisco, but all things that I'm supremely comfortable in.

"What are you thinking?" Sloane asks from the doorway, his eyes completely fixated on me.

"I really have lived a double life, and it's all right here. Both of my lives," I whisper as I turn back around to take in my shoes, the expensive bags, and accessories that I have.

"Which one is you, Imogen?" he asks gently.

"I don't know," I admit.

"Want to know what I think?" he asks. I spin around, curious as to what his thoughts might be on the subject. "I think that you've been living this life and thinking it was temporary.

I think that you'd go back to Frisco and play dress up to please our families, but you've been waiting for something to change so you haven't found *you* yet. All the while, I fucked around, fucked you up, and selfishly did whatever the fuck I wanted to, with no regard to you or your feelings."

I nod because I'd come to the same realization not long ago, but I don't know how to fix it. I also don't know if I should even attempt to fix it—especially since I'll be leaving soon.

My body practically weeps at the idea of walking away from Sloane. He's the only one who knows me that way. He's the only one who, no matter the circumstances, can make me ignite.

"What do you want to wear, sunshine?" he asks, interrupting my thoughts.

I bite the inside of my cheek as I look around my closet, and I shrug.

"What makes you happiest?" he asks.

"I don't know," I whisper truthfully.

"Your fancy shit make you happy? Or your jeans and tee's?" he asks, his voice deep and gravelly. "Whatever makes you happy, sunshine, that's what I want you to have."

"I don't feel like I'm the jeans and plain tee girl, but I don't feel like I'm the society girl either. I don't feel like I belong anywhere at all," I admit.

Sloane closes the distance between us and wraps his arms around me, pulling me into my chest.

"I've fucked up, for so goddamn long," he rasps.

"No, it's me, this is all on me," I say.

He looks down at me, shaking his head. "Bullshit," he barks. "I fucked around on you, fucked you over, and I was a complete fucking asshole. You were eighteen when I married

195

you. We should have been building this life together, instead of me doing *whateverthefuck* I wanted to do and hurting you repeatedly in the goddamn process. Instead of me leaving you alone and ignoring you. My drug use and the women, *fuck*, they completely obliterated you. I completely obliterated you."

"Sloane," I murmur.

"It's the truth, and it fucking sucks that I wasted so much of our time that way. I wish there were better words for me to say but, sunshine, I'm *so* sorry. I wish I could be a better man for you, a man who could walk away from you because, honest to fuck, Imogen, I should."

I blink. Then, without another thought, I wrap my arms around him. My towel falls to the floor, but my nakedness isn't what I'm focused on right now. Right now, I'm focused on the words I never thought that I would hear him say with sincerity.

I'm sorry.

Two words that alone don't count for much, and sometimes when they're said they don't really mean much. Sloane has only ever said them one other time, and that was just recently. I know that he truly means them, they are from his heart.

"Jeans and a cute top," I whisper against his neck.

"What?" he asks as I step back.

"I think I'm jeans with a cute top. A mix-match," I shrug with a small smile.

"And I think you're fucking amazing. See you in a few. Get ready, baby."

I watch him turn and walk out of the room, and it's as though a huge boulder has been lifted from my chest. There's something lighter in the air. This all needed to be said, it needed to happen, and I'm glad for it.

Then my mind shifts to Graham and that lightness disappears. I have a feeling that Graham's dark cloud is going to follow me for eternity.

I wish that all of this with Sloane would have happened about ten years ago, but life hands us pieces of happiness to grab a hold of, and I've finally found my piece. I plan on riding it to the bitter end.

Soar

I try not to let the guilt consume and eat me alive. The asshole I was, for the length of time that I was, I probably should. Pulling my phone out of my pocket, I call Kipling. I need to make sure he's good. It's been a couple of days, and he's got a ton of shit on his plate for an adult, let alone the eighteen-year-old kid he is.

"Sloane," he murmurs quietly into the phone.

"You asleep?" I ask in surprise.

Kipling is nothing like me. In fact, he's my exact opposite. He doesn't sleep in. He's up at the ass crack of dawn doing whatever it is the good kids do. I wouldn't know; I was never a good kid. I was up all night long and sleeping all day.

"Yeah," he grumbles.

"Talk to me, Kippy," I bark.

"Drank a bunch last night. Dad's expensive shit. My *fuck you* to the bastard," he says. I can practically see him shrug.

"Kip, that's not you. Don't let him turn you into someone

you aren't. His actions do not have any bearing on you," I say. He grunts.

"He had six other fucking kids. *Six,* Sloane."

"I know, and he's a fucking piece of shit, a bigger piece of shit than I imagined. He knew about them; to what extent, I'm not sure I ever want to know, but you know what?" I ask.

"What?"

"That doesn't change the fact that you are Kipling Huntington, a man who has been accepted into Harvard; a man who will do great fucking things without Sloane Huntington, II. You make me so goddamn proud, Kippy. Every day, I wish that I could be half the man you are," I admit.

"Sloane," he moans.

"I'm serious. You're driven, you're fucking smart as shit, and you're going places. Do not let that asshole drag you down. Don't fucking do it. You do, and you'll wake up one day like me," I whisper. "You'll wake up having wasted twenty years of your life on drugs and whores. Hurting a woman that you love with all of your being for almost fifteen fucking years, for no other reason than drugs and daddy issues. Don't do that, man."

We sit in silence for a moment and I can tell that my words have hit him hard. Kipling has known and loved Imogen his entire life. I know that the past three years, as he's grown closer toward manhood, he realizes how I've treated her. He knows, in general, what I've done, and he hasn't liked it. His many angry letters that were delivered to my prison cell stated just that.

"I love you, Sloane, but I don't want that for me," he whispers.

"No fucking shit, Kippy. I don't want that for you, either.

Why do you think I'm being a dick?" I chuckle.

"You're not being a dick. I've been drinking and feeling sorry for myself," he admits.

"Mom situated with a new place?" I ask, changing the topic.

Kipling tells me that she's found a place, he hired movers, and that all of dad's clothes and useless *shit* are out of the house. He says they're going to keep all of his office documents and anything that looks important to go through later.

"So mom's situated. I think you need to head to Harvard on Monday," I announce.

"Sloane," he murmurs.

"Not fucking with you, Kip. I want your ass there. Dad's paid for the first semester, I'm paying for the rest. You're fucking graduating. Don't let mom's *anything* keep you from it. I'll take care of her, make sure she's settled."

"But you don't live here," he points out.

"Little brother, it's not like I live in another state. Not a fucking hardship to check up on her," I state.

"Okay," he relents.

"Serious as shit. I'll be making your flight arrangements, and you're going."

We end the call and I turn around to see that Imogen is standing in the living room with a smile on her lips. She looks sexy as shit in a pair of holy tight jeans, some fancy flowy top that she's got tucked in, and a jacket.

Her hair is down and wavy, just like I prefer it, and her makeup is minimal—again, how I prefer. I grin when I see that she's got a pair of sexy as shit heels on her feet. A perfect mixture of the society girl meets Old Lady.

"You're a good big brother," she whispers as she walks up

to me.

"How much of that did you hear?" I ask, wrapping my hand around her hip.

"Enough to know how amazing you are. Enough to know that when we get home from the store I'll be on my knees sucking your cock," she exhales.

"Goddamn," I grunt, moving my hand to her ass and giving it a squeeze.

"I love you, Sloane Huntington," she breathes as I lower my face to hers.

"Mmm, I love *you*, Imogen Huntington," I murmur against her lips before I take her in a gentle kiss.

We kiss for only a moment and then I clear my throat and tell her to take her sweet ass to the car. I think about taking hers, but I've missed driving mine, so we'll go in muscle car style to the city and buy her fancy as shit, expensive as fuck, groceries.

Once we arrive, I grab the cart and follow her to the candy aisle. I swear, I feel like we're teenagers again, standing in the candy aisle with my girl.

"Imogen, that's fifty bucks for fucking jelly beans," I state as she loads up a bag of candy.

"They're the only ones I like," she says, shrugging her shoulders.

"Babe, its candy. What are you, eight?"

"When you're gone, I usually eat jelly beans and drink wine," she shrugs. My eyes widen.

"No wonder you're too skinny," I grunt.

"*What*?"

"You heard me, sunshine," I murmur, wrapping my hand around the side of her neck and tugging her close to me. "I don't want to come back in a couple days and find you even an ounce lighter."

"Days?" she asks.

"I'm leaving in a couple days. I'm going to make sure Kip is set up and on the plane to school, and then I have to go."

"I didn't know you could leave state lines," she mutters as she ties a string around her jelly beans.

"I can't," I say. When she sucks in a breath, I give her neck a squeeze before I lower my head and whisper into her ear. "I'm not going out of the state, sunshine. I have no desire to go back to prison, not ever."

She lets out a sigh of relief and together we finish shopping for her expensive as shit groceries. Personally, I'm fine with whatever is found in a gas station for food, but Imogen is an all-natural foods nut; so whatever she wants here, it's hers.

chapter eighteen

Soar

Walking away from a sleeping Imogen to go on a run is not something I want to do. For the first time, in a fuck've a long time, I find myself wanting to spend as much time with her as possible. I've had moments where I haven't wanted to leave her, but nothing like I've been experiencing since being sober and back together.

There's something different about her now, a vulnerability that I feel the need and want to protect. Then there's her smile, fuck me, I want to put it on her face every day and keep it there. It shines so goddamn bright.

Shaking my head of thoughts of Imogen, I load up some guns into my trunk. "This shit isn't normal, is it?"

"Not typically, but they found themselves in short supply, and it's their shit," Grease shrugs.

202

"So, just deliver it to Kirill?" I ask as I slam my trunk closed.

"Yeah, deliver it to him, and make sure he doesn't have anything else he needs from you," he murmurs before he turns and starts to walk away.

"So, you made Serina your Old Lady?" I arch my brow before he gets too far away from me.

I watch as he turns around and a stupid as fuck grin appears on his ugly as shit face.

"Yeah. Not conventional, I know," he says.

"You look happy. Pleased for you," I say, lifting my chin.

"Glad to see you worked your shit out with Genny. Must be fun to fuck the bitch outta her ridged ass," he smiles.

"You have no idea," I say, laughing before I walk over to my driver's seat.

"Glad you're cleaned up, brother," Grease says in seriousness.

I lift my chin to him in acknowledgement as I slide into my seat and start the engine.

I head out of the clubhouse parking lot, turning my car toward Los Angeles, toward Kirill, to drop off a trunk full of dope and guns. Probably not the smartest shit to do while on parole, but who the fuck cares. It's only stupid if you get caught, and since I'm stone cold sober, I don't plan on ever getting caught again.

Imogen

Waking up alone, showering and dressing for a day of absolutely nothing is… pointless. I do it, but only because I need to. I can't even think if I'm not showered and dressed. I don't know how to be that woman who lays around in her pajamas all day with unkempt hair. Sometimes I wish I could be like that. It sounds relaxing as all hell.

I decide to make a batch of brownies, organic and all natural. Tonight, I'm supposed to meet up with a bunch of the Old Ladies for dinner and dessert.

Since they all have kids now, instead of going out to restaurants or bars, they've been meeting up at one girls house bi-monthly to just hangout. I'm pretty nervous that I was not only invited but practically begged, by Mary-Anne herself, to join.

My phone rings just as I slip the brownies into the oven.

"You're coming tonight, right?" Ivy asks in my ear as soon as I answer her call. I make a non-committal noise and Ivy sighs.

"You need to be there. It's fun, it's relaxing, and you've missed out on a lot of what's been happening the past three years," she says.

I'm surprised at how much different she seems from the girl I first met a few years ago. Granted, she's a married woman now with a baby on the way, but she's definitely not that shy girl who snuck around behind her brother Grease's back with her man.

"I think I'll be there," I say. She lets out a sigh of obvious frustration.

"Genny, you were a bitch for a long time. We all knew why. We didn't understand your dynamics with Soar, but we all know now. Nobody will hold your past against you. We're a family in this club; and believe it or not, you *are* part of our family."

"Yeah, okay Ivy," I mutter.

"If you're not there, we're going to come and get you," she states before she ends the call.

I spend the rest of the day reorganizing the kitchen and moving little things around the house. It's still clean from a couple days ago, when I got down to business and deep-cleaned it from top to bottom, so there isn't a whole lot to do. Nevertheless, I still need to feel productive.

A knock on the door surprises me just as I take the brownies out of the oven. I have an hour before I'm supposed to be at Mary-Anne's, so I was just getting ready to head back to the bedroom to get dressed.

I furrow my eyebrows together, wondering who could be knocking. I answer the door without looking, assuming it's one of the girls to make sure I'm coming.

"Hello, darling," Graham's voice sneers as he pushes his way inside the house, slamming the door behind him before locking it.

"What are you doing here? What do you want?" I ask him with false bravado as I back away.

He doesn't look the same as he did in that parking lot. He looks much like he did the night he hit me. He appears aloof, but behind his eyes there's an evil lurking that sends chills down my spine.

I try to back my body toward the sliding glass door, so that I can try to run from him, but Graham is faster than I anticipate. He wraps his hand around my bicep, his grip tight, unwavering, and strong.

"It's time for you to come back, Imogen. You've had your fun, you've gained your closure, and now we're getting married," he announces with a grin.

"Graham, we're not getting married. I'm already married to Sloane, and I'm staying married to him," I say gently, afraid to speak too loud.

"No," he barks. "This is not how I planned things," he rambles as he runs his hand through his hair.

He shakes me and then his hand comes out and lands across my face in a hard blow. My entire body moves to the side, but he doesn't let me fall to the ground, his grip on my arm still, too tight. I don't get a chance to say anything before he starts rambling.

"Your father promised me. He fucking *swore* I'd have you. He promised I'd have control over your money, and I had it all planned out. It was a perfect fucking plan, and Sloane fucked me over, again."

"What did you have planned out?" I ask, trying not to let my tears from the pain fall, or my bottom lip tremble in fear.

"*Everything*," he hisses before he throws me across the room.

My entire body crashes into the hard wall, and his fist smashes against my head before I can even blink.

I fall to the floor, and his foot connects with my ribs, taking all of the air out of my lungs. "I was going to have control of your trusts, all of them. I was going to knock you up and then," he sneers, "I was going to leave you penniless. My final *fuck-you* to Sloane," he laughs. "None of that works if I don't get you."

"Sloane?" I ask, trying to push myself up. Graham's shoe connects with my ribs again.

"Yeah, Sloane. You didn't think that I actually wanted *you*, did you?" He laughs and shakes his head before he crouches down to my level on the floor. "This was all so that I could win. Sloane has always won, always. He always got the pussy, he always got the attention, and he was always better at everything. I fucking tried, and he was still better. Since we were kids," he cries.

"Every guy wanted in your cunt when we were in school. Perfect little Imogen. Blonde hair, light brown eyes, and sweet as sugar. We all wanted that tight snatch, but only Sloane got in there. Fucking asshole had already fucked the entire school, and then he got you, too," he screams.

"Well, let's see if he wants you after I fuck up that pretty little face," he laughs demonically.

I open my mouth to scream, but then pain radiates from my face as his fist lands on my cheekbone.

Everything goes black.

Ivy

"I knew she wouldn't come," Mary-Anne murmurs as she takes the casserole out of the oven.

"I talked to her, she seemed like she was coming," I say.

I want to be confident that she'll be here, but she's almost an hour late, and she still sounded hesitant when I ended the call. I shake my head. "I'm going to go get her," I announce.

Standing up from her seat, Colleen calls out, "I'll go with you."

Once we're in my jeep, we drive toward Genny's house. When we turn down her street, I suddenly feel sick to my stomach. I press my hand against my belly, thinking maybe the baby is moving around and making me feel nauseous, which she does do some days; but that's not what this feels like.

"Do you feel that?" Colleen asks me. I nod. "It's foreboding. Something is wrong," she whispers.

We pull up to Genny and Soar's house, and the feeling seeps into my bones, it's so bad.

"Maybe we should call one of the guys?" I ask as I chew on the corner of my lip.

"C'mon, I'm sure we're just overreacting," she laughs as she opens the door and hops out onto the ground.

I follow suit, not quite hopping, but definitely sliding down until my feet gently touch the ground. Walking behind Colleen, I slowly make my way up the dark walkway and onto the porch.

There's a light on inside, but as I press my ear to the door, I don't hear anything. Colleen rings the bell and still—nothing. We both call out her name while I knock, and still—nothing. I pull my cell phone out of my pocket and call her, but the phone just rings and goes to voicemail.

Colleen tries the door, and the handle turns. When she opens the door, peaking her head inside, she lets out a cry before she slams it closed.

"Call Camo and MadDog, now. Do not come inside," she warns. I blink a few times, my mouth opening and closing. "*Now*, Ivy," she barks, shaking me from my stupor.

I watch as she goes back inside, carefully closing the door behind her. Then I pull out my phone and I do as she asks. I call Camo.

"What's up?" he asks, sounding distracted.

"I'm at Genny's and somethings wrong. Colleen won't let me in the house, but when she peeked inside she screamed. I think something happened to Genny," I whisper.

"Genny's dramatic, you sure?" he asks.

"West, I'm serious. This isn't a joke. Something is wrong," I state firmly.

"All right," he grumbles. "I'll be there in a minute."

Annoyed with my husband, I decide to call MadDog next. He sounds much more concerned than Camo did and swears he'll be here as soon as he can. I don't walk inside of the house, too afraid to see what's on the other side of the door. I hope Genny is okay, but I also know that based off of Colleen's immediate reaction, she isn't.

West shows up first and looks irritated as shit that I've dragged him away from whatever it was he was up to. I'm surprised when he walks up to me and wraps his hand around my back, lowering his head to press his lips to mine.

"Sorry I was short on the phone, baby," he murmurs against my lips, his beard tickling me. "You feelin' okay?"

He presses his hand to my belly, and I get shivers, just like I always do when he's anywhere near me.

"I'm okay, just worried about Genny," I admit.

"Let me go inside. You stay here," he rumbles and lowers his hand to squeeze my ass before he releases me and walks inside.

I watch his ass, encased in his perfectly fit jeans, and I sigh like a teenager, still unbelieving that this man is mine. I don't care that we're married and he's mine forever, I'm still in complete shock that it's all real. He's real. We're real. I don't know if I'll ever fully believe it, either.

"Do you know anything?" MadDog asks, taking me out of my thoughts.

I hadn't even heard his bike pull up. I turn to face him,

shaking my head as my answer.

"Colleen and West are in there. I was told to stay outside," I shrug.

Camo

Fucking shit.

Looking down at the bloodied body of Genny makes my stomach turn. Colleen already checked for a pulse, and it's there. She says it's weak, but it's there. So I guess there's that.

MadDog walks in, and I hear his boots freeze just as Colleen and I are discussing whether to take her into the emergency room, or if we should call an ambulance.

"What the fuck?" he whispers.

"No clue. She's got a pulse," I state.

He points to me, "Call an ambulance," he orders.

I don't say anything in response. Pulling out my phone, I call 911 and tell them about my emergency.

"Christ," MadDog hisses as he crouches down.

"Who could have done this to her?" Colleen asks on a whisper.

"The guy she was dating. He hit her hard enough to leave a mark when she broke it off," MadDog announces as I hang up with the emergency dispatch.

"This is more than a slap across the face, prez," I mutter as I look down at the blood that's started to dry all over her face. I don't let my eyes travel down further, noticing her clothes are ripped and torn all to shit. "Could it be the Aryan's? Devil's took another woman and kid and moved them to Canada just the other day."

"Could be, but I don't think so. This shit is personal looking," he mutters.

The EMTs burst through the door, and we all take a step back from Genny. I decide to join Ivy outside, knowing she's probably a ball of panicked nerves at seeing the ambulance pull up.

"West," Ivy cries out from beside the front door.

I walk over to her and quickly pull her, as far as she can go, into my chest. Her belly is growing bigger day-by-day, so she can't be flush against me anymore, but I need to shield her from Genny right now.

"Is she dead?" she whispers. I look down into her worried eyes, shaking my head once.

"She's alive. There's a heartbeat," I murmur.

"But she's hurt," she whispers. I close my eyes with a nod.

"Why? *Why*? Who would hurt Genny?" she practically screams.

I hold her a little tighter and run my hand up and down her back.

"Let's get to the hospital and make phone calls, yeah?"

She nods, and I turn her away from the front door just as the EMT's start to run with the gurney to the ambulance. MadDog calls out that Colleen is going to ride with Genny. He's going to his place, where the rest of the Old Ladies are, to tell them and round them up to meet us at the hospital.

"I knew something was wrong," Ivy whispers as I help her into the passenger side of the car.

"Baby, if you hadn't come down here when you did, no telling when someone would have found her. You probably saved her life," I murmur as I press my lips to her forehead before I close the door.

I curse myself for what I was doing when all this happened. I wasn't doing anything good, and I sure as fuck wasn't thinking about stopping the bad I was doing.

Goddammit, I'm a fucking asshole. My pregnant wife is over here helping our friend, a woman who was lying on the floor in a mass of blood and flesh, and I was fucking around, almost fucking up completely.

Starting the engine, I take Ivy's hand in mine and squeeze it tightly. I love her. My wife. She's real and she's mine, and she's so goddamn beautiful. I need to keep reminding myself how much I love her, and how I would feel if she was taken from me. I almost ruined everything tonight.

"I love you," she whispers, wrapping her other hand around my forearm.

"Love you so much, baby," I murmur.

She'll never know what almost happened. It doesn't matter, because it's never going to *almost* happen again.

chapter nineteen

Soar

The drive down to LA is uneventful, and I'm fucking grateful for it. When I arrive, I send MadDog a text, informing him that I've made it before I shove my phone back into my pocket.

Pulling up to Kirill Baryshev's house is almost surreal. It reminds me of Frisco, of my parents' and their friends' money. His view is worth a million bucks alone, never mind the actual house.

Knocking on the door, I'm surprised when a young teenage girl answers. She appears to be around sixteen or so, and she looks exactly like Kirill, with her long body and dark hair. When she grows into a woman, she's going to be breathtaking.

"I'm here to see your father. Is Kirill around?" I ask.

She eyes me up and down, not a hint of fear or trepidation

in her gaze before she juts out her chin.

"Stay here, I'll get him," she announces before she turns and walks away, leaving the front door open and me on the porch.

I shake my head with a chuckle. She has a lot to learn. Her bravado is admirable, but she definitely has a lot to learn. You never leave a man you don't know on the porch with your door unlocked, let alone open, and walk away—for starters.

My thoughts are interrupted when I see a gorgeous blonde carrying a baby walk by. She freezes in her place as her eyes zero in on my cut and then her gaze turns wary.

"Can I help you?" she asks, no tremble or fear in her voice whatsoever. Goddamn, this man's women are strong. Fucking unwavering.

"Here to see Kirill," I shrug.

"He's expecting you?"

"Yeah. Your daughter went to go get him," I shrug.

I watch as her eyes lift to the ceiling and she lets out a sharp curse.

"Teenagers," she says, shaking her head. "I'm Tatyana," she offers.

"Soar."

"Hmm, you're from up north?" she asks. I nod.

"Soar," Kirill's voice carries before he appears. "Come on inside. Apologies for my daughter, Kiska," he shrugs with a lighthearted grin.

I step through the front door and tell him no problem. Tatyana offers me a drink, but I decline, not wanting to put her out.

"Come out in the back. We'll talk. View is spectacular out there," Kirill offers.

"Nice to meet you, Tatyana," I offer with a grin as I walk by the stacked as fuck woman. Goddamn, Kirill is indeed a lucky man.

"Same to you," she smiles before she walks away.

Kirill and I walk outside to the backyard. He's wrong—the view isn't spectacular, it's out of this fucking world. The city lights glitter below, but it feels as though you're above it all, above everything, peaceful and serine—totally alone. It's the best of both worlds, being close to the city, but with the feel of the mountains and the serenity.

"Apologies if my daughter wasn't polite. She's struggling right now," he offers as he pulls out a cigar and offers me one.

I take it, not because I particularly care for cigars, but because I don't want to be rude.

"Everything all right?" I ask out of politeness as I take a lighter out of my pocket.

"I've chosen a man for her to marry. She isn't happy," he shrugs.

"Chosen?" I ask curiously.

"Or rather, he's chosen her, and I've agreed. In our organization, it's better to arrange marriages, especially between leaders. As her father, as a *Pakhan*, it's important."

"You and Tatyana?" I ask.

"Arranged," he grins. "Now, let's get down to business, yeah?"

I nod, ignoring my phone that seems to be buzzing like crazy in my pocket. Kirill and I walk around the side of the house to my car and I pop the trunk. I show him the merchandise, and he nods before he turns to me with a grin.

"Excellent. Let's unload it into the garage."

I spend the next few minutes unloading the trunk into his

garage, stopping to admire the merchandise every so often. When we're finished, he thanks me with a pat on my back.

"You need anything while you're in town?" he asks.

I know what he's asking. Do I need any women or any dope? I shake my head.

"I'm just going to crash at the hotel before I drive back to town. Need me for anything tomorrow before I head back home?"

"*Nyet*, I'm good. This was what I was waiting on," he grins as he holds out his hand. I take his in mine and give it a firm shake. "You need anything, contact me and I'll get it over to you tonight."

I nod, knowing that for the first time in years, I don't even *want* anything or any*one*. I take my phone out of my pocket before I sit down in my car and start the engine. I back down Kirill's steep driveway, then I thumb my phone and look through the ten missed calls from MadDog.

Fucking hell, he must be really concerned that I wouldn't deliver this shit to Kirill without incident. I drive straight to the hotel before I call him, not wanting to break California's no phone policy. I'm not even going to give the police an ounce of ammunition to pull my ass over.

Once I'm checked into the hotel and settled in my room, I decide to call MadDog back.

"Where the fuck are you?" he barks without even saying hello.

"I just dropped that shit off to Kirill, and I'm settled in my hotel. What's up?"

"You need to get back here," he murmurs.

"I'm leaving in the morning, stopping by my mom's on the way home. What's the problem?" I ask.

I feel a sense of dread fill me, and I know something is terribly wrong. Fucking horribly wrong. MadDog has never beat around the bush, ever. I walk over to the window and look at the city, and the cars headlights and taillights that line the freeways as I wait.

"It's Genny," he rasps.

"What about her?" I snap.

"You just need to get back here, brother."

"Prez, it's an eight-fucking-hour drive. You're going to have to give me something," I demand.

I feel my stomach clench when he murmurs, "She's hurt. She's in the hospital."

"What happened?" I ask as I reach down and grab my bag, thankful I hadn't even opened it.

I run out of the room, heading toward the stairwell as I wait for him to continue. He tells me that he doesn't know much. Colleen found her and she had a pulse when the ambulance took her away.

The whole club is at the hospital, but he doesn't know anything. It pisses me off that I'm so far away, and that I wasn't there to keep her safe.

"I'll be there as soon as I can," I choke out.

"Don't get pulled over," he warns.

"I won't," I confirm as I throw my shit in the back seat before I start my car.

It's after six in the morning, my adrenaline keeping me alert enough to drive throughout the entire night. The hospital appears, and it's as though I can finally take a breath; like I had been holding my breath for the past eight hours as my focus

217

was on the road, on driving, on my destination and nothing else. MadDog sent me a text telling me what floor they were on so that I don't have to waste time asking reception.

"Where is she?" I call out breathlessly as I run into the waiting room where I see all of my brothers and most of their Old Ladies.

"Soar," MadDog calls. I turn to him and see a grim expression set on his face.

I see nothing around me, I'm hyper focused on MadDog and the words he's about to say to me. "Where is she?" I demand as the room melts away.

My heart pounds in my chest, and I'm vaguely aware that I didn't even feel a quarter of this when my father was in the hospital dying, but my Imogen? She means more to me than any other person, aside from Kipling, in my life. She can't leave me, not when I've just got her back—got *us* back.

"We haven't heard anything," he admits.

"It's been eight fucking hours, where is her goddamn doctor?" I shout.

MadDog reaches out for me, but I shrug away from his grasp as I turn to find a hospital staff member. I don't care if it's the goddamn janitor. Somebody is going to give me some information on my fucking wife, right this goddamn minute.

I march over to the nurse's station, where they're sitting around looking like they're doing nothing but sticking their thumbs up each other's asses, and I demand to know the status of my wife.

"If a doctor hasn't come out yet to discuss your wife's status, then there's nothing we can tell you," one nurse says.

She's young and she looks like she's about to shit herself. I'm in a fucking bad mood and I'm worried as shit, so I don't take her feelings into consideration when I speak.

"I haven't been here. I just fucking walked in the god-damn door. Now I don't care who the fuck you have to get down on your knees and blow to get me a status update, but I want it, and I want it right fucking now," I sneer.

"Soar," a soft voice says behind me. I ignore it.

"I—uh—I…" she stutters before she bursts into tears.

"Fucking ruthless," a voice says beside me.

I see Camo, who is giving me a dirty look for acting like an asshole. I ignore him and turn back to the nurse who is crying.

"You aren't moving," I snap.

Her body jolts and she whispers that she'll find a doctor before she runs off.

"I'll be surprised if security isn't in here in a few minutes dragging your ass out of here," Camo says dryly.

"She was brought in here over eight hours ago. I want a goddamn update," I announce.

"Understandable," Camo mutters. "Maybe not the best idea to make the staff cry, though, brother."

I turn away from him, ignoring him completely, and walk back into the waiting area where everybody else is standing. It's then that I notice the room is quiet. For as many peo-ple that are here, it's almost completely silent. I run my hand through my hair and drop my head, looking at the ground.

"Sir?" a little voice calls.

I look over to the nurse who is standing by me, ring-ing her fingers together nervously, her face splotched from crying.

"Yeah, babe?" I ask, my voice softer than it was a few minutes ago.

"The doctor is almost finished with surgery, and he'll be in here as soon as he's able," she says.

I watch as she physically braces herself, but I don't blow up at her. I softly thank her and she blinks once before she turns and runs away from me.

Ivy walks up beside me before she murmurs, "She's going to be okay." I grunt as my answer and continue to stare at the door, waiting. "She's strong."

"Stronger than she should be," I mutter. I can feel her questioning gaze on me. "No need to pretend that I wasn't a fucking piece of shit to her for years, Ivy. You saw it, everyone saw it. I mean I fucking hit on Cleo before I went down," I announce before I clench my jaw tightly.

"Soar," she sighs. "You fucked up, but you've changed."

"Only took me twenty years to fix my shit, and now she's hurt, really fucking hurt," I grind out.

Ivy doesn't say anything else. The doctor interrupts our conversation by walking into the room, a chart in hand and bloody scrubs on his body. I walk straight up to him and notice that he looks fucking tired. I feel the same goddamn way.

"Family of Imogen Huntington?" he calls.

"I'm her husband, Sloane," I state as I place my hands on my hips and wait for the heavy news to be thrown my way.

"She sustained some serious injuries. The reason it took so long for me to get out here was that we had to send her out for testing and wait for results. She has some major contusions to her head and her torso. I wanted to check her brain swelling and check her for internal bleeding. In all, she doesn't have any life-threatening injuries. I want her to stay in the hospital for another forty-eight hours under observation, but I feel pretty confident that she'll make a complete recovery. Your wife was very lucky," he states. I don't miss the way his lip curls, as if I did this to her.

"Can I see her?" I ask.

He nods slowly, and I follow behind him, not bothering to look back at the room full of people who were no doubt listening.

Once the doctor stops outside a room, he turns to face me, all calm and gentleness completely gone from his features. If I was a man who was easily intimidated, I might find him as such.

"You do this to her?" he asks.

"Imogen is my wife. I'd never hurt her," I state, my gaze never wavering. Surprisingly, neither does his.

"I've seen a lot of husbands and wives in here over the years. She didn't fall down the stairs, she didn't fall down anything. This woman was beat, and I want to know, plain and simple, if you did it," he practically growls.

"I'll tell you again. Imogen has been mine since she was fifteen years old. I've done a lot of shit, but physically harming her is something I would never do. Now if you don't step the fuck aside and let me see my wife, *I'm* going to move you," I growl.

The doctor nods and steps to the side, but I can feel his gaze still on me. I could give a single fuck. I open the hospital room door and close it behind me before I look up at Imogen. My breath is stolen from my goddamn body at the sight of her.

She's hooked up to a bunch of machines, wires draped all over her, but my focus is on her gorgeous face. She doesn't even look human. She's so fucking swollen. Every single inch of her face is triple its normal size, and I can't even see her eyes.

She's black, blue, red, purple, and completely unrecognizable.

My feet take me to the side of her bed, and I fall to my knees. I wrap my fingers around hers and press my forehead to the back of her hand. I'm alone, so I don't try to hold them back, to choke them back or to keep them from coming.

I cry.

My wife, she's so fucking hurt, so fucking broken, and it's my fault. It doesn't matter who did it to her, I wasn't there to protect her, to help her, or to keep her safe. I'm never fucking there for her, not ever. I'm the biggest piece of shit that's walked this earth.

The pain in my chest is so excruciating that I find it's hard to simply breathe. Who the fuck could hurt her like this? Then I lift my head, and it dawns on me.

Graham Bayard.

That cocksucking piece of goddamn shit. *It was him.* I know it without a doubt. Wiping my face, I take another look at my beautifully broken wife and decide there's only one thing left to do. I'm going to kill him.

I storm out of her room and into the waiting area to see that MadDog is watching me warily. I walk straight over to him, speaking low so that the entire hospital can't hear me.

"It was Bayard," I mutter.

"We don't know that for sure," he says. I can tell he feels the same way.

"I need someone to stay with her while I handle this shit," I announce.

"Soar, you cannot do anything stupid. You're on probation," he warns.

"Do I look like I give one single fuck?"

Colleen stands before she calls out, "I'll stay with her."

"I'll stay, too," Ivy murmurs.

"We'll all stay. The kids are all together, everything is handled for today," Mary-Anne mutters.

"You don't go alone," MadDog states.

"I could give a *rat's ass* who goes with me. But I'm driving down to Frisco today, now," I announce before I turn and walk away.

I storm down to my car, firing up my engine before I speed off. I don't bother even attempting to go inside of my house. I don't want to see the aftermath of how Imogen ended up the way she did. I have one focus, and one focus only, Graham Bayard bleeding and fucking *dead*.

chapter twenty

Soar

We pull up to Graham's fancy as fuck place in *Parker Heights*, an all brick mansion on a corner. No doubt, costing more than ninety percent of the population could earn in their lifetime. The outside looks simple, albeit large. I have no doubt that the inside is impeccable and ostentatious. No way would it have the homey feel of Imogen's Frisco house.

"What's the plan?" Camo asks as I swing my leg over my bike.

"No plan. I'm killing the fuck," I shrug as I walk toward the front door.

"Soar, you need to get your shit under control," MadDog barks.

"I'm perfectly calm," I lie.

Ringing Graham's doorbell, I wait in full view of his peephole so that he can see me and shit himself. The door opens slowly, and I'm surprised to see that he actually answers and not some staff member of his. He looks me up and down and grins.

"Sloane, how good of you to show. Make sure you wave to my cameras," he grins.

I growl. I should have known and anticipated that he would have his place monitored. I should have known because my father had the same shit at his place.

"You hurt my wife?" I ask bluntly.

"Why would I hurt Imogen? We're to be married," he says. I hear Camo snort behind me.

"Imogen wouldn't marry you if I were dead, man, and you fucking know it," I say.

"I couldn't even see her give this pencil dick the time of day," Camo says. If I turned to look at him, he'd probably be shrugging.

"Tell your minions to shut the fuck up, Sloane," Graham growls.

"You do have a pencil dick," I chuckle. "I remember seeing that shit in the locker room in high school. We all felt sorry for you."

I watch as his face turns red. He's so fucking easy to rile up. "Shut the fuck up," he shouts.

"You're clear, brother," MadDog rumbles.

That's when I know that he's called Oliver, the tech guy who works for the Russian's, to cut and manipulate Graham's cameras.

I lift my chin and force my way inside of his house, my brothers at my back.

"You can't come in here," he cries just as I hear the door close.

"Did you hurt Imogen?" I ask again as I take a knife out of its holster at my belt.

"The fucking tease played me and went back to you," he shouts. "I had her and her family's money in the palm of my hand. I was going to strip her of everything, leave her a pile of worthless nothing, and you fucked it all up, once again," he says as he actually stomps his foot like the child he is. "Her dad was still going to give it to me, then all of a sudden he decided not to. Such bullshit."

I can feel the air in the room crackle as my brothers hear Graham's plans, of stealing Genny's money and leaving her broken and alone, come to light.

Texas, MadDog, Camo, and Torch slowly circle around him, but they don't get too close; just close enough that if he tries to run, like the pussy he is, they'll be able to stop him.

"You're done, Bayard," I announce, pointing my knife in his direction.

"What are you going to do, shank me? Something you picked up in prison?" he laughs. I can tell that he's scared.

I shake my head as I close the distance between us. To his credit, he stands firm, even though his eyes are darting from side to side.

"I did kill a man in prison, how'd you know?" I ask.

I reach out and drag the tip of my knife from the hollow of his throat to his belly button. He sucks in a breath, and I almost laugh at what a pussy he really is.

"Stop bullshitting me, Sloane. What do you want?" he asks, his voice trembling. "How much?"

"Your life," I shrug. "You think you can hit *my* woman,

then beat her half to death, and that I'll just let that go?"

"Like you give a fuck about her. She told me how much you fucked around on her. You don't really give a shit," he states.

I shrug, though inside I fucking *hate* how much he knows about my relationship with Imogen. Wrapping my hand around his shoulder I shove my knife into his belly. The fuck has really let himself get soft over the years. Then I lean forward and whisper into his ear.

"I love Genny. I've loved her since she was fifteen years old. She's mine. She's always *been* mine, and she'll always *be* mine," I murmur. "You touched what was mine, and now you fucking pay," I state as I twist the knife in his soft gut. I yank it up his body until it hits the bone of his ribcage.

"Think he's dead, brother," Torch murmurs.

I take a step back, noticing all the blood mixed with some guts, and shrug. "He didn't suffer enough."

"Nope," MadDog states.

"We can't set this place on fire. How are we going to get rid of him, and all the blood, in broad daylight?" Camo asks.

"Anybody touch anything?" I ask, looking around. They all shake their heads.

"I have contacts in SFPD. You all head out the back. I'll call my guy," I state.

"How the fuck do you have contacts here?" Camo asks.

"You aren't a bad society boy, with rich as fuck parents, without having some cops and judges in your back pocket, brother. My father didn't want his name in the papers because I'd shamed him. I also assume he had about a million skeletons in his own closet to cover up throughout the years. I'll meet you guys back at the clubhouse," I call out as I wipe down the handle of my knife and throw it next to Graham's bloody body.

Everybody moves out of the house except MadDog.

"I'll stay with you until you're cleared for sure," he states. I nod as I take my phone out of my pocket and start placing phone calls.

Imogen

I moan, my body feeling heavy and my face pulsing with pain. I try to move my lips, but they don't go anywhere. All I hear are other people's voices in the room. I can't open my eyes, and I feel my heart starting to race in panic. I lift my hand and press it to my face, but it all feels funny—swollen, puffy, and not right at all.

"Genny—oh, honey, don't do that," Colleen's voice whispers through the room.

I feel her grab my hand and I turn my head toward her, but I still can't open my eyes.

"Wha Ha-en?" I gurgle, unable to form actual words.

"You were hurt pretty badly, honey. You're in the hospital," she coos gently. I can feel her hand on my hair. "We called your parents and they're on their way, so is Soar's mom," she informs me. She doesn't say anything about Sloane.

"Swoan?" I ask, but it hurts my face, my throat—my *everything*.

"He'll be here as soon as he can, babe," she whispers.

"Oh, my god," I hear my mom's voice.

She sounds completely horrified. I have a feeling it looks

just as bad as it feels, and I don't know if I ever want to look in the mirror again.

"Did that piece of shit do this to you?" my father asks.

I try to relax and think about the night. I hear Colleen in the background talking to my parents, and I'm grateful for that as I try to retrace the evening. I remember talking to Ivy about going to Mary-Anne's. I took brownies out of the oven and someone rang the bell. I thought it was Ivy. It was Graham. Then it all comes flooding back to me. Graham kicking and punching me until everything went black.

"I'll kill Sloane," my father roars. I choke out a laugh.

"Gwam," I mumble.

"What?" my father asks.

I can feel him come closer. I can smell his expensive cologne, and I wish it were comforting, but it isn't.

"No, Swoan. Gwam," I mumble again.

"Are you trying to tell me that Graham did this to you?" I nod but my father scoffs. "Graham is refined, Imogen. He would never do this."

"Sloane is a complete barbarian. Graham adores you," my mother chimes in.

I hear Sloane's harsh bark of laughter fill the room. I can do nothing but listen to my parents and Sloane talk.

"Graham already marked her once. I have never touched Imogen in anger before, not once," he growls. "Besides, I was in Los Angeles visiting a friend."

"What was her name?" my mother huffs.

"Not a woman. Not that it's your fucking business. You two can fucking leave," Sloane says.

I imagine he's waving his hand around in annoyance. He's always had a short temper where my parents are concerned.

Not that I can blame him; they drive me insane as well.

"I will not leave my daughter, not in this sub-par hospital," my father snorts.

"Then you can sit on the couch with your goddamn mouths closed," Sloane barks.

I hear my father sputter, but I'm getting tired and fading quickly.

"Go back to sleep, sunshine," Sloane's voice mutters.

I feel his lips on the back of my hand as he presses a kiss there, and then I do as he requests. Again, his blanket of safety wraps around me and I feel at peace. I go back to sleep

"Will there be any permanent damage? I can call my plastic surgeon," I hear my mother's voice say.

"I think we'll know more once the swelling goes down, ma'am," a stranger's voice mutters. Then I feel him come closer.

"Can you try and open your eyes for me today, Mrs. Huntington?" he asks. I feel his warm touch on my ribs, my stomach, and then my face.

I try to open my eyes, relaxing my face as much as I can, and am surprised when I see light and then a shadow.

"There you go, let's see those pretty brown eyes of yours," he murmurs. "Can you make anything out, or are you just seeing shadows at this point?"

"Shaowes," I rasp, unable to pronounce certain letters still.

"Good, good. Hopefully as your swelling decreases you'll get your sharper vision back. Now, you've been monitored for twenty-four hours and everything is looking really good.

I want to keep you here another twenty-four hours, maybe forty-eight, depending on how quickly your swelling reduces. Other than the pain in your face, how are you feeling?"

"O-aay," I state.

"You're on some pretty powerful pain meds and you've got a catheter in. But I'm going to have the nurse take that out and get you up and moving today. The more you move around, the sooner you'll be able to get out of here," he says soothingly. I nod. "Now, do I need to call the police so you can make a report? Your husband was here and he says that this wasn't him. I have to ask these things," he murmurs.

"Wa-n't him," I say with a shake of my head.

"Okay," he says, sounding disappointed. Then I hear his footsteps and the door closes behind him.

The room is bathed in silence for a few minutes, and I let out a heavy sigh, knowing my mother has something to say.

"I know Sloane wouldn't hurt you," she finally whispers. I don't speak, waiting for her to continue. "I know he's liked his women, maybe done some drugs, and, with his little group, some questionable things. He's not like his father, not like that. And even Sloane's father never left Kalli as battered as you are."

I make a noise in the back of my throat, wishing she would stop. She doesn't.

"It's no secret that I've never liked the boy. Not because of him, but because of the way you allowed him to treat you. You're better than that; you're better than a Huntington. You were always so starry eyed over him, and he was a handsome boy. He still is a very handsome man, so I understand. I just didn't want you to fall in love with looks and settle," she takes a deep breath. "I didn't want you to settle like me. Settle for a pretty man who wouldn't treat you well, because women love a pretty man with money."

Tears fill my eyes and fall down my face at what my mother is implying about her relationship with my father. My mother and I don't get along, we never have, but she's also never really been involved in my life. She's always been more concerned with herself, or maybe she was just lost inside of her own head, dealing with infidelity exactly like I always have.

"But you ended up exactly like me, didn't you?" she asks. I can't help but agree with her. "I'm sorry I didn't teach you what kind of man you should have looked for."

I start to open my mouth, but then I hear the door open.

"I'm just going to head out now," my mother says.

I turn my head, opening my eyes as widely as I can, and I see a shadow standing in the doorway. It's a shadow I recognize. It's a shadow that I would know no matter where I was.

It's Sloane.

"Fucking hell, sunshine," he rasps. I hear him dragging a chair across the room to the side of the bed. He gathers my hand in his and he lets out a breath. "Sorry I wasn't here. I had to get some shit handled. Not leaving you now, though."

"Go home tomorrow," I say slowly, trying to enunciate every word.

"Yeah? Can't wait. How are you feeling?" he asks.

I shrug.

"You never have to worry about Graham again, sunshine," he whispers.

I wait for him to continue, and I'm surprised when he does. "I took care of him. He'll never hurt you again, baby," he whispers. "I want you out of here. I want you better and home with me."

"Home," I say, my lips trembling.

"Yeah, sunshine. I want to help you get better."

I shake my head, thinking of my mother's words, wondering if staying with him is where I should be. Maybe I should just leave California, leave the country, go far away and start over. Find a man who isn't sexy and attractive; find a man who loves and adores me and sees no other woman in the world but me.

Then I think about the way Sloane told me he loves me. I think about all the stuff we've been through the past few weeks, and I know that I would endure everything all over again to have him. I love him, and time or distance couldn't make that love dissipate, let alone disappear.

It's him for me, and nobody else can compare. I'm willing to let him keep my heart, in the hopes that he won't break it into a million pieces again. Foolishly, I'm pretty confident right now that he won't.

I *love* this man.

This *beautiful* man.

This *rich* man.

This *rough* man.

chapter twenty-one

Soar

I watch her sleep. Her face isn't as bad today as it was yesterday. The swelling has receded a bit, but she's still got a long road to recovery ahead of her. I close my eyes tightly and curse to myself. This was all me. Me and nobody else. If I had better protection over her when I left for LA, then Graham wouldn't have been able to get to her.

Fuck, if I hadn't let her into this life, then she'd probably be married to some straight-laced fucker right now, in a mansion with three kids. Graham wouldn't have ever been on her radar, and I wouldn't have pissed him off enough to take his anger out on her. None of this would have happened and she'd probably have a much better life.

No matter how you look at it, this is all my fault.

"This isn't your fault," a familiar voice says from the

doorway. I turn around to see my mother standing there.

She's wearing designer, as per usual, her bleached hair styled to perfection and her makeup impeccable. She looks like the society bitch she is, but I've always just called her *mom*.

"You finally get sober enough to drive over here?" I ask, feeling the heat of my resentment at the woman rise.

"I knew her parents would be here, and I knew they didn't want to see me, so I waited," she shrugs as she takes a few more steps into the room. "Goddammit, that man is a fucking monster," she gasps, abandoning her perfect language for curse words, which I prefer.

"Something like that," I state, not wishing to look over at Genny again. Staring at her will not make her better. It will not make the damage disappear.

"I hope you took care of him," my mother states as she walks over to the sofa and slowly sits down.

"I did," I say, but lift my brow in surprise that she'd even direct me to do so. My mother hates the club, hates my life, and hasn't hidden that fact—*ever*.

"If you're going to be in a group like that, I'm glad that it's good for something," she huffs.

"Yeah, well, he's no longer an issue."

"I'm all moved in to my new place, your brother is gone, and now this. Everything's just falling to pieces, Sloaney," my mom whispers, using a little nickname she had for me when I was a kid.

"You upset about dad being gone?" I ask curiously.

"Hell, no. That man was wretched. I did contact the mothers of his children. There are three," she says quietly. "I'm meeting with them next week. I know their children are now financially taken care of, but I guess I just wanted to know the women he preferred over me, and maybe get some closure."

"That could do more harm than good, mom," I warn.

"I know," she nods. "Kipling has been a mess. Thank you for getting him gone sooner rather than later. He's taking it all very hard."

"I offered to pay for his schooling after this first semester," I state. She shakes her head.

"There's no reason to. I have plenty of money," she says with a wave of her hand.

"As long as the business does well."

"No, Sloaney, *I* have plenty of money. My family had money, too, you know. Not as much as your father was worth, but I have more than most of the people in this world, and I'm going to put my boy through Harvard. I also plan on spoiling your children, if you'll ever have any," she says.

"Okay, mom," I say, shaking my head. "But I'm taking care of his second semester. You want to pony up for the rest that's cool, but I have some funds that I want to use on it."

She nods and doesn't argue, which I'm grateful for. "I love Imogen. I always have. I wasn't always nice to her because she reminded me so much of myself. I wanted more for her than I had," she murmurs. "I saw the way you were, it reminded me so much of your father. You aren't him, are you, son?"

I think about her question. Three years ago, I was more like the man I despised than I care to admit, especially when it came to women and the way I treated my wife. Though I never physically hurt Imogen, emotionally? I completely broke her, shattered her into pieces. I didn't give a single fuck when I did it, either.

I was chasing a high, always chasing that fucking high.

I never looked back at the damage, or pain, I was inflicting on this woman who only wanted my love. This woman, who wanted to love and wanted to be loved. I fucked her over time and time again.

"No, mom, I'm not him. Not anymore," I whisper.

"Good. Be better than your father. My only hope in this life is that you and Kipling show the world that the Huntington name still stands for something good," she says as she stands up and smooths down her pants.

"I'm not sure I'm the man for that task, mom."

I watch in silence as my mom walks directly over to me, cupping my cheeks in her hands as she looks down into my eyes, watching me for a breath before she speaks.

"You're a better man than your father. You left and have never asked for a single thing from us, from him. That pissed him off to no end. He wanted you to fail and come crawling back to him, but I knew. I knew that my Sloaney was smart and he would take care of himself without incident. Love Imogen the way she deserves. You only get one life. Please, Sloane, be the best man you can be for her, but most importantly, for you."

I stare at my mom in shock as she drops her hands and bends over to place her lips on my forehead. Then she takes a step back and turns to walk toward the door. I watch her, still totally speechless.

"I'll see you both at the summer party," she says as she opens the door and walks out, leaving Genny and me alone again.

"You know she's right," Genny mutters from next to me. I look up in surprise to see she's awake. "You're better than him."

I close my eyes and let out a long heavy sigh.

"Get some sleep, sunshine."

Imogen

Home.

I never thought I would want to step foot inside of this place again. Let alone call it home. But it is. This is my home, and today I'm back. I'm thankful for the other Old Ladies who cleaned up the evidence of my attack.

It doesn't look as though it's even been touched, let alone that a woman had been beaten here. I talked to a grief counselor before I left the hospital and she warned me about all types of things like flashbacks and such. I should be worried about that, but I'm just far too happy to be back.

"Do you need to get into bed and rest?" Sloane asks.

Sloane is another reason I'm not more of a mess. He's been absolutely wonderful. I feel safe and completely at peace with him at home with me. It's not a completely new experience, as I've been feeling this way lately, but it's different to have him take care of me.

I like it.

I like it a lot.

Though my face hurts like hell, and the doctors still don't know for sure if I'll have permanent damage, I would consider doing it all over again just to have him care after me like this.

"Maybe just a bath," I shrug.

"Yeah, sunshine, I can handle that," he smiles.

He wraps his warm hand around mine and gently tugs me toward the bathroom. My ribs hurt like hell, so I can't walk very fast. I'm excited to soak them in warm water to ease the aches and pains.

"I have some Epsom salt stuff under the sink," I mumble.

I watch as he digs around and pulls out my Epsom salt soak and bubble bath. Then, with avid fascination, as he starts my bath and adds in the salts and bubbles, I watch him. Without a word, he turns to me as the tub fills and gently starts to remove my clothes. I've still yet to look in the mirror, and I am avoiding it. I don't know if I'll ever want to look at myself again.

"Your poor fucking body, Imogen," Sloane hisses as he strips me bare.

Thankfully, my eyes aren't as swollen as they were just a day ago, and I can actually see again.

Unfortunately, I can see the complete pain etched on his face as he looks me over.

"I'll be okay," I say, trying to reassure him and myself.

Sloane's fingers trail from the hollow of my throat, down the center of my chest to my belly, and then back up before he wraps them, gently, around the back of my neck. He drops his head but doesn't touch my forehead with his own. I can feel his breath fanning my face, and I watch as he swallows heavily.

"Imogen," he rasps. "I know you'll be okay, sunshine. You shouldn't *have* to be okay, but I know that you will be. You're so strong, and you're going to be just fine. It kills me that you've been hurt, baby. Absolutely fucking kills me."

I place my hands on his waist and wait for him to open his eyes. Looking at the pain that's deeply etched into his gaze, I give him a shaky smile.

"I will be okay, Sloane. *We* will be okay. He hurt me but he didn't break me," I whisper.

"No, he fucking didn't. I sure broke him, though," he growls.

"Did you?" I ask with a small smile.

"Fucking shattered into a million goddamn pieces," he chuckles as he leans forward and softly presses his lips to mine. "Now, let me help you in this bath and I'll get us something to eat while you soak."

"Yeah?" I ask as he lets me use his arms for stability to get inside of the warm water.

"Probably just ordering pizza, sunshine, don't get too excited."

"I can't remember the last time I had pizza," I sigh as the warm water envelopes me.

Sloane doesn't say anything, and I'm too busy soaking in the heavenly tub to wonder why. After days in the hospital, using their shitty shower, and then being in so much pain, I honestly didn't care if I was clean or not.

This tub right here feels like heaven. I'm going to have to wash my hair in the morning, but right now, I don't care how dirty it is. I'm home, Sloane's here, and we're both breathing. That is all I care about.

"You didn't," I whisper in feigned horror.

"That pussy had it coming," Sloane says as he takes another bite of pizza.

We're sitting in bed, eating pizza straight from the box, and talking. It's like a dream come true. Sloane reaches over to me and threads his fingers with mine before he tosses his slice into the box. I finished a long time ago, but I've been having fun talking with him. I'd forgotten how funny Sloane was, and how much I enjoyed just conversing with him.

He throws the box onto the floor and rests back against the headboard. Tugging me gently, so that I'm lying against him. The back of my head is on his chest and my arm is curled around him.

"I still remember exactly what you were wearing the first time I saw you," he whispers. "You had on this tiny little skirt with buttons down the front, with a little sweater that your stomach peaked out of just a little. Fuck me, it was sexy as shit. And knee socks. You were like every wet dream I'd ever had. Your hair was long and straight, and I didn't think I'd ever seen a prettier girl in my entire life."

"Sloane," I whisper as tears well in my eyes.

"I was such a fucking punk back then. Hell, I was a punk for twenty years. I wanted you, but I wanted everything else on two legs, too. *You*, the thought of another boy even looking at you sent me into a rage. My head was so fucked up, and I'd get blitzed, fuck around, feel guilty until the next time I got high. It was a vicious cycle. Only when I sobered up completely did I truly realize the damage I'd done to you, to us."

"I was really young. I chose to see what I wanted to see, and I chose to stay when I could have very well left. We're both to blame for the way things happened, Sloane," I whisper, looking up at the ceiling.

"Don't do that," he warns. "Don't take the blame off of me when it's all me, sunshine. You did nothing but love me. When I fucked you over, you reacted. None of that is on you. All of that is on me."

"I hate that you were with other people. I hate it more than anything else. I hate it more than the fact that we didn't have children. I just fucking hate it," I cry. He holds me a little closer.

"I wasn't with anyone else when we were dating. I said that because I was being a dick. I'm sorry, Imogen. I wish I could go back in time. Fuck me, do I wish that I could. You're going to have babies, Genny. I'm giving them to you, as many as your heart desires," he whispers, pressing his lips against my hair.

I fall asleep in his arms. My mind on babies and the past, on the missed memories, on *what-could-have-beens*, and *what-should-have-beens*.

I flutter my eye lids open, unsure of the time, and there he is. *Graham*. Staring right at my face. He sneers at me, and I let out a scream. I try to back away, but he reaches for me. Right before his hand connects with my skin, the bedside table light goes on, and he's gone.

"Genny?" Sloane's husky voice calls out in confusion. I roll over to face him, trying to calm my breaths, trying to gain control over myself.

"He was here," I whisper.

"Who, sunshine?" he asks in confusion, his hair mussed up from sleep.

"Graham," I rasp.

Sloane's tightness in his body relaxes and he shakes his head before he slides back down into the sheets and rolls to my side, wrapping his hand around my hip.

"He couldn't be here, baby. I killed him," he admits

truthfully. Sloane didn't just get *rid* of him—he *got rid of him.*

"You *killed* him?" I breathe.

"What did you think I meant when I said I got rid of him? And that he'd never touch you again?" he asks as a smile tugs the corner of his lips.

"I don't know. Not that."

"Well, he's gone. He can't hurt you anymore. It was a flashback, and you knew it was a possibility," he murmurs. "Do you think you can get some sleep? Or do you need my help on that?"

"Help?" I ask curiously.

He shrugs, "I could eat your pussy until you're exhausted and you pass out." It sends chills over my entire body, and my belly heats at the thought as I press my thighs together.

"Mmmm," he hums.

Before I can even say another word, my nightie is shoved up, and my panties are pulled down.

I let out a long moan as Sloane's tongue slides over my entire center and then circles my clit.

"Don't move too much, baby. I don't want to hurt your ribs," he murmurs against my core.

Sloane eats me. He's gentle but purposeful, and it doesn't take me long before I'm writhing beneath him and crying out his name as I tug on the strands of his blond hair.

When he slips two fingers inside of me and begins to pump in and out of my core, I know that I'm done for. I can't hold on a second longer, and I completely disintegrate beneath him as I come.

His lips touch the inside of my thigh, but he crawls up the side of my body instead of my middle, and starts to gently run the pads of his fingertips up and down my skin, touching my breasts and around my nipples while I try and catch my breath.

"Sloane," I whisper.

"Can you sleep now, sunshine?"

"What about you?" I ask, knowing he must be hard and ready to go.

"I'll survive the night, baby," he murmurs. "That was for you and you alone."

I sigh as he presses his lips to the side of my head and curls his body around mine. It doesn't take long for me to fall asleep. Less than five minutes.

I wonder if Sloane will put me to sleep like this every night from now on.

chapter twenty-two

Soar

"Kirill said everything was good," MadDog states from his position at the front of the long table.

Church. Not the place I want to be right now. I'd much rather be buried inside of my wife's sweet cunt. However, it's mandatory, and I'm here. Seeing as I missed so many of them when I was locked up, I need as much catch up as I can get, anyway. It's just too bad Genny is refusing to leave the house so she won't be waiting for me when it's over.

"Good," I lift my chin.

"There are some issues they're havin' in New York—their business, not ours. However, he wants some trusted brothers on standby if they're needed. Figured I can count on my guys here and some of Fury's men in Idaho for sure to fly on over," he states. Every man in the room nods.

The Russian's have had our back on more than one occasion, so it's a fair trade. The deal has been working smoothly for a few years now. Kirill seems solid enough, so if he needs help, I'll fully volunteer my services.

"Soar can't leave state lines, so we can't have him on the rotation for at least two years traveling to Denver. But he's our man to load at the docks. We're using the Humboldt docks permanently now. I want Soar, Torch, Mammoth and Camo handling the dock work between the four of them for a while. All their Old Ladies are knocked up, and Soar's stuck here," he announces. "The rest of the men I'll be making a new schedule for today, and I'll post it on my office window."

"Any other business?" he asks, looking around.

"Any news on the Aryans?" Texas asks.

"Nothin' new to report, really. Seems like we've hit a dead end. We're lucky to have found the women and children that we did. Unless problems arise, I say we let those fuckers stay hidden in their bunkers. I have a feeling that without Drifter feeding them information anymore, their well will dry up completely."

I sit up before I speak, "What about those highway patrol cops that were up in my shit?"

MadDog shakes his head. "We got nothin' on that, brother. Hopefully with Graham being put down that'll be the end of it." He lifts his chin before he turns to the rest of the group. "With nothin' else, what do you all think about allowing the prospect, Joel, to patch-in? Ready to vote?" MadDog questions.

We all grunt, and then we each state our verdict. I don't know the guy well, but I'm not allowed to be a neutral party.

I am just like every man in this room, a complete patched member.

Nobody votes no, so it's easy for me to cast a positive vote as well. MadDog throws down his gavel and adjourns the meeting, but before we leave the room, he sends Grease out to get the punk ass little fuck.

Once Joel is brought in, MadDog tells him his fate, and I swear I see the kid tear up before he gives us the brightest, widest smile I've ever seen.

"You're blinding me with those pearly whites," I jokingly shout.

"*Blinder*. That's fuckin' it," MadDog yells.

"My dad's a dentist. I get free zoom whitening," he shrugs with a chuckle.

"Well, Blinder, better keep at it. You have a road name now to uphold," I say as I walk past him and clap him on the shoulder.

"Patch-in party tomorrow night," MadDog yells as the other men congratulate Blinder and follow behind me out of the room.

I walk up to the bar and lean my forearms against it as I signal to the prospect tending that I need a drink. He hands me a beer, and I lift my chin in thanks. I'm only one pull in when I feel a set of tits press against my forearm. I look down at my arm and then into the eyes of the girl I fucked when I first got out of prison. The little bitch that made Imogen cry in the grocery store.

"Destini," she says sweetly.

"Help you?" I ask.

"Wondered if you were ready for another round? I know your woman's been out of commission, so I thought I'd offer up my services," she says, pouting her lips to give me a bit of a show.

I don't have to even think to know my answer. Nothing about her, not even her puffy lips, are worth hurting my wife again. I've done that shit enough.

Making her promises to stay sober, stay faithful, and be the man she needs me to be is my main focus. I've had enough strange to last me a lifetime. In the end, it didn't make me feel half as good as seeing my wife smile up at me, love and trust shining in her eyes.

"Got an Old Lady, out of commission or not, doesn't matter," I shrug.

For the first time ever, I truly feel that way deep in my bones. I've never felt it before. I've *said* it, and maybe I've meant it, but *felt* it? Fuck no, not like I do right now.

"I'm not like the others. I can keep quiet, Soar. I know you like to play a little. I still remember how you felt inside of me. Nobody would have to know," she whispers.

I laugh. It's a full-on belly laugh, and I should feel super shitty for it because this girl is young. She's young and fuckin' dumb. I've already told her no before, and she's offering herself up for another form of rejection. *Christ*, how stupid can you be.

"I highly doubt you remember what my dick felt like, babe. You've had so much cock in your snatch since then, I don't see how you could," I laugh, shaking my head. "I know without a doubt I could fuck you and my wife wouldn't find out. That's not the point. The point is, I don't *want* to fuck you. You're young and you have a hot little body, but soon enough, you'll be gone and nobody here will care. Not me, not anyone. You keep hounding me after I've told you no repeatedly, you'll be out on your ass soon."

I turn away, abandoning my beer and walk toward the door. I don't need to fuck whores, I don't need to party it up, not without Imogen. And maybe in a few months both of us will feel okay with me being down here without her; but right now, to me, it doesn't feel right. I need some more time, some more time with her, some more time with my sobriety, and some more time being free.

"You okay, brother?" Torch asks as soon as I step outside.

"Turned down an offer from Destini," I state, shoving my hands in my pocket.

"Hard to do?" he asks.

Shaking my head, I know it wasn't hard. In fact, it was easy—too fucking easy. And that shit makes me feel shitter than anything else. Turning her down was so goddamn easy that I should have been doing it this whole fucking time.

Torch interrupts me mid-thought, "Lot's goin' on in that head of yours, I'm sure. It's different, being free and being sober all at the same time, plus dealing with feelings and the consequences of your actions when you were fucked in the head. It's a fuck've a lot to deal with. Add to that what Imogen just went through," he says, not looking at me, but instead up at the stars that fill the sky.

"No fucking shit," I say, letting out a puff of air from my lungs.

"You're handling everything really well. Really fuckin' well. Got to be honest, we're all kind of watching and waiting for your breakdown," he states. I shake my head once.

"Me too," I admit.

"Really fuckin' proud of you, Soar. I didn't know you well before you went in, but I gotta say you're a standup brother, a good man, and I'm proud we're on the same team."

"Thanks. I just, *fuck*," I say, lifting my hand to rub at the back of my neck. "I'm too old for this shit. Do you know how much I missed by being a fucking douchebag for so long?" I ask angrily.

"Yeah, brother. I do," Torch states. I cut my eyes over to him.

He knows because he stayed away from his wife, suffering from PTSD for years, abandoning her, thinking it was better for her that he stayed gone. Maybe at the time it was. Maybe I should have done the same thing. A more selfless man, like him, probably would.

I'm selfish, though—born and fucking raised to be a selfish fucking prick. I kept Imogen just at arm's length, continuing to hurt her repeatedly over the years. Hurting her so fucking badly and being too goddamn high and too fucking stubborn to change—for her, for me, or for us.

"Imogen is thirty-five. She wants a baby, and I never wanted them. She wants a whole fucking house full, but I never gave that to her. How do I make up for that?" I ask, turning my head to look at him.

"Cleo's thirty-five and she's about to have a baby," Torch states. "Genny wants a kid, you give that to her. Now. Not later, but now. Make the second part of her life worth the pain you put her through for the first half," he says.

"I swore I would," I admit.

"Then come through."

I think about his words. Then I admit the truth, something I hate to say aloud. I say it anyway. "I'm scared I'll relapse. I'm scared I'll get blitzed and fuck whores, and she'll be at home with my kid and I'll go right back to that routine.

goddamn father."

"Don't let that happen," he shrugs as he takes a step away from me and turns to go inside. As though it's that fucking simple.

"How?"

"Be fucking better, Soar. Be better for her, be better for your kid; but most importantly, be better for *you*."

Torch walks back inside, and I let out an exhale before I start to walk toward my bike. Be better for Imogen, for our kids, and for me. I don't know if I can hack this shit, if I can really *be* better. I want to try.

Just as I straddle my bike, my phone rings from my pocket and I pull it out to answer it. Kip's name flashes on the screen, and I grin. *Be better for Kippy, too,* I think right before I click accept.

Imogen

Turning off the television, I decide to turn on my eReader to see if there's a book I haven't read yet. I need something to keep me company, and to keep my mind off of exactly where Sloane is tonight. He's down at the club for Church. He asked me to go with him, a first, really, and I probably should have just taken him up on his offer; but I'm not ready for anyone down there to see me, yet—especially not the whores.

The swelling in my face has gone down quite a bit, but it's not gone. It's also a million different shades of blue and purple mixed with brown and yellow. In other words, it's a hot fucking mess.

No way in hell am I going to let those skinny bitch whores see me like this. Especially that one that came up to me in the grocery store. Next time I see that little bitch, I'm going to look like a ten, not a puffy disaster.

"Sunshine," a voice calls out. My spine straightens in surprise. Glancing down at my clock, I notice it's not even midnight yet. "Hey, you're up."

"I am," I say with a shaky smile.

"You all right, baby?" Sloane asks as he shrugs his cut off before he places it on the bench at the foot of our bed.

"I didn't expect you home so soon," I state. Honestly, I didn't expect him home at all.

He grins, shaking his head. "Didn't feel much like partying. I was missing my woman."

"Oh, yeah?" I ask, cocking my head to the side in wonder.

Sloane *Soar* McKinley Huntington III never misses a party, not unless there's a damn good reason.

"Not the same anymore. I'm sober and," he pauses as he takes his shirt off before shoving his jeans down his legs.

I watch as he toes out of his boots and then he's on the bed, removing his socks before he pulls his jeans the rest of the way off. He crawls up next to me. "I missed my Old Lady. I missed you. All I could think was that you were here cooped up alone."

"Is that all?" I ask.

"Honesty?"

I nod and wait for his answer, bracing myself for whatever it is that he's going to throw my way.

"I'm so scared of completely fucking up, sunshine. One hit, one drop of X, one line, and I'm back in the joint," he murmurs before he turns to me and pulls me into his arms. "One whore, and I'll hurt you, probably lose you forever. I'd die without you, baby, and I'm so scared of ruining everything we've got going for us right now."

Closing my eyes, I think about his words, about his fears. He's right. One night with a whore, and I'm gone, for good this time. There will be no sweet words to bring me back. No matter how much I love him, I just can't let myself be that pathetic person anymore, letting him make me feel completely *worthless*.

"Sloane," I whimper.

He rolls on top of me, his lips brushing mine so gently that it sends chills over my body. Then he just stares into my eyes, his hips between my thighs, his elbows holding his body up on either side of my head. His green eyes bore into mine with an intensity that I've never felt before.

"I love you, Imogen. The last thing I want to do is hurt you again. I think I've hurt you enough to last for ten lifetimes. You get honesty from me, and that's me being honest. I'm scared, sunshine."

I nod at his words. I'm scared, too—terrified.

"I'm scared, but we're going to work, baby. You and me," he murmurs before pressing his lips to mine again.

His tongue slides out to taste my lips, and I moan as he slips further into my mouth. I can feel the firm length of his erection pressing against my center, and I throw back my head on a cry.

We haven't had sex since my accident, but he's brought me pleasure on more than one occasion. It's just not enough. I want to feel him inside of me, taking, owning, *pleasuring* me like only his cock can do.

"I want you to ride me, Imogen," he rasps against my neck as he kisses his way down to my collar bone. His tongue tastes my skin and I let out a long groan.

"My face," I whisper.

"Is fucking gorgeous. I can't be on top, sunshine. I'll hurt your ribs," he mutters against my skin.

I nod, completely unbelieving of his kind words about my face. He rolls onto his back and I watch as he yanks off his boxer briefs. I quickly remove my sleep shorts and tank set, trying not to think about the bruises on my face or on my stomach and sides as I straddle his hips.

Sloane's hands slide from my knees to the outside of my thighs, the sides of my waist and up to cup my breasts. I let out a shuttered breath as he pinches my nipples and tweaks them slightly.

"You still on your birth control?" he asks. My entire body freezes.

"My what?" I whisper in surprise.

"Your birth control, whatever the fuck you take, you still on it?" he murmurs, his eyes zeroed in on his fingers playing with my nipples.

"I, uh," I sigh as I close my eyes, relishing how good it feels when he touches me. "It's a pill. I take it every morning."

"Throw that shit in the trash, Imogen."

"Sloane," I whisper.

"Sink down on my hard cock, sunshine. No more birth control. No more waiting. We're making a baby. We're living this life to the fullest. That shit starts now," he announces.

"What about your fears? Everything you just said?" I ask in confusion.

He grins and tugs on both of my nipples before he slides

his hands down to my waist, giving me a gentle squeeze.

"I'm scared. But, baby, I'm going to be scared about slipping tomorrow and every day after for the rest of my life. Especially since the damage I would inflict wouldn't only be on me but on you, too. There's no guarantees, but if we sit around scared to death, we'll never live. You won't have your babies, and I won't have a wife that smiles so bright she blinds me like the goddamn sun. So, no more pills, sunshine."

"I want you to be sure. This isn't something you can take back or change your mind on," I warn.

"Almost forty years old, baby. I think it's about time I stop thinking about myself all the time and start working on making your dreams come true, don't you?" he asks. He tucks a bit of fallen hair behind my ear, careful not to hurt my face.

"Sloane," I whisper as tears fill my eyes. "I want you to be happy, too, and you don't want them."

"Promised you babies, sunshine. I'm delivering that promise to you. Told you that I didn't want them because of fear, not because I couldn't love them. You're going to be a beautiful mama, and I'm going to be their roughneck daddy. Now climb up on this dick, Imogen," he growls.

I do as he asks and sink down on his hard length, sighing when I'm fully seated down around him. I look into his eyes, and he only smirks at me before he gently bucks up, causing me to gasp slightly.

"Ride me nice and slow, baby," he murmurs.

Leaning back, my fingers gripping his thighs, I do as he demands. I ride my man slow, with purpose, and with complete delight. Every roll of my hips sends shivers up my spine. When his thumb presses against my clit, I let out a moan of appreciation.

"You're going to make me come too fast," I whimper.

"You don't get there, sunshine, and it'll be over," he murmurs. "The sight of you enjoying yourself the way you are, your tits swaying with each move you make; goddamn, I'm on edge, baby."

I smirk as I continue to move in a way that is apparently keeping him on edge. Except, with the added pressure of his thumb against my clit, I find myself in the same predicament. I shudder and cry out as I come all around him.

My pussy pulses, and he thrusts up inside of me a few times before he lets out a groan of his own. With heavy breaths, I look down at Sloane. His blond hair is messy, but his eyes are bright and his smile is wide.

"Love you, Imogen," he murmurs. "Most beautiful woman I've ever laid eyes on."

"I'm a disaster," I whisper as he gently rolls us over so that we're on our sides facing each other. I lose his length from inside of me, and I miss him already.

"No matter what, Genny, you've always been stunning. Swear to fuck, sunshine, no matter what," he rasps before his lips press against mine.

"Get some sleep, baby."

I close my eyes and do as he asks.

Sleep finds me almost immediately.

chapter twenty-three

Imogen

A loud noise causes me to jump. I sit straight up, my hair a ratty mess, and my body bare. The loud noise happens again, and I realize that it's someone at the door. I glance to Sloane's side of the bed, but he's gone. The pounding noise sounds again, and I hurry to grab Sloane's discarded shirt from the night before and a pair of panties.

Looking through the peephole I gasp at who is on the other side. Pulling my brows together, I answer the door just as the man lifts his hand to bang on my door again. "Can I help you?" I ask immediately.

"Hey there, Mrs. Huntington," he says smoothly.

It only takes me a second to realize it's the highway patrol officer who pulled me over. I don't respond as I stand at the door and just look at him.

"Sloane's probation officer is on his way. I suspect he's got some drugs in this place, maybe some guns too," he murmurs as he places his hand on my stomach and pushes me to the side.

He walks into my living room and looks around. "Alone tonight?" He smirks.

"What do you want? There's nothing in here, and I didn't invite you in," I state.

He grins, "Sweetheart, you don't have to invite me anywhere. Your husband is an ex-con on parole, this is his residence, and I can walk in here any fucking time I want to."

His cocky grin is too much, too wide, and way too sure of himself. I wrap my hands around my stomach as I press my lips together. Another man walks inside and he looks from me to the cop.

"Tell me you did not drag my fucking ass out of bed for a home visit about a model prisoner and model parolee?" he grumbles.

"Excuse me, what's happening here?" I ask quietly from my place against the wall as I try to tug down Sloane's shirt.

"Sorry ma'am, I got a report from this officer that he has suspicions that your husband had a weapon and illegal drugs on the premises," the probation officer murmurs.

My eyes dart from man-to-man and I nod. He explains that he has the right to check the place. I glance at the clock and notice that it's three in the morning.

I don't know where Sloane is. I watch as the two men go about searching my house. Then they request access to my bedroom. I give them a nod, even though I don't want them anywhere near my room.

A few minutes later, they emerge, and the probation

officer shakes his head. "Sorry for disturbing your sleep, ma'am. Nothing was found." He then turns to the police officer. "The next time you wake my ass up at two in the fucking morning, your shit better be solid." He turns and walks out of the door, leaving me alone with the officer.

"He's a lucky fuck," he murmurs as he walks closer toward me. My back is pressed against the wall. He gets so close that I can feel the heat of his body, and I shiver in disgust. "Next time I bring him back, he'll find something. This was just a dry run."

"What do you want?" I whisper.

He grins as his top teeth sink into his bottom lip, "Sweetheart, I want what was promised to me. Bayard has all but disappeared, and I've yet to have those sweet lips wrapped around my cock."

I open my mouth to say something, but no words come out. He leans forward a little more and wraps his hand around the outside of my thigh. "Your lips are going to be wrapped around my cock. Your pussy is going to strangle me, and then I'm going to fuck your ass, Imogen. Sweet little society slut like you, I bet it's going to be fucking fantastic."

I press my lips together to keep from throwing up in his face. His hand moves to the inside of my thigh, and I press my legs together as my heart starts to race. "As soon as Sloane's ass is locked back up, I'm taking what Bayard promised me," he whispers.

"Do you mind taking your hands off of my wife, *officer*?" Sloane's voice roars through the room. The officer, *Houston*—according to his name badge—smirks, not looking away.

"Yeah, I'll take my hands off of her, convict—for now," he grunts before he pushes away from me and walks away.

I stay with my back against the wall as my knees shake, threating to buckle beneath me.

I watch as Houston walks up to Sloane, so close that their noses practically touch. Sloane doesn't say anything. His jaw ticks and his fists clench at his sides. His green eyes track Houston's every move.

Houston grins his cocky fucking grin. "Watch your back, Huntington. Your wife's got a sweet little body. Can't wait to fuck the shit out of her when you're all locked up," he cackles before he walks away.

Once the door closes, I watch as Sloane's body jerks, then he walks over and flips the lock. I don't move from my spot against the wall as he starts to stalk me. "What the fuck just happened here?"

"Sloane, I-I-..."

His hand wraps around the front of my throat, and I snap my mouth shut. His eyes are ablaze with anger. "That fuck put his hands on you. He walked into my house and he put his goddamn hands on you, and I couldn't do a fucking thing about it."

I lift my hand to wrap around the back of his neck as I look into his eyes. "Sloane, he doesn't matter," I murmur.

"Like fuck he doesn't matter," he shouts.

Lifting up on my toes, I press my mouth against his before I whisper against his lips. "I love you. Please don't do anything that will take you away from me."

His hands wrap around my waist and fist in the shirt I'm wearing before his mouth consumes mine. His tongue fills me as he picks me up and presses my back against the wall. I lift my legs to wrap them around his waist as he fumbles with his belt.

My panties are ripped from my body, and then he's inside of me, filling me. "No man touches what's mine," he growls against my mouth as he slams into me.

"Sloane," I gasp as my fingernails dig into his shoulders.

He grunts, his hips thrusting against mine, his pelvis grinding against my clit, causing me to gasp with each pump of his hips. I can feel my nipples hard against the soft cotton of his t-shirt, scraping against the fabric and sending goosebumps to break out over my skin.

Sloane's soft grunts fill the air as his body claims mine, my back pounding against the wall with each pump of his hips. "Come," he demands.

My head hits the wall hard, and I do just as he's instructed. I come all around him. Sloane groans as his hips thrust with several, hard, quick strokes before he explodes inside of me on a shout. "He touches you again, and I'll fucking kill him—cop or not."

He pulls out of me and takes a step back, his hand sliding through his hair before he zips up his pants.

"Your parole officer was here, he searched the house with Houston," I whisper. Sloane's eyes lift to me in surprise. "Where were you?"

He shakes his head. "I had some club shit come up and I was only gone an hour. I didn't want to wake you."

"Let's go to bed," I suggest.

He runs his hand over his face and nods. "They got me by the balls, sunshine," he whispers.

I hurry toward him, wrapping my arms around him and pressing my mouth to his.

"Don't let them affect you. It's what they want."

Sloane's forehead falls against mine and he exhales. "Love

you, Imogen," he breathes. "Let's get to bed."

We walk to the bedroom hand-in-hand, not saying a word. Before we climb into bed, I slide his shirt from my body and drop it on the floor. His arms wrap around me and tug me against his body. It doesn't take but a moment to fall asleep, and I know why.

At the end of the day, no matter what's happened, I always feel safe wrapped in Sloane's arms.

I roll over what seems like minutes later and find that the sheets are cold and empty beside me. With a frown, I sit up and touch my hand to my face, part of my new morning routine to check my swollenness. It actually feels better to the touch, so I slide out of bed and use the restroom before braving a look in the mirror.

I let out a breath as I stare at myself. For the first time in days, I'm recognizable. I look like me, albeit battered and bruised, but my features are mine and they're staring right back at me.

I can see my eyes are bright and shining with tears at the sight. I let out a scream when I feel a warm hand slide around my waist. I'm so focused on my face that I hadn't realized he was walking up behind me.

Sighing, I turn my head as Sloane lowers his and brushes his lips across mine.

"What're you doing, baby?" he rasps.

"Looking at my face. All of the swelling is almost gone," I murmur.

"Fucking beautiful, sunshine," he mutters as his hand slips down to cup my bare pussy.

I shiver in his arms. I move to wrap one of my hands around his wrist that's at my pussy and the other around the back of his neck, touching the back of his hair.

"*Sloane.*"

"Ride my hand, baby," he rasps, slipping two fingers inside of me.

He presses his palm against my clit as his tongue snakes out, licking the side of my neck before he gently sucks.

"Oh, god," I moan, doing what he asks.

Riding his perfect hand, his fingers fucking me and his warm bare chest pressed against my back, I cry out to god, *again.*

"You're beautiful, Imogen," he states, wrapping his hand around my jaw and forcing my face to the mirror, keeping me forward. My eyes fly to meet his instantly. "Look at yourself, baby."

My eyes move from his face to mine, my hips still jerking in his hold, riding him and bringing myself closer toward a climax.

"Do you see just how beautiful you are?" he asks. I try to shake my head, but his grasp is too firm. "My wife, more beautiful today than ever."

"I'm still bruised, still marked," I say, denying his words.

"Yeah, you're marked, right here on your hip," he grunts as his hand falls from my chin to wrap around and squeeze my tattooed hip. "But I'm talking about your face, sunshine. This face, it's the most beautiful face I've ever seen. Rendered me speechless when you were fifteen years old, and still renders me fucking speechless now. A couple bruises won't change that."

"Baby," I whisper as I turn my head and press my lips to his.

My orgasm quickly consumes me, and my thighs shake,

my pussy pulsing around his fingers and my tongue slipping inside of his mouth. He lets me be in control of the kiss until my body finally relaxes against him.

Sloane removes his fingers from inside of me, and in one lightning fast thrust, replaces them with his cock—to the hilt. I let out a gasp and tilt my hips for him, throwing my head back and bracing my hands on the edge of the vanity.

"Your face renders me speechless, you're so goddamn beautiful, Imogen. But like this, your pussy filled with my cock, you're spectacular. Arch back for me a little more, sunshine," he softly asks.

I do. For him, I do, and I always will.

I lift my face and lock eyes with his. Watching as he sinks his teeth into his bottom lip, he completely focuses on me, on my eyes, and on my face as he slowly fucks me. Sloane is in control now. He gave that to me last night, but not anymore.

My breasts sway with each thrust from his hips. His eyes glance down and his teeth press further into his bottom lip as his fingers squeeze my hips a little tighter. Driving his cock up inside of me causes me to shiver in delight.

"I plan on filling this sweet pussy of yours with my cum, sunshine, and filling your belly with my baby," he rasps as his gaze shifts from my breasts to my eyes again.

I open my mouth to speak, but Sloane leans over and bites my shoulder, making me moan.

"Touch that pussy, Genny. Make yourself come," he demands.

I shiver and release one of my hands from the vanity to press two fingers against my clit.

"C'mon, sunshine. Come on your man," he murmurs against my ear.

Without another word, he lifts his chest from my back and starts to fuck me with earnest. I let out a cry as my fingers stroke myself fast and hard, with one purpose and one purpose only—*to come*. Our gazes stay connected as he takes from me, takes my body like only he can. I let him. I offer it to him.

I come around him in a high-pitched squeak before I let out a low groan. My entire lower-half goes completely limp. Sloane wraps his arm around my waist and holds me up while he drives up inside of me a few more times before he releases his own groan as he fills me with his cum.

"*Goddamn*, Imogen," he rasps as he slips out of me.

Without another word, he turns and starts the shower, holding his hand out for me. I place my palm in his and, together, we shower.

"I want you to come with me tonight, sunshine," he murmurs as he massages my scalp with shampoo.

"Tonight?" I ask on a moan.

"Patch-in party at the club," he states.

I feel as though ice has flooded my veins. I start to shake my head, but he spins me around to wash the soap out of my hair, totally ignoring my freak-out.

"Sloane," I whisper once my hair is clean. He ignores me again, spinning me back around to condition me.

"I want you to come with me, Imogen. Everyone knows what happened to you, and nobody gives a fuck that your face isn't perfect. I want you at my side because you're my Old Lady, and it's your earned place; but I also need you there because I love you."

I close my eyes and allow him to spin me once more to wash the conditioner out. I, personally, would let it soak for at least ten more minutes, but he's being sweet, so I'm not going to bitch about it. When the conditioner is rinsed, I lift my head and look into his green eyes, eyes that are waiting for my answer.

Bringing my hand up to cup his wet jaw, I smile softly. Then I lift to my toes and press my lips to his before I wrap both of my hands around his shoulders and press my breasts against his chest.

"If you need me there, baby, that's where I'll be—always at your side, always where you need me," I whisper.

He grins before he lowers his head and captures my lips with his in a soft kiss, still careful not to cause me further pain. Though my face has lost most of its swollenness, it will still take weeks and weeks to heal completely.

"Pleased as fuck, sunshine," he grins.

We finish our shower and then Sloane makes me breakfast. It isn't anything fancy, just eggs, bacon, and toast, but I can't deny that watching him cook for me in the kitchen is something that I will never, ever forget as long as I live.

"What time do I need to be ready?" I ask when he sets my plate in front of me.

"Nine," he grunts as he walks around the kitchen island and sits at the barstool next to mine.

"I wish I had time to visit your mother for another bruise hiding makeup tutorial," I mutter before I cover my mouth as my eyes widen, just having realized what I've actually said to him.

"She that good at it?" he asks, shoveling some eggs into his mouth, seeming unaffected.

I nod before I take a bite of toast and then speak. "She is. You couldn't even tell I had a bruise by the time she was done with me."

"This will be the last time in your life you'll ever have to worry about it," he growls.

I place my palm on his forearm and squeeze him gently with my fingers before nodding.

"I love you, Sloane."

"Love you too, baby," he murmurs, turning to his plate and finishing his food.

We don't speak for the rest of our meal, and then he informs me that he has some more club *shit* to do. He says he'll be back around eight to get ready for the party, and I need to be ready to roll by nine. I agree.

Before he walks out of the front door, he kisses me, filling my mouth with his tongue. I taste the promise of later, and I know that tonight we're going to have fun, even if that fun doesn't start until after the party is over.

"Pack a little bag, we'll stay in my room at the club tonight," Sloane announces before he slams the door behind him.

I blink and turn to my bedroom. I need to call someone for help. I can do my makeup, but I'm not an expert. I wonder if my mother-in-law would travel this far to help me, and then I decide I need to just stop being a pussy bitch and call the other Old Ladies. I consider these women my friends, so I need to stop keeping them at arm's length.

I don't even have to guide my bike as I go to the clubhouse from my house. It's an easy ride, something that only takes a few moments. If I wanted, I feel like I could close my eyes for the entirety of the trip.

MadDog should have the scheduling done by now, so I can give it to Genny. I also want to get a man on her while I'm gone working. I'll never allow her to be home alone again.

I'll never leave her vulnerable like that again, not ever. She's been left vulnerable too many times as it is.

"Hey, brother," Texas booms as I walk into the main bar area of the clubhouse.

I lift my chin at him and glance around the room. I'm not surprised to see Serina draped over a naked Grease. They're both passed the fuck out. I shake my head as I walk over to the bar and ask the prospect for a bottle of water.

"Taking it slow tonight?" Texas asks.

"Got a piss test in an hour," I chuckle.

"At least it's not tomorrow," he laughs, toasting my water with his beer bottle. I let out a sigh and his brow furrows. "You doin' okay?"

"I am, really good. Imogen and I are trying for a baby," I admit.

That bite of panic that I expect to consume me at the words that have just left my lips, it isn't there.

"Yeah? Congrats, brother. I hope your swimmers take," he grins, slapping me on the back.

"Me too," I admit, jutting my chin out.

Texas watches me for another beat before his face goes serious and his voice dips low. "You have any issues with your sobriety, we're here for you, brother. Not one of us wants to see you fail, wants to see your marriage fail. We were all concerned when Genny left the way she did; would be a million times worse she took your kid with her."

"Yeah, we actually talked about that last night," I admit.

I'm not one to really talk about my feelings and shit much, but being sober has kind of forced that out of me lately. It's brought all my feelings to the surface. On more than one occasion, I've felt like I might explode if I don't get my shit out.

"Everything good?" he asks when I don't expand.

I nod with a grin and clap him on the back before I stand and head toward MadDog's office.

I knock on the door and wait for him to call me inside before I walk in. He and Mary-Anne fuck like rabbits, and there's no way I want to risk walking in on them. Though I've heard it's hot as hell, I'm not really into watching my prez fuck his pregnant wife.

"C'mon in," he grunts. I turn the handle before walking inside, then I freeze.

MadDog's got a kid standing on his thighs while his hand is wrapped around her little belly, and another one is sitting on the floor in a pink dress, an array of *Barbies* and their clothes strung out all around her. I can't hide my smile at the sight. It's cute as fuck, and not what I'm used to with my prez.

"Just wanted to know if that schedule is done, but I can see you've got your hands full," I say with a smile.

MadDog looks up and he gives me a wide smile. I've never seen him look so fuckin' happy. It sends a pang of regret to my heart. If he can be this happy, if he can find his happiness, why couldn't I be man enough to give that to Genny these past years?

"You asking about a schedule or you looking for an ear to unload on?" he asks, his voice raspy and deep.

"Both," I admit.

"Riley, girl," he calls.

Her little head pops up before her body follows and she

rushes to her daddy's side. He bends down low and murmurs to her. She nods her head and then scurries past me.

"She's gonna run to the kitchen and grab, Mary," he mutters. "We'll talk without little ears."

"*Maxfield*," Mary scolds as she walks into the room, not even realizing I'm here. "You sent Riley in there, and she walked right past Grease and Serina, passed out naked."

"Sorry, sweetness," he states a with a shrug, sounding the least bit sorry.

"Well, you will be when they're teenagers and think they can do that shit," she says as she walks over to little Finley, who is smiling widely at her mama.

"They better fuckin' not," he growls.

"Well, they keep seeing this stuff, they think it's normal, they'll be acting just like their aunties and uncles," she says as she wraps her hands around Finley's middle and brings her to her hip.

"All right, sweetness, you made your point," he murmurs, wrapping his hand around her hip.

She rolls her eyes and bends down, pressing her lips to his. I feel like a voyeur as I watch them kiss. It isn't anything deep and overtly sexual, but it's still intimate.

"I'll come get them when I'm done here, yeah?"

"Okay," she breathes as her face completely softens.

I watch as he pats her ass and then she giggles slightly as she slips past me with Finley in her arms, closing the door behind her.

"You're scheduled to work this week, and every other week. They've upped the shipments to weekly. Don't know why, don't give a fuck. All I know is that it makes our wallets fatter," he shrugs. "And I have colleges to save up for," he grins. "You needed to talk?"

"I want to have a man on Imogen when I'm at the docks," I announce, watching as he slowly nods.

Then I explain to him about what happened early this morning. I tell him about my probation officer and the officer Houston showing up at my place.

"The fuck you say," he whispers in a lethal tone.

Normally, it would be something brought up in church, maybe even voted on, and I'd be asking and not telling. This is my wife, and I refuse to take any more chances with her safety.

"The protection?"

"I'll approve it. You can have one of the prospects watch out for her on those nights. I understand your hesitancy, and I'm cool with that. Nothing wrong with keeping your woman safe. How is she doin', by the way?" he asks with concern laced in his voice.

"Better. She'll be here tonight," I shrug. He doesn't hide, nor could he probably, his surprise at that announcement.

"How are *you* doin'?" he asks, switching topics.

I tell him exactly what I told Texas, except he's my president so I elaborate. I talk to him a little bit about my fears, and he talks me down. He's good with advice, and he's been through it all, so I take in everything he says and soak it up. When I leave his office, I feel like a weight has been lifted off my shoulders.

I make my way to my probation officer's place and do my piss test, knowing without a doubt that it'll come back clean as a fucking whistle. I'm also going to ask him just what in the fuck went down a few hours ago.

My woman should never have to be woken from bed to

deal with that shit. I want to kick his ass and worry about the repercussions later, but I have too much to live for to go back to that hell hole.

I have a woman, a whole slew of brothers, Kipling, and soon, maybe I'll have a kid of my own. Fuck yeah. I have way too fucking much to live for to pop a dirty test and get sent back to the joint.

chapter twenty-four

Imogen

"I look like I'm trying to cover bruises," I state as I gaze at my face in the mirror.

I have a thick layer of makeup on, and while it looks better than just my clean face, it still looks like it's exactly what it is—caked on makeup to cover bruising.

"I'm not sure how else to get maximum coverage," Cleo whispers as she looks over my face.

Ivy looks over my face, scrutinizing me, "What if we tried contouring a little more."

"Well, unless you're a pro, I can't contour for shit," Cleo states.

"Times like this, I wish Kentlee lived here. She was so good at makeup when she worked at the strip club," Mary-Anne sighs as she places her hand on the swell of her belly.

"I think this is as good as it's going to get," I mutter.

"You're still beautiful; but the bruising is so dark, I don't think it matters what we do, it'll still be there," Cleo states softly.

"The bar in the clubhouse is dark, the lighting sucks there, which is good. Plus, your outfit is hot as hell. Nobody will be looking at your face," Mary-Anne grins widely.

My eyes automatically go over to the minuscule outfit that the girls brought over when I called them to help me with my makeup. It's an extremely small black dress. It doesn't even look like my left thigh would fit inside, but Mary-Anne claims it *stretches*.

Ivy goes through my shoes and brings out a pair of metallic gold, Valentino, strappy gladiator, high heels, with matching gold studs adorning the straps up to my ankles.

"You want me to wear *Valentino* to the clubhouse?" I ask, my eyes widening as Ivy sets my shoes down next to my bed.

"All your shoes are expensive. I didn't see any knockoffs in there," she says, practically rolling her eyes.

"I guess it doesn't matter," I mutter.

"They're sexy. I think you should wear them, knock your husband's socks off," Teeny whispers.

I look over to the small woman, and she tips her head to the side, giving me a wide smile. Shaking my head, I lift a shoulder and agree to wear the damn shoes.

I can't believe my fifteen hundred dollar high heels are going to be on that disgusting clubhouse floor. They'll probably get some kind of liquid spilled on them, too.

"Okay, we have to go and get dressed as well," Mary-Anne announces as she stands up.

All of the women excuse themselves and start to make

their way out of my room, but Mary stops and wraps her hand around my shoulder, giving me a squeeze.

"I'm glad to have you back, Genny. Honestly, I can't tell you how glad I am that you're so happy," she says, giving me a wink.

"Me, too," I admit.

"The roads that are the hardest, at the end, what's waiting for you, it makes the journey so totally worth it," she whispers before she walks away, leaving me alone in my bedroom.

I don't think any more about her words. If I do, I'll cry. Instead, I walk over to the dress and drop my robe as I reach for the minuscule fabric. I test the elasticity, and as Mary-Anne ensured, it has some serious stretch—though I'm not quite sure it will be enough.

Letting out a breath, I step into the dress and shimmy it up my completely naked body. I walk over to my closet, where I have a full-length mirror, and I take a look at myself. The dress is tight and short, almost indecently short. The way it holds everything in, and together, I cannot deny that I look sexy. On top of that, I *feel* sexy.

Hearing the front door open and then slam shut, I run over to my shoes and clutch, grabbing them before I lock myself in the bathroom. I still need to fix my hair, and I don't want Sloane to see me until my look is one-hundred percent complete.

"Sunshine?" he calls out.

"In the bathroom, just finishing my hair and stuff," I call out.

He informs me that he'll shower in the guest bath and he'll be ready to leave in just twenty minutes, so I better *hurry my ass up*. I smile at his order. It's so *normal*. Not normal for us, but just normal. I can't help but love it. I'm glad that our relationship is shifting, and I'm enjoying that shift immensely.

Once my hair is styled in waves that tumble down my shoulders, I buckle my *Valentinos* and look at my clutch. Deciding I don't want to keep track of it all night, I leave it right on the counter. I'll be back tomorrow, and the only person who would call me is going to be right next to me the entire evening. Anybody else can contact him if they want to get a hold of me.

"Ready, sunshine?" Sloane asks, rapping on the door with his knuckles.

"Yeah," I breathe as I take another look at my make-up-covered face in the mirror.

I don't look completely disastrous, but I don't look like myself, either. Shaking the thoughts out of my head, I turn and open the door. I'm surprised to see Sloane is standing right at the doorway, his eyes travelling from my feet up to my face so slowly that I start to squirm in my spot. He lets out a shaky breath and then his gaze connects with mine.

"You can't leave this house looking like that, Imogen," he rasps, his breathing shallow and his nostrils flaring.

"*What*?" I ask in confusion.

I know my face doesn't look that great, but I'd hoped the girls were right when they said my dress would detract from it. Apparently, everybody was wrong. I watch as Sloane lifts his hands and curls his fingers against the top of the doorjamb.

"I'm about two seconds from ripping that flimsy looking material you're trying to pull off as a dress, and fucking you until you can't walk. If I feel this way, I have no doubt in fuck every man down at that clubhouse will feel the exact same. I don't want them thinking of my wife that way," he announces.

My eyes widen and my mouth opens slightly in an O shape.

"Sloane," I whisper as I take a step closer to him.

"Hangin' on by a thread, sunshine. Don't come at me with your sweet whispers," he mutters.

I don't stop. I continue to walk up to him. Without a word, I sink to my knees once I've reached him. He lets out a guttural sound as I work the button of his jeans and his fly before I swiftly pull his pants and underwear down just past his ass, exposing his hard cock.

I don't touch him. Instead, I lick the underside of his length, circling my tongue around the head of his dick. I hear the wood of the jamb cracking beneath his fingers, and I can't help the excited thrill that shoots up my spine and down to my pussy.

"I don't want to hurt you, baby. But if you don't suck my cock, I'm going to fuck your mouth," he warns.

Opening my mouth, I take him as far as I can down my throat. He lets out a deep groan, and I feel it wash over me.

"Look at me, sunshine," he orders.

I open my eyes and look up at him through my lashes. My gorgeous blond husband. My eyes shift to his forearm, and I see my name permanently etched in his skin. I can't help but moan. *Mine.* He's all mine. It spurs me on to suck harder and faster. I reach up and cup his balls in my hand, massaging and tugging on the soft flesh as he growls deep from his chest.

"I'm about to come, baby," he warns.

It's been years since I've swallowed. Blow jobs themselves were few and far between in our dysfunctional relationship. When I was young, swallowing just seemed gross. By the time I was comfortable with my sexuality, we were so fucked up that I only did it a few times before I refused, just because I could.

I want that part of him again—all of him. As he grows larger in my mouth, I welcome the warm spurts of his release down my throat as he lets his head fall back. I watch the beautiful column of his throat when a loud roar escapes his mouth.

Sloane takes a step back and sinks to his knees in front of me, his hands at my waist before he gently tugs me closer. To my surprise, he presses his lips against mine. Then he forces his tongue in my mouth and tastes me, no doubt tasting himself as well.

His hands slip down to my ass and he squeezes my flesh roughly, the pads of his fingers digging into me before he lifts his head just slightly and lets his forehead rest against mine.

"Fuck me, baby," he rasps. "Took all of me, in control, in charge, but sunshine you took it all."

"You made me feel beautiful when I wasn't sure how I felt about myself," I murmur, letting out an exhale.

"You know you're gorgeous, sunshine. You don't need me to tell you that," he murmurs.

"My bruising...I don't feel it and you know that. I wanted to thank you," I smile.

He laughs softly and moves one of his hands to my hair. He twists it in the strands at the back of my head, and the other presses against the small of my back. "Best thank you for a delivered compliment in my whole fucking life." Sloane's hands flex, tightening in my hair and pressing against my back even more.

"Baby, I know you're vain and that looks really fucking

matter to you, but believe me, Imogen, you're still gorgeous no matter what," he assures.

I close my eyes with a small nod. He presses his lips at the corner of mine before he stands up, helping me to my feet before he fixes his pants.

"Need to redo your lipstick, my sunshine," he whispers.

My eyes widen, and I turn around to face the mirror, making a strangled noise. Sloane laughs softly behind me.

"My dick's got that red lipstick all over it. Fuck me, I'm going to be hard all goddamn night just thinking about it," he grunts as he leans against the jamb and watches me fix my face.

"Sloane," I hiss as my eyes move to his. They sparkle as they take me in. I can't stop my belly from fluttering.

"Mean it, baby. Can't wait to get you back up to my room tonight and fuck you all night long," he grins.

"All night?" I ask as I lift an eyebrow.

"All fucking night. I'm putting a baby inside of you tonight. Then maybe right before you fall asleep—" he mutters softly as he walks up behind me and places a hand on my belly. "—maybe I fuck that pretty ass of yours. Been a while, baby."

His warm breath washes over my neck, his words making me shiver, causing my legs to shake with anticipation. It has been a while; so long, in fact, that I'm pretty certain it's going to hurt.

When we were good, and then when we would go through long spells of being good, that was something we both enjoyed. I kept it from him when he hurt me. No way could I trust him to go there with me.

So, while it's been a really long time, I trust him more

now than I ever have, and I want that. The connection we share when we're together, when I'm completely at his mercy like that, it's like nothing I've ever experienced in my life. I love it.

"It's been a while," I admit with a whisper, my eyes connected to his in the mirror.

"You feel comfortable with that?"

I could kiss him for asking. I nod once, biting the inside of my cheek, trying not to show how nervous I am—but I want it. I want him every way, and I want a new start to us, in every way possible, even in this.

"Make you feel good, sunshine," he mutters as he presses his lips to my neck, nipping my skin before he licks me.

"I know you will, Sloane. You always do," I admit on a whimper.

I'm so wet, between making him come with my mouth and this talk, I'm afraid that my need is going to start sliding down my thigh at any second. His hand slides down my belly and his fingers gently slide through my slick center.

"No panties," he grunts as he presses his semi-hard cock against my back.

I rock against his fingers, urging them to play with my clit or slip inside of me, anything. "Dress is too tight," I mutter.

"So wet, but you're going to have to wait. We're late, sunshine," he murmurs. I can't help the whine that escapes my lips. "Mmmm, I'll take care of you, I always do—eventually."

Sloane removes his fingers from beneath my dress and takes a step back, jutting his chin toward the mirror in a silent command for me to finish my lipstick. It takes everything inside of me not to stomp my foot like a child, but I don't.

I finish my lipstick, and a few minutes later, we're on our

way out the door. I head toward his car, but he makes a tsking sound and guides me toward his motorcycle. I haven't ridden on the back of his bike in years, and I can't stop the thrill of excitement as it rolls through me. Then there's the fact that I'll be completely exposed, and plastered against his back, with no barrier between my naked center and the rest of the world.

He loads my small bag in his saddle pouch and straddles the machine. I lick my lips at the sight of his thick thighs straining in his jeans and shiver. His head tips to the side as he watches me climb up behind him.

"Press that sweet bare cunt against my back, baby, and let's ride," he grunts.

My thighs shake as I do exactly what he asks. He starts the engine as my hands grip his shirt, and he roars down the road toward the clubhouse. I shiver at the sensations that roll through me. as his bike vibrates down the road.

Grabbing onto his shirt, clutching it in my hands, I try to bite back the moan as he moves through the curves of the mountain roads.

Soar

The drive to the clubhouse is quiet. Mainly because we're on my bike and we can't talk. Genny holds on tight, her sweet bare cunt against my back. I can feel her heat pressing against me and then, she shifts, and I hear her moan. *Fuck me*. She's getting off. I try to focus on the road—that shit is not easy. Pulling over to the side of the dark shoulder, I stop.

Without speaking I turn around and wrap my hand

around the back of hers, shoving her face in my neck while I slip two fingers into her wet pussy. She cries out as I curl my fingers inside of her and place my thumb against her clit.

"Get yourself there," I growl in her ear. She whimpers and doesn't say anything as she shifts, and rolls her hips, finding her release. When she comes it's with a cry against my neck, and a sob. "You okay?"

She lifts her head, her eyes shining brightly, and a small smile playing on her lips. "Yeah, Sloane," she whispers.

Fuck me.

Yeah.

Nothing else is said. I turn around and take off toward the clubhouse again. Her now, sopping wet pussy, pressed against me. Fuck, it's one of the best feelings in the world.

My mind starts to wander, to think and I'm grateful for it. This will be my first true test. My first real party since getting out. Sure, the guys threw me something when I was released, but I got drunk as shit and fucked a whore, maybe two. I honestly don't remember. It wasn't the same as what's going to happen tonight.

Nervous.

I feel fucking nervous.

Imogen's hand wraps around my thigh and she gives it a squeeze. "Sloane?"

"Just thinking," I grunt, squeezing my handlebars a little tighter.

We pull into the clubhouse parking lot and I don't make a move to get off of my bike.

She lets out a sigh and crawls off behind me only to crawl over my thighs, and straddle me. Her knees on either side of my hips. Parked in front of my club, I move my hands to wrap around the outsides of her thighs, my eyes looking into hers.

"Are you scared you'll be tempted?" she asks.

Admitting it makes me feel weak, but if I can't be honest and truthful with my wife, then who the fuck can I be honest with? I nod my answer and she smiles softly. "By drugs or women?" she asks.

My heart fucking aches that she even has to ask, but I understand why.

"Only one woman I want, Imogen," I mutter, running my nose alongside hers. "Just you, my sunshine."

I don't kiss her, not wanting to mess up her lipstick again, but press my lips to the corner of her mouth. When I squeeze her thighs, I explain a little more about how I'm feeling.

I tell her that I haven't craved the drugs since I've been out, but I'm worried that in this environment, at this party, I will. And if that craving is strong enough, I'm afraid I won't be able to deny it. If I don't deny it, I'll hurt her, and the probability of me being locked up again is high.

"Sloane," she sighs as she cups my cheeks when I'm finished sharing my pussy-assed feelings. "You're assuming a lot of things. You're worried and you don't even know how you're going to react yet. You cannot worry about what could happen. If I did the same thing, I wouldn't be right here with you."

Thinking about her words, I nod. She's right. If she stressed about me, about my fidelity and the future—our future—then she definitely would not be where she is. My track record is fucking shit, but I promised a change, I promised my faithfulness, and I aim to deliver. Part of that means no dope. My head has to be in the right place, and I can't let my own self sabotage ruin our life.

HAYLEY FAIMAN

"Ready to have some fun, sunshine?"

She smiles beautifully, nodding as she answers, "Yeah, I'm so ready."

I squeeze her thighs and help her off of me, watching as she shimmies her skirt down and tries not to flash the empty parking lot with her bare pussy. I get a peek anyway. When she's situated, I get off of my bike and wrap my hand around her waist. I tuck her close to my side and turn us toward the clubhouse.

"These rocks are going to ruin my shoes," Imogen huffs next to me as we crunch through the gravel.

I reach down and pick her up, slipping my arm beneath her knees and my other behind her back. She throws her hands around my shoulders and looks at me with surprise.

"Shoes are hot as fuck, sunshine. I expect to see you in them in the future. I'm also going to fuck you in those shoes later."

She shutters in my arms as her lips part in awe, and I know she's imagining me fucking her hard, wearing nothing but the hot as shit shoes.

My sunshine can't wait.

chapter twenty-five

Imogen

Sloane sets me down just outside of the main clubhouse door. I can already hear the loud music blaring from the bar, and I know the party must be in full swing. We're late, but not overly so. Regardless, I know that these men like to party, and they like to party hard. He asks me if I'm ready, and although I'm not, I smile brightly and nod.

Walking into the hazy room, I look around and see that many whores have already lost their tops, or perhaps they never had them on to begin with. I'm not sure.

Sloane guides me away from them and toward another side of the room, the side where the couples always seem to congregate. Not that I came to club parties often, but when I did, this was where I hung out.

All of the Old Ladies smile as I step up to the group.

Colleen's eyes take me in, and when she reaches my face they soften. I'm surprised that I don't see pity in them, but I don't, and I'm relieved. Sloane stays directly at my side the entire night, never leaving, ordering a prospect to deliver our drinks throughout the evening.

Perched on his lap, I spend my time chatting with the other women. It's fun. Relaxed. It's easy to ignore the other side of the room, the side where sex is assuredly being flaunted without reservation.

Mary-Anne and MadDog are the first to leave, followed by Ivy and Camo, then Mammoth and Teeny, then finally Torch and Cleo leave. The pregnant women, all looking as though they were at different levels of exhaustion.

I talk with Colleen and Bobbie for another half an hour or so, but they also decide to retire for the evening. It leaves just me and Sloane. I'm tipsy, but not exactly tired.

"How's your pussy?" Sloane whispers against my ear from behind, his hands wrapping around my waist and squeezing.

"Neglected," I admit as I let out a shaky exhale.

"Turn around and straddle me," he mutters.

I shiver in his arms as I slip off of his knee. I shake my head and he tips his lips in a grin. "I'm not fucking you out here," I say, waving my hand around.

"I was just going to play with you, baby," he states.

Shaking my head again, I hold out my hand for him. He slips his inside and stands, his stomach brushing against my chest as he looks down at me. Then he tucks a piece of my wavy hair behind my ear before he lowers his face. "I want to give you all of me, Sloane. I want wild fucking, but I don't want anybody to see that."

Wetting his lips, I hear a low groan deep inside of him

as he dips his head even more, his mouth at my ear before he speaks. "You're definitely getting a wild fuck tonight, sunshine. Now go up to my room and wait for me. I want you in nothing but those heels," he rasps.

"Sloane," I gasp.

"Hurry now, baby."

I turn away from him and head toward the bedrooms, stopping at the bathroom first to take care of business. When I'm washing my hands, of course, Destini walks in—her tits not moving an inch, even though she's bare breasted. She smirks at me, and I can't help but feel the need to scratch her damn eyes out.

"I honestly can't believe he's kept you around. It must be a pathetic existence, being you," she laughs as she washes her hands.

"Why is that?" I ask before continuing. "I'm not here for one purpose only, to spread for whatever man requests it, or for any member that happens to amble on in here."

"Snooty bitches like you never can keep a man. Eventually, they all come to girls like me, girls who have no boundaries. Girls who know how to suck, how to fuck, and how to take what we're given with no backtalk."

I try not to, but I burst out laughing in her face. She narrows her eyes on me and raises her hand. I catch her wrist before she can strike my healing face. I squeeze her too-skinny wrist, knowing she probably lives off of booze and cigarettes to stay scarily thin, so she's weak as hell.

"Snooty bitches like me get claimed. We get branded and put up in nice houses, with nice cars, money and jewelry. Snooty bitches like me get their last names, their children, and most importantly their respect. Maybe you get one of them for a time or two, but they're doing nothing but using you. When you're too old, too stretched out, or generally of no use to them, they'll toss you aside and another little cunt will take your place. But snooty bitches like me will still be here."

I release her hand and turn my back to her. I take two steps away from her when she reaches out and grabs the back of my hair. A low, immature move if I ever saw one.

"You may think you're something special, but I already know your man can't keep that cock of his in his pants, so you better believe I'll be right here to take care of him when he's feeling like he wants some strange. Then when you suck his cock, I bet you'll still be able to taste my pussy on it," she laughs as she releases my hair. I school my features and turn to her as I take a few steps backward.

"I pity girls like you, I really do," I state as I continue to back up, my hand on the handle of the door.

"Why?" she asks in confusion.

"You have no self-worth. None."

"Like you? A woman who keeps taking her man back even though he's fucking everything with a pussy?" she laughs harshly.

"I'm a woman who has been in love with the same man since she was fifteen years old. Big difference."

"Not from where I'm standing," she laughs.

Opening the door, I take another step out and give her a shrug. "Maybe not; but I'm not being used, either."

I turn and leave her in the bathroom, trying to not allow her words to affect me. I can lie and say that they don't, but they do. Words like that, words that talk of my husband's numerous infidelities over the years probably always will, no matter what our relationship looks like at the time.

I'm not going to let her words ruin my night, though—not like she wants them to. I'm too tipsy, too needy, and too excited to have my husband in every part of my body.

Once I make it into his bedroom, I look around. It's been a long time since I've stepped foot into this room, and I'm surprised to find the bed made and the space actually clean. I shimmy out of my dress and place it on the empty chair that sits in the corner.

Then I fold the comforter over a few times until it's at the edge of the bed. I'm just finishing smoothing it out, noticing that the sheets also appear to be clean when the door opens.

Sloane is standing at the entrance to his room, his eyes taking me in from top to toe and back up again. He sinks his teeth in his lower lip and smirks as he walks inside and closes the door, flipping the deadbolt before he removes his boots, leaving them right in front of the door.

"Are you wet for me?" he whispers as he removes his cut and sets it on top of my dress on the chair in the corner.

I turn to face him, watching him as he removes his shirt. My breathing turning ragged at the sight of his muscular frame, I itch to touch him. His thumb pops the top button of his jeans and he shoves them, along with his boxers, down his legs, stepping out of them. He takes one after another slow step toward me every time he loses an article of clothing.

"Are you?" he asks again.

I wasn't.

I am now.

I nod.

Once he's in front of me, Sloane lifts a finger and touches the center of my chest, letting it drag down to my clit but not applying the pressure I crave. I bite the inside of my cheek, and he grins.

Then, without warning, he bends down and wraps his hands around my knees, flipping me onto my back. My ribs protest slightly, but the small twinge of pain isn't enough to keep my excitement at bay.

His hands wrap around the inside of my thighs, and he presses them open as his mouth descends on my center. The flat of his tongue slides along my entire core, and when his mouth sucks on my clit, my back arches off the bed. My hands automatically find his hair and hold onto him.

"Oh, god, baby," I moan as I slip my legs over his shoulders and dig my heels into his back as I force my pussy closer to his face.

Sloane reaches under my ass and tips me up, angling me and eating me like never before. It's so good, and I've been on edge all night. I come hard and fast, riding his face as my body shakes uncontrollably.

He flips me gently onto my stomach. With my knees holding me up, my calves and feet hanging off of the bed, his mouth is on me again. I cry out when his tongue flicks my still sensitive clit, but his hands wrap around my hips and he forces me against him, holding me still while he takes and gives all at the same time.

It doesn't take me long to work back up again, to be on the edge and then to topple over. I fist the sheets at my head while I try to climb away from him, on sensory overload. His lips press against my inner thigh as he backs away, and I collapse on the mattress, face down.

"You ready for my cock now, sunshine?" he asks on a chuckle.

I roll over and push my hair out of my face only to see his green eyes shining as he grins, looking down at me. "Look at you. A hot fucking mess from your man making you come. *Christ,* you're beautiful, baby."

I shake my head and smile up at him, unable to speak, my lungs still trying to catch their breath. He wraps his hands around my calves and lifts my legs so that my ankles are resting on his shoulders, my legs straight and locked. Then he enters me, slowly and to the hilt.

"Feels so good," I moan as he pulls out and then gently glides back inside of me.

"Taking you slow, sunshine. This night is going to last a long fucking time, and I don't want to wear your sweet pussy out too quickly, now."

"Baby," I rasp.

Sloane does as he promises, fucking me slow and with purpose, sending me over the edge again. Then he flips me over and fucks me a little harder until he comes deep inside of me, promising this time we've created a baby, for sure.

Imogen. My sweet wife. She's fucking exhausted. Yet, I'm not through with her. I need more from her body, and I aim to take it. She turns her head to look back at me. Her face is covered in a light sheen of sweat, and a small satisfied smile is tugging on her lips.

I bend over her back and press my lips to hers, slipping my tongue into her mouth and tasting her, tasting *us.* Fuck, she's so goddamn perfect for me.

"Are you ready?" I ask against her lips. She sucks in a deep breath and nods.

"Yeah, baby," she says through trembling lips.

"Been a while, we can play, instead," I offer, feeling a little guilty about wanting so much, and her not being ready to give it to me.

Shaking her head, she reaches behind her and wraps her hand around the back of my head to pull me down a little more. "I need you, I need all of you, Sloane. I know that this is part of you, part of us, and I need you to re-claim every part of me."

I can't control the growl that climbs up my throat at her words. "I'll never abuse your trust again, baby."

She smiles but doesn't say anything. I press my lips to hers again before I stand up and take a step back from her. I move to my dresser and grab a brand-new bottle of oil. Silently, I make my way back to her.

The party is still in full swing in the bar, the music thumping throughout my room, but it all fades away as I look to my wife and everything she's offering me. She's moved to the center of the bed and is lying on her stomach.

I coat my dick with the oil and crawl up the bed, not satisfied to look at the back of her head this first time. I need to see into her eyes. I want that connection, and I'm pretty sure she *needs* it. I gently roll her over and ignore the look of surprise on her face.

Wrapping my hands around the backs of her knees I spread her wide for me, pushing her legs up a little. Her pussy is swollen from my mouth and cock. I stopped counting her orgasms when she reached five. Her cunt looks so pretty, pink and sensitive.

"Sloane," she rasps.

Releasing one of her legs, I drip the oil on that swollen pussy and let it slide down to her ass. I'm sure it's more than enough, but I can't tear my eyes away from the oil as it drips, coating her. Then she lets out a moan, and I grin. My sunshine likes her ass play, and it's been so fucking long.

I slide my fingers through her oiled cunt and dip them inside, pumping her gently, curling my fingers and petting her the way she likes, which makes her arch her back and moan again. Then, when she starts to whimper, I remove them and slip them into the tight ring of her ass.

Her ass is so warm and so tight, I know that I'm not going to last long once my cock is buried deep inside of her. I gently fuck her ass with my fingers, adding a third to prepare her for my dick. I go slow, not wishing to cause her pain. I know she's past any pain she may feel when she starts to meet my fingers' thrusts.

"Ready for me?" I ask, pulling my fingers from her ass.

"Please, Sloane," she whispers.

I wrap both of my hands around the backs of her knees again and spread her wider as I push her legs as close to the sides of her face as possible. I rest one of them over my shoulder while I press my cock against her entrance.

"Relax, my sunshine," I murmur gently.

I watch as her body physically loses its tension, and I push my way further inside of her.

My gaze stays connected to hers. Nothing could shatter this between us right now. Nothing else in the world exists but her, me, and my cock in her ass. Once I'm fully seated inside of her, I press my lips to hers.

I slip my tongue inside of her mouth and start to fuck her mouth with mine. I know she's fully relaxed and becoming excited when she starts to fuck my cock on her own, moving her hips.

I take her cue and gently pull out as I fuck her with my tongue and my dick. She whimpers into my mouth before she rips her lips from mine and throws her head back. I move one of my hands to her pussy and press my thumb against her clit, which makes her eyes widen and her head snap up so that our eyes connect again.

"Want your pussy filled with my fingers, sunshine?" I ask, my voice tight as I try to keep from coming inside of her.

"Yes, Sloane," she whispers. It tugs at my heart, the sweetness of her voice.

I fill her cunt with my fingers, pressing my thumb against her clit and rubbing her firmly. I feel her pussy flutter against my fingers, so I start to fuck her a little harder.

When she cries out, her hoarse voice filling the room as her pussy and ass squeeze me, I fuck her in earnest—harder than I should, my body unable to harness even an ounce of control. I throw back my head and roar as I come, filling her full of my seed. My muscles tremble as I keep my body from smashing hers against the mattress.

It takes everything inside of me to actually ease myself from her body, wanting to stay there for as long as I can. She lets out a deep groan once I'm completely out of her, and I release her legs, lying my head against her stomach to catch my breath. I wrap my arms around her back and hold her to me, my chest laying against her warm, oiled, center.

"It's never felt that good before," she whispers as her fingers start to play with my hair.

I grunt my response, my body completely worn out. I massage her slick skin with my thumbs before I speak. "Since I've been back, since *we've* been back, everything has felt phenomenal and better than before. Maybe because I'm sober, but I think it's really because I love you so fuckin' much, sunshine, and I'm grateful as fuck that you're so goddamn forgiving."

"I don't want to be a doormat, but I know I've forgiven you too easily," she whispers as she continues to play with my hair, "and I don't care. If I didn't, I wouldn't be right here, right now."

I turn and press my lips to her belly before I speak. "Let's get cleaned up and get some sleep, sunshine."

"I love you, Sloane Huntington."

"Love you, baby," I grunt, pressing my lips to her belly again as I stand.

I turn, grabbing a shirt and pulling it on over her naked body before I pick her up. Together, we walk to the communal showers. Obviously, I didn't think about the cleanup when I decided this is what we would do tonight, but I wouldn't take one fucking second of it back.

chapter twenty-six

Soar

A week later, I find myself kissing my wife goodbye. She's still sleeping in bed, but her eyes flutter open as she looks up at my seated position. She looks at me with confusion and then realization dawns on her. I won't be back until tomorrow sometime.

Tonight, I'm driving up to Humboldt to load up the truck with merchandise. Normally, I would try and come back the same night, but MadDog warned that this shipment is double the size of the last, so I have a feeling it's going to take twice as long to load.

"I'll miss you," she murmurs.

Looking at her face, there is still some light bruising, but most is yellowed. It's almost completely cleared of the horrors she suffered. I reach out and touch my finger to her nose, then drag it down to her lips, tracing them. Lips that were wrapped around my cock last night; lips that sucked me completely dry. Lips that are mine.

"A prospect will be outside the front door all night long. You need anything, you fear anything, you tell him," I rumble.

"Okay," she breathes before her tongue peeks out and tastes my finger. Shaking my head, I lean down and press my lips to hers.

"Gonna be late. Can't fuck you, sunshine."

"When you get back?" she asks on an exhale, her lips still touching mine.

"Yeah, when I get back," I grunt.

It takes everything inside of me to stand up and turn away from her. She's warm, curled into the sheets, and I know that she's still naked from last night. Goddamn, my woman knows how to make me smile.

Swear to Christ, I don't think I've been this happy my entire life. I don't think I've ever allowed myself to be this happy, either. Wish I would have found this inside of me, this strength, this ability to allow her to love me and me love her, a lot fucking sooner.

"Don't go inside. Your job is to watch the outside. I want you going on a perimeter check at least once every hour to check the doors and windows. My wife may or may not leave while I'm gone. If she does, you follow her at a distance. You don't talk to her and you sure as fuck don't look at her," I growl.

"Yes, sir," the prospect says, grinding his teeth together.

I lift my chin and leave him on my front porch. Maybe I'm being a dick, but we've all been there. I don't give a fuck if this guy was a staff sergeant for the army or not; to me, he's just a fucking *boot*—green, a new recruit, and not yet worthy of my respect.

Driving to the clubhouse, I don't bother going inside of the bar. I walk out to the warehouse where the truck is. Torch and MadDog are already waiting for me, and it takes about ten minutes for MadDog to go over our route again. Once we're finished, he slaps me on the back, then does the same to Torch before he wishes us luck.

"Ready?" he asks.

I can't help but remember the last time we were together like this, I ended up in prison for three years. I smile to myself, knowing that no way in fuck is that ever going to happen again.

"Fuck yeah," I grin as I start the engine.

We drive a little way out of Shasta and are on our way to Humboldt when I see cop lights behind me. I furrow my brow and look to Torch as I pull over. I watch as he walks up to the truck and I recognize him immediately. It's Houston, the fuck.

"Know I don't have to ask this shit, but you clean?" he asks.

"Haven't touched anything other than beer since I've been out," I state. He grins.

A different California highway patrol officer walks up to Torch's side and asks us both to get out of the truck, our information in hand. Luckily, my gun is stowed, as is Torch's, in a hidden compartment, so I don't have to worry about that. I hop down from the truck and walk around the back, also thankful that we haven't picked up our load yet.

"You boys headed out of town?" he asks, looking at our cuts.

"Yeah, helping a friend move," Torch states nonchalantly.

I listen to the officer call out for wants and warrants for both of us, and he narrows his eyes on me when the dispatcher says we're clear. He walks over to his car and sits in the front seat, typing some things on his computer before he walks back over to us.

"Gonna need to talk to Mr. Huntington alone, please," he says.

Torch looks between us, confusion etched on his face, but he backs up and away from the officer and me.

"You obviously have a hard on for me. What can I help you with today?" I ask, taking him in.

"I'm still just waiting for you to fuck up. When you do, I'm going to take you down," he rasps.

I roll my eyes. "I'm not going to fuck up. Bayard isn't paying you anymore. You need to get the fuck on with your life."

"Not Bayard paying me anymore," he quips. "Mr. Stewart is a very determined, man you know?"

"Why, because my father-in-law paid you too?" I ask, arching my brow.

"Scum like you are the reason I became a cop," he spits.

I shake my head with a grin. Then I pin him with my eyes. "Better the devil you know, cop. My father-in-law has a reason to shove my ass back in jail, I'm sure—none of those you would probably agree with. In fact, you knew them, they'd probably make you sick to your stomach, unless you're a sick fuck just like him. Which, based off of your obsession with my wife, I can assume you are," I shrug.

"What's that supposed to mean?"

"You do know he tried to force Imogen into marrying someone who beat her. When she told him, and showed him the evidence, he didn't bat an eyelash. In fact, he didn't give a fuck and told her she needed to marry him anyway," I inform him.

I watch as he blinks and cringes before he fixes his features. "Who his daughter marries is none of my concern. I'm concerned with you and your illegal activities."

I snort. "Women getting beat because they refuse to fuck a guy they're dating isn't your concern? Good to fucking know the law is on the side of the citizens. You want to rape her though, right? So why would you give a fuck about her being hurt. Man, I could give a fuck about my father-in-law, about you or anybody else, but someone lays a hand on a woman? I take major fucking issue with that. Are we done here?"

"You talk to your probation officer?" he asks with a smirk.

"Check in every week. Saturday's, sometimes Sunday's, whatever works for his schedule. I haven't popped dirty once," I shrug.

His jaw clenches hard, and I watch as a muscle ticks in his cheek. Then he lets out a puff of air, lifts his chin, and turns to walk away from me. He doesn't even say we're free to go. He tosses our ID's out the window of his cruiser and speeds off.

"The fuck?" Torch asks as he rushes after our flying paperwork to keep it from going into the street.

"My father-in-law is trying to get my ass landed back in jail so he has full control over my wife," I mutter.

"*Shit*," he curses as he takes his phone out of his pocket.

I hear him talking, and I assume it's to MadDog but all I can think about is Imogen. What her fate would be if I was locked up again. She'd leave me, assuredly, and her father would try to control her.

Odds are, he would win. I can't let that shit happen—not

to my Genny. Though Graham is gone, he'd just find some other man and get into some kind of scheme with him, using Imogen to sweeten the deal. *Fuck that.*

"MadDog says to continue as planned, but instead of leaving in the morning we need to leave either as soon as we're loaded or tomorrow night. Try to fly out under the radar." I nod in agreement and walk back to the truck, hopping inside and starting it up.

"You okay, brother?" he asks.

"I'll be fine," I grunt.

Fuck that, I won't be fine.

I'll deal, but as long as I'm breathing free and Imogen is at home waiting for me, I'll be okay.

Imogen

I stretch and climb out of bed. I wish I could stay beneath the warm sheets all day. I could, if I really wanted, but I'm not going to. Today I'm going to bake a cake. It's Sloane's birthday tomorrow, something he probably thought I'd forgotten.

We haven't celebrated birthdays together in years. He would choose to be with his club on his, and I would leave and go shopping in the city for mine. I can't even remember the last time we bought each other birthday presents.

Since he's out of town for the day and all evening, it's the perfect opportunity to make a cake and have it ready for tomorrow. He's already informed me that the club is doing a birthday thing on Friday, but I'm glad that I get to spend his actual birthday with him.

Just me and him.

After I'm showered, I dress in a pair of low slung, holey jeans and an oversized shirt, letting it drape off of one shoulder. I throw my hair up in a messy bun and forego my makeup, knowing my face looks better but still not completely healed. Since I'm home alone, it doesn't matter.

Once I've gathered all of my cake ingredients, I flip the television on and look for something to watch while I bake. I settle on *Friends* reruns. They're doing some kind of marathon, and I'm excited to have something light and funny in the background as I make my husband the first birthday cake I've baked since I was eighteen years old.

While the cake is baking, I remember that Sloane said there would be a man guarding the door all day long. I pour a glass of ice water, knowing he'd probably appreciate a beer instead; nonetheless, he's getting water.

Once I make my way to the door, I open it and look to the side to see him. He's younger, probably mid-twenties, and I find myself curious as to how he's ended up in this life. Clearing my throat at him, he turns to face me and I step outside of the house as his eyes widen.

"I'm sure you're hot, or bored, or both. I wanted to at least give you some ice water," I say with a shrug.

"Thank you, ma'am," he mutters.

"Ma'am?" I say, scrunching my nose up. He winks with a smile as he takes the plastic cup from me.

"I'm not going to be heading out anywhere, today; just wanted to let you know," I smile.

He nods and turns his face to the street. I let him be, knowing Sloane probably told him not to talk to me, or to focus on his job. *Who knows.* Turning, I make my way back inside of the house right as the timer goes off, informing me that the cakes are finished.

Another episode of *Friends* comes on as the cakes cool and I start the frosting. I take out a crystal blue cake stand and place the cake on top. Then, I add a thick layer of icing for the filling before I pop the top layer directly on top.

I decorate it simplistically. Nothing fancy, just a thick layer of buttercream icing, keeping it light and clean. I find a decorating bag and dye, coloring a small amount in blue and write, *Happy Birthday Sloane* in the middle.

By the time I've finished, it's late in the evening, so I set the cake in the center of the kitchen island. Then I make my way to bed, my dinner being cake batter and buttercream frosting. Unhealthy, but delicious. I shower and dress for bed, crawling beneath the sheets and not realizing how tired my legs are after spending all day on them, until now.

I check my phone before I fall asleep and don't see any missed texts or calls. I decide to send Sloane a text, letting him know I'm going to sleep and that I love him. He texts me back just a few seconds later saying he loves me. The goofy smile that tips my lips is ridiculous.

It seems like I've just fallen asleep when I feel something heavy pressing me into the mattress. My eyes fly open and they're met with familiar green ones staring back at me. I gasp in surprise and then smile.

"Sloane," I murmur, my voice husky with sleep.

"You made me a cake," he states.

I nod as he lifts his hand and cups my cheek while his body presses me a little more into the bed.

"Happy birthday, baby," I whisper.

"Fucking, shit," he groans.

I open my mouth to say something, but his lips are on mine and his tongue fills me. Moaning, I reach up and wrap my hand around his wrist at my cheek.

"Sloane," I murmur against his mouth.

"I'm going to fuck you, then we're eating that cake in bed, naked," he announces. I feel my belly heat at his words.

"Okay," I grin.

Sloane sits back on his haunches and quickly removes my clothing and then his. I wait for him to pounce on me, but he doesn't. Instead, he traces my entire body with his fingertips. He circles each my nipples, then following the side of my breast down to my stomach.

I hold my breath when his fingers make their way to the crease of my thighs. By the time he's finished touching every inch of me, I'm a whimpering pile of need.

From his knees, he guides his dick inside of me and yanks my bottom half up, so that my lower back rests on the tops of his thighs. His eyes watch as he fills me over and over with his glistening cock. Sloane's teeth sink into his bottom lip on a growl.

"The way you take me, fuck sunshine, always so goddamn pretty," he growls.

"Baby," I whimper as my body breaks out into a sweat. I'm so close to toppling over the edge, I feel like I might actually weep.

"Fuck, Imogen. I could stay inside of you forever, baby."

"I need to come. Please, Sloane," I practically beg.

He releases my hip with one hand and presses his thumb against my clit as he continues to slowly fuck me. It's too slow, but with the added pressure of his thumb, I shiver at the sensation. Licking my lips, I ask him for more. *Harder*.

Faster. Anything.

Pushing me up the bed, he shifts so that he's above me, and then he slams inside of my body. I throw back my head with a cry as he does what I've asked him to do. He fucks me, hard, fast, and with raw determination.

"Oh, god, Sloane, holy shit," I cry as I come, my hands flying up and my nails digging into his biceps.

He grunts a few more times and then lets out a cry of his own as he fills me with his release. Sloane slumps against me, his face going straight to my neck and nuzzling me as he works to catch his breath. I take the moment, feeling his weight against me, and loving it completely as I catch my own breath.

"Fucking hell, sunshine," he murmurs against my neck.

"I could say the same," I laugh.

Sloane moves his hands under my back and rolls us over so that I'm straddling him, keeping us connected. His hands run up and down my back, and I swear I purr at the sensation.

"You okay?" I ask after a few beats of silence.

I lift my head so that I can hear his answer, and he tries to shake his head. I arch my eyebrow, and he lets out a breath.

"Your dad paid off that CHP officer to try and nail me in something illegal and send my ass back to prison. I thought it was only Bayard, but apparently it's your father in on it, too," he finally admits.

"How do you know it was my dad?" I ask in surprise.

"I asked him why he had such a hard on for me. Told him Bayard wasn't paying him anymore and I was clean as a whistle. His reply was that Bayard may not be paying him but Mr. Stewart was. Fucking shit, sunshine," he curses as he pulls me a little closer to him. "I just got you, I just got myself, and we just got back to us—a better us than we've ever had before. Last thing I need is to be thrown back in there."

Pressing my lips to his, I kiss his nerves away, or at least I try. I don't know what my father is doing, or why, but I aim to find out. I can't tell Sloane that. He'd probably try to stop me.

No, I'm going to find out exactly what my father's problem is once and for all. This isn't about me being a rebellious teen and marrying a man he doesn't approve of; this isn't about *me* at all. I have a feeling it's about much more.

Sloane smiles widely, "Let's get some of that cake, sunshine. Smells so fucking good, baby."

We spend the rest of the early morning hours of Sloane's birthday naked, in bed, eating cake. Sloane whispers that it's the most perfect birthday morning he's ever had before. We don't fall asleep until well after five in the morning.

chapter twenty-seven

Imogen

It's two days after Sloane's birthday. He's just informed me that he has to do *shit* at the clubhouse all day long. I mention in passing that I'm going to drive to Frisco and check in on his mother and also my own. My parents' summer party is just in two-week's time, and I usually help her every year with last minute details anyway.

"I don't know, Genny, that shit with that cop doesn't sit right with me. I'm not sure that I want you traveling alone like that," he murmurs.

I wrap my hand around the side of his neck. "Nothing will happen, baby. I'm just going to visit your mom and come home," I explain.

He shakes his head before his eyes meet mine. "You'll have a prospect on you."

"But—"

His jaw clenches before he speaks. "But fucking nothing. You'll have a prospect on you, Imogen. That fuck wants to rape every part of you, and I'll be damned if you're unprotected. He won't have the opportunity to even look at you sideways let alone do anything to you."

I gulp at his words. His face is set deadly serious and he looks worried. I relent. "Okay," I whisper.

"He'll follow you, but nothing more. He won't have contact with you unless it becomes eminent." I nod.

He lowers to give me a swift kiss before he squeezes my waist and tells me he loves me. Then he's out the door.

With a heavy sigh, I think about how I can ditch my guard. I shouldn't. Sloane's right. That cop is more than just a little frightening. Maybe I can talk my guard into keeping a teeny-tiny secret for me?

I need to visit my father.

Sloane won't suspect that I'm actually going to add in a trip to see my father in my visit as well. I want to know what his problem is, and why he wants my husband to go back to prison so badly that he would pay a police officer to try and catch him doing something illegal. I have no doubt that Sloane does do illegal things, but I'm not so convinced my father is actually a good man, either.

When I arrive in the city, I don't go to my mother or Kalli. I drive straight to my father's office building. Dressed in an expensive sheath dress, and even more expensive high heels, my makeup perfect—as well as my hair—I look every bit the part of Imogen Carolina Stewart-Huntington.

With my head held high, too high, I walk right past reception into the elevators. I continue right past my father's secretary, who tries to stand and chase after me, but she's too slow.

I close and lock the door to my father's office without even looking in his direction. I hear him clear his throat, and I make my way to the chair in front of his desk. I sit before I lift my gaze to meet his cold-dead one.

"Good morning, father," I state. He looks peeved. No— beyond that. He looks *pissed*.

"Can I help you?" he asks, narrowing his eyes on me, as if to intimidate me.

"You can call off your police officer. What is your exact reasoning for wishing to send my husband back to prison?"

My father's eyes widen and then he clenches his jaw. "What are you talking about?"

"Personally, I thought you were smart enough not to pay off a stupid policeman. I figured you'd at least find someone who was smart enough *not* to throw your name out there. Or one who at least doesn't threaten me with rape every time he's in my vicinity," I shrug. His face gets even redder as he becomes angrier. If I loved him the way a daughter should, I would be concerned over his heart. "Tell me what you and Graham had cooked up, and exactly why you want my husband gone, and don't bother saying it's because I can do better. We both know that you could give a shit about whatever man I have and how he treats me. This is all about something you have to gain."

I watch as he leans back slightly in his chair, smiling like a fool. "Maybe you really are my daughter," he states.

"Of course, I am. We look exactly like each other. Now, tell me, I have other shit to do today."

"Graham was going to invest in some shit he had insider

information on. He's no longer around. I assume your husband took care of him for beating the shit out of you. Too bad he couldn't have waited until the information he had came to light. Luckily, I didn't give him the account information yet," he explains.

"So all this was so you could make more of something you have plenty of—money."

He shrugs with a grin. "You can never have too much money, Imogen. In that regard, I've always wondered about your paternity. You don't crave it like I do; you don't spend it like your mother does. You seem to be content in that shitty little town, living in a house a quarter of the size of the one you can afford, and being with a man who is scum."

"Like you're not a criminal?" I ask, arching an eyebrow. "You've answered why you pushed for Graham, but not why you want to send my husband back to jail."

"I have the chance to take over a company. Its profit would be more than Graham's little scheme, and it would be a long-term investment with an infinite amount of return," he sighs. "The man is in his sixties, single and looking. He likes you, thinks you're gorgeous. He's seen you around at social things the past few years. He gets you, and he'll retire, selling his company to me for much less than it's worth. In the end, it won't matter. You'll get my money anyway, as my only child," my father explains.

Shaking my head, I press my hand to my stomach to keep from throwing up all over my father's carpeting. He's trying to pawn me off like chattel. Arranged marriages happen, especially in our circle.

If I were single, I might at least go on a date with this guy—except, he's my father's age. Not to mention, I'm very married and very in love with my husband. The manipulative way my father is trying to get what he wants is what makes me more sick than anything.

"No," I state. "Keep all your money. Write me off, give it to charity, burn it, I don't care. It doesn't matter if my husband is sent to prison or not, I'm not marrying this man. I'm married, and I'm staying married. There's no other man for me, father. I'm sorry that you don't know what it feels like to have love, but even if Sloane dies, I won't remarry. He's it for me, daddy," I whisper using a word I haven't called him since I was a child.

He flinches at the sound, and his eyes come back to me, a hint of the man I knew as a child beneath his cold stare. It leaves quickly.

"Imogen, you don't know what you're giving up. You don't know what you're keeping. I have pictures," he murmurs.

"I don't care. I love him."

I watch as he reaches into a drawer in his desk and pulls out a stack of enlarged pictures and tosses them to me. I catch them and try not to, but I look at them. It's Sloane. He's fucking a girl from behind, his eyes open. When I focus on them, I see that he's high as a kite.

"This was dated four years ago, father. I'm sorry, but this man is not the man I'm married to now," I state.

"Look at the next one," he grunts.

I flip to the next picture and look at the date. It's only a few months ago. Actually, it's the day he got out of prison. I only know the date because I distinctly remember Kip calling me the day he got out. It's burned in my memory banks. And now, the vision of him fucking that new whore who confronted me in the grocery store is also burned in my brain.

"Not four years ago," my father states. I look up to see he's grinning as my eyes fill with tears.

"Doesn't matter," I whisper through the knot in my throat. "There is so much more happening and I want to know what it is."

"It doesn't matter? I think it does, Imogen. And what? Money isn't a good enough motivation? Graham thought it was a good enough one to marry you and knock you up. He wanted my money and knew it was the only way he could get it all."

"Nope, this picture doesn't matter," I say, popping my *p* as I stand. I let all of the photos, except the one I'm holding, fall to the ground. "Call off your hounds. I'm not marrying your friend."

Without another word, I turn around and I walk out of his office, my nose not quite as high as it was when I entered. At least my tears don't fall until I'm in my car, alone.

I don't go to Kalli's or to my mothers. I decide to go to my home. I'm meeting the real estate agent at five this evening to have her take photographs so that she can list it for me to sell.

Right now, I just want to be alone. I power down my phone as I pull into the garage and close the door. I slip my shoes off as I walk straight to the master bedroom, and I pull back the sheets before I crawl beneath them and wrap them around my body.

The man watching me probably calls Sloane immediately, but I don't care. I need to be alone for a little while. I need to cry and maybe scream. I need to process.

I cry, but I don't scream.

I sob and wail. I knew he'd been with the girl before we officially got back together, but seeing it, seeing his eyes looking clear of drugs and sober as he fucks her. It tears another piece of my heart out of my chest. I grip the picture in my hand. I don't plan on holding any of this against him, but fuck—it hurts.

I'll be okay in a little while, only because I know that this man in the photograph is not the Sloane I've had for weeks. Eventually, I fall asleep from my crying jag, thankful for the break from my tears.

Soar

Dialing my mother, I can't help that sick feeling in the pit of my stomach that something is wrong. I've texted and called Imogen about ten times, but her phone goes straight to voicemail and all messages are unread. Something is wrong.

I should have had a prospect with her when she's gone into the city today. Not just following her, but with her person. It was fucking stupid of me not to. I don't think anything has really happened, the prospect would have called me. I decide to check in with my mother before bothering him.

"Sloane?" my mother asks, sounding fairly chipper.

"Looking for Imogen. She come by to see you yet?" I bark, unable to exchange pleasantries with my mom, not until I know where my sunshine is.

"I wasn't aware that she was to come by today."

I curse, running my hand through my hair as I start to pace. I explain that she said she was going to the city today to meet with her mom about that stupid fucking party, and then she said she was going to check on her.

"You don't think something's happened, do you? I've been home all day," my mother says, sounding worried. I'm beyond worried. I'm downright panicked, and I'm too far away to do anything.

I thank her, and she tells me to keep her informed and that if she can help to just let her know. She sounds nothing like the mother I remember, and I can't help but be grateful that my piece of shit father is finally dead. My mother hasn't sounded so lucid in the early afternoon as she has the past few times I've called her. Maybe there's something salvage-able between us. I hope so, for my children's sake.

The prospect doesn't answer my call, and I bark at his voicemail, instructing him to call me immediately before I start to walk toward the front door. Texas' hand wraps around my shoulder and clamps down just as I take a step to leave.

"Where're ya goin'?" he asks.

"I can't get a hold of Genny. She's not where she's sup-posed to be, her phone's off, and the prospect I had on her didn't answer my call," I state, trying to shake him off.

"Have Camo drive you. Last thing you need to do is lay your bike down because your head is not in the right place."

I look up to Camo, who is standing beside him, and I nod in agreement. My gut churns, knowing down to my bones that something is not right. Even at her most pissed off at me, Imogen has always, always been reachable—if even only by text.

Camo and I run to his truck. He starts the engine and pulls out, sending his tires spinning, dirt and gravel flying everywhere before he speaks, "Where are we going?"

"Frisco, fast as you can without getting pulled over," I announce.

He nods and, thankfully, doesn't say anything else. I spend the ride calling her mother, who, like mine, hasn't heard anything from Genny. I then dial the prospect's number over and over again. *Goddammit, where the fuck is my wife?* I close my eyes and try to calm myself down, try to keep from crawling out of my own skin with worry.

"That guy who hurt her isn't an issue anymore, remember that brother," Camo murmurs next to me.

My eyes pop open and I turn to him, giving him a chin lift, afraid to speak. Yeah, Graham may not be a problem anymore, but that doesn't mean that she's one hundred percent safe. That fucking cop has been sniffing around and making threats.

She's *Imogen Huntington*. Someone who wants money could hold her hostage or hurt her. In fact, her father could do all of those things to get whatever he wants from her, since he obviously wants *something*.

The rest of the ride is in complete silence. When I see the city in sight, my heart starts to pound in my chest with panic. I don't know where I'm going to tell Camo to go. Maybe we'll try her father's office first, then go from there. Maybe I can scare the absolute fucking shit out of the old man.

"Where to?" Camo asks.

I give him the address to Genny's father's office building and then help him with navigating downtown Frisco. Once we're parked in the garage, I slide out, checking to make sure my gun is at the small of my back. Camo slams his door, and I look over at him in question.

"You stay here," I grunt.

He chuckles, shaking his head, "No way in fuck am I letting you go in there alone. You're a loose cannon, brother," he murmurs.

I lift my chin and start to walk toward the building's entrance. I can hear him behind me, his boots heavy and pounding the floor with each step.

I ignore the girl at the front desk and walk straight over to the elevators, stepping inside and pressing the button I know will lead me to Stewart's floor. Camo and I don't speak as we ride up.

Once the doors ping open, we step out and make our way over to Stewart's office. The door is open and the secretary is gone, probably to lunch. I turn the knob and walk inside of my father-in-law's office.

Unfortunately, I walk in on him fucking his missing secretary. His head pops up, as does hers, and she lets out a scream as she tries to cover her naked tits. She's sitting on his lap, reverse cowgirl, so I get a full view of her young, naked body. Fuck me, it's like he and my dad are the same goddamn man.

I watch as she stands and gathers her dress, covering herself as she slips into the bathroom that I know must be to the left of me. All of these big offices have bathrooms in them. I know my own father's did.

These uptight fucks are too pretentious to share one ounce of space with anybody else, even while they're taking a shit.

"How may I help you today, Sloane?" he asks, tucking his dick back into his pants and pulling them over his hips.

"Where's my wife?" I growl.

I watch as his eyes widen in surprise. Then he smiles and laughs. "She finally left you this time, then?"

Shaking my head, I pull my gun out and point it at him.

"Don't move," I warn as he reaches out, no doubt to call security or his cop buddy. "Where the fuck is my fucking wife?"

"You're worthless, an absolutely fucking worthless thug," he grinds through a clenched jaw.

"Like I've ever cared what you think of me," I growl, taking a step forward. "Where is my wife?"

He smiles. When he does, he looks like the cocksucking snake he is. "Not sure where she could be. With access to her trust, she could be anywhere by now. I made sure she had a parting photograph of you to always keep with her."

"Photograph?" I ask, gripping my gun tighter, grappling with the war inside of my head.

Part of me wants to pull the trigger, the other part knows he isn't worth shit. He definitely isn't worth going back to the pen over. Killing Graham and having my contact cover it up is one thing. He's nobody but some rich asshole who works for his daddy. Stewart is a completely different story.

"Oh, you didn't know that I've had a PI following you since you said *I do*? I should give him a raise. He's obviously good at his job. I have pictures of you and all of your whores, Sloane. I knew they'd come in handy eventually. Imogen was visibly upset at the picture of you and your coming home party fuck," he says, smiling widely.

"You didn't," I rumble.

"Why wouldn't I? She's useful to me, and I need her. I'll do whatever I have to. It's not like I forced you to fuck that young thing. You did that all on your own," he laughs.

My phone rings in my pocket, and I reach for it, my eyes never leaving Stewart's. I answer without looking at the caller ID. My mother's voice is on the other line, and the three words she says to me makes my heart ramp back up again.

Relief floods my entire body—*I found her.* Thanking her, I end the call and then finish this shit with Imogen's father once and for all.

"Leave my wife alone. She's mine. She's not yours anymore. She hasn't been since she was eighteen years old. Whatever game you want to use her as your pawn in, forget it," I state. "And call that fuckhead cop off of me and her."

"Or what?" he asks, arching his brow.

"You think you're the only one who can play games, old man? I meant it when I said you didn't scare me when I was a teenager, and you still don't. I know what you love and I know how to take it from you, piece by piece," I murmur.

He smirks, cockiness written all over his face, but I can see the fear behind his eyes. "I don't love anyone," he shrugs. I know he doesn't love any*one.* I'm not an idiot—not completely, anyway.

"I know you don't love any*one.* I know *what* you love, so watch yourself," I say, shoving my gun back in my jeans.

Turning around to walk away from him, Camo at my heels, I hear him spouting something. I don't give much of a shit about what he has to say. He fucks with me or Imogen one more time, and I'm tearing down his precious company and stripping him of his cash—penny by penny if I have to.

"Do you remember where Genny's house is?" I ask as Camo and I slide into his pickup truck.

He nods. "Yeah."

"My mom called while we were in there, that's where she is," I say.

Camo drives toward Genny's and I stay silent, thinking. I'm sure seeing me and Destini upset her; it would anyone, but she knew it happened. I can only hope that she doesn't hold it against me. When we pull up to the house, I'm surprised to see the prospect leaning against the front door. "The fuck?" I whisper.

"He ain't gonna earn a cut anytime soon," Camo mutters as he throws the car in park.

We both get out and I march up to the little fuck. He's playing a goddamn game on his phone. Silently I reach back and punch him in the side of the head. "Take care of this weak punk," I announce before I pound on the fucking door with my fist.

chapter twenty-eight

Imogen

A knocking sound startles me awake, and I roll over to see my mother-in-law, Kalli, standing at my back porch door. Her hand is on her hip, and her glasses are focused directly on me. I don't know how she got on my back deck, but I don't question it. She's Kalli Huntington. She gets whatever she wants, no matter what that is. If she can't do it herself, she hires it done. Slipping out of bed, I stumble over to the door and open it, not waiting to see if she walks in or not before I turn around and crawl back to my comfortable bed.

"Well, now, this is new," she states as she sits down in the chair across from me, crossing her legs. I glance at the red-soles of her low heels and focus on that, instead of her face. "You want to tell me what my son did to make you run from him?"

My eyes snap up to hers, and I reach down to the photograph that's on the floor and hold it out for her. She gently removes it from my hand, and I hear her hum as she takes in the way her son is fucking that whore. That *young* whore. Maybe her age shouldn't affect me so much. He's always fucked whores and, in general, they're all fairly young. Perhaps it stings a little more because my father and Graham both made mention of how I'm now *old*.

"I can understand why you unplugged and hid out here," she says. "Who gave this to you?"

I shift my eyes away from her before I bring them back and answer, "My father."

"Why do you think he did that?" she asks, sounding far too sober and logical for my taste.

I have a feeling she only has more to say, and she knows the answer anyway.

"He wants me to leave him and marry some sixty-year old guy, so that he can take over his business. He's willing to sell his business to my father, but the trade-off is me."

She snorts and shakes her head, "You're playing perfectly into your father's hands."

I agree, knowing that she's right; that is, if I were going to leave Sloane over this. If infidelity was a sole reason to leave, I would have left a long time ago. Unfortunately, I'm too stupid in love with Sloane, and I always have been. I knew he'd been with this girl, the way he brushed me off when I confronted him about it after she spewed her nonsense in the grocery store, he couldn't deny it. It doesn't take away the hurt at having it shoved in my face, yet again.

"I'm not leaving, Sloane. I just needed some time to be alone," I shrug.

"You know that this man, fresh out of prison, he is not the man you have now, don't you?" she asks.

I nod, releasing a long exhale. I know she's right, and yet, that doesn't make my heart or my stomach stop twisting and aching. "I know."

A loud pounding on the front door makes me jump, and my eyes widen as she gives me a small smile. To her credit, she looks at least a bit sorry. I know she must have called Sloane. Though how he made it here that fast, I don't know.

"Work it out," she says, reaching to take my hand as I sit up in the bed. She gives my hand a squeeze as she stands, and then she walks toward the front door.

I know she's going to let Sloane into the house. I'm stuck in my spot. Sitting on the edge of the bed, my breathing shallow as I wait for Sloane to appear.

My eyes stay trained to the ground in front of me as his shadow darkens my vision. I don't look up. I can't. If I do, then I'll surely cry.

Sloane doesn't give me an opportunity to not look at him. He falls down to his knees in front of me and cups my cheeks with his hands, gently forcing my face up. When my eyes meet his light green ones, the tears fill them. I'm unable to control my tears or my trembling bottom lip.

"Sunshine," he rasps.

I shake my head as I try to control myself. I don't want to hear anything, no apologies, no promises, no *more*. "I'm tired of hurting," I whisper truthfully.

"If I could take it back, if I could take them all back, I would. Fuck, baby, I would take it all back—every single one of them. None of them mean anything to me. I don't even…"

I stop him before he continues. "Don't tell me that they

322

meant nothing to you, or that you can't remember them. It just makes me feel even shitter. Because if I was something to you, if I meant anything to you, you wouldn't have done that to me. If they meant nothing, then you wouldn't have been with them—especially if I meant even the slightest bit of *anything* to you," I whisper.

"It wasn't ever about them. Fucking shit, it was about the dope. *It's always been the goddamn high*," he practically screams, his eyes showing every ounce of pain. "Christ, sunshine. Don't do this. I can't excuse my actions, but baby, you know—you know that I would change all that shit if I could."

His thumbs wipe my falling tears away, and I allow him because I love him. I always have and I always will. Even if that love sometimes hurts, apparently, I'll take the pain. For whatever reason, I go back for more, again and again.

"I know, Sloane. I love you so much and seeing that picture hurt. I just needed a few hours to wallow in my own bullshit. I'm okay now," I say, giving him a smile.

"Never again, sunshine. Since getting back with you, I haven't touched another woman. I swear to you, baby. I wouldn't lie about that, not ever again," he murmurs.

Reaching up, I cup his cheek. "I know. I believe you and I trust you," I whisper. "I'm not mad. It was a surprise to see, and it knocked me on my ass for a minute. I'm okay."

I close my eyes and gasp when his lips touch mine. He kisses me sweetly, gently, and he doesn't push further, his teeth nipping my bottom lip before he pulls away and rests his forehead against mine.

"I love you, Imogen. I want to erase that part of my past, not for me, but for you. It kills me that I hurt you for so long. I was nothing but a selfish bastard, always looking for a high of some kind. I never wanted to lose you, either. You grounded me to some degree. I treated you like shit for so fucking long, and I'm so goddamn sorry, sunshine. All these years, and I wasted them, fucking wasted them and hurt the shit out of you."

"I love you, too, Sloane. When you're alone with me, and you're *my Sloane*. It's hard for me to love Soar, but I'm starting to," I admit.

He lets out a heavy breath and his hands move from my face to the outsides of my thighs. He pushes my dress up to my hips. I suck in a breath when his hands move to my ass and he pulls me to the edge of the bed. His mouth opens, and he blows hot air on the material of my panties, on my center. He nips me, and then he sucks. I feel his tongue press against my clit, causing me to moan and fist my fingers in his hair.

Without a word, he hooks his fingers in my panties and pulls them down my legs as he sits back slightly. Then his face is back at my core, and his tongue flicks my clit before it fills my pussy.

"Sloane," I gasp, fisting my fingers in his hair as I push myself closer to his mouth.

He lifts my legs and throws them over his shoulders as his hands cup my ass. He pulls me, angling me, and I use my grip in his hair to keep myself upright as I ride his face.

Moaning, Sloane's fingers dig into my ass a little harder. His tongue works me, fucking me, and then nipping and licking before flicking my clit. It feels so good, and I have no problem chasing my orgasm as I grind against his face, his eyes focused on mine. When I come, it's with a long moan.

I fall back once he releases me, my legs as limp as the rest of my body. I don't hear him unbuckle, unzip, or the sound of his pants falling, but I do feel him when he slides inside of my wet center. I lift my legs, wrapping them higher around his waist as my eyes flutter open to look into his.

"I love you, sunshine," he murmurs as he slowly pulls out of me before he sinks back inside.

I open my mouth, but he doesn't allow me to speak. He interrupts me. Every time he sinks down inside of me, he tells me he loves me. Every single time. I can do nothing but watch him, watch the way he looks at me, watch his eyes, how they hide absolutely nothing and shine with love.

"Come on my cock, baby," he rasps. I feel his arms trembling above me, and his *I love yous* become more strained.

Lifting my legs a little higher, he grinds against my clit with his pelvis. It sends me over the edge. My pussy clamps down around him while I whimper through my release, and then he fucks me without restraint.

I accept every thrust from his hips, every slam against my center; and when he throws back his head with his release, he calls my name as he comes. Then he slumps forward and nuzzles my neck with his face.

"I love you," he rasps, again.

"Love you, too, Sloane," I murmur as my fingers trail up and down his slick back.

He lifts his head and his eyes connect with mine before he speaks. "You coming home with me tonight?"

Using my finger, I trace his lips, and I smile. "Yes, baby, I'm coming home with you tonight. After the real estate agent leaves."

"Real Estate agent?" he asks, looking confused.

"I wasn't coming here just to meet with my father, your mother, and mine. I was putting this place up on the market, too," I shrug. "I don't want it anymore."

"No shit?" he asks, looking surprised.

Shaking my head with a small laugh I repeat, "No shit."

Camo left, with the prospect in tow, while we were in the middle of making up, leaving me a text that he was headed back up north. My mother left before I even walked into the house. She hugged me, told me I had been an asshole, and to fix my shit before she turned away without a backward glance.

Imogen and I clean up, and I watch her make the bed so that it looks showroom ready again. Once she slips her shoes back on, I reach out for her from the corner chair in the room and tug her down to my lap.

"Sloane?"

"I really am so damn sorry, sunshine," I confess. She nods once, her tongue peeking out to taste her lips.

"I know you are. No more apologizing. What's done is done. Now we just move on," she states. I wrap a hand around the back of her neck and tug her face closer to mine.

"Never. Again," I grind out.

"Baby…" She doesn't finish her sentence because I press my lips to hers and push my tongue into her mouth to taste her, my sweet wife.

"I hope you're still this in love with me when I'm as big as a house and nine months pregnant," she grins with a wink.

I throw back my head in laughter as she narrows her eyes on me, but I'm unable to control myself. She's too fucking hilarious for words.

"Guaranteed, Imogen, you'll be the sexiest pregnant woman I have ever laid eyes on. Let's get you pregnant so I can prove that shit to you," I grin.

She opens her mouth to reply, but the doorbell rings. She huffs and slides off of my lap. I watch her sweet ass as it flounces to the front door, I walk the entire way watching her ass and smiling.

This is my wife, my woman, and my sunshine. A woman who forgives me of my sins, but isn't afraid to tell me her worries. She's not afraid to take yet another leap of faith with me. She embraces all that is me. All that is us.

Once the real estate agent is finished photographing the house, we walk to the garage and I slip Imogen's car keys from her hand. I also ask her for the picture her father gave her. She hands it over as she presses her lips together, and I don't hesitate to take the lighter out of my pocket and light the fucker on fire. Once it's completely burned, I stomp on it to put out the fire.

"You want to visit your mom before we head home?" I ask as I start the engine of her car.

This is the next thing to go. It isn't as safe for her to have this in the mountains. She needs a *Land Rover* or something more suitable for the snow.

"Not really. I'll just call her," she murmurs.

I wrap my hand around her thigh and give her a squeeze, "Not a problem, sunshine, if you want to go see your mom."

"I know, I just—I don't feel like seeing anybody. I just want to go to bed with you," she grins as she turns to me, her eyes looking soft and inviting.

I drive in silence for at least an hour, maybe two, my eyes

slicing over to her a few times to see her in the same position, her head turned to the side, looking out the window. She's watching the scenery, and it's starting to change from the city to the mountains. Maybe she's regretting coming back with me.

"Tomorrow's the birthday party," I say, afraid of her reaction.

Smiling, she turns her head to face me and she nods. "I have the perfect outfit."

"Not worried about your clothes, sunshine. I'm concerned about everything that happened today, and if you're going to be all right there?"

She frowns slightly before she lifts her chin. Her hand comes out to squeeze my thigh. With a heavy sigh, she finally speaks. "The club isn't my favorite part of our lives. The man you have to be, the assuredly illegal things you do, I don't love it. Most of the men and the women, aside from the whores, that aspect I enjoy. They're more of a family than we've ever had. There's more love there than we've ever had from our own blood relatives.

"So, I guess, I understand it. I hated what it turned you into, but looking back, it wasn't the club that turned you into anything. You did it to yourself. It wouldn't have mattered if you were working in your father's office or not. You were going to look for new highs, however they came. I've forgiven the club, and I'm trying to focus on all of the positive aspects of it. I still might take that little bitch to the ground, though," she shrugs.

I can't help myself, I chuckle at her words as I give her knee another squeeze. I love her, all of her, every single part of her. I can't imagine my life without her. I can only hope that she always feels the same, and that I can make her half as happy as she makes me.

"No need to knock a bitch out, sunshine. I'm all yours. I was searching, back then. I didn't know what I was searching for, but I didn't feel like I'd found it. I was scared of turning into my father, but I did anyway. The drugs and the women, fuck me, I turned out exactly like him," he takes a breath before he continues, "But swear to fuck, when I dried out and got my head out of my ass, those were the best moments of my life. Just you and me, like this."

She huffs and narrows her eyes at me. "It's not that. It actually has very little to do with you, and very much to do her, being a complete bitch." She whispers her next words. "You're not your father, Sloane. Please believe that. I agree that you were searching and you didn't know how to find what you needed."

"Okay, sunshine," I murmur. "Some days, I look in the mirror, and all I see is his reflection staring back at me. When I would look in your eyes and see that hurt I'd caused, all I could picture was the look my mother always wore. Staying clean and sober, it seemed like the best thing to do, and fuck, I tried. But I wasn't strong enough back then. I was weak," I smile sadly.

She reaches across the seat and wraps her hand around my thigh, giving me a squeeze. "He can't hurt you anymore, Sloane. You aren't him, I'm not Kalli, and he's gone," she whispers. "You're a man now."

"I am, that," I agree.

"You're not weak anymore." she states.

Shaking my head, I pull over on the side of the road before I turn to her. "Sunshine. I'm the opposite of weak, now."

Imogen reaches up and wraps her hand around the side of my neck as her eyes take me in. "I see that, Sloane. I believe you and I trust you," she whispers.

Her words wash over me and I grin. "You can beat Destini's ass, though. I'll even watch. Fair warning, after you fuck her up, I'm going to need to *fuck* you," I state, changing the subject as I pull back onto the road and head toward home.

"*Sloane*," she says, feigning a gasp of surprise.

"Seriously, baby. You beating the shit out of some little whore, all because she said some shit about me, about her and me? It's bound to make me hard as nails."

"Fine, if I ever stoop to that level, you can fuck me in the bar," she shrugs.

I swerve the car to the side of the road and slam on the breaks. Turning to face her, I see that she's giggling, her face red and her eyes widened in surprise.

"You want that? You don't have to make bets, sunshine," I murmur, my eyes boring straight into hers. She takes a gulp and looks down.

"No, I mean, no," she shakes her head. "I'm not brave enough," she says.

"Whatever you want like that, if you want to try anything, you just ask me, baby," I mutter.

"Okay," she breathes.

Christ. I turn back to the front windshield and drive us home, my cock hard the entire time. Once we're back at our house, I pick Imogen up and carry her to the bedroom, demanding that she rides me slow and hard.

My woman delivers. My woman always delivers.

After we've both come, I hold her as she sleeps. I can't

imagine her fucking me in the bar, in public, at the clubhouse. Maybe she'd enjoy watching others do it? I always keep her on the other side when we're there, away from the real parties.

Sure, she could turn her head and see some stuff, but she doesn't know that if we walked into one of the other rooms off of the main one, that's where the orgies are, where people fuck each other; where there are no rules. You walk into that room, and everything is fair game.

Yeah, Grease and Serina put on a little show, and sometimes guys get their dicks sucked or have a whore ride them in the main bar area, but the other room is where the serious action happens. The other guys keep their wives away from that room, and I doubt any of them even know it exists. Maybe after our friends leave next time we're there, I'll take her in there, not to participate, but to watch.

I grin—*Happy fucking birthday to me.*

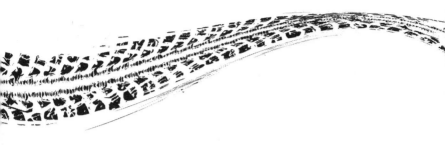

chapter twenty-nine

Imogen

*F*ace—healed.
    Makeup—flawless.
Dress—skin tight.
Heels—sky high and expensive.
Husband—waiting.

Everything is in place to leave, and yet I find myself staring into the mirror. I don't know why, but I feel anxious. Maybe it's because of everything that happened when I went to the city, or maybe it's just me being a complete wuss.

"Sunshine, you ready?" he asks, rapping on the bathroom door.

I take in a deep breath and tell him yes before I open the door. He's standing on the other side, his eyes dragging from my black Louboutins to my bright red, bandage, strapless, mini dress with a thick gold zipper that is the entire length of the front. Then he scans my hair, long and in soft waves, his eyes take in my face before they finally settle on my gaze.

"Maybe we should stay home?" he grunts.

"Not this again. Let's go," I state, turning to grab my purse from the counter before I start to walk toward him.

He doesn't move. I stand just inches away from him, waiting for him to step back. He doesn't. Instead, he lifts his hand to tangle it in the back of my hair. He tugs me closer, forcing me to press my body against his. I grab hold of his hips to keep from falling down. His nose skims alongside mine, and his breath fans my face in a sigh.

"So beautiful. I don't deserve you at all, sunshine," he whispers. I close my eyes and let out a breath of my own at his words. "I want to give you the world; not just shit we can both afford, but the shit that's priceless. A family, love, and happiness."

I feel my eyes watering, but I beat back the tears, not wanting to have to re-do my entire face before we leave. I inhale deeply, trying to keep from crying as he tugs my hair slightly, forcing my head back so that I'm looking into his green eyes.

"I love you, Sloane," I whisper.

"Love you, too, baby," he murmurs before he presses his lips to mine softly, careful not to smear my red lipstick. "Let's get going, so I can fuck you later."

A thrill shimmies up and down my spine at the thought. The last time we were in his room at the club, he gave me so many orgasms, I swear it took me a full week to recoup. It was fantastic.

I smile and nod as his hand slides from my hair down my

spine, running over my lower back before he gabs ahold of my ass, giving it a rough squeeze with a grunt.

We take his car, and I am so thankful he isn't making me ride his bike in this dress. I honestly don't think it would even stretch enough for me to straddle his seat. Sloane's fingers tease the inside of my thigh, and I let out a trembling exhale, wishing for them to travel further up my leg. They don't.

The clubhouse parking lot is packed full, and I wonder just who the hell is here. It seems like way too many cars, trucks, and bikes. I turn to Sloane and he is looking around the parking lot as well, except he doesn't look confused.

"This is a lot of people," I mention, trying to figure out what's happening.

"It's a party, baby—an *open* party," he shrugs as he opens the door and climbs out.

He walks over to my side and helps me out of the car, but he doesn't allow me to even take a step before he's picking me up and cradling me in his arms.

My eyes widen in surprise as I let out a yelp. "What are you doing?"

"Expensive shoes. I know them when I see them, sunshine."

I wrap my arms around his shoulders, pulling myself closer and resting my head against his shoulder as I press my lips to the underside of his jaw. *My sweet, rough man*—a thought I didn't think I would ever have about Sloane Huntington.

"Kippy called me yesterday," he mentions as he walks. I wait for him to continue. "He sounds better. Now that he's away and he can tell mom's doing okay, he seems more at ease."

"Poor Kip. That was a lot to happen at once," I murmur.

He grins and holds me a little tighter. "He contacted a sibling. She's only a year younger than me," he rumbles.

"Seriously?" I cry.

"Didn't even know who dad was. Didn't know who her own father was. I told Kip, though he was an asshole, at least we knew where we came from," he murmurs. "You call him on Sunday, maybe, talk to him. You guys have a special relationship. Make sure he's really doing okay for me."

I smile, pressing my lips to the underside of his jaw again before peeking my tongue out to taste his skin. As always, he tastes delicious as all hell. He squeezes me close then sets me down on my feet at the entrance to the clubhouse.

I see the prospect leaning against the building, the same one that I gave ice water to a few days ago. I smile at him, but he ignores me and looks from me to Sloane, with a little fear in his eyes.

Once we're inside, I instantly feel claustrophobic. Since I wasn't one for MC parties, I have never been to one like this before. I came to some of the family things, but in general, if I wasn't hanging out with the other Old Ladies, I wasn't anywhere near this place.

Sloane wraps his hand around mine and tugs me forward. He then turns to me and leans down to whisper in my ear. "I should have made sure your brand was visible. Sorry, sunshine. You have to stick to my side all night long, no matter what."

I shiver at his warning and nod, my hand gripping his a little tighter than before as I plaster the front of my body to the back of his. I feel like a doe caught in headlights as I look around at the crush of people. They're everywhere, and I don't recognize any of them. That is, until they part a little bit and I'm brought over to the same corner where the couples always are and I see my friends. All except Ivy.

My brow furrows as I look for her.

"Ivy's not feeling well," Colleen states. "And Teeny is on bedrest."

Sloane thrusts a beer in my hand, and I turn from Colleen to thank him. I don't even get to say the words because his lips touch mine and his hand travels down to my ass and gives it a squeeze. I can't help the squeak that escapes me. Sloane pulls me down on his lap. We spend the evening talking to our friends. The music is loud, and the smell of pot wafts through the air.

I keep glancing up at Sloane to see if he seems edgy or needy for drugs, but he's acting completely normal, aloof, and relaxed. I find myself relaxing even more.

This is the second party we've been to since he's been clean. I can't help the smile that forms on my lips that this man, this version of Sloane, seems as though he's here to stay.

Mary-Anne and I chat about her new baby boy a little, but she asks MadDog to take her home early, due to the amount of smoke that's quickly filling the room.

Texas and Colleen are next to leave, and then Torch and Cleo. I can tell Cleo is tired as she yawns and rubs her belly. Once they've all left, Sloane turns us toward the crazy part of the room. There are naked women walking around everywhere.

We walk over to the pool tables, and I'm not surprised to see Grease fucking Serina from behind as she sucks some stranger's dick. It's when I notice that Grease is actually fucking her ass, because there's another man beneath her, that my eyes widen.

Sloane walks us over to the bar. Even though it's extremely crowded, he has beers in his hand, along with a couple of shots that are placed on the bar top, almost immediately. I reach for the shots and take one, watching as he does as well before he hands me my beer.

He then presses his palm to my lower back and pushes me through the crowd. I drink my beer, wondering where on earth we're going when we pass the pool tables, the sofas that are against the wall, and then turn left down a hallway that I've never been to before.

I know that the whore's rooms are down here, so it's not like I've ever wished to come down here; but I'm surprised to see a big room off to the left. I'm even more surprised by the activities happening inside of this room.

There are naked people everywhere. Not one person has clothes on, except for a few people who are sitting on the leather sofas that line two of the four walls. There is plush carpeting and a few lounge chairs that people are screwing on in the middle of the room. Most, but not all, are with multiple partners, and it makes me wonder what exactly is happening here.

"Sloane?" I whisper, my voice strained with worry.

"We're just gonna watch, baby," he murmurs as he presses his lips to my forehead and guides me over to a sofa. He doesn't let me sit. He pulls me down across his lap. "You mentioned what you did about Destini and the bar. I'm not sure I could fuck you in the bar like that, or even in here. If you wanted me to, I would, but I think you said that more out of shock value," he says, whispering against my shoulder, his lips touching me with each word he speaks. "But I thought maybe you might want to watch a little."

"Sloane," I say shakily.

"See those three in the middle?" he mutters.

My eyes turn to the four people in the middle of the room. It's a whore I've seen before. I can't remember her name, but she was here before I left three years ago. She's lying down with a man fucking her pussy. There's a woman sitting on her face as she eats her out. Then there's another man sucking on the girl who riding the whore's face.

"I'm sure you like that," I snort, thinking about how any man would love two women.

"Mmm, I couldn't let another man touch you. I'd be too fucking jealous," he grunts against my shoulder before he nips my skin with his teeth.

"The feeling is mutual," I state.

I feel his fingertips grazing the inside of my thigh, and then he wrenches my panties to the side as he slips two fingers inside of me. His tongue tastes my shoulder before he moves up to my neck, behind my ear and kisses me there.

"You like watching, though," he whispers.

I lift one of my legs higher to give him more room, without showing everybody my center. I don't answer, because it's true. Seeing these people, their inhibitions shoved to the side as they pleasure each other, it's sexy as hell.

"Will you come when they do?" he asks.

I whimper, my breathing shallowing as his fingers curl inside of me. I watch the three of them, the woman riding the whore's face throws back her head as she starts to shake, her orgasm on the cusp of imploding. The man groans as he starts to thrust into the whore harder.

"Sloane," I gasp as his thumb presses against my clit,

applying pressure as he fucks me with his fingers.

Nipping my shoulder, he tells me to come, and I do right as I hear the man groan and the woman cry out with her own release. "If we don't go to my room, I'm two seconds from fucking you right here and not giving a flying fuck who watches."

I stand and hold out my hand for him as I adjust my tiny dress. I pull him toward his room as fast as my high heels will take me. Once we're at his door, he presses me against it, his hips pressed close to my lower back as he pushes his hard cock against me. "I'm going to fuck you until you scream, sunshine," he murmurs.

"Yes, please," I whimper as I reach for the handle of the door.

He moans as his teeth sink into the lobe of my ear. "Maybe I'll just fuck you right here, take you in the hall against this door?"

"Please do," a voice laughs from behind us.

It's like cold water is being doused over my entire body.

I close my eyes and curse to myself as soon as I realize who just spoke. I don't turn completely around; my cock is hard and this cunt isn't worth my full attention. I tip my head to the side before I speak to her, feeling Imogen stiffen beneath me.

"Don't you have some cock to suck?" I ask.

"Are you offering, baby?" she coos.

339

I laugh. It causes my entire body to shake, but this bitch is pretty hilarious. "Bitch, I'm not offering you fucking shit. Take your little ass right on out of here. Learn when a man doesn't want you, especially when a patched *Devil* doesn't want you. You don't learn that really quickly, you'll find your whore ass working a street corner instead of being in a nice warm clubhouse. Now get the fuck out of the hallway before I march your raggedy ass out."

I turn my head away from her, not wishing to see her reaction, mainly because I don't give a fuck about her. I care about the woman in my arms, who is still stiff as a fucking board. I turn the handle of my door, pushing us inside before I slam it behind me and flip the lock closed.

"Sunshine," I murmur.

She turns around to face me, her eyes bright and her smile wide. Then she laughs. It's absolutely stunning.

"I wish that I could have seen her face," she giggles as she shakes her head.

I grunt and grin at the same time, loving how happy she looks as she laughs. The heat has left, but I don't mind. I'll have fun building it back up again. Personally, I'm enjoying her smile and the fact that she didn't let that whore get to her.

My eyes widen when she starts to unzip her dress. When she's finished, it falls to the floor and she's standing in front of me wearing her heels, black lacy panties, and a black strapless bra. My mouth goes fucking dry.

"Come on," she says lifting her chin.

I shake my head as I strip out of my clothes, and then I stalk toward her, wrapping my hands around her small waist. "Can't wait to make you scream, baby."

340

She grins before she whispers, "I'm planning on it. I'm planning on this whole building knowing you're making your wife come."

"Fuck, yeah," I grunt before I press my lips to hers, hard.

My fucking wife, so goddamn hot it sends a shot of fire down my spine.

Unhooking her bra, I let it fall to the ground before I pull her panties down. She steps out of the lacey material as I back her up against the edge of the bed.

My cock is close to exploding, and I close my eyes to try and calm myself down. I need her to torture me a little the way she likes, on top and with full reign.

"Ride me, baby. I want to watch you," I murmur as my lips travel down her neck.

I bend a little further to draw one of her breasts into my mouth, sucking on her nipple before I flick the hardened bud with my tongue.

"Yes," she hisses.

I release her with a pop and climb onto the bed, holding out my hand for her. She slips hers inside as she climbs over me, lining my cock with her slick, hot entrance.

I let my hands glide up her sides and cup her breasts, pinching and tugging on her nipples as she sinks down on top of me, taking my cock deep inside of her tight body. She doesn't move, and I'm grateful for it, knowing I'm seconds away from exploding too early inside of her.

"Ride me nice and slow, sunshine," I whisper, my jaw clenched tightly. "I want you to come again. Make yourself. Use me."

"Sloane," she says, trembling above me as she starts to roll her hips.

Imogen gives me a goddamn show to top any other show she's ever given me. She fucking tortures me, and I let her. It's the most beautiful torture I've ever received. My woman, my wife, enjoying my cock—a cock that is, for the rest of our lives, only hers.

chapter thirty

Imogen

The warm weight against my back is suddenly ripped from me, and my eyes widen as I let out a short scream. Sloane is being hauled out of bed by a police officer. I pull the sheets up my body to cover myself as best as I can.

There are several police surrounding us in the room, and one of them tosses a folded blue paper at me. I recognize him as the highway patrol officer, Houston. I open the to see it's a warrant.

"What is this?" I ask quietly.

"We have reason to believe that these men are transporting illegal arms and drugs. This is a warrant to search the premises."

I hear Sloane grunt from his place on the floor, an officer's knee lodged in his back. "Can I get some fucking pants on at least?" he growls.

Another officer throws a pair of pants in his face, and I hear his muffled words. "You need to get up, ma'am. We're starting here, first," an officer says, his eyes pinned to where my hand is holding the navy blue sheet against my naked breasts.

"Can I please have some privacy to put some clothes on?" I ask.

I watch as three of the officers smirk, including Houston. One flat out smiles, and another has the nerve to look at me with pity.

"Sorry, sweetheart, no can-do. We don't want you trying to cover anything up for your husband now, do we?" Houston states.

I open my mouth to speak, unsure of what I'm going to say, when Sloane's enraged yell fills the room. "You fucking pieces of shit. Let my wife fucking put some clothes on. You know she knows fucking nothing about anything. She's innocent."

I watch as Houston kicks Sloane in his ribs, causing him to groan. "Shut your fucking mouth, convict."

"It's okay," I whisper as I close my eyes and take a gulp of air, trying to get some damn balls.

The only man who has ever seen me naked is my husband. Now, I'm about to show it all, every single part of me, to a room full of police officers.

I stand on shaky legs with the sheet still wrapped around me, hoping I can get past these men to the drawer of Sloane's nightstand, where I know he has at least a t-shirt and maybe even gym shorts stowed away. Maybe I can get by without showing anything at all.

As soon as I'm standing, Houston reaches out and grabs

the sheet, yanking it from my body and forcing me to stand, shocked and frozen still, in front of them. I hear Sloane rustling around on the ground, but I can't look anywhere but at the officer in front of me.

"Didn't know you boys could get such pretty pussy in your beds. Knew I'd get you eventually, Imogen," he laughs coldly.

I hear Sloane's voice muffle something that sounds like *fuck you*. I feel so pathetic for not moving, but I can't. It's as though my feet are physically cemented to the ground. "How about I fuck her pretty little mouth?" he asks before he laughs. "You know Bayard promised me that much."

My eyes widen and my feet finally react to his words, my brain telling me flight or fight. I'm too weak to fight any of these men, so I flight. I'm not fast enough, though. Houston wraps his hand around my bicep and halts my movement.

"James," the one who looked at me with pity warns.

"Oh, shut the fuck up. She's a whore, just like the rest of them. She's used to sucking strange. She'll be fine," he spits. "Sluts are sluts, society or club ones."

"You're a goddamn idiot, James," Officer Pity growls.

My heart races and I can feel my breathing shallow as panic consumes me. I'm going to be raped, right here in front of my husband, and there's nothing anybody can do about it. I have a feeling all of the other men are being detained as well, including whoever stayed over after the party.

"You need another report in your file like a whole in the head. You better just back the fuck away. I have a feeling Mrs. Huntington won't just accept your scare tactics. Plus, I'm standing right here, and I'm more than willing to testify against your dirty ass."

Houston's hand releases me immediately, and I rush over

to Sloane's dresser, grabbing the first black shirt I can find and, thankfully, a pair of athletic shorts he keeps around. Once I'm covered, I feel stronger, like somehow the vulnerability of my nakedness is now gone, and I can think again.

"You all right, Mrs. Huntington?" Officer Pity asks.

"No. My husband has been kicked, is being held on the ground naked, and we were ripped from our sleep. I certainly am *not* all right," I snap. I watch as Sloane looks toward me and grins.

"How about I escort you down to where we're holding everyone, and you can join your... friends, there?"

I nod, but don't take a step, and I certainly don't take his offered hand. "How about you let my husband stand up so that he can join the rest of *his* friends?" I ask, arching my brow. He shakes his head with a grin and tells the other men to do as I've requested.

I ignore the looks as I walk over to Sloane. Sinking to the ground I help him with his jeans. Once I bring them up his body, I gently tug his zipper up, and button the top button. I'm careful, and then rise to my feet, my eyes focused on his.

"Thank you, sunshine," he murmurs.

I press my lips to the center of his chest before tipping my head back and giving him a wink. Then I turn, with my head held high, and walk out of the room toward the bar, where I have a feeling everybody else is located.

"Nerves of steel, woman," the officer chuckles behind me.

"Your friends are jackasses," I announce.

He laughs even harder, and I feel his fingers wrap around my wrist before he tugs me to a stop, gently turning me around to face him.

"They absolutely are. They're also all my superiors, and

your husband is possibly in deep shit," he states.

I nod, ignoring his words. If he hadn't recognized me for who my family is, then the outcome would have been much different. Sure, he may have felt badly, but he wouldn't have done anything to stop it. He's not good, either. In this building, there is no good or bad side; they're *all* bad, just wearing different uniforms.

I see Bobbie and walk straight over to her. She's is sitting at a barstool, and when she notices my clothes, her eyes widen. There are mostly whores, party girls, and a few Old Ladies in this room, which means they're keeping the men separately.

"You okay, honey?" Bobbie asks.

"I am," I murmur.

"You look shaken," Serina says from my other side.

I don't know her well, just that she's an ex-clubwhore turned Old Lady, but she wraps her hand around mine and gives it a squeeze.

I cough, clearing my throat, "There was an incident, but everything is okay. I'm okay."

"Fucking pieces of shit. You know they won't find anything, right? Our men are not stupid," Serina practically growls.

"Let's hope not," I state.

I glare daggers at the fuck who tried to assault my wife. I'll have his goddamn job for that shit—or maybe I'll fuck with him personally. I'm getting really fucking sick of seeing this prick around. I grin to myself at the thought. Yeah, forget his job, I'll fuck with his life instead. Piece of shit woman abuser.

The men and I are all lined up against one wall, hands cuffed behind our backs as the cops search the place. All of the police officers, except for two that are placed in charge of watching us, take off and spread out. They aren't going to find shit, except maybe some recreational drugs—none of which are in my room, unless they plant them there.

An hour later, Houston returns, looking pretty pissed off. He, along with his partner, start to un-cuff us.

"I'm guessing you didn't find what you were looking for?" I smart off.

His head snaps up and he spits on the floor before he speaks. "Watch your goddamn back, you piece of shit."

I don't say anything else, not wishing to agitate him further. I have plans for him, plans that will bring him to his knees. All of the police officers leave with very little fanfare, and the men all stomp toward the bar area, toward women or drinks or both. I don't want drinks. I want Imogen, and I want to make sure she's okay.

Walking into the bar, I see her sitting with Serina. She gives me a smile and scoots off of her chair, walking toward Grease, I assume. Imogen turns to me. Expecting to see a look of disgust in her eyes, I'm surprised that she's smiling and looks fairly at ease.

"You okay, sunshine?" I ask, tucking a piece of her hair behind her ear.

Her brown eyes meet mine, and I see a mix of fear, hesitation, and apprehension in them.

"Church in two hours," MadDog announces in the bar.

I wrap my hand around Genny's and tug her off of her

stool as I start to quickly walk toward my room. I know she is struggling to keep up with me, but I need to ensure that she's okay. I can't do that with a room full of people. Once we're inside of my room, I spin around and walk toward her until her back is pressed against the closed door.

"Sloane," she breathes as her eyes search mine.

I dip my head and press my forehead against hers, closing my eyes and inhaling her scent before I speak. "I thought he was going to hurt you. I swear to god, Imogen, I've never been so scared in my entire fucking life. I was helpless. I couldn't protect you," I whisper.

"It wasn't your fault," she breathes. I let out a humorless laugh and lift my head from hers.

"Yeah, sunshine, it fucking is my fault. Anything that happens to you because of the club, because of my involvement with it, anything I can't protect you from is my goddamn fault."

I gaze into her pretty brown eyes as she lifts her hand and cups my cheek. "You cannot control the actions of other people. In this building or outside of it. I was scared, terrified even, but just like you couldn't control Graham's actions, you could not control that police officer's," she says gently.

"If that other one hadn't said anything, nobody would have stopped him," I mutter.

She wraps her other hand around my waist, and my body does a tremor as her hand touches my bare skin. "I know he wouldn't have, but it still wouldn't have been your fault, baby."

This softness from her, I haven't had it in so long. I didn't earn it. Now, it's too much; she's too fucking sweet, and it makes my goddamn heart ache. I lower my head again and press my lips to hers. Without hesitation, she opens for me.

Though I don't deserve it, I take from her anyway.

I yank her pants down. I unzip my own, pushing them down past my ass before I bend slightly and pick her up by the backs of her knees. I slam inside of her tight cunt, with one hard thrust. Her head falls back and hits the door with a thud. I kiss her neck, licking and sucking as I drive into her, surely bruising her back as it slams against the door.

"Sloane," she groans as her nails dig into the flesh of my shoulders.

"Fuck, sunshine," I murmur, fucking her even harder.

Imogen's pussy flutters, and I can tell she's climbing closer—but I'm not ready for her to come yet. I bite down on her neck, and she shivers in my arms. Goddamn, she feels so good—so good. "Don't come yet," I murmur against her skin.

"Sloane, I'm close," she pants.

Reluctantly, I pull out of her completely. She growls, which causes me to smile. Picking her up, I walk a few feet closer to the bed and toss her there before kicking off my pants. I watch as she removes her shirt.

I sink my teeth into my bottom lip at my wife, spread out completely naked, flushed from my cock. I don't know that I've ever seen anything more beautiful—that is, until she actually comes. That is fucking gorgeous.

I crawl up the bed and gather her in my arms, not wanting to fuck her from behind, needing to have her brown eyes focused on mine.

On my knees, with her tits pressed against my chest, and her eyes connected to mine, I wrap my arms around her back. Then I lower Imogen onto my cock.

Holding her still and against my body, I lift my hips and surge inside of her tight heat. Her legs instantly wrap around mine as I hold her body flush against my own.

"I love you, baby," she whispers, lifting her arms to wrap around my neck and holding the back of my head with her hands.

"Nobody touches you, nobody but me," I growl.

She shakes her head as tears fill her eyes. "Never," she whispers.

I wish I could stay buried inside of her forever, but when her pussy starts to flutter again, I don't try to stop her from coming. I want to feel her squeeze my cock and take her pleasure from me.

That's exactly what I do, and she presses her lips to mine as she shakes against me with her climax. I pull her down on my cock a few times, swallowing her cry as my release shoots deep inside of her, marking all of her as mine.

Unable to hold her up much longer, I lie us down on the bed, slipping from her pussy before I pull her against my side. Imogen doesn't speak. Her head rests on my chest, and her fingers gently stroke my side.

"This, what's between us, it feels so different than it did before you went away, and even from when we were first together," she states.

I lift my hand into the back of her hair and tug her head so that I can look into her eyes.

"We're not the same people we were when we were kids. And we sure as fuck aren't the same people we were three years ago," I mutter.

"You make me happy, Sloane. I never thought I would say that again, but you really do. I love you more today than I ever have."

Running my fingertips over her lips, I sift them through

her hair at the side of her head and search her eyes. My wife, this woman whose heart is bigger than anything I could ever imagine. The way she accepts me, loves me, and has forgiven me is beyond anything I could ever imagine possible.

"Love you, Imogen, more than you could ever know," I admit.

She smiles before she presses her lips to my chest and lays her cheek against me. I hold her for as long as I can before I have to get up to meet the rest of the brothers for church.

chapter thirty-one

Imogen

I smooth down the skirt of my dress and then take another look in the mirror. My parents' summer party is what they call *informal*; but to the rest of the world, it would be considered very formal.

I'm wearing a chiffon, billowy, long sleeve maxi dress that is bright blue, with big, bright, deep fuchsia flowers printed on it. It has a kimono style top that exposes the center of my entire chest down to just above my belly button, with a thick band around my waist. The skirt flows to the ground from my waist but has a slit cut high, all the way up to almost my hip.

Grabbing my purse, I slip on my gold high heels—Louboutins. I think I could have an addiction to them, it seems they're all I buy. I smile as I look down at them.

They have triangle cutouts along the bottom, trimmed in

metallic gold leather, with small gold spikes all over. *I freaking love them.* I'm sure they'll get stuck in the grass more times than I care for them to, and I'll probably end the afternoon barefoot, but it's all in the grand entrance. This outfit is sure to make my entrance exactly that.

"You planning on taking off your robe and putting your dress on anytime soon? If we don't leave in the next ten minutes, we're going to be late," Sloane states.

I turn from the mirror with a smirk on my lips. "This is my dress. I'm ready to go. My clutch is on the bed if you'll grab that," I say, fastening a delicate rose gold chain onto my wrist.

"What do you mean, that's your dress? Your tits are hanging out," he growls.

I look down at my chest, but nothing is showing—not even a hint of cleavage. Though the dress has no center to my chest area, it completely covers each breasts.

"My tits are not hanging out. There's not even a hint of boob, Sloane; not even side boob."

His eyes narrow, and I watch as a muscle jumps in his jaw when he clenches his teeth together. I close the distance between us and press my chest against his.

For the first time ever, he's wearing his cut to one of our family's functions, and it was by my request. Sloane's hands cup my ass, and he pulls me even closer to him, pressing his length against my belly.

"I'm going to be hard all fucking day, sunshine," he murmurs.

"I'll let you fuck me in my childhood bedroom," I whisper.

He grins, and it turns from small to a full-blown, wide smile. "Is it still hot pink?" he asks.

"Exact same bed. My mother hasn't redecorated that room yet. She can't decide what she wants to do with it," I nod.

I don't know that it's not that my mother can't decide what to do with it, exactly. I think maybe she's avoiding it for whatever reason. It's as though my childhood bedroom is locked in a time warp.

"Let's get the fuck out of here, then. Never did get to fuck you on those pretty pink sheets. Been waiting almost twenty years to do it."

I throw back my head and laugh at my husband. This man. My entire world. He brushes my lips with his and squeezes my ass one last time before he releases me and walks toward the door. He lifts his chin, and I follow behind him. He walks over to his muscle car and we slide inside.

"I didn't realize this had a slit up to your pussy, sunshine," he rumbles, his hand on my knee as we head toward Frisco.

I frown slightly and turn to him. "Do you not like it?"

My breath hitches when he moves his hand up the inside of my thigh to the center of my panties and slips his fingers beneath them, straight to my core. His fingers pump in and out of me a few times, and I can't stop my hips from searching for more, or my mouth from letting out a moan.

"I don't want you to come, sunshine," he rasps.

My eyes pop open as I turn to him, his thumb pressing against my clit at the exact same time.

"*Why*?" I whine.

"When I make you come, it's going to be in your bedroom, on that bed, an image I jacked off to about a million and five fucking times as a teenager. You spread out for me for the taking on those pink sheets," he grins.

I laugh, "You are such a pervert."

"Fuck yeah, I am," he grunts, as he continues to curl his fingers inside of me.

I can't think anything else as he continues to touch me, bringing me closer toward my release. I bite my bottom lip with a whimper as I try not to come all over his fingers. The car stops and my eyes snap open. The vision in front of me is my parents' home.

"Sloane," I hiss as he slides his fingers out of me.

I watch as he brings them up to his mouth and sucks them clean. Then he leans over and presses his lips to mine, shoving his tongue deep inside of my mouth, swirling it around. I taste myself on him.

I reach over and grab onto his cut with a moan. Then a knock on the window has me jumping. I turn my head to see my father standing beside my door, his arms folded across his chest.

My door is wrenched open and my father reaches down and grabs my bicep, dragging me out of the car. My ankle twists as I try to gain my balance.

"You want to take your goddamn hands off of my wife?" Sloane growls as he rushes to my side.

He wraps his hand around my waist, yanking me closer to him. I have to gain my balance again, but at least he's holding onto me tightly as I do.

"I didn't think you'd have the balls to show, or that you wouldn't be locked up in jail."

Sloane lets out a humorless laugh. "Or that Imogen would still be at my side and not play into your dirty little hand like you'd planned?"

My father's face turns beat red, and he lets out a low

growl before he calms himself almost immediately. It's a little scary, but perfectly normal for my father, who is scary in and of himself. I smooth my dress down and then my hair as well, trying to regain my faculties.

"You look like goddamn trash, the both of you," my father sneers.

"Well, I'm glad you think so highly of us, but I could care less what you think. I'm not here for you, I'm here for mother and Kalli," I state as I take a step toward the front door. "Father, it doesn't matter what you think of me or Sloane. We're married, happily. Your plan didn't work, but it almost got me raped by some dickhead cop. Please stop." Sloane stiffens beside me, but I don't allow him to wait another second to hear anything else my father has to say.

"I can't believe you just said that," he growls in my ear as his hand tightens around me.

"He needed to know, and I don't want to get into a discussion about it. It's over and done with," I shrug.

We don't say anything else as we enter the backyard of the party. There are at least two hundred people milling around, but finding my mother is easy. She's wearing a maxi dress as well, except it's a solid color, bright lime green. It actually looks lovely against her skin. We make our way toward her, and her eyes light up at the sight of me before they shift to Sloane in surprise.

"I'm sure your father loved seeing the vest, Sloane dear," my mother says with a smirk before she leans over and gives him cheek kisses. She does the same with me. "You look lovely, Imogen."

"Thanks," I grin.

My mother and I have started to chat lately. It's something

new, but I'm starting to enjoy our communication. The same goes for Kalli, who floats toward us in a white chiffon skirt and a pale pink sleeveless top, accented perfectly with a thick gold belt around her waist.

Kallie wraps her arms around me in a tight hug then turns to Sloane and does the same. "I would love for you to meet someone," she murmurs. I look from her to a very dashing man standing behind her.

"This is Calvin," Kalli says as her cheeks tint pink.

I hear Sloane grunt beside me, but I can't help but smile. I reach out my hand, and the man brings it up to his lips, brushing my knuckles.

"Imogen Stewart, it's a pleasure to finally meet you," he murmurs.

He has silver hair and looks to be around his mid-sixties. I blink and wonder if this is the man my father was trying to set me up with.

I clear my throat as he releases my hand. "Do we know you?" Sloane asks on a growl, taking the words out of my mouth.

"No. Imogen's father has been trying to do business with me. Though, I admit, it was a tempting offer, but I'm sorry dear. You're just too young for me. I prefer a mature woman who knows how to handle a man. If you see your father, tell him I'm sorry it didn't work out between us, businesswise or family wise. It seems as though you've found someone your own age."

I blink at his words, unbelieving of what he's saying. I shouldn't be surprised that my father flat-out lied to me. A part of me is a little shocked at the entirety of the situation. Then I burst out laughing. My mother, Sloane, and Kalli all stare at me.

"Oh, Calvin. I'm actually Mrs. Imogen Huntington. I do believe my father was trying to fool us both. I'm so glad that you've found Kalli, as I'm very much in love with her son and have been since I was a fifteen-year-old girl," I say. He grins and nods before he expresses both his agreement and relief.

"You better start talking to me, sunshine," Sloane whispers against my ear.

I turn to him and smile. "Why don't we head into the house and I'll tell you what happened?" I ask with a smirk.

I watch his lips twitch as he does his best to scowl at me. Then he reaches for my hand and tugs me toward the house.

Soar

"You want to explain to me about Calvin out there?" I ask as I lock the door to Imogen's bedroom behind me.

She laughs as she takes off her dress, leaving her in only her high heels and panties. She's gone braless today, and the thought of her tits being bare, all day, makes my mouth water and pisses me off all at the same time.

I watch as she steps out of her shoes and then her panties before she climbs onto her bed and turns around. She spreads her thighs in the middle of her pink bed. All thoughts of her father and this Calvin guy completely disappear.

"You've just made the seventeen-year-old me's fantasy come true, Imogen, baby," I murmur.

With a smirk, she trails her fingers down the center of her chest to her pussy and dips them inside. I strip my clothes off, unable to control myself. I need her tight cunt wrapped around my dick, not her fingers.

Crawling between her spread thighs, I wrap my hand around her wrists and give her a gentle squeeze. She moves her hand out of the way, and I replace her fingers with my cock.

"On your stomach," I demand.

She shivers and moves to her stomach, lifting her ass in the air. I bite my lip as my eyes scan her perfect round ass, splayed against the soft sheets of her childhood bedroom. Fuck me, I've jacked off to this image right here for most of my late-teen years.

"*Sunshine*," I rasp.

"Baby," she whispers, looking back at me.

I spread her ass with my hands and squeeze her flesh before I align my cock with her wet pussy. I can see how slick she is just with a glance. Pressing my cock to her entrance, I gently slip the head inside of her, causing her to sigh.

"Sloane," she whimpers.

Slipping my hand down her spine, I grab a handful of her hair in my hand, tugging it as I slam deep inside of her sweet cunt. Sinking my teeth into my bottom lip, I watch as my cock disappears inside of her tight heat, over and over. Tugging her hair back, I groan as her back bows and I sink a little deeper inside of her.

Neither of us speak, my grunts filling the air, as she gasps softly every so often. "Make yourself come on my cock, baby," I rasp as my hand connects with her ass.

Imogen's hand slips underneath her body, and I feel her nails graze my balls. I tighten my fingers in her hair a little more at the sensation. Her breath hitches as her body shivers.

"Sloane," she gasps. "I'm going to come."

I grunt as I fuck her a little harder, my hips slamming against her ass and filling the room with the sound of slapping skin. When her body tenses, I feel her pussy contract around me. Then she lets out a sob. I speed up my thrusts before I bury myself inside of her as deep as I can go. I come, hard, my cock twitching and filling her with my cum.

Lowering my head and chest, I twist her head around so that I can press my lips to hers. "I love you, sunshine," I murmur against her mouth.

"Let's go home, Soar," she whispers.

"Soar?" I ask in surprise.

She grins, pressing her lips to mine before she gently jerks her head back so that she can look in my eyes. "Yeah, Soar. My Old Man, my husband—mine. Let's go home, to where we belong. This life, it isn't us."

"You sure?"

Imogen cups my cheek, and I feel her cool fingers against my face before she speaks. "We're Soar and Genny. Imogen and Sloane checked out a long damn time ago. Soar and Genny have an awesome life full of ups and downs; but it's also full of laughter, love, and good friends. I like them."

"Fuck, sunshine, I like them, too," I grin.

After only being at her parents' party a total of one hour, we say our goodbyes. My mother asks if she and Calvin can come and visit us next week. She then informs me that they'll be flying out to spend some time with Kip.

She wants to mend their relationship and introduce him to this man she's so obviously into. I'm happy for her. She deserves someone a lot fucking better than my father was. My mother and I won't ever be perfect, but maybe we can be more than just family. Maybe we can be friends.

Imogen hugs her mother and tells her goodbye before joining my side. I turn and look back at all of the people. I know most of them, I grew up with them, but Imogen is right. These aren't our people anymore. This isn't our life. We're Soar and Genny.

Imogen

I don't bother saying goodbye to my father. I don't know if we'll ever be anything more than cordial to each other. He's done too much to try and tear me down and tear Sloane and I apart for nothing other than his personal gain.

I have so much more to look forward to in this life that I can't hold onto shit in the past; I can't hold onto hope that my father will change. I know it's possible for people to change—Sloane did, and each day he proves it to me.

"We going straight home?" Sloane asks as we get a little closer to town.

"There a party tonight?" I ask.

He nods with a grin. "You want to party?" he asks.

I shrug. I don't really want to party, but I do have an announcement to make. It's all brand new, but, If I know my Sloane, *my Soar*, he'll want everybody to know. So it will be easier to tell them all at once.

I don't expect the lights in the rearview mirror. "Fucking shit," Sloane growls as he pulls the car over. I glance in the side mirror as the officer exits his car, and I groan.

"I'm getting really fucking tired of this asshole," I whisper.

Sloane smiles, though it doesn't reach his eyes as he rolls the window down.

"Officer Houston, how may I help you?" Sloane calls out with both of his hands on the steering wheel.

"Hey there, boy, where are you coming from on this fine evening?"

I don't know how this douchebag seems to be everywhere, but I'm getting really tired of seeing his slimy face and cold eyes. I think about that one officer that stopped him from abusing me, and wish he were here right now.

"Went to a family party, sir," Sloane grunts.

The officer grins before he talks into the radio at his chest and then turns back to us. "I think we'll do a little search of your vehicle right about now. Hop on out."

I don't bother looking at Sloane, I don't need to. I can feel the anger radiating from him. I open the door and get out of the car. Standing to the side, I watch as Houston puts cuffs on Sloane's wrists. Then he slowly saunters over to me. He rests his hand on the belt at his hips before he tips his head so that he has Sloane in his line of sight.

"You let your wife dress like one of the whores, people are going to assume her pussy is up for grabs," he chortles.

I take a step back from him. Sloane growls, but I can't look at him, all I can see is this asshole who has a taser and a gun at his fingertips.

"He doesn't let me do anything. I'm an adult, officer Houston. I can do what I want," I state.

His eyes heat, and I see his smirk turn into a full-fledged grin. That's when I know that I've made a mistake. A colossal mistake. I take another step back, stumbling on a rock and almost falling on my ass. Houston stalks toward me, and Sloane grunts behind him.

I can't look away from Houston. The evil darkness in his eyes has me frozen in fear. Taking another step back, my foot twists, and I cry out as I fall to the ground. Houston laughs. "Perfect, less work for me to do. Why don't you take those panties off for me too, sweetheart?"

"Fuck you," I whisper.

I open my mouth to scream when the sound of a bike's roar pulls up. Houston's head swivels to the side and he freezes. Looking around him, I see Camo, Torch, and Texas pull up. "The fuck," he whispers.

I can't stop the smile from curving on my lips, but I don't say anything.

Staying planted on my ass, I watch as the guys get off of their bikes. Camo and Texas walk toward Houston and me, and Torch makes his way toward Sloane.

"Didn't realize this was your jurisdiction," Camo murmurs as he walks closer toward us. Texas' eyes flash at me, and I see anger in his gaze.

Houston grunts, "It's a road, and I'm an officer of the law. I can do whatever the fuck I want to."

"Wrong, you dirty fuck," Sloane's voice rings out.

I watch as Houston's body jerks, and then he falls forward. Sloane walks over to him, his hands now free of the cuffs and a gun in them. I jump as he pulls the trigger three more times, emptying bullets into the back of his head.

Sloane turns to me and my gaze clashes with his. "Get up, sunshine," he orders.

I scramble as ladylike as I can and try to stand on my shaky legs and high heels—a combination that isn't the best.

"Come to your man."

His tone is one that invites zero room for argument, and I close my eyes as I step over the now very still, and extremely dead body of officer Houston. Sloane reaches out when I'm within arm's length and tugs me against his side.

"I'll call a cleanup crew," Camo mumbles as he and the other men walk away.

I don't look at them. My eyes are focused on the man in front of me, the man whose chin is tipped down and his jaw is clenched.

"Are you okay?" he whispers.

Lifting my hand, I cup his cheek, feeling his stubble before I lift up and press my lips against the side of his. "I'm fine, Sloane. You make me feel so damn safe."

"How in the fuck do you feel safe? That piece of shit has been gunning for you to hurt you," he rasps.

I smile up at him. "I feel safe because you protected me. You kept me safe, again."

He shakes his head in disbelief. "You good to get in the car? I need to talk to the guys."

"I'm good," I whisper.

I kiss him one more time, then I hurry toward the car and slide inside, completely ignoring the dead body on the side of the road. I watch as Sloane talks to his brothers, for about twenty minutes before he jogs back to the car and slides inside of the passenger seat. I'm completely stoic. I feel like I should be panicking, screaming, or feeling something—anything. I feel, almost numb.

"Everything okay?" I whisper.

Sloane jerks his chin up. "Yeah, he called in when he was here. The guys have to cover those tracks. Nothing to worry about. They have it handled. Ready to party a little?"

"You still want to go?" I ask. I want to go home and silently freak out. I want to forget all of this ever happened.

He smiles. "Yeah, baby, we'll have fun." We don't say anything else as he drives us toward the club. We ignore the entire situation that just happened. Once we pull into the parking lot, Sloane looks over at me with a frown. "I don't want you to worry about what just happened. You're good, right?"

I tip my head to the side as I give him a small smile. "He was planning on hurting me, Sloane. It was self-defense." He grunts at my words as though he doesn't believe me. Thankfully, he drops it.

"You look too fucking sexy still. You should go change first," he mumbles.

I slide out of the car and start to walk toward the front door when he runs up behind me and scoops me in his arms. "Can't ruin those expensive as fuck shoes now," he grins as his lips touch mine.

Looking into his clear, green eyes, I decide, not for the first time, that yes, sober looks good on my Old Man.

Once we're inside, everything about the past hour disappears. He sets me down, and I look away from his face to see that the room is focused on us. It's still early, the music isn't too loud, and the naked bodies aren't on display yet.

"I have an announcement to make," I shout. I feel Sloane stiffen behind me. "There's going to be another baby Devil in eight months or so."

Sloane's hands reach out and wrap around my waist before he spins me around to face him. His face is pale and his eyes wide as he searches mine. "Are you fucking with me?" he rasps.

"No, I'm pregnant. I just found out," I whisper.

"Holy fucking shit. Holy goddamn fucking shit," he breathes before he smiles and looks up to face the room. "*I'm going to be a dad*," he calls out.

The room erupts in cheers, and the men come up to him, patting him on the back and congratulating him, then me.

"Oh, my god, this is so amazing," Mary-Anne says as she hugs me. Her belly is in the way, but she does her best to embrace me just the same.

"How many babies does that make in less than a year?" Teeny asks, looking around. We count, "Five," she states.

"A new generation of Devils," Ivy says with a smile.

"Shit, this world is in serious trouble," Mary-Anne laughs.

We spend the rest of the evening with our friends, our family, and I've never been happier than I am in this exact moment. Sloane wraps his hand around my waist and tugs me against his side as his lips brush mine.

All of the drama forgotten, and although I'll probably have some kind of guilt about it later, there is so much to be happy and thankful for right now. I push all of the scary shit aside.

"Love you, sunshine," he murmurs against my mouth.

"I love you so much, baby."

He places his hand on my stomach and his grin widens as his eyes almost sparkle. "Have I made up for my years of bullshit yet?" he asks softly.

"You're getting there," I whisper.

EIGHT MONTHS LATER

Soar

I watch, from across the street, with a sick satisfaction as my father-in-law pulls up into his driveway from a long day at work. His clothes are strewn all over the lawn, and a very expensive looking television has been thrown in the middle, beat to shit with a hammer.

It's completely out of character for my mother-in-law, but I can't help but smile. He steps out of his car and walks over to all of his shit in the middle of the front yard, his hands on his hips as he tips his head to the sky as if to ask—*why me.*

"Brother, his television?" Torch asks from my side.

"He threatened to practically sell off Cleo, and hired a cop on the hook to put your ass away, giving him permission

368

to have his way with her, what would you do?" I ask with a frown.

"Burn his house to the ground after I killed him," he shrugs.

I laugh. He would do that, too. I personally don't like murder. It's a little too messy, and it means he wouldn't be living with the consequences for his actions for too long. Like with Graham and Houston, the satisfaction of their deaths were just a little too hollow. "I prefer watching him suffer from afar."

"How'd you know he was cheating on his wife with his secretaries?" he asks as we walk toward our bikes, which are parked a block away from my father-in-law's estate.

"Man like that? Man that threatened to do what he tried to do to his own daughter, my woman? He had skeletons for sure. I just had to figure them out. Plus, I walked in on him fucking a secretary not too long ago," I shrug. "It wasn't that he was cheating, she probably knew that already."

"What was it then?" he asks.

"It's that he was keeping several of them, putting them up in fancy as fuck apartments in the city, spending time with them, taking them on vacations. He was giving them wife privileges."

He snorts. "Don't fuck with Soar."

"Bet your fucking ass," I grunt.

It only takes us a few minutes to walk to our bikes. Torch waves as he goes in a different direction, and I head toward where I need to be. I've been gone for too long, anyway. I need to be back in that room with her. Walking into the building, I hurry to her floor and I stop dead in my tracks at the sight before me.

Imogen is sitting up, her hair unkempt, yet gorgeous, and my son is at her breast. His blond hair is the only thing I can see of him as he's swaddled in a blue blanket. Genny looks over at me, and I can see just how tired she is; but when her brown eye's catch mine, she smiles.

"How you feeling, mama?" I ask as I make my way toward my wife and child.

I place my hand on Everett's head. Everett, a name Imogen chose. She said because we were both so wild, he's destined to be the same, and that's what it means. The difference with him and us is that we won't ever try to tame him the way our families did us. Fuck, yeah. Rett. It's a perfect name for our little man.

"I'm tired, but he's hungry," she murmurs softly.

I lean over to press my lips to hers. She's my goddamn hero, carrying him and then safely bringing him into this world to share with me—a fucking hero. With my lips still touching hers, I whisper that as soon as he's finished eating, I'll change and hold him.

"Thank you," Imogen sighs.

"Where'd you go?" she asks as soon as he's finished eating and I take him, throwing a cloth over my shoulder to burp him.

"Had something to do. Nothing for you to worry about, okay, sunshine?"

"Mmm," she hums. I look over to find that she's fallen fast asleep.

I smile and take Everett over to the plastic bassinet. Changing his diaper, I'm slow and scared I'm going to hurt him; but he just looks at me the entire time, as if he's trying to figure out exactly who and what I am. When I'm finished, I wrap him back in his blanket and walk him over to the shitty recliner they leave for us dads.

I lay him against my chest and I pat his back as I talk to my little man.

"You're going to be a good man, you hear me? You aren't allowed to do half of the shit your old man has. The other half, I'll teach you about," I laugh when he makes a gurgling noise before he sighs. "Never thought I wanted a little man like you. Waited thirty-nine years, and here you are. Aside from your mama, you're the best thing that's ever happened to me, Rett," I whisper.

A knock on the door interrupts our bonding, and I watch as my little brother walks through the door, my mother and her new husband, Calvin, trailing behind.

"Oh, my god, he's absolutely gorgeous," my mother coos, careful not to be too loud.

They all three sit on the sofa. As much as I should probably hand him to my mother, I hand him to my baby brother instead.

I place him in Kip's arms, "Here, Uncle Kipling, meet Everett."

"Holy shit, something this perfect came from my *dumbfuck* brother?" he asks with a laugh.

"Hey, he's mine, too," Imogen says, her voice raspy from the bed.

I walk over to her and sit on the edge next to her, taking her hand in mine.

"He's perfect, Genny," Kipling says, unable to take his eyes off of my son.

"He is, isn't he?" she asks in a grin.

"He absolutely is, and so are you," I murmur as I lean

down and press my lips to hers again.

Imogen smiles and she squeezes my hand. "Are you happy?" she asks.

"Have I made up for my years of bullshit, yet?" I ask. It's a question I've asked periodically throughout the past year.

"You're really, really close," she grins.

"What else do you need, baby?" I ask as I run my thumb over her bottom lip.

"More of this, all of it."

I smile widely. "You got it sunshine. A whole fucking lifetime of it."

ROUGH & REAL
Notorious Devils #7

Ivy

It is official.

I've let myself go.

I know it. My husband West knows it. Hell, the entire *Notorious Devils* club, including the whores, know it, too. I see the way they dismiss me as their eyes always lock onto my husband's.

My Old Man is hot. He's been mine since I was twenty-one years old. Now, fifteen years later, I think he looks even better than he did the day I met him. Unfortunately, time hasn't been as kind to me. Three children, twenty pounds, and the overall *mom-look* isn't a gorgeous sight to see when you look at yourself in the mirror.

It doesn't help that I'd overheard West talking about me just last night. I guess he didn't realize that the bedroom window was open. He was outside talking to one of his brothers, a newer guy they call Tinker, who had been telling West that he was thinking of making some girl his Old Lady.

"Don't do it brother," West chuckled.

"Why's that? You got an Old Lady," Tinker points out.

"Yeah, few years down the road, after a few kids, they let themselves go, man. That sexy as fuck bitch that's on the back of your bike, now? She's gonna be a member of the PTA in mom jeans and an oversized sweatshirt, carrying around an extra

thirty pounds from kid number three that she's too fuckin' lazy to lose," West states.

I sat in our bedroom, the bedroom where we made our three children, and I cried. That was last night. Today, I make a change, and not for him—for *me*.

I didn't know he thought of me that way. How could I? Certainly, not when he told me more often than not that he loved the curves of my body, knowing his babies put them there, while he fucked me.

West and I aren't perfect. We're married. We argue. We've gone through weird moments off and on throughout our marriage, but what we never have done is go through dry spells. I've never once worried that my husband is fucking whores at the clubhouse, not once.

We have sex almost every single night of the week. Exhausted or not, I always make time for my man. After hearing him talk to his *brother* last night, now I'm not so sure. That conversation alone makes me question everything about us.

"Finley is picking me up and we're going to the mall," Rosalie, our thirteen-year-old daughter states from the doorway.

Finley is the president of the *Notorious Devils'* sixteen-year-old daughter. "Is Bailey joining you?" I ask, speaking of the youngest Duhart, a thirteen-year-old boy—a boy my daughter is very much in puppy love with. She blushes slightly and nods. I sigh, knowing this day was coming, yet never truly ready for it. My brown haired, blue eyed daughter is growing up.

"Have fun. Be home by dinner time," I murmur.

"Thanks mom, you're the best," she squeals as she runs in

to give me a quick hug.

A few minutes later, Remi, our ten-year-old son, and Reid, our eight-year-old son, come rushing into my bedroom. They ask if they can go two houses down to their cousins to play legos.

One of West's sisters, lives two houses down from us. His other sister lives across the street, and his mother lives three houses down in the opposite direction.

Some days, I enjoy his family being so close, especially since my only family is my brother, Barry. Other days, I want them to stay out of my business.

With the children out of the house, I decide to go online and research gyms and trainers. No more feeling shitty about myself. No more hearing my own husband tell his friends about my supposed thirty-pound weight gain, even though it's only twenty—*no fucking more.*

I call the gym and the trainer has an opening right away, so I text my sister-in-law to let her know that I have an errand to run and I leave. If I'm going to do this, I need to just go and handle it immediately. If I wait around, I'll over think it and avoid it.

Once I arrive at the gym, I let the front desk know that I'm here and wait for the trainer. He arrives, and I try so hard to keep from letting my mouth fall to the floor. He isn't much younger than me, maybe five years, but he's ripped, totally and completely ripped. Immediately, I want to turn and run.

"Ivy?" he asks, his voice softer than I imagined it would be. I stand and take his outstretched hand. "I'm Chad."

He tells me to follow him into his office and we talk. He asks me about my health, about my fitness level—which is pathetic—then he weighs and measures me. When I see the numbers, it makes me sick to my stomach.

How did I let this happen?

"Don't stress, Ivy. You are not in bad shape. I've seen so much worse. I predict in just a few weeks, if you follow the plan we set forth today, you're going to see a drastic change. Let's talk about your goals," Chad smiles.

I leave the gym with a workout schedule and a food plan. Our first session starts at eight o'clock tomorrow morning, when the kids are in school and West is gone, doing whatever it is he does all day long.

This is the chance for me to better myself, to change my body and to love myself. Maybe my husband will look at me the way he did when we first met each other all those years ago, when I worked in this little dessert bar downtown. *Carlotta's.*

West

I lift my chin to Tinker, who is curled on the sofa in the bar with his woman. I shake my head, knowing he's going to make her his Old Lady. She's a nice girl, but I can tell that she's into him for one reason, and one reason only. *For a brand.*

After fifteen years in the club life, I can spot the girls like her from a mile away. I tried to warn him off of her the only way I knew how. I told him she was going to get fat and lazy if he branded her. She probably will, too; she's the type. I curl my lip and make my way toward the Prez' office.

"You are absolutely not going to that college. It's nothing but a party school," I hear him growl.

I can only imagine he's talking to his oldest daughter, Riley. She's got it in her head that she wants to go to Chico State, and no way in *fuck* is her father gonna allow that shit.

"Daddy, all my friends are going, and I'll be so close to home," she whines.

"No, and that's final," MadDog's voice booms.

A few seconds later, an emotional teenager flies out of his office and past me.

"Don't laugh. You're fuckin' next," MadDog growls as I walk into his office and close the door.

"Don't I know it. Rosalie is already all starry-eyed over Bailey. I'm definitely not ready for that shit."

"Fuck," MadDog grunts. "I don't know what's worse, trying to keep all the dicks away from my girls, or trying to keep my son's dick from going after all the girls," he rumbles.

"He better keep his little pecker to himself," I state, giving him a hard look.

MadDog laughs and shakes his head. "Kids, man, who the fuck said we should do this shit? I'm too goddamn old," he murmurs.

"I recall you telling Mary you wanted one more after Bailey was born and she put her foot down," I say, arching a brow.

"Bullshit," he barks. I can't help but laugh.

We shoot the shit for a while and then we stand and head to church together. We have a meeting today. As a group, we have some important decisions to make about the future of the club.

Unfortunately, there have been murmurings of another club trying to start shit and hone in on our territories, a new club that we don't know much about. Hopefully, Soar and

Torch have some more information about it, since they've had a week to dig some shit up.

I pass by Grease, my brother-in-law, who gives me a chin lift. I grin at him as I continue on my way. I've been in love with his sister for fifteen years. Though he hated me for it at first, we've handled our differences. Now, we're not just brothers, we're friends.

My mind quickly drifts to my wife. She's not the same person now as the day I met her. Time has changed her, it's changed us. She's a mother to three kids, and she's damn good at it. She handles our house, the kids—and at night, she handles me.

But lately, I feel like we're in a complete rut. I don't know how to change that. We aren't spontaneous, we can't be as parents. And our sex life, while it's consistent, it's a little boring. It fucking kills me to even think that.

I pass by the free-for-all room and I pause. There's a couple prospects fucking one of the whores, together. She's on her hands and knees, sucking one cock, while another fucks her from behind. I watch.

This seems to be where I've been finding myself more often than anywhere else. I shouldn't even look, but I can't fucking help myself—it's sexy as shit.

"Let's get this meeting started," MadDog announces breaking me of my thoughts.

also by
HAYLEY FAIMAN

MEN OF BASEBALL SERIES—

Pitching for Amalie
Catching Maggie
Forced Play for Libby
Sweet Spot for Victoria

RUSSIAN BRATVA SERIES—

Owned by the Badman
Seducing the Badman
Dancing for the Badman
Living for the Badman
Tempting the Badman
Protected by the Badman
Forever my Badman
Betrothed to the Badman (October 2017)
Chosen by the Badman (February 2018)

NOTORIOUS DEVILS MC—

Rough & Rowdy
Rough & Raw
Rough & Rugged
Rough & Ruthless
Rough & Ready
Rough & Rich
Rough & Real (January 2018)

STANDALONE TITLES
Royally Relinquished: A Modern Day Fairy Tale
Personal Foul (December 2017)

Follow me on social media to stay current on the
happenings in my little book world.

Website: hayleyfaiman.com

Facebook: www.facebook.com/authorhayleyfaiman

Goodreads: www.goodreads.com/author/show/10735805.
Hayley_Faiman

Signup for my Newsletter: hayleyfaiman.us13.list-manage.
com/subscribe?u=d0e156a6e8d82f22e819d1065&id=4d4aefa

about the author

As an only child, Hayley Faiman had to entertain herself somehow. She started writing stories at the age of six and never really stopped.

Born in California, she met her now husband at the age of sixteen and married him at the age of twenty in 2004. After all of these years together, he's still the love of her life.

Hayley's husband joined the military and they lived in Oregon, where he was stationed with the US Coast Guard. They moved back to California in 2006, where they had two little boys. Recently, the four of them moved out to the Hill Country of Texas, where they adopted a new family member, a chocolate lab named Optimus Prime.

Most of Hayley's days are spent taking care of her two boys, going to the baseball fields for practice, or helping them with homework. Her evenings are spent with her husband and her nights—those are spent creating alpha book boyfriends.

acknowledgments

I want to thank all of my fans, everyone to took a chance on *Rough & Rowdy* and then decided to continue on with this series! There is so much more coming your way so sit back and hold on, these men of the Notorious Devils are not through with you yet!

I always say a special thank you to my husband, my best friend, and the man who supports me in every single one of my dreams. He's the man who has owned my heart for the past seventeen years. *Thank you babes.*

My mom, she's always supported wholeheartedly everything I have ever decided to take a leap of faith on, including my writing. She's the kindest, most loving, and most supportive mom in the world. Thank you *Banana Boots.*

Rosalyn my editor, my bestie, my confidant. Thank you for helping me with this hot mess express of a book! We seriously put in some major hours with this one! All the words have been said, they'll be said repeatedly, I'll never tire of saying them. God brought us together for a reason, in a time where we truly needed each other's guidance and friendship.

My sister from another mister, Nisha. Thank you for being my friend and always having my ear and always making a bitch laugh.

Celia, my oldest friend, from the git-n-go until today, thank you for being such an awesome friend. Thanks for the laughs, the cupcakes, the brownies, the cruises in the Mustang, and all of the years together.

Cassy Roop, thank you so much for always making these covers so hot and sexy!

Crystal Snyder thank you for loving my book men, for Beta reading for me, and being such a beautiful person inside and out!

Tammy Cole, thank you for loving Soar!!!

Stacey Blake. Sending my manuscript to you is never "scary" because I know that you'll always make it absolutely gorgeous! Thank you for being so fantastic!

Enticing Journey—Ena and Amanda—I always know that my PR work is safe with you, that you'll represent my book and me in a way that only you can—THE BEST WAY! I truly appreciate all of the hard work you ladies put into everything!

A special thanks to all the Blogger babes that have taken a chance on me...

Thank you from the bottom of my heart.

Made in the USA
Columbia, SC
14 September 2017